features some of the characters who appeared in Margaret Murphy's *Darkness Falls*

'*Darkness Falls* is a model of what the modern suspense thriller should be – tense, scary, page-turning and stomach-churning – because we care most of all about what happens to the characters. Set aside a day – you won't be able to put it down once it has you in its grip' *Val McDermid*

'A skilfully plotted story with strongly drawn characters' Susanna Yager, *Sunday Telegraph*

'Margaret Murphy has managed to produce another out-standing psychological thriller . . . *Darkness Falls* is a powerul work . . . Readers of her previous work should certainly not be disappointed, whilst those fresh to her output will find this book provides an enticing introduction.' *Sherlock*

'Exemplary chiller . . . If Murphy's appointed task is to scare the reader . . . she succeeds brilliantly' *Literary Review*

'A piece of absolutely terrifying writing . . . This is crime's most compelling, chilling book ever' *North Wales Chronicle*

'Menacing psychological thriller with a clever plot' *Glasgow Evening Times*

'Just what British crime writing is crying out for – a compassionate, grass roots British novel with the pace, energy and impeccable research of an American thriller' *Mo Hayder*

*Also by Margaret Murphy
in New English Library paperbacks*

Darkness Falls

*About the author*

Margaret Murphy is the author of five novels, all concerned with the psychology of both the violent criminal and the victim of crime. Her first, *Goodnight My Angel,* was shortlisted for the First Blood award for debut crime novels. A graduate in environmental biology, in 1998 she went back to university to gain an MA in writing. She is the founder of Murder Squad and an active member of the Crime Writers' Association. She has been a countryside ranger, biology teacher, dyslexia tutor and creative writing teacher. She lives on the Wirral.

# MARGARET MURPHY

# Weaving Shadows

**NEW ENGLISH LIBRARY**
Hodder & Stoughton

copyright © 2003 by Margaret Murphy

First published in Great Britain in 2003 by Hodder and Stoughton
A division of Hodder Headline
First published in paperback in Great Britain in 2003
by Hodder and Stoughton
A New English Library paperback

A CIP catalogue record for this title
is available from the British Library

ISBN 0 340 82055 1

Typeset in Plantin by Hewer Text Ltd, Edinburgh
Printed and bound in Great Britain by
Mackays of Chatham plc, Chatham, Kent

Hodder and Stoughton
A division of Hodder Headline
338 Euston Road
London NW1 3BH

For James and Brenda Wright

# ACKNOWLEDGEMENTS

Sincere thanks to Inspector Dave Griffin of Cheshire Constabulary whose continued help and boundless generosity has been both inspiring and humbling.

For the background on counselling, I have found the following texts helpful: Shattered Assumptions by Ronnie Janoff-Bulman and The Theory and Practice of Counselling by Richard Nelson-Jones. Dr A.D.M. Davies' lectures on clinical psychology at the University of Liverpool also provided useful insights, and I am grateful for her encouragement and support.

# PROLOGUE

———◆———

The tail end of August, and hotter than hell. Clemence wound down the window, glancing around to check for nosy neighbours as he did so: with the window open, he was conspicuous. The mingled scents of overblown privet and new-mown grass buffeted his face like a solid mass. He noted with alarm that the sun had crept round, slicing sharply across one edge of his camera, resting on the passenger seat. He snatched it up. It was warm. *Shit!* For a moment he held it to the cooler air at the window, but shifted it when he got a curious look from a kid walking past.

He watched until she became a blurred tadpole shape in the distance. A combination of heat haze and the residual effects of twelve years staring at nothing further than thirty feet away. A slight deficit in visual perception, the doctor said. It would right itself, with time. The girl turned the corner and he settled back. The 28–200mm lens he had chosen for its versatility was a comforting weight in his lap.

He armed the sweat from his forehead and a spiky trickle crabbed its way from his chest to the waistband of his chinos. If she didn't come soon, he would have to move the car somewhere cooler.

He squinted up into the shimmering mosaic of the sycamore canopy above him; the leaves had a hard, brittle quality, not yet tinged with autumn colour, yet well past the soft greens of spring. He would have to wait another year to see that on the outside.

A couple of streets away, an ice-cream van clanged 'Greensleeves' at a mad pace, speeding to its favoured pitch, and for a moment the stink of privet was displaced by a childhood memory: running into the street after tea, the pavement a hot, searing white, coins slippery in his seven-year-old palm. Reaching the juddering, custard-yellow van and breathing in the heady combination of raspberry syrup and diesel fumes.

The years inside seemed grey by comparison – leached of colour by their sameness and deadened by fear and rage. Those years, when the predominant smells of boiled cabbage and stale shit seemed almost interchangeable, had made him greedy for sensory stimulation of a more wholesome kind. He closed his eyes and breathed deeply, purging himself of the prison smells, relishing the prickling sensation of the privet's scent on his palate and at the back of his throat.

A car pulled up almost opposite and Clemence slumped lower in his seat, cupping his hand protectively over the zoom lens in his lap, then, cautiously lifting the camera to waist height, he turned his head slowly, his heart thumping painfully in his chest. It was her.

He experienced a curious mixture of excitement and anxiety: this woman represented a goal – perhaps even an ambition. It had taken some time to build to this moment. He had sought her out, and now he was determined that he would get what he came for.

She got out of her car and walked towards the house with the faded red door, broken fence and overgrown privet hedge. He had imagined her somewhere grander – more picturesque – with neatly pruned shrubs, and borders planted with meticulous reference to the colour wheel: no clashing oranges and purples for her, but tasteful drifts of graded tints, and a carefully considered marrying of texture and form.

She reached the front door and he zapped off a few shots as she turned into the sunlight to rummage for her keys in her handbag. He liked catching women unawares: it was at such moments that they often exhibited an unselfconscious grace.

She went through the door and he waited. No point in startling her. Give her a few minutes to kick off her shoes, hang up her jacket, maybe put the kettle on. She might even offer him a cuppa. The anxiety had been replaced by a growing sense of dread. Group therapy sessions during his final three years inside had taught him to recognise the often confusing emotions he felt. They had also practised anger management: identify the signs and deactivate the rage or, if it got past control, walk away. Not always an option on the inside, but being on the outside made things easier on that score – it was so *big* for one thing; there were so many places you could go. And managing the anger had unexpected advantages: putting distance between what you might call the incitement, and the retribution made detection more difficult.

He checked his watch. He'd given her long enough. He rolled up the window and reached for the door handle. A moment of doubt like a spasm of pain. What if she wouldn't speak to him? He forced himself to take a few breaths. She would – he would talk, and she would listen. He would persuade her.

He got out of the car and crossed the street.

# I

Michaela O'Connor had that look on her that said she would pursue the case to its natural conclusion, which generally meant until she got her way.

'Mitch, you know I'm grateful.' Clara Pascal gathered up her papers, trying to avoid her friend's eye. 'I mean, for the work – and . . . well, everything.'

This was a conversation they had had many times, and Michaela – Mitch to her friends – showed no sign of tiring of the argument. 'So do this,' she said, obdurate, implacable. 'For me.'

Clara shot her a look.

'I'm a lawyer,' Mitch retorted, answering as though Clara had voiced her disapproval. 'Unscrupulous manipulation is in the job description.'

It was such an outrageously inaccurate portrait of her friend and colleague that in other circumstances, Clara would have laughed. As it was, she finished packing her bundle to prepare for tomorrow's case and set her briefcase upright on the scuffed oak desk top. She looked into Mitch's frank, fearless face, and it pained her to see love and frustration, both directed at her.

'It's a woman, Clara,' Mitch said. 'Not some fifteen

stone, testosterone-crazed thug. She's just a woman who couldn't take any more. She's not denying she did it. She's not trying to fool anyone, or get away with anything. But she wants justice.' She left a silence that Clara, despite her resolve to get out quickly and agree to nothing, felt she had to answer.

'She has a strong case, Mitch, anyone could—'

'I don't want just anyone,' Mitch insisted. 'She needs someone experienced. Someone persuasive.'

'She could do worse than have you for an advocate,' Clara said, forcing a smile.

'I'm dealing with the unfair dismissal.' Understatement was one of Mitch's more disarming attributes: although she made it sound routine, this one looked like being a test case.

Clara felt sick. 'God, Mitch, please don't ask me to do this.'

'I *am* asking, Clara.'

Mitch had been among the first to call after she had been released. She hadn't been embarrassed like so many others who had left messages of goodwill, but *God forbid* that Hugo should disturb the invalid. Mitch had demanded to speak to Clara and immediately asked if she was up to a visit.

'Is it important?' Clara had avoided people right from the beginning. 'Can't we talk over the phone?'

'Sure it's important.' Mitch's Dublin accent was always strongest when she was delivering home truths to her friends. 'And no, we can't do this over the phone – I want to be able to see you when you tell me you're fine, so I can look you in the eye when I call you a liar.'

Since that day, Mitch had done her a hundred favours and she was asking for just one in return. If it weren't for the cases Mitch's practice had provided over the past months, Clara would have no reason to get out of bed in the morning. Her caseload at Jericho Chambers had dried to a slow trickle because she was so choosy about which she would take on. Within a few weeks it would be little more than a drip. But even the *thought* of taking a criminal case brought her out in a cold sweat.

She looked into Mitch's oval, pleasant face again and said quietly, 'I'm sorry. I'll do civil, I'll do family – I'll do the bloody *filing*, if it helps! Just don't ask me to do criminal law.'

Outside, she went through the ritual that always made her feel ashamed: looking both ways before stepping out onto the narrow pavement, crossing the road and walking up the gated path to Kaleyards car park, her car keys ready in her hand – for easy escape, or as a weapon. Kaleyards was hemmed in by the shops on one side and the sheer sandstone bank of Chester's city walls on the other, but it was infinitely preferable to the grey concrete confinement of the multi-storey in Pepper Street. She checked over her shoulder as she pressed the remote door release, her heart pounding, her breathing as ragged as if she had been running. The worst part was getting the door open and sliding behind the wheel.

When she was a child, she was afraid of something that hid on the landing; when she had to come downstairs alone, she always counted the steps. By the seventh, she knew it had crept to the bars and was peering down at her. By the tenth, it was at the top of the stairs, ready to pounce, the nameless, shapeless terror that lurked in the dark corners of her childhood. The trick was to get to the bottom fast and rush to the sitting room without looking back. Sometimes she thought she heard its heavy tread on the stairs at her back, and once, she felt a draught of warm air as it swiped at her and missed, but it never caught her. Not then.

She had waited till adulthood to meet the bogeyman. She knew now that the bogeyman had a name and human form. She had looked the bogeyman in the eye.

Pippa no longer ran to the door to greet her in the evenings. But Trish came into the hallway, as she always did, smiling a welcome.

'Good day?' she asked, wiping her hands on a towel. She had pulled her hair back into a ponytail, and her plump, friendly face was flushed. Trish had been with them since Pippa's infancy, first as a nanny, later as child-minder and part-time housekeeper. She was the same age, and had similar tastes to Clara. They all regarded her as one of the family. In recent months Pippa had clung to Trish as the one steady, calming influence in an uncertain world.

She kept her distance, but Clara knew Trish well enough to be sure that if she showed a moment's weakness, a hint of receptiveness, Trish would seize her in a fierce hug, trying to squeeze the pain out of her.

Clara hung her jacket in the cloakroom and kicked off her shoes. 'What's for dinner?' she asked, her voice a touch too loud, a touch too bright. *Brittle, Clara. You sound brittle.*

Trish half-turned, uncertain if she should give the news. 'I think Hugo . . .'

He appeared from the kitchen. He always had a hunched, slightly bruised appearance these days; nevertheless, he towered over Trish. 'I thought we might go out,' he said. 'Give Trish a break from cooking.'

*It's not just me who sounds brittle.* Clara suffered a brief spasm of anguish. *So much love, and for what?* She clamped down on that. Clamped down on it and stamped on it, hard.

'Good idea,' she said, closing the cloakroom door, not wanting to see his pleased expression because a moment later she was going to disappoint him. 'You three go. I've work to do.'

'It's just an hour or two . . .' She couldn't see the reproach or the hurt on his face, but it was clear enough in his voice.

'I can't spare two hours,' she said. 'This case—'

'*What* case?' Now he was angry. 'It's not as though you're inundated with work . . .'

She glanced up sharply, and Trish, embarrassed, sidled past Hugo, returning to the kitchen.

'The case I'm working on,' she said evenly.

He bit back a reply and took a step towards her, regret and concern getting the better of his impatience.

'I'll be in my office.' She headed for the stairs.

'Pippa barely saw you over the weekend,' Hugo protested.

'I'll be sure and kiss her goodnight when you get home.'

'Don't *bother*.'

Pippa stood at the top of the stairs. Her father in miniature: the creamy skin was tanned a shade or two darker than his after a summer holiday spent mainly out of doors, but her hair was the same glossy black as her father's and her eyes were the same startling blue. Her little body bristled with injured pride. 'I wouldn't want to put you out.' She stalked past and Clara realised with detached interest that she felt nothing: no remorse, no hurt – not even anger at her daughter's resentment.

Hugo caught her as she stamped down the hall. 'Apologise to your mother, young lady,' he said.

'No.' The answer was unequivocal. She stared defiantly up at her father, the little frown line between her eyebrows a replica of his own.

'*Apologise*, Pippa.'

'Hugo, it really doesn't matter,' Clara said.

'See?' Pippa demanded. '*She* doesn't care.'

But Hugo was not about to let this one go. After a second or two, Pippa relented. 'All *right* then. I'm sorry.' She shook free of her father and stormed off, shouting, 'I'm sorry for being such a bloody nuisance!'

Hugo called after her, but she slammed the kitchen door, rattling it in its frame.

'She's confused, Clara,' he said. 'She doesn't understand why—'

'I'd better make a start,' Clara interrupted.

'We'll stay then.'

'For God's sake, Hugo! Will you just *go*?'

She knew she was driving him away and a part of her wanted that. She was angry with everyone and trusted no one. But why was she angry with Hugo? She would not let herself think about that – did not even admit it to herself consciously – but her rage against Hugo was real and powerful. She lashed out verbally. And sometimes she wanted to lash out physically. She hadn't – not yet – but the ferocity of her feelings frightened her. She closed her eyes, willing away the urge to apologise, masking her guilt with anger.

He spoke quietly: 'I don't like to leave you here alone.'

She laughed. It sounded bitter and harsh, even to her own ears, and she barely recognised herself. 'You needn't worry,' she said. 'Trish keeps the paracetamol locked away these days.'

Hugo looked more puzzled than upset. 'I didn't mean that.'

She knew he didn't. What he meant was he didn't like to leave her all alone in their big old house with its creaky boards and sighing timbers; with the shufflings and thumps that kept her awake every night. Part of her wanted to go to him and smooth the worry line from his forehead, but the hard, self-destructive voice that had gained such power over her in the preceding months spoke with cold disdain: 'I think I can manage for an hour or two on my own.'

Half an hour after they left, Clara was back on the road, heading for Upton-by-Chester. Marcia Liddle lived in a big nineteen-twenties semi, backing onto the golf course. She conducted her therapy sessions in a high-ceilinged room with ornate cornices and honey-coloured floorboards, overlooking the golf course. In winter, a coal fire burned in the hearth, augmenting the central heating, but today the fireplace was resplendent with a huge vase of late summer garden flowers. The window sashes were thrown wide, admitting wafts of night-scented stock and occasional bursts of birdsong: wrens and robins and the two-tone creaking of great tits.

'I'm pleased you came back,' Marcia said, smiling a welcome and showing her to a chair. 'I wasn't sure you would.' This was only their third session, and the second had ended acrimoniously.

Clara bit her lower lip. 'About last week . . .'

Marcia didn't speak, and Clara recognised it as one of her ploys: there was no polite negation of bad behaviour or emotional outbursts in Marcia's sessions. No blame, either, but explanations were elicited, and she was capable of monumental silences to get the answer she sought. Clara tried letting her mind wander, taking in the shelves of books on counselling and psychology, the tape deck that Marcia sometimes used in her sessions, the porcelain masks she collected as a hobby.

Marcia waited and Clara, unable to bear the silence any longer, said, 'I was angry.'

'Why?'

'*You're* supposed to tell *me*.'

'We're working on this together, Clara.'

'I'm fed up with guessing games, Marcia,' she said. 'I don't understand the rules.'

Marcia looked at her in mild surprise. 'There are no rules. Not in the way you mean. If there is a rule, it's that we both try to make you well.'

'I'm not sick.'

'You're not *well*, either.'

Marcia was in her mid-fifties; she wore her fine, greying hair in a short crop cut. The only make-up Clara had ever noticed was her lipstick, which was a little too bright for the pallor of her skin. She held Clara with her kindly, myopic stare and Clara wanted to lash out at her, to dent her imperturbable calm. She closed her eyes, alarmed by the violence of her thoughts. It was a mistake: she should never have resumed her counselling sessions. She felt a prickling at the back of her nose and her eyes felt hot and wet. *I will not do this. I will not cry!*

She swallowed, took a breath and opened her eyes. 'Sometimes, I feel so full of rage . . .' She stared at a porcelain Pierrot mask on the bookshelf behind Marcia, willing herself not to break down.

'It's a defence, Clara,' Marcia explained. 'The anger. A way of allowing you to feel you have some control.'

Clara recognised this. Her kidnapper had robbed her of her liberty, but worse, he had denied her right to basic human dignity. He terrorised, brutalised and humiliated her, and during that long, cold, terrible incarceration her fear had turned to anger. Only her anger – only her downright fury – had kept her from despair. Now it served a different purpose: it stopped her from feeling helpless.

'I don't want Hugo to treat me like an invalid,' she said.

'Even when you behave like one?'

'What?'

'You're afraid to go out. Afraid of the dark, of being alone, of enclosed spaces, of crowds, of practising your chosen career—'

'Now wait a minute,' Clara interrupted.

Marcia raised a hand to silence her. 'You're sending out confused signals. You're saying "look after me" and as soon as anyone makes a move, you fight them off, tooth and nail. Do you think you *deserved* what happened to you, Clara – is that why you refuse their sympathy?'

'I don't have to listen to this,' Clara said, standing up and walking quickly to the door.

'No – you don't. So why did you come?'

Clara rested her hand on the door handle, ready to escape. 'I thought you'd help.'

'But you don't need help. You're not an invalid.'

Clara leaned her head against the glossy paintwork of the door. It felt cool, comforting.

'Who are you most angry with – yourself, or Hugo?'

The question was so bizarre that Clara turned to face her counsellor. 'Why on earth would I blame Hugo?'

Marcia raised her eyebrows. 'Blame?' she repeated. 'I didn't use the word "blame", I suggested that you were angry.'

'You're twisting my words,' Clara said. 'I'm not angry with him and I don't blame him.'

'Why not? After all, he didn't save you.' Marcia's voice was calm, warm, but insistent.

Clara laughed in astonishment. 'That's preposterous.'

'Is it? What about the irrational part of you – the part that hyperventilates at the thought of going into the basement of a building? Isn't that part of you boiling mad because he did nothing to prevent your abduction?'

'How could he? You're not making sense . . .'

'That's the whole point of these awful events, Clara. Nothing makes sense any more. Our whole view becomes distorted. We no longer see ourselves as worthy – the world as benign.'

'It never was,' Clara said.

'You're right,' Marcia agreed. 'It's all smoke and mirrors. But what do we have, without our illusions? An indifferent world? A hostile world? Worse yet – a dangerous one?'

Clara closed her eyes briefly. 'This doesn't help,' she said, 'Going over and over it. I've been doing that for the last nine months, and all it does is make me more angry and more afraid.'

Marcia nodded agreement. 'The panic attacks are getting worse, and you're developing more phobias because you've replaced your illusions with irrational fears.'

'How can you say my fear is irrational, after what I went through?'

'When a whiff of cigarette smoke can induce a panic attack, I think I'm justified in calling it an irrational response. You were in a horrible situation in which you were horribly frightened, and you were subjected to cigarette smoke. So now, smoke equals danger. Classical conditioning.'

'It doesn't make it any less real.'

'I know. And as you've said, it doesn't help, continually churning it over. The question is, what are you going to do about it?'

Clara listened to the sound of her own breathing. 'I don't know, Marcia. I wish I did.'

Marcia gazed at her intently for some moments, then she gave a short nod, as if satisfied that Clara was ready to hear what she had to say. 'Illusions and irrational fears are both based on false premises, Clara. But given the choice, I'd go for the illusion every time. It makes life bearable. It helps us to get out of bed in the morning. Unfortunately, you can't re-establish an illusion. Once it's shattered it cannot be remade. But you *can* rationalise. You can apply logic, statistics, the laws of averages if you will.'

'But it doesn't *help*,' Clara cried, wild with despair. 'Don't you think I've told myself all of this – "It's only cigarette smoke", "only a courtroom"?'

'They're learned behaviours,' Marcia said. 'Learned behaviours can be *un*learned.'

'I tried that with my last therapist – it didn't work.'

'You tried desensitisation?'

'Yes.'

'How long did you try for?'

Clara looked out of the window.

'How many therapy sessions?'

Two men tramped silently across the golf course, a couple of hundred yards away.

'Clara?'

'Three.' When she looked back, there was amusement in Marcia's eyes. She didn't need to say anything: she had made her point. Clara smiled reluctantly, feeling a little foolish.

'What do I have to do?' she asked.

'We'll begin with relaxation techniques. We'll tackle your phobias here in the therapy sessions initially, decreasing the level of anxiety you feel just thinking about these stimuli. When you've got that under control, then we'll slowly introduce the stimuli themselves. We'll work on managing your anger. I'll set homework tasks: techniques for you to practise, relaxation, visualisation, rationalisation. We'll go very slowly – you dictate the pace.'

Clara nodded slowly. This sounded manageable. 'Okay.'

'Explain what we're trying to your husband and friends – you'll need their help.'

'No.'

'I'm sorry?'

'Hugo doesn't know. Nobody does.' It had been a relief when Hugo had told her of their plans to eat out: at least she wouldn't have to lie about where she was going. Marcia waited and Clara sighed impatiently. 'There's nothing sinister in it. It might not work out. I just didn't want to build up his hopes.'

'And you didn't want people asking awkward questions. After all, it's easier to drop out if nobody knows but you and me . . .'

It was true: Clara had arranged sessions during the working day, at night, changing the times so that neither Hugo nor Mitch suspected. She had even lied to Hugo about working out of town, anything rather than tell him what would give him hope – because she didn't truly believe that she would see it through to the end.

Marcia leaned forward in her chair, animated, eager, her professional detachment suspended for the moment. 'You're surrounded by people who love you. Let them help you. Give it a try. What's the worst that could happen?'

'I fail.' Clara swallowed. The thought was almost unbearable. 'I lose them.'

'And if you don't try? What happens then? D'you think you'll keep them?'

# 2

You tried to talk her round, but she wouldn't listen. It wasn't your fault. She wouldn't see sense.

You feel sick – you won't enjoy this – but you can't deny there is also a measure of triumph. Because she's pleading. She'll do anything. *Now* she'll do anything. Now that it's too late. Now that things have gone too far.

The first swing, you're so frightened it won't be hard enough that you overcompensate. The crunch of bone and cartilage makes you think of treading on snails. Her eye socket shatters. Blood spatters everywhere. Oh, God . . . Blood and something else, grey, the texture of blancmange, lands with a splat on the wall. You feel weak with nausea. Too much force. Your heart is beating so hard you feel as if your chest will explode.

She twitches and makes a gagging sound, but even now you know that she's gone. Wait long enough and she's gone. She's not struggling. Take your time. You can stop now. All you need do is wait.

But you can't stop. It scares you how much you hate her. She fucked up your life. She refused to do what any decent human being would do. You want to wipe her out. To obliterate her. Face (*smack!*) body (*smack!*) mind (*smack!*) . . . You lose count how many times. You're panting. Out of breath with terror and rage. Enough.

The smell in the room makes you heave. Butcher's shop. Butcher's slime. There's a taste in your mouth like sucking pennies. You hear a sound: a faint expulsion of breath. *Dear God! Won't she be quiet?*

'You're dead, damnit! You're dead! Why won't you die?'

You wait. For a few dreadful seconds her body twitches, her legs jerking and her hands flailing. Her head is a bloody mass, but her body won't accept its death. It defies the reality. You want to scream. You want to run and hide, but you have to stay until she is dead, until you're certain she can't identify you. You cannot go to prison. You *will* not.

How long do you wait? Until at last she is still. Until the fine pink spray from the pulpy mess that was her lips has ceased, and when you uncover your ears, you can no longer hear the ugly wet gurgle of blood and air in her throat. Until you grow cold as her body chills and your legs and back and head ache with the waiting.

Clearing up is the hardest part. *Harder than bluffing your way in? Harder than that first crack with the hammer?*

Yes. Because at the start, you had the anger to keep you from running. But now – what is there to rage against? It doesn't even look like her any more. The legs and arms and torso are there, but she is not. She's nothing but a smear on the sole of your shoe. You think again of snail shells crunching underfoot and you dry-heave.

Stop. Stop and think. You have to keep a clear head. This stage is crucial. This is where most mistakes are made. Concealment is the next step. And disposal – of the weapon and of your clothing.

You know you'll have nightmares about this. Before, you told yourself to expect to see her bloody face in your dreams; blood and flesh and bone. But now you know for sure, the one thing you will recall is seeing her blue moccasin slipper, lying on its side by her naked foot.

And even as you clean up, you know that the worst, the hardest part is yet to come. You will have to face people, knowing what you have done. And every time you will have to tell yourself that when they look at you they can't see what's in your heart. They can't read what's in your mind.

Liars know that. And cheats and con-artists and adulterers . . . and murderers. When people look at you, they see what's on the surface and they judge you by what they see.

# 3

By six a.m., the thin mist that hugged the ground in pockets was all but gone. A dew pearled the neatly trimmed squares of lawn marking the boundaries between private property and public footpath, but the south-facing houses in Leahurst Street were already warming in the sun.

A wood pigeon crooned mournfully across the empty roadway and the air, still pungent with the spicy-sweet scent of honeysuckle, blurred the margins of night and day.

Mark Tidswell's milk float wheezed down the street, stopping every twenty yards. He was a neat, wiry man and he worked fast. There were more orders for orange juice in the hot weather, and this August had been a right scorcher, which meant making the deliveries at a trot if he was to keep to schedule.

Number twenty-nine was up early. The front door was open and the milk bottles gleamed on the step. Nice-looking bint, that one. He engaged in a mildly erotic fantasy as he bent to pick up the sun-warmed empties and replaced them with one pint of milk and one of orange. He wasn't sure what made him turn back. Something he had seen, but which didn't register on a conscious level. What he told his wife – but not the lads at the dairy – was that the hairs on the back of his neck stood up, and he felt a dark presence at his back.

When he looked again at the white uPVC door frame, he saw blood. A wide track of blood, as if something very wet with it had brushed past, leaving a slick ten centimetres wide. There was blood on the door handle, too, like someone had tried to pull the door shut on their way out. He looked down and saw that the doormat was rucked and a corner caught at the bottom of the door jamb, preventing the door from closing.

Tidswell eased the empty bottles back onto the doorstep, wincing at the faint *clink* of glass on glass. He dipped inside his uniform jacket, took his cell phone from his shirt pocket and punched triple nine. His finger hovered over the 'call' button as he pushed the door open, taking care to avoid the smears of blood.

His heart was hammering; he felt both foolish and terrified. After all, what did he know? She might have cut herself pruning the roses – or it might not be blood at all – he might just open the porch door and see her padding about in her nightie, munching a piece of toast. The notion no longer had any erotic allure.

He was about to step inside when he realised that he had nothing heavier than his mobile phone to heave at an attacker, and he bent to pick up a full bottle of milk. The hall was empty and still, almost as if the house held its breath.

'Hello?' he called, ready to back out fast if anyone replied. He took a couple more steps and called again. 'Hello?' He couldn't remember her name – number twenty-nine – a pint a day and orange juice on Wednesday and Saturday, he knew that, but not her name.

There was more blood on the door of the front room. On the broad wedge of carpet, visible through the open door, a footprint: large, man-size. And a smell. Like a butcher's slab. His breathing grew more shallow and rapid. *Press call and wait for the cops*, Mark, he told himself. But pride made him go on. He would feel a prize prat if he called them out and Mrs twenty-nine came trolling downstairs wanting to know what the hell he was doing in her hallway, and why the police were clumping up her path.

So he eased the door open, calling again, glad that the lads couldn't hear that tentative, poncy 'Hello-oo?'

She lay on her back, her feet towards him. The milk bottle slipped through his fingers and bounced on the carpet. The pressure lifted an edge of the foil cap and it leaked silently onto the floor, turning pink as it mingled with a patch of blood. Her face was covered with a cushion, taken from the sofa near the window, but there was no doubt as to how she died. No doubt at all.

He moaned, backing for the door, unable to take his eyes off her. Once in the hallway, he ran. Bolted for his milk float and collapsed on the step, his head between his knees, waiting for the faintness to pass. It wasn't until five minutes later, when number forty-seven came across him on his way to work, that he remembered the phone in his hand and made the final keystroke that brought the police.

DS Phil Barton arrived at the same moment two uniformed officers pulled up outside the house in a marked car – Leahurst Street was just three streets away from his own; his wife, Fran had taken the call as he towelled off from the shower.

Barton was a stocky man, with an air of both authority and physical vigour. His hair was thinning and he wore it cropped close to his scalp; today it bristled with two days' growth. He showed his ID to the uniformed sergeant and police constable as they got out of the car.

'Who's the informant?'

The sergeant nodded towards the milkman, still sitting on the step of his float, wringing his hands. 'Mark Tidswell,' he said. 'I'll have a word with him, shall I? See if I can get anything useful out of him.'

The constable set about shepherding a group of people, gathered at the front door of number twenty-nine, back onto the roadway. Barton stopped one of them at the garden gate. 'Who's the owner of the house?' he asked. 'Do you know?'

The man shrugged, apologetic. 'You don't see much of folk. 'Less you're home during the day.'

Barton raised his voice. 'Does anyone know her?' All he got was shamefaced looks. 'All right,' he said, rubbing a hand over the fuzz of growth on his head. 'Give your names and addresses to the constable, in case we need to speak to you again.'

He walked to the house with his head down, almost as if he intended to shoulder-charge his way in. There were some who weren't affected by this kind of thing. He wasn't one of them. At the front door he took a deep breath, then stepped into the cool shadows of the hall.

The smell was sickly sweet, with undertones of something sharper and more metallic. Blood. The door to the left of the porch was open. He edged in to the room, taking care not to touch the door. Barton's first task was to establish that they had a crime scene; his second was to preserve the integrity of the scene for the forensics team.

He stood in the doorway and took a long, hard look. A dark, drying stain had spread in a halo around the victim's head, the edges now crusted and almost black. A table had been overturned in the struggle and its lamp lay broken beside it, but the bulb was intact and it was switched on. So the victim was attacked during the hours of darkness. Maybe.

A milk bottle, half its contents leaked onto the carpet had mixed with some of the blood. It reminded him of the strawberry milk shake Timmy was so fond of, but he banished the thought before his digestive system could react, concentrating instead on the detail, keeping strictly to the facts, and suppressing any associations, any emotions.

There was a lot of blood spatter – walls, skirting

boards, even the ceiling. Was that grey matter on the walls? Jeez! He was grateful he wouldn't have the responsibility of photographing this lot in all its close-up, fast-film glory. He thought he understood the cushion over her face, too: repugnance, if not of the deed, then at least of the aftermath.

He felt a tremendous sadness, and a sense of outrage for the woman, not least because she had been so casually disregarded: the cushion seemed a final insult to her. But nothing could have compelled him to remove it – after all, he told himself, it wasn't his job to establish they had a corpse: leave that to the police surgeon.

A soft shuffle, followed by a *thump!* Barton's heart-rate picked up a notch. Upstairs. *Bloody hell!* Was the killer still in the house? He took out his Casco baton and, walking at the edge of the stair treads, avoiding touching the banister, began a cautious ascent.

A sudden sharp rattle of wood on wood. He ducked, freezing mid-step, and waited several beats before moving on. Near the top of the stairs, he heard the rattle again, a familiar sound, and yet so incongruous given the setting that he rejected the evidence of his own ears. He paused again, waiting – there it was – this time he knew for certain.

*A baby! My God – there's a baby in the house!*

He ran to the bedroom. Outside the door, he lowered his baton and listened for any sign that there was someone in there with the child. There was nothing except the rattle of little hands batting the wooden bars of a cot and the incomprehensible burble of a child in quiet conversation with itself. He turned the handle, slowly opening the door.

The little girl stood up in her cot, fair hair curling in wisps around a face slightly distorted by a teething rash on her right cheek. She couldn't be more than a year old. She looked like she had been crying but now she was curious about the stranger at her bedroom door.

Her eyes opened wide with astonishment and she shook the cot bars excitedly, sticking out her padded rump and calling 'Mummummum.'

Barton lifted her out. She twisted in his arms, pointed with one pudgy finger to the door, and made a surprised exclamation.

*Where's Mummy*? Barton thought. She wants to know where her mummy is. Had she been awake when the killer battered her mother to death? Had she heard her mother's screams?

He bent to pick up a teddy bear from the floor – the thump he had heard on his way to the front door – and handed it to her. She gave a cry of delight, burying her face in it. She was hot, despite the short-sleeved vest and pants she was dressed in. He reached into her cot for a teething ring. He thought she would be needing a comforter during the next few hours. She took it and immediately began to chew on it, dribbling onto her vest and the sleeve of his jacket.

'Let's go and see what we can find outside,' he suggested.

The baby squealed and jiggled up and down on his arm in excited approval. Barton shifted her to his left arm and flicked the Casco baton to full length before making his way carefully downstairs.

# 4

Ian Clemence worked in total darkness. It was a skill recently acquired, and one which gave him a thrill he couldn't explain. Maybe it was the manual dexterity it required. Maybe it was knowing the task so well that he could literally do it blindfold. He had prepared everything in advance: the solutions were mixed, measured and warming to twenty degrees Celsius in a tray he had improvised as a water bath.

He prised the top off the film cassette with a bottle opener and took out the film, taking care to handle the edges only. Then he trimmed the film leader and felt for the plastic spiral on the counter in front of him, winding the film onto the spool before placing it in the light-tight developing tank and snapping on the lid. The rest of the process could be done in the light.

He pulled the cord and checked the temperature of the developing solution. Almost ready. He was proud of his dark-room; Walker, the landlord, had insisted that the adaptations were easily removable, so he had fitted the hardboard blackout to the window with turn catches. He wasn't too keen when Clemence said he wanted to rip out the single sink unit and wobbly cupboard that represented the entire fixtures and fittings of the old kitchen, but he came round when he saw the improvements Clemence had made by scraping off fifteen years of grease and dirt before painting and fitting units he had scrounged from a house refurb. up the road. Course, old Walker wasn't too keen on black – said it didn't really fit with kitchen ambience.

'I was thinking more of Mediterranean colours,' he said. 'Terracottas and blues.'

Clemence had to promise a repaint if he ever moved on. He was a bit concerned that the room was airtight as well as light tight, but he would take care of that if he stayed much longer.

He timed each stage carefully: developer, stop bath, fixer, then on to the rinse, placing the tank in the double sink and feeding the mixer hose into the top. The rinse would take thirty minutes. He heard a door slam in one of the rooms above him, then the rapid thud of footsteps on the stairs. His kitchen dark-room had originally been a pantry, built under the stairs of the old house. Initially he had been worried about dust falling from the stair treads onto his drying negatives and prints, but he solved that problem by lining the treads with foil and finishing the job with panelling.

As the front door slammed, he lifted a strip of thirty-six negatives he had developed the previous night, scanning for anything interesting. He found half a dozen of the woman in the little top with the shoestring straps. Her bra-strap showed, he remembered. These days, it seemed, showing a thin ribbon of bra-strap was all right.

He smiled, running a finger along the contour of her

face. It was a source of constant surprise and pleasure that photography allowed him such licence. He couldn't imagine any other circumstances in which he could stare so fixedly at a woman without giving cause for offence. Not that he was a perv – but it had been a long time and, although he did like to look, it would take him a while to trust himself again around women in a social setting.

He would make the contact prints now. He brushed the negs off with an artist's brush, then turned on the safe light before flicking off the white light. He had thought that the confinement of this little, stuffy room would be a problem, but he discovered a serenity in the stillness and dark. He smiled, remembering something he had read in one of the photographic text books he had borrowed from the library: 'Pictures,' the author had lyricised, 'are like women. They require your full attention – and your most delicate work is done in the dark.'

Developing and printing was a new departure for him. Inside, he had no choice – all the photography class's work was sent to a photo lab and, having worked in one since his release, he knew that there was no scope for artistic interpretation or even technical skill. All he did at the lab was load the films and check the paper levels; the machine did the rest. Still, he had learned a thing or two about camera technique and the manager had allowed him to take some waste material home – off-cuts and dregs, he'd said. And if Clemence was a little free in his interpretation of end-of-roll, and if, from time to time there happened to be more than a drain of fixer in the canisters, who would blame him for liberating it for himself?

He cut the thirty-six negs into strips of six and laid them side-by-side in the contact printer's lid, then placed an eight-by-ten piece of printing paper on the baseboard and transferred the lot to the enlarger. Fifteen seconds exposure would be plenty. Timing it to the second, he switched off the lamp and transferred the sheet to the developing tray.

This stage had been a new revelation. Watching the pictures ghost onto the paper the first few times, seeing them rapidly take form and substance, he had to remind himself not to hold his breath. And he had overdeveloped a few, being so mesmerised by the sharpening of the image. Now he timed everything to the second, following the instructions on the solution bottles. He enjoyed the apparent contradiction that resulted in good photographs: the combination of science and art, honesty and artifice.

Time up. He lifted the prints out of the developer with a pair of tongs and slid them into the stop bath. Shit. Even without a magnifying glass he could see a mistake. How the hell did he miss it? Behind the woman, scaffolding on the sandstone backdrop. Distracting and aesthetically displeasing. He had followed the maestro's advice a little too closely, giving his full attention to the woman, when he should have looked at the setting, too. He should have used a wider aperture, reduced the depth of field and blurred the background a little. It was tempting to bin the lot, but he decided to continue the process through to completion. Maybe he would try making one of those vignettes – fogging the background with under- or over-exposure. Might be worth a try.

Sometimes, he thought, you just have to coax the picture you want out of the picture you've taken. He hadn't read that anywhere, but he had discovered for himself that sometimes the picture was hidden in the development and sometimes it was the sitter who was playing hide-and-seek, flirting with the camera.

Clemence knew all about hiding. He was a master of concealment. For twelve years he had avoided discovery, hiding his feelings, his fears, his wants and desires. He had even learned to conceal pleasure. Inside, a smile was interpreted as a gesture of appeasement; most of the places he had been banged up, you might as well crawl on your belly as go around with a smile on your face. Smiling was for ponces; smiling was for victims. If you wanted to stay safe, you didn't smile, and you learned to make eye-contact only when you intended to back it up with action.

He hadn't realised just how complete his disappearance had been until he noticed that his co-workers stayed clear of him when he started at the lab – well clear – as if he had a three-foot barrier around him and they were wary of invading his personal space. It had taken a conscious effort to relax his face muscles, to smile occasionally. And gradually he had gained their trust.

When he looked at one of his black-and-white portraits of a con and saw something the man thought he had hidden, that was a moment of real excitement.

Sometimes he saw sadness betrayed in the droop of an eyelid, defensiveness in the lift of the chin. Cons were masters of concealment, but the camera, although it did lie – of course it did, otherwise, where was the pleasure? – it was also capable of great honesty.

Survival on the outside required a different sort of concealment – new rules. The image that had served him so well all those years – con, hard man – did not serve so well when people were free to walk away from you. You had to learn to get on with people in a different way, and it didn't always involve strength. If you wanted to take pictures of people, you had to make them feel relaxed, safe.

Developing and printing was the same. You had to coax the right contrast, balance the light and shade, keep it from becoming too hard, push it on from being too soft. He had learned a lot from the text books, some more by trial and error, but mistakes were expensive – in photography just as much as in life – and he didn't have cash to spare. He had grappled with how to achieve texture and depth and movement and, more than anything else, clarity in his pictures.

Not the kind of clarity that relates to focus and depth of field. This clarity was about ways of seeing. It was about catching the essence – of the person, the situation, even of the quality of light. It was about finding the picture in the scene, capturing the moment, distilling the feeling of that moment in the turn of the head or – Yes, in a smile.

He gave names to his pictures; names, times and dates, and he catalogued and filed them carefully.

They were a history, a record of his progress and, in a more undefinable way, they represented a return to life. The very difference of the scenes, the people, the settings he captured on film was a testament to his freedom.

The luminous face of the clock reminded him that it was almost time for his shift. The rest would have to wait until later. He picked up his camera and opened the body. The film was already rewound into the cassette. He tipped it out, snapped in a new film and closed the catch, listening with satisfaction to the autowind preparing it for the first shot. He placed the completed roll in a cylinder and clipped on the lid.

He cleared the foodstuff from the cupboard above the bench and, using a penknife, he flipped the catches and eased the backboard out a fraction, levering it the rest of the way with his fingertips. The gap behind the board was just sufficient to accommodate the film.

The pictures on it weren't his best work, but then conditions hadn't been ideal. Using a flash had been out of the question and he'd had to get the shots and get gone fast. Still . . .

He threw the tube in the air and caught it again. Worth the risk.

# 5

The radio played at low volume. A local music station. Hugo and Pippa chatted at the kitchen table; Trish was coming to take Pippa to the zoo, and Pippa was looking forward to one of Trish's famous picnics.

'It's a pity they don't do elephant rides at Chester Zoo any more,' Hugo said. 'I could have told you how you get down from an elephant.'

Pippa stared at him, wide-eyed. 'How *do* you get down from an elephant?'

He grinned. 'You don't get down from an elephant, you get down from a duck.'

She giggled and elbowed him in the ribs. 'You're such a Sad Dad.'

For a moment they were silent and the clink of their spoons against their breakfast bowls chimed with the alarm call of a blackbird. Though the kitchen windows stood open, barely a breath of air circulated: it was going to be one of those still, suffocating days when the consultation rooms at Wrexham County Court would be stiflingly hot.

Clara hoped it would not put her client in a bad mood. She was representing Jill Quigley, a twenty-year-old, in a wrangle with her ex-husband over access.

Clara believed that in their hearts neither truly wanted to deprive the other of time with their child, and yet twice when he had called to pick up Daniel, their son, Gary had found the house empty. It was difficult, Jill said, when she had to rely on public transport, adding that he had no such excuse when he had brought Daniel back late from his last visit, making her miss a hospital appointment.

Clara suspected that each was trying to tell the other, first by poor timekeeping, and now through the courts, that they were hurt. That they had thought love was for ever, that it was supposed to make up for lack of money and poor housing. It was supposed to make life sweet and instead, before either of them had reached the age of twenty-one, they were consumed with bitterness and made helpless by an absence of hope.

Clara sighed and Hugo reached across the table and squeezed her hand. She glanced up, surprised. Pippa looked from her father to her mother and back again, a wary expectancy lighting her face, then the letterbox rattled, breaking the spell. She jumped down from her chair and pelted out into the hall, yelling, 'I'll get it!'

Hugo stroked the crease between Clara's thumb and forefinger. 'Okay?' he asked.

'Why wouldn't I be?' She saw that slight retreat she had seen so many times in recent months. It was as though his focus shifted away from her – only by a fraction – but enough to create a safe distance between them.

*For God's sake, Clara – he's not accusing you of anything. Can't you at least be civil?* She put her hand over his, preventing its gentle withdrawal. 'Sorry,' she said. 'I'm fine.'

He leaned forward, increasing the pressure on her hand and the hope in his eyes nearly broke her heart.

Pippa found a clear space at the end of the table and began sorting the post into 'Mummy', 'Daddy' and 'junk' piles, keeping up a constant commentary. The radio news had just started and Clara cleared the breakfast dishes, listening with half an ear. The news reader listed the main items in brief, each separated by synthetic drum beats. The third item gave her a jolt.

She stood at the fridge door, the butter dish in her hand, and the cool draught that had been a welcome relief in the already sweltering air, became an icy chill.

Hugo flicked the radio switch, and in the silence she heard again the piping of the blackbird, sounding the alarm: predator on the loose.

Hugo turned to Pippa, who had stopped her sorting with two envelopes still in her hand. 'You get yourself ready for your day out, Poppet,' he said, smiling reassurance.

'Daddy . . .'

'Trish will be here in no time – I bet she'll take you to the café first thing and buy you an ice lolly.'

Pippa gave a quick nod and her hair bobbed and fell back into place. She had grown it out for the summer; it hung in a glossy black sheet, breaking on her bony shoulders.

Clara waited until she heard her daughter's footsteps on the stairs then she walked across the kitchen and switched the radio back on. The second item was just finishing Clara listened, holding her breath.

'Cheshire police have launched a murder hunt this morning,' the news reader began in suitably solemn tones.

'You don't have to listen to this,' Hugo said, talking over the commentary.

Clara turned up the volume.

'– the woman's badly beaten body was—'

'It doesn't mean that you're not safe.'

Clara glared at him and increased the volume again.

'Police say the shocking discovery was made by a local milkman on his rounds—'

'All right. *All right!*' He leaned past her and turned down the volume. 'But you don't have to make *her* listen.'

'Do you want her to think she's safe because Mummy and Daddy are here to look after her?'

'Don't, Clara. Please, don't do this.'

'Do *what*, Hugo?'

She felt tears prick the back of her eyes, and the strength of emotion surprised her. She *could* feel – for Pippa, anyway. But these were tears of hopelessness, and she wouldn't allow herself that indulgence. She fought them back angrily.

'What happened to you was—'

'Bad luck?'

'It doesn't happen all the time, and it doesn't happen to everyone.'

He was dealing in logic. What she felt was something more primal. Her abduction had wiped out every notion she had of security in the world. 'Every day,' she repeated. 'Women are raped. Beaten. Terrorised. Vanished.'

'It isn't going to happen to you.'

*Why can't he understand this didn't end with my safe return home?* 'This isn't about me.' They both knew that was a lie, but she went on, 'This is about a woman beaten to death in her own home, not more than two miles from where we live.'

'It won't happen to you,' he repeated. 'And it won't happen to Pippa.' He reached for her hand again, but she snatched it away.

'How can you *know* that?'

He seemed puzzled by the question, and she laughed, astonished by a sudden insight. 'You're thinking nothing so horrible could happen twice, right?'

He raised his shoulders.

'Who's going to stop it happening, Hugo?' Marcia had been right: as irrational as it seemed, she was angry with Hugo, because he hadn't been able to prevent it happening to her – all his strength and love were not enough to keep her safe. And now, restored to her family, even in his arms she was afraid.

Diva Legal Services was in a converted shop, mid-terrace, built of pink rustic brick, just outside the city walls on Frodsham Street: with its jumble of Tudor-style buildings and modern, flat-fronted shops, it had a cosiness that Clara found comforting. The pavements were narrow and busy with lunch-time shoppers, and Clara had to step into the gutter once or twice to let people pass.

'Diva' was a pun on Chester's Roman name and an oblique reference to the fact that Mitch O'Connor allowed only female barristers through the doors of her practice. Clara thought that the arc of gold lettering looked a little old-fashioned, but Mitch insisted that people found the traditional frontage reassuring. Clara's theory that it reminded Mitch of the 'owld cunthry' had earned her a clip round the ear from the Diva herself.

There was no revolving door and no security access here. The outer office was bright and clean, and wooden blinds on the windows provided privacy for the clients, but the furniture, though carefully matched, was gleaned from a warehouse clearance and the carpet was industrial quality cord.

Mitch dealt mostly in family law, and legal aid was rarely granted in such cases. Added to this was the problem that few of Mitch's clients were wealthy. She employed a sliding scale – clients were charged what they could afford to pay, the better off subsidising the poor – but since Diva Legal Services' fees were modest by most standards, nobody had yet complained.

Fliss, the receptionist/secretary was on her lunch break when Clara arrived and Mitch came out of her office to check who had come in. She winced at Clara's expression.

'Bad morning?' she asked.

'The judge sent them home. Told them not to waste the court's time until they have some positive suggestions about resolving the situation.'

'I thought you were confident of a settlement today.'

'I was. But I'd reckoned without Gary calling un-announced last Sunday, demanding to take Daniel boating on the Dee. Jill refused. They argued. It got ugly. Now neither is willing to compromise and Jill's trying to get a restriction order on him. Insisting on supervised visits.'

'So major set-back wouldn't be an exaggeration?'

'Total disaster wouldn't be an exaggeration,' Clara said.

'You'll feel better with coffee and carbohydrate inside you.' Mitch locked the front door and led the way through to the little kitchen at the back of the building. Diva Legal Services lacked the state-of-the-art drinks vendor that Jericho Chambers boasted – and if you wanted coffee, you made it yourself – but Mitch did keep a fresh supply of good filter coffee grounds.

Clara reached for the jug, but Mitch waved her away. 'That stuff's been stewing all morning,' she said. 'It'll curdle in your stomach.' She dumped the dregs and threw the old filter in the bin. While she prepared fresh, Clara dropped her briefcase in the corner and shrugged out of her jacket.

'You look like you need this,' Mitch remarked. 'Not sleeping?'

Clara shrugged. 'The pills knock me out, but I feel like I've climbed Snowdon by the end of the night.'

'Did you try that relaxation tape I gave you?'

'Can we change the subject?'

Mitch set the jug on the hot plate and the water began trickling through the filter, filling the kitchen with the rich, nutty aroma of Colombian coffee. 'All right,' she said. 'What's the plan?'

Clara frowned.

'Jill and Gary. What are you going to do?'

'Oh,' Clara relaxed a little. She had thought that Mitch was about to deliver one of her lectures on the general theme that accepting help was not a sign of weakness. 'If I can get Jill to see sense, I'll try for an early hearing. It might mean travelling out to Rhyl, to fit into the judge's timetable, but it'd be worth it.' She shifted uncomfortably under Mitch's gaze: she wasn't going to like this next bit. 'I thought I'd pop round this afternoon.'

'Pop round?' Mitch said. 'Pop round where?'

Clara looked away. 'To see Jill Quigley.'

'At her *house*?'

'I'm not planning to move *in*, Mitch. If I see her on her own territory – if she sees I'm concerned . . .'

Mitch folded her arms. 'Oh, and by the way, it means you'll be able to "see" the boy as well?'

In reply, Clara scooped a couple of mugs up from the table and took them to the sink to wash.

'Clara,' Mitch said, her tone disapproving. 'You've read the court welfare officer's report. Everything you need to know is in there.'

'I know what Jill Quigley wants,' Clara said, stolidly scrubbing and rinsing the mugs while the coffee machine spat and gurgled, steadily filling. 'I think I know what Gary wants. I'd like to be sure I know what Daniel wants.'

'He's five years old. He wants his mummy and daddy to stop shouting at each other.'

'And if she heard that from him . . .'

'You know as well as I do that these cases are decided on the paperwork,' Mitch insisted. 'The court welfare officer talks to the child and makes a report. We read it. We talk to the client and we present the case. Lawyers *don't talk to the child*.'

Clara turned to face her. 'Maybe that's part of the problem,' she said. 'Maybe that's why my client is being so bloody minded – because nobody really talks to the child.'

Mitch took the clean mugs and carefully poured the coffee into them. Twice she took a breath, then, with a shake of her head subsided. Only after she had added milk to Clara's mug and handed it to her did she speak. 'I know—' she began, then thought better of it. 'I *realise* how hard it's been for you. I understand your need to be as sure as you can be. But Clara, it wasn't just you that made a mistake, it was the court.'

This was the same argument Marcia had used; the same Clara herself had used a hundred times in trying to excuse herself, to lessen her burden of guilt, but she was never convinced. 'If I'd gone with my gut feeling . . .'

'Feelings are destructive when applied to the law. Feelings have nothing to do with justice. No—' she said, firmly quelling Clara's attempt to interrupt. 'Hear me out. I've waited a long time to say this.' Her Irish accent became stronger in her agitation, the 't's softening and the vowels rounding, so that the 'i's became 'oy's. 'No matter how bad it looks, no matter how damning the evidence, the accused has a *right* to a fair hearing and a competent defence.'

'I was more than competent, Mitch.'

Mitch smiled, deliberately misinterpreting the comment. 'Talent will out,' she said. She had a wide, generous mouth, and an infectious smile, but Clara was in no mood to be flattered.

She frowned, dismissing the compliment impatiently. 'I'm saying I wasn't just competent, I was *driven*. I pursued that case with a ruthlessness that had nothing to do with justice – to hell with justice, I was hungry for success. I wanted my result. I wanted colleagues to talk about the case. I wanted them to say how I'd beaten Peter Telford. Because Peter Telford is the best.'

Mitch didn't answer at first. She seemed to take all of this in, measuring her words before replying. At length, she sighed. 'You did the best job you could. That's what the law is all about, Clara. The defence does their best to prove their client's innocence; the prosecution do their damnedest to prove him guilty. That's why we don't have the mother or father of a hit-and-run victim try the driver. We appoint juries, and we rely on the good sense and common decency of reasonable people to decide innocence or guilt.'

# 6

By mid-afternoon, Detective Inspector Steve Lawson was making his second visit to the murder scene. The electoral register gave the householder's name as Amy Dennis. Identification would be confirmed from personal effects and dental records – physical identification was out of the question, given the extent of her injuries. He had met most of the enquiry team – some of whom he had worked with the previous year – and allocated roles to some.

He had been stationed in Warrington for the last six months, leading a CID team; plenty of variety and a fair clear-up rate, but he had missed the buzz of a major enquiry. DCI McAteer was the SIO on this one, and Lawson would be sharing an office with DS Phil Barton – he had worked with both men on the Clara Pascal kidnap the previous winter, and he liked and trusted them.

He parked halfway down Leahurst Street: press and local TV and radio had got hold of the story and their cars and an outside broadcast van had taken up all the available parking space nearest to the police tape. They waited together on the westerly edge, keeping the sun behind them, sweltering in their shirt-sleeves.

Lawson gave himself a few moments to take stock: they couldn't be expecting much to happen; the body had been taken to the Countess of Chester Hospital mortuary an hour previously, the search of the house and gardens and the public pathway at the back of the house continued, but there wasn't much to see. They held on, nevertheless, hoping that some grisly discovery would come to light.

The removal of the body and interviews of the neighbours had provided enough copy for one day, and the assembled media representatives were in relaxed mood. They lounged near the tape, chatting, flirting; one or two had even rolled up their sleeves to catch the sun. If Lawson moved fast he might reach the tape before they realised who he was.

He locked his car, avoiding using the remote, in case the flashing lights attracted attention, and walked quickly towards the crowd. Within two steps someone had spotted him.

'Inspector!' The man stepped forward, sweating, red-faced in the heat. 'Sir, when will the victim's name be released?'

Another reporter shouted a question: 'Is it Amy Dennis, Inspector?' Lawson knew, of course, that the police weren't the only ones with access to the electoral roll, but the press had moved fast on this one. Presumably word had got out about the severity of the victim's injuries. The journalists crowded round, barring his way.

He stopped walking and waited for the assembled media to settle. Standing still, he could command their attention. Media training had also taught him that pushing through the crowd, muttering 'no comment' would have the effect of making him look harried. So Lawson stopped, and while he waited for silence he decided what he could say without really saying anything.

'As soon as the relatives have been informed, we'll let you know,' he said. On the local TV news round-up, later, he would look cool and elegant. 'But I'm sure you appreciate the importance of respecting the feelings of the bereaved.'

'Yeah,' someone grumbled. 'But we've got deadlines to meet.'

'I've every sympathy,' Lawson said with dry good humour. A few of them smiled. They weren't hostile, and he was glad of that. 'But I'm sure none of us would like to hear of the death of a loved one on the news.' The reporter who had spoken shuffled a little, and muttered something under his breath. 'And we'll have a press briefing at four p.m. – Cheshire Police Headquarters.'

The radio and TV crews were mollified, but not all the press were happy with this arrangement: if there was something new to print, those who had evening editions to catch were already close to the cut-off point.

A dark-haired woman with thin, chiselled features and a touch of sunburn asked, 'Is it true the victim was battered with a hammer?'

'Four p.m., ladies and gentlemen,' Lawson replied, and moved on. This time they gave way with reasonably good grace.

The SOCOs had laid down aluminium staging to protect the carpets from contamination caused by the investigation team tramping in and out. Access was limited to Scene of Crime Officers and the pathologist, to try to reduce the risk of cross-contamination. The staging creaked and clattered as Lawson made his way inside. He found one of the SOCOs in the kitchen, packing his case ready to leave.

'All done here?' he asked.

The SOCO nodded. 'Not a moment too soon.'

'It must be like a sauna in that lot,' Lawson sympathised: the air was heavy with the sweet-sour smell of stale blood and the SOCO was kitted out in a zoot-suit – hood up as per regulation – and he was masked, gloved and booted.

Lawson coughed, trying to clear the metallic tang from the back of his throat. 'What've you got?' he asked.

'Apart from the front room which is pretty much awash – some blood in the hallway, on the doors, some on the carpets. Nice footprint in the living-room. Not a trace anywhere else – upstairs or down.'

'Fingerprints?'

'A few. But the bloodstains on the doors look like glove-prints. They're smooth. We might get something from the fibre lifts, but that's lab work – it'll take a while.'

Through the kitchen window, Lawson could see half a dozen uniformed officers searching the shrubs in the borders. Beyond that, on the dirt path that ran behind the houses, more officers inched slowly, prodding the undergrowth, picking bits of paper out of the hedge-row, bagging and labelling the detritus of a thousand careless walkers in the hope that one cigarette stub, one piece of torn cloth might provide a vital clue.

'Seen Sergeant Barton?' he asked.

The SOCO jerked his head towards the side door. 'In the garage, sir. We've given that the all-clear.'

Lawson retraced his steps, emerging with some relief into the fresh air. The heat and the glare felt like a physical barrier and he had to take a breath before he stepped out, ignoring the expectant faces of the journalists and walking around to the garage. Barton had left the side door open.

'Wow.'

Barton looked up from a pile of document wallets he was thumbing through. 'Not what you'd expect, is it?'

'Last time I looked, my garage was jammed with old furniture and bits of a motorbike I've been promising myself I'll rebuild for the last five years.'

Barton grinned. 'Isn't everyone's?'

'Apparently not.' Lawson gazed appreciatively around the room. The garage had been converted to a dark-room and office. The windows were blacked out, so light was provided by an overhead strip light and the small amount filtering through from the open door. An extractor fan hummed quietly at the far end of the dark-room, and although there was a faint whiff of chemicals – bleach, or some other alkali, he thought – it was far more pleasant then the oppressive stench of death in the house.

Barton took an armful of the buff-coloured folders

and sat on a blue-green leather sofa pushed against the end wall. The office area had wood laminate flooring and was furnished with bookshelves, a computer, filing cabinets and, incongruously, a playpen. Over all, a fine dusting of fingerprint powder.

Barton saw him glance at the playpen and asked, 'How's the baby?'

'She's fine,' Lawson said. 'Social services will probably place her with her grandparents for now.'

'Has the father been traced?'

'He's being interviewed now.' Lawson took a moment to scan the rest of the room, leaving Barton to continue sifting through files. Two-thirds of the room was given over to film development and processing.

The right side housed a sink, shallow plastic trays, a chemical storage rack, drying-racks containing prints and a line to which strips of negatives were pegged. Various jugs and measuring cylinders were ranged on the shelving over the bench and above this, a red wall-mounted safe-light with a pull-switch. Opposite was a dry area, with what he took to be two photographic enlargers; above one was a second safe-light. A trimmer lay next to a green gel cutting-board, and below the bench was row upon row of cabinets with shallow drawers, all labelled.

He walked over and slid one of the drawers open. A portrait of a man lay on top; his skin so tanned and wrinkled that it reminded Lawson of an elephant, as did the dark, intelligent eyes that peered out from the hatches and grooves of the ancient face. He found a pair of tongs on the bench above and picked up the photograph by the edge, tilting it. There were traces of fine, chalky powder on this, too.

'They did the top few,' Barton said. 'They put them all back in case you wanted to catalogue them. If you want the rest doing, they say they can come back, but there's barely a print in here, except for one or two from the baby. She seems to've been pretty obsessive about keeping the place dust-free – the SOCO photographer said it ruins the negs.'

'She wouldn't approve of this.' Lawson ran one finger over the surface of the bench, coming up with a silky patina of fingerprint powder. He counted the cabinets: twenty, the length of the dark-room, each with between five and ten drawers, each drawer containing dozens of pictures. 'Better lift this lot and put someone full-time onto checking them – I'm assuming she was a professional?'

'Most definitely.' Barton indicated the bookshelves opposite him. 'The ring binders are all lecture notes, as far as I can see. She worked part-time at Birkenhead Tech. These—' He held up the buff folders he was checking through '– These are students on a distance learning course – "Arts for Everyone".' He handed a few to Lawson.

Lawson opened the top folder. On the left of the top sheet was a photograph of a smiling woman with an eager expression and a broad, self-deprecatory smile. A box to the right gave her personal details: name, address, roll number, occupation and so on. Below this were several headings:

**Personal background**

**Previous experience in photography**

**What do you want from the course?**

The student had answered the questions conscien-
tiously, filling the three or four centimetres of space
between each heading with close, neat handwriting. A
bundle of sheets behind this one were copies of Amy
Dennis's reports on the assignments.

'We'll have to talk to all of these people,' Lawson
said, slipping the papers back into the folder. When
Barton didn't respond, he looked up. 'Found something?' he asked.

He handed Lawson the folder he had been reading.
'You might want to start with this character.'

Another student profile, this one a man, unsmiling,
staring out of the photograph as if trying to catch a
glimpse of the reader's face. 'Ian Clemence. You know
him?'

'Of old.'

Lawson glanced at the top of the page. 'He's banged
up,' he said.

'For twelve years – thirteen, come September.
Which means he just might be out by now.'

Lawson flicked quickly through the stack of reports
and letters; there were pages and pages of comment
and questions pinned to each assignment. It seemed
Mr Clemence considered his personal tuition very
much a dialogue. He skimmed the contents, deciding

to take this folder back to base to study. 'Thirteen come September,' he repeated, frowning slightly at the sergeant. 'But you knew him straight off . . .'

Barton gave him a slightly queasy smile. 'You never forget your first murder, do you, Boss?'

# 7

Fliss was at her desk when Clara returned from her visit to Jill Quigley. She smiled, handing Clara her phone and fax messages. Fliss was a slight, serious girl with a small mouth and glossy brown hair cut short and feathered to her face. In that brief eye contact, Clara knew that she had been expertly and thoroughly read.

'Jericho Chambers called,' she said. 'Wanted to know if you'd be in this week.'

Clara felt dread settle like a stone in her stomach. 'I don't suppose . . .'

Fliss reached for the phone. 'I'll ring them, shall I?'

'Tell them I'll call in tomorrow,' Clara said. 'And Fliss – whatever we're paying you, it isn't enough.'

Officially, she worked out of Jericho Chambers, but of late Clara had found it more and more difficult to walk through the doors: Jericho Chambers meant criminal cases, and Clara wasn't ready for criminal cases – not yet. She had been telling herself 'not yet', as though it was just a matter of time, for nine months now and she didn't like to admit that it wasn't getting any better; so she worked out of her friend's chambers instead, accepting Family cases and filling the time with unnecessary preparation, checks and counter-checks.

She walked through to the offices, nodding politely to a blonde woman and a distraught-looking man who sat almost facing each other, holding each other's hands.

A fresh pot of coffee was brewing in the tiny kitchen and a white patisserie box tied with string had been placed in the centre of the table. A small card had been slipped under the string and Clara picked it up, smiling as she shrugged off her jacket.

*For Clara,* it read. *Emergency carbohydrate.* Fliss, it seemed, had delayed her just long enough for Mitch to lay the bait. She pulled the string and the lid popped open. Inside was a doughnut, a strawberry tart, and two Danish pastries. Clara's stomach growled, re-minding her that she hadn't finished breakfast and had skipped lunch. She turned the card over and read Mitch's business address and phone number on the back.

'I read somewhere that hypoglycaemia was the sec-ond biggest cause of attacks on the person, after alcohol.' Mitch leaned against the door frame, her arms folded across a thick bundle of notes, trying to gauge Clara's mood.

'Better believe it,' Clara said happily, sinking her teeth into the doughnut, savouring its yeasty scent and the hint of vanilla in the dough. A drop of jam squeezed from the centre onto her palm and she set the bun down to lick the jam from her hand.

Mitch grinned, taking this as a sign of truce. She put

down the files she was carrying and poured coffee for them. 'I think this is where I came in,' she said.

She waited until Clara had finished the doughnut, watching her thoughtfully over the rim of her coffee cup. She had the kind of Irish colouring that gave a russet dusting of colour to the cheeks even in winter; with a light summer tan she had a coppery glow that seemed to reflect the warmth of her nature. Clara rinsed her hands and ran a finger over her lips, checking for stray sugar crystals. Mitch took a breath.

'Clara—' she began.

'Mitch, please.' Clara interrupted. 'I know you don't approve, but you've got to let me deal with cases as I see fit. As it happens,' she rattled on, 'it was the best thing I could have done. Jill Quigley was charmed to think that her barrister should come to see her, and Daniel—'

'*Clara*—' Mitch repeated.

'What?'

'I wasn't going to ask about the Quigleys.'

'You weren't?' She searched her friend's face, immediately suspicious.

'No, I wasn't. I was going to ask you about the Tobins. But I'm glad you sorted things out.' Mitch fell silent.

This was a ploy that Clara had seen her use to excellent effect on occasion: if she felt that her colleagues were paying insufficient attention to her snippet of court gossip, or a case she wanted them to take, she would start the story, then leave it – often in mid-sentence. The trick to was follow the prologue with a pause; the more significant the silence, the better. Clara sighed.

'Am I going to have to drag this out of you?' she asked.

'What?'

'The Tobins,' she said wearily. 'Who are they? Why did you want to ask me about them? And am I to infer that they're special enough to put my trip to see Jill Quigley right out of your mind?'

'Well . . .' Mitch began.

'Oh—' Clara interrupted again, remembering the patisserie box. 'And inspire you to buy me cakes.'

A smile played around the corners of her friend's mouth. 'I was kind of hoping you'd share the cakes . . .'

Clara studied her for a few moments longer. 'I've a feeling I'm going to regret this,' she said. 'Go on, then.'

Mitch smiled as if to say *I thought you'd never ask.* She pulled the bundle towards her and tapped the top folder. 'The Tobins, since you're interested, are the couple outside.' Clara remembered them, clinging to each other.

Mitch ploughed on. 'Bethany was supposed to see them, but her youngest has had an asthma attack – she's had to go to the hospital. That poor couple have been waiting an hour already, Clara. Everyone else is in court today, and I've got a meeting about the unfair dismissal in—' Mitch glanced at her watch. 'Ten minutes.'

Clara began to shake her head.

'Look,' Mitch said, forestalling an outright refusal, 'their brief has put together a strong case. All they need is someone to present the arguments to the judge.'

She made it sound so simple. 'You know I need time to prepare.'

'I *know*, but they've had this hanging over them for four months already.'

'So one day more won't make any difference. Tell them to make an appointment. I'll talk to them in the morning – after I've read the notes.'

'You've seen them – how can you say a day won't make a difference to them? They're desperate, Clara.'

Alarm bells started to ring. 'If this is a criminal case—'

'Visiting rights' Mitch reassured her, a little too hastily, Clara would realise later when she'd had time to reflect. 'It's a contested case.'

'Give me time to read the notes.' She slid the folder from the pile and began skimming the top sheet.

Mitch gently closed the file. 'Talk to them, Clara,' she said. 'Make notes as you go. You don't even have to take the case – just get the gist so I can pass it back to Bethany.'

Clara laughed. 'I know I said I'd do the filing, but this is ridiculous!'

Mitch flashed her another smile and then she was serious. 'It's late. They're almost out of their minds. We can't send them away without at least giving them a little reassurance. He's a right to see his baby.'

Clara narrowed her eyes. She knew when she was being manipulated, and she got the feeling that Mitch was making an oblique reference to her own outburst that morning, about taking the child's wishes into consideration.

'I'd love to stay,' Mitch said, already backing for the door. 'But . . .' She tapped the face of her watch.

'Mitch—'

'Gotta dash. Give it an hour – you'll have it all clear in your mind.'

Clara had noticed the tension on her way in, and the husband's evident distress, but she hadn't really looked at them. Diane Tobin was small and blonde. She wore her hair in an Alice band, and Clara's first impression was of someone incredibly young and vulnerable. She led them through to one of the consulting rooms, carrying the bundle of documents that Fliss had taken from the files on their arrival.

Turning to invite them to sit, Clara experienced a disorientating sideways shift in her perception: Mrs Tobin's face was more lined, the skin less vibrant than she would have expected from the twenty-something age bracket she had estimated at first glance. Looking at her more closely, Clara revised her estimate upwards by ten years. One thing that did remain, even on closer examination, however, was the essential fragility of the woman: she looked delicate, in need of protection.

Clara retreated behind the desk, needing the formality of this arrangement, feeling at a loss without her careful study of the paperwork before meeting her clients. She introduced herself, giving them what she hoped was a reassuring smile. Chris Tobin shot his wife an anxious look and she squeezed his hand. He was a tall, etiolated man, who looked like he had never quite got over a teenage growth spurt. He wore baggy chinos fastened too high at the waist, with a dark green shirt tucked in to them. Unlike his wife, who seemed cool and freshly powdered despite the afternoon heat, Mr Tobin sweated freely, and Clara had the impression that he had been crying.

She picked up a pen and pulled her notepad to her, inviting the couple to be seated with a gesture of her hand. They were too polite to move the chairs closer together, but as soon as they were seated, they reached across the gap and held hands again. It was a curiously touching gesture and Clara had to blink tears of sympathy from her eyes.

*Start with an innocuous question, one just to get them started.*

'What contact do you have now?'

'Weekends,' Mrs Tobin said. 'She's allowed to stay Friday night to Sunday evening.'

'Your daughter . . .' Clara glanced down at the file.

'Helen,' Mrs Tobin supplied.

Clara jotted the name down on her pad, circling it. 'How old is Helen?' she asked.

'Eleven months,' Mr Tobin said.

Mrs Tobin tucked her hair behind her ears, a girlish gesture that reinforced the impression of vulnerable youth.

'I take it that you asked for more visiting contact . . .' Clara hoped they would fill in the gaps.

'Staying contact, I think they call it,' Mrs Tobin said.

Mr Tobin broke free of his wife, flinging her hand from him. 'That's irrelevant, now!' he exclaimed. 'I want my daughter home with me, where she belongs.'

Clara looked with a growing sense of dismay at the four-inch stack of papers in the file. Somewhere in there was the answer to what was puzzling her. *Damnit!* She shouldn't have allowed Mitch to hustle her into an interview she was ill-prepared to conduct. She took a breath. *Go on Clara, impress them.*

'I should explain that my colleague who was to have talked to you this afternoon was called away to a family crisis. Normally, we would have asked you to come back another day.' She felt she was excusing her lack of preparation to herself as much as to them.

'I understood that we were to discuss visiting and staying contact – your right to see Helen and to have her stay with you,' she explained, thinking that perhaps they had misunderstood their solicitor. Mr Tobin did not respond, but his wife gave a short nod. 'But from what you've just said, you're thinking of a residency order . . .'

Mr Tobin spoke up. 'I'm sorry,' he said. 'This has all happened so fast. We asked for more visits. We wanted Helen to be able to come away on holiday with us, but her mother . . .' His face twisted in a spasm of pain.

'Her mother was difficult,' Mrs Tobin went on. 'We've tried to be reasonable. Chris only wanted what is his right as Helen's father.'

'It took the court welfare officer sixteen weeks to come up with a simplistic report in her favour,' he said bitterly.

'Which explains why you're contesting the case. But a residency order is something quite different,' Clara said, with a bewildered smile. 'If the welfare officer recommended against an increase in *visiting* contact, what makes you think you'll get a *residency* order in your favour?'

They exchanged a look. Mrs Tobin took her husband's hand again; she was to speak for both of them. 'She's dead.' Her voice was icy calm, but she gripped his hand with a fierceness that bleached the knuckles of colour. 'She—'

Mr Tobin shook his head, frowning at her to be quiet. 'Helen's mother died quite suddenly, Ms Pascal.' His pain was real, and his regret.

'I'm sorry,' she said softly.

'And now,' Mr Tobin added, 'they—' His chest heaved, and for a moment, Clara thought that he would break down. 'They took my little girl away from me.'

'Social Services,' Mrs Tobin explained. 'They placed Helen with her grandparents.'

'Have you spoken to them?' Clara asked.

He frowned, staring hard at the blotter on her desk, struggling to keep his composure. 'They told me that Helen didn't belong to me. They're going to fight for custody.'

Clara began to understand his agitation: not only had he been refused the chance to see more of his daughter, he now felt that he might lose her altogether.

'All right,' she said, determined to restore some kind of balance in his life, to send him away with some measure of hope. 'First of all, your visiting and staying contact remains the same as before Helen's mother died.'

He looked at her with a wary glimmer of hope in his eyes. 'You're sure of that?'

'The terms of the original order stand, unless and until new provisions are made at another hearing.'

He tilted his head back and his Adam's apple bobbed.

Clara gave him a moment to catch his breath, then she asked, 'Where do you both work?'

'What the *hell* has that got to do with anything?'

Clara felt an immediate rush of fear. She recalled her counsellor's frequent reassurance that most people play by the rules. Well, Mr Tobin looked ready to scratch the rules, and his arms looked long enough to reach right across the table. She moved back in her chair.

'The courts like to feel that they are sending a child to a stable household – preferably one in which at least one partner works,' she said, relieved to hear that her voice was controlled, that she sounded calm.

Mr Tobin was chastened. 'You have to get her back for me, Ms Pascal.' He was no more than forty, but the skin around his eyes was deeply lined and his cheeks had begun to sag. His was a face made for tragedy. He put a trembling finger to his eyebrow, smoothing and worrying it in turns.

Mrs Tobin took the lead. 'I'm a photographer,' she said. 'I lecture two evenings a week at Birkenhead Tech and I do a bit of freelance tuition, but at heart, I'm a creative artist.' This was said with no hint of irony. 'Chris, is—'

'I lecture in journalism, here in Chester, at St Werburgh's University,' he interrupted, rousing himself from kneading his eyebrow.

'So you're out, what – eight-thirty until six Monday to Friday?'

He nodded. 'Give or take.'

'Your freelance work,' Clara said to Mrs Tobin. 'It must take you away from home a lot.'

Mr Tobin sat up straight, his eyes wide with alarm. 'I'm sure the university will find a place in the nursery,' he said. 'It's on site. I could pick Helen up on my way home.'

Clara smiled, making a note of the day care option. 'It's all right, Mr Tobin,' she said gently. 'I'm on your side.' He flushed a little and Clara went on, 'But you should check with the nursery. Is there anyone else who can help out? Your parents, perhaps.'

He shook his head. 'They live too far away. It wouldn't be practical. If her maternal grandparents would like to . . .' He shrugged. 'We've no objection to them seeing Helen, and if they want to help out . . .'

Clara couldn't imagine that Helen's grandparents would be content to babysit for the man against whom they were making an application for a residency order, but that observation would wait for another day.

He looked straight at her and she saw that she had underestimated Mr Tobin. There was single-minded strength and determination in the man. 'How can we get custody of my daughter, Ms Pascal?' he asked.

'The process starts afresh, I'm afraid,' Clara said. 'You need to go back to your solicitor—'

'No! We've waited all this time. You can't send us away!'

'I'm not "sending you away" – this is how the system works. You talk to your solicitor, who briefs your barrister. Your barrister presents the case to the court.'

'We know the legal process,' Mr Tobin said coldly. 'And it's already wasted four months of our lives.'

'Our case comes up at Wrexham County Court in two weeks. Can't we just turn up and talk to the judge?' Mrs Tobin asked.

'Your application was against Helen's mother, Mrs Tobin,' Clara explained. 'Since she is now deceased – and Helen's grandparents have put in an application for residency – it changes everything. The hearing will be postponed whether you appoint a solicitor or not.'

'I'm asking for your help, Ms Pascal,' Tobin said. 'Won't you help us?'

Clara looked into his face. His eyes were red-rimmed and raw. At least she could talk them through the process. Then, when they were calm and had time to think about it, she would tell them to instruct their solicitor. She would argue the case for them in court, but it was ludicrous paying barrister's fees for solicitor's work. 'You must make an immediate application for a residency order,' she said. 'That entitles you to access to medical records, to decide on medical intervention, should Helen need it – it gives you all the legal rights of a parent.'

'But they say I'm not Helen's father . . .'

'They'll have to prove it. They will probably ask for a

declaration of paternity. You would have to take a blood test.'

'And if I refuse?'

'The court would order it. Best to pre-empt the request.'

He thought about it.

'Mr Tobin, if you are in any doubt as to your paternity—'

'I am not!' he responded angrily.

'So,' she said, firmly, 'It shouldn't be a problem.' She held his gaze and he flushed, looking away. 'And you really will have to curb your temper, if you're serious about this residency order,' she added. 'The court won't like placing Helen with someone so volatile.'

'I'm not usually . . . I just don't want to lose her—' He stopped short, clamping his jaw tight.

Clara glanced at Mrs Tobin. Two pink spots appeared on her cheeks. She hadn't imagined it, then: Mr Tobin had almost said, 'I just don't want to lose her, *too*.'

Clara felt a confusing mixture of compassion and irritation with Mrs Tobin. Why did she put up with it? 'The good news,' she said, after a pause, 'is that you've a number of points in your favour: you're the birth father; you see your daughter regularly; you're young.' She smiled at their surprise. 'It's all comparative,' she said. 'Helen's grandparents are how old?'

Mr Tobin shrugged. 'I only met the grandmother once. Late sixties – seventy, perhaps?'

'How solid is your marriage?' She asked the question

bluntly; this time she was ready for an angry response and Mr Tobin did not disappoint. He half-rose, placing his free hand flat on the table, invading her personal space.

'What sort of question is that?' he demanded.

'The sort you'll hear a lot if this case comes to court,' Clara answered. 'From what I gather, Mr Tobin, Helen is the result of an extra-marital affair.' Neither of them contradicted her and she went on. 'You are asking the court to believe that your wife will love and cherish the child of this liaison as her own. That demands quite a leap of faith.'

Mrs Tobin tugged her husband's hand, distressed and embarrassed by his outburst, and Mr Tobin lowered himself slowly back into his chair and stared at his clenched fist in his lap.

'My husband made a mistake, Ms Pascal,' Mrs Tobin said.

'Is that how you see the affair, Mr Tobin?' Clara asked. 'As a mistake?'

He swallowed and for a few moments remained silent. When he spoke, he sounded almost in awe. 'Helen is the best thing that ever happened to me.'

A fleeting emotion, brief but strong, registered on Mrs Tobin's face, but was gone before Clara had the chance to analyse it. She reflected that it must be almost unbearable to hear that the best thing in your husband's life came out of an experience that was personally humiliating and painful.

Mr Tobin seemed to sense this, because he added, 'I regret having hurt Diane – of course I do.'

*Big of you*, Clara thought.

'But I don't regret Helen's existence. She's—' He coughed, then closed his eyes. His eyelashes were wet.

'We were both going through a bad patch,' Mrs Tobin said with a determined lift of the chin. 'I was finding it hard to get commissions – a bit of freelance photojournalism, tuition on a correspondence course – but it didn't pay well. We argued a lot. I . . .' For a moment, Clara thought that she, too, would falter and stop, but she seemed to find a new impetus and went on, 'I drove Chris away.'

Mr Tobin exclaimed, but his protestations were half-hearted and had a hollow ring.

'I remember what it was like, Chris,' she insisted. 'I was bitter. I let my bitterness poison our relationship.'

Clara admired the woman's courage: it couldn't be easy to admit that, and to a stranger.

'We have always wanted children – a child,' she corrected, as if more than one was asking too much. 'Since the first year of our marriage, we've planned a family.' She glanced at her husband. 'Ten years . . . We tried IVF – we were considering adoption when—' She couldn't bring herself to say it, but Clara could read it in her face: *When Chris's lover fulfilled my role as a wife and gave him a baby*.

'Their affair nearly destroyed me. But the very first time Chris brought Helen home – from that moment, she felt like she was mine – ours. She's the answer to a prayer.'

If she could get her to say that in court, the case was in the bag. 'Is your name on the birth certificate, Mr Tobin?'

'Of course,' he said.

That would work in his favour. 'And you're registered with the CSA?'

He nodded. 'I provide support.'

'That must put a strain on your finances, particularly since you've had difficulty finding work, Mrs Tobin. How did you feel about that?'

She found the question offensive, Clara could see that, but Mrs Tobin had the intelligence to realise that these were questions that had to be asked. 'Of course I wasn't thrilled,' she said, with admirable control. 'But one has to face one's responsibilities – take the consequences of one's actions.'

'I love my daughter,' Mr Tobin said, his voice roughened by emotion. 'I'd do anything to keep her. I can't bear to see her in care.'

'She's with her *grandparents*, Mr Tobin,' Clara said.

He gave her another determined, unyielding look. 'She's my child,' he said. 'She belongs with me.'

# 8

Sebastian Enderby shook the hand of his new financial backer. He should be euphoric: honoured by the Chamber of Commerce only the previous evening, given the unequivocal endorsement of his peers, and now another substantial investment in his enterprise, yet he felt sick with worry.

Often, in the mornings, he would try his hand at moving some stock. He used an online broker – it was only for fun – his equivalent of a caffeine kick-start; a sure cure for hangovers and overindulgence, and one that didn't even require him to break sweat. Until this morning: his morning toe-dip had been a miserable affair. He was nervous, buying stock just before a downturn, selling too early. In thirty short minutes he lost just shy of three thousand pounds; small change, given his current business interests and his bankability as a business associate. Nevertheless, it troubled him.

His anxiety was, at least in part, caused by the business card in his wallet. He had taken it out at least a dozen times during the day and stared at the name and telephone number hastily scribbled on the back of it. On several occasions he had even got part way through dialling, but he hung up each time, unwilling to begin a chain of events that might ultimately destroy his reputation, his business, his marriage – his life.

And now, as the early evening rhythm began to assert itself and traffic turned homeward, he checked his watch and wondered if he could make it back to his office in Chester before six. If the M56 wasn't too busy, and he put his foot down, he could make the trip in thirty-five minutes. As he walked through the town towards his car, he was calculating how much his staff needed to know. He hoped that the drive would clear his head. If he remained calm, it might not be necessary to use the phone number. His spirits lifted a little; yes, he might just get away with it.

He paced the emptying streets with the steady, even tread of a heavy man whose health has not yet quite been ruined by business lunches and negotiations conducted in wine bars. Walking past boutiques and antique shops, some already shuttered for the night, he continued thinking about his predicament, his mind circling round and round the problem. How could he have been so rash? So damned foolish?

The walk made him hot and he loosened his tie, then, increasingly uncomfortable, he slipped off his jacket and carried it over his arm. At his car, he juggled his briefcase and jacket, finally switching the jacket to his left hand, bunching it over the handle of the brief-case and worrying absently about creasing it. He retrieved his car key and used the remote to open the doors.

'Mr Enderby?'

Enderby's shoulders drooped. Another reporter looking for a filler for the business section of one of the local weeklies.

He turned. 'I'm Sebastian Enderby,' he said, trying not to sound irritated.

The man raised his camera arm and Enderby adjusted his features ready for the anticipated snapshot. The shape was wrong. He registered this first. It took a fraction of a second longer for him to recognise what the man held in his hand.

*A gun. My God! He's got a gun.* Enderby panicked, lifting his briefcase in a feeble attempt to protect himself.

The man calmly batted the briefcase away, pointed the gun and fired.

# 9

The probation service came up with an address for Clemence. Chris Thorpe handed the slip to Cath Young and slid behind the wheel of his Montego. DC Young glanced at it and then set it to one side, studying instead the picture of Clemence that had been faxed through from Clayton Open Prison.

'Look at enough of those,' Thorpe said, 'you begin to see a family resemblance among villains.'

Young tilted the picture to catch the dusty afternoon light; drawing her eyebrows down in a parody of concentration, she looked from the photograph to Thorpe and back again. 'You're right,' she said, 'I'm seeing villains everywhere.'

'Now that's funny,' Thorpe replied, nudging the car into reverse and backing out of the parking bay. 'You're a real comedian. Time was, you hung on my every word.'

'Time was, I thought the Spice Girls were cool,' she shot back.

He leaned across her and hit the button on the glove compartment. 'Find the map of Chester,' he said. 'See if you can read that without making me laugh.'

Young grinned. She thought Chris wouldn't look so

much like the mug-shots in the albums if he shaved the stubble on his chin and let the fuzz on his head grow out a little. At least he'd stopped wearing his mugger's hat for the summer. He might look like a thug, but there was a core of strength and decency in the man that she could quite fancy.

They turned right, the sandstone walls of the city rising above them like a sheer cliff, and below, the car park of the Little Roodee glinted with hundreds of cars, baking in the heat. Beyond the racecourse, the Welsh hills were just visible, shimmering in a bluish haze.

They followed the ring road anticlockwise then headed north-east on Hoole Road, over the railway bridge, where the Georgian architecture changed abruptly to soot-blackened Victorian red brick.

'Next left,' Young said. An immediate right after the turn took them into Clemence's street. Thorpe pulled up opposite number forty-one and killed the engine.

'We're only here to ask a few questions,' Thorpe reminded her. 'Could be our man was tucked up in bed at his old mum's at the time of the murder.'

'Yeah,' Young said. 'And could be I'll make Chief Constable by Christmas.'

She got out and pulled her shirt straight over her trousers. A disastrous first appearance in a skirt on her first day as a DC had resulted in a brief, and hated, spell with the nickname Babe; since then, Young had doggedly refused to wear a skirt, much to the disappointment of the male officers in the division. She slammed the car door and turned, her attention caught by a glint of orange evening sunlight: a reflection from the gleaming black door of number forty-one. A man stood on the threshold for a second, lifting his face to the sun. Dark hair, cut short and slightly ruffled. Clemence. In his right hand he carried a black sports bag. He trotted down the steep concrete steps, light on his feet in the way a dancer or a fighter is light on his feet.

Young gave a cursory glance left and was forced to wait while a red Sierra swept past, its stereo booming a dance rhythm. Clemence turned right, away from her, his head down, moving fast.

Young crossed the road diagonally, intending to intercept him. She heard Thorpe slam the car door and his footsteps hurrying after her.

'Excuse me, sir,' she said, remembering to keep her voice low and strong. He carried on walking, if anything picking up the pace a little. 'Sir? Ian Clemence—' She felt a stab of the old fear of being ignored, before impatience saved her from humiliation. '*Oi*, Clemence!'

He swung round, startled. 'Sorry,' he said. 'Are you talking to me?' A northern accent, even after all those years moving around the country from prison to prison.

'Is your name Clemence?' There was bulk beneath the white T-shirt, and judging by the meat on his arms, it was solid muscle. Young drew herself up, matching the man's curious stare, Thorpe was a reassuring presence at her back.

Clemence blinked. 'Who wants to know?'

*Nice touch*, Young thought: ambiguity was always

useful in a defence argument. 'I was scared stiff, Your Honour. I thought they were muggers. They came at me from behind.'

He was ten feet away, but he knew. He had seen them when he set foot outside his front door. He knew they were cops. She saw it in the set of his shoulders, in the pleasant look that managed somehow to exude a warning. She showed him her ID. 'DC Young,' she said. 'And this is DC Thorpe.'

He relaxed, the tension leaving him instantaneously. He even smiled a little.

It put Young off her guard for a fraction of a second and in the moment she stepped towards him, he threw the sports bag at her and ran. She deflected the bag with one arm and gave chase. She heard Thorpe calling for back-up; he would pick up the bag before he followed them, so she was on her own.

It was hot, but running was Young's sport; it kept her fit – sometimes she thought it kept her sane – and while Clemence looked like he took care of himself, he had the stocky build of a weight-lifter. Not much scope for marathon running Inside, she reflected. He would soon tire.

She kept pace with him, dodging around cars, watching for an alley he might disappear into, keeping him in sight and biding her time until he wore himself out. Then he turned another corner and she saw Hoole Road ahead and heard the constant thrum of traffic. Thorpe was losing ground; she could hear his flat-footed run fading into the distance. If Clemence jumped the barrier into the traffic she would lose him – or worse, someone might swerve to avoid him and she would end up with a death on her hands.

*Bugger!* she thought. *This is going to hurt.* She put on a spurt of speed, catching him in seconds. His breathing was harsh and rasping; only adrenaline was keeping him going. She aimed low, her shoulder hitting the back of his thighs. His knees buckled and he crashed to the ground. He rolled, turning, reaching.

She snapped the cuffs on his left hand and got to her feet, levering his arm forward and up, twisting at the wrist and forcing him back down. He was strong and he was mightily pissed off. He placed his right hand flat on the ground, resisting her, and she knew she hadn't the strength to hold him and bring his right arm round behind his back.

'Lie still!' she yelled. 'You're under arrest!'

'Like fuck!' He bucked suddenly, struggling to his knees, screaming against the pain as she increased the pressure on his shoulder. He was slippery with sweat. She was losing him.

'Thorpe!' she yelled. 'Where the *hell* are you?' Her hand slipped a little further; her leverage was weakening. Clemence sensed it, too: he grunted, trying harder, rotating his arm, and she felt it slide under her fingers. She roared, leaning her entire weight on his hand, knowing that it wasn't hurting him any more; she had lost the wrist lock.

Then suddenly Clemence was on the ground again, flattened by Thorpe's elbow on the back of his neck. Thorpe grabbed Clemence's right arm and clicked the right cuff on his wrist.

It took two of them to get him to his knees to prevent him lashing out with his feet. They had an arm each and even Thorpe's bulk was barely sufficient to keep Clemence from throwing them both off while Young cautioned him.

A squad car screamed around the corner, siren blaring, and fetched up nose in to the kerb next to them. Two PCs leapt out, ready for trouble.

'All right,' Clemence said. 'You can let me up.' There was a tension in the muscles of his shoulders, but he had stopped fighting.

Young looked at Thorpe and he nodded. They released the pressure slowly, waiting for him to kick off again, but he didn't. His T-shirt was smeared with dirt and the right sleeve had come adrift at the shoulder, but he was unmarked. *How nice for him*, Young thought. She could feel a stinging throb in the heel of her right hand: she had skinned it tackling Clemence to the ground, picking up a sackful of grit in the process.

'Have a look what's in the bag,' Thorpe said.

Clemence pulled back, but Thorpe tightened his grip and when one of the PCs stepped forward to take Young's place, he seemed to give up. He waited, his face still and impassive, but his eyes simmering with impotent rage. Thorpe had dropped Clemence's sports bag a few yards away.

Young picked it up, surprised that it was so light, and unzipped the u-shaped flap. There was something inside. At first she thought it was a patterned shirt, then the smell hit her and she had to swallow hard to keep from gagging. *Not in front of the boys, Cath*, she told herself.

Keeping a carefully blank expression on her face, she crooked her little finger and snagged it, lifting it far enough out of the bag for the men to see. A white T-shirt, soaked in blood.

The custody suite was busy for a Tuesday, and Young had to join the queue: the heat made people fractious and thirsty, and when you're twenty and male, you reach for a cold lager to quench it, in preference to something more wholesome.

'You're bleeding, DC Young,' the sergeant observed. Young attracted a few appreciative looks – even sweating and dusty from her struggle with Clemence, she was a stunner. 'And who have you got in your bloody mitt?'

Young glanced quickly at Thorpe. 'You bagged him,' he said. 'He's all yours.' The looks of appreciation acquired a hint of admiration: even handcuffed, Clemence was intimidating.

While Young detailed the circumstances of the arrest, a ragged queue built up behind them. The sergeant's desk was separated from the cells by a dividing wall with no door; the rule was officers waited the other side of the divide with their prisoners until called, but a tall, pale-skinned youth kept craning forward, trying to get a glimpse of Clemence's face. He had a tattoo of a web and spider in blue ink at the angle of his jawbone and an arc of ear studs in the curve of his left ear lobe. Clemence sensed his scrutiny and turned, looking over one beefy shoulder.

'You really waste someone?' the boy asked, as though it was an unfulfilled ambition.

Clemence stared at him. 'You the duty solicitor?' The boy licked his lips nervously. ''Cos if you are, I'm thinking we should talk somewhere private.' Clemence lowered his voice confidentially. 'Right to silence – all that.'

The boy sniggered. This *was* a joke, right?

Young touched Clemence's arm and they moved towards the cells. As he passed the youth, Clemence scrutinised the spider's web in the angle of his jaw. 'Nice tattoo,' he said. 'Make sure you get that one on the system,' he told the arresting officer. The youth touched his jaw, not sure how to react.

Clemence winked. 'Good as a bar code to the Dibbles, a distinctive tattoo like that,' he said. 'You've marked yourself out, pal.'

'Move it, Clemence,' Young warned.

As Clemence moved on, the youth took a swing at him. Thorpe caught his fist and tutted mildly. Clemence faced the boy, his eyes hard and glittering. The boy's bravado was fragile and he quickly looked away. Young tried to shove Clemence backwards, but he was solid, immovable. The queue was getting restless, sensing a possible ruck and the arresting officers tensed, ready to act, but unwilling to say anything that might spark off a fight. Unexpectedly, Clemence shrugged and allowed himself to be escorted out. 'Like I said, Spider,' he muttered, 'You've marked yourself out.'

It was over in seconds, but Young felt wired. The

adrenaline rush left her limbs feeling jerky, not quite under control. She took Clemence to cell M4, as instructed by the custody sergeant and, with Thorpe looking on, she removed the handcuffs. Her fingers shook slightly and Clemence turned his head, bringing his face offensively close to hers.

'Need some help with that?' he asked.

She answered him with a cold stare and he smiled, massaging his wrists when she released him, watching her out of the door. She turned the lock and leaned against it for a second or two with her eyes closed.

'OK, Cath?' Thorpe asked.

She thought about it. Anyone else would get a quick smile and a glib answer, but Chris Thorpe deserved honesty, and she explored her feelings, probing gently, as if testing a fresh bruise. She nodded. 'Yep,' she said. 'Apart from pebble-dashing my hand.'

He took it, examining the damage. 'Let's find a pair of tweezers,' he suggested. 'I'll pick the grit out of the scabs.'

Young sighed and fluttered her eyelashes at him. 'Gee, Chris,' she said. 'You really know how to treat a girl.'

DC Fletcher came in as Thorpe taped a piece of gauze over Young's smooth and freshly disinfected palm. 'What a touching scene,' he sneered.

'What's up, Fletch,' Young asked. 'Bet on a three-legged donkey again, did you?'

Thorpe wriggled his eyebrows comically at her and muttered, 'Time was . . .'

She beamed back at him. *Time was* just the sound of Fletcher's voice could make her cringe. *Time was* the smell of his after-shave could make her physically ill.

'Fall over in the playground, did we?' Fletcher asked nastily. 'Graze our pretty knees?' He had bullied and harassed Young during her difficult first week in CID. Now, almost a year later, things were different.

'Another masterclass in detection from Fletch the Letch.' Young dropped Thorpe a slow wink. 'As a matter of fact, we've been arresting a murder suspect, haven't we, Chris?' The curdled look on Fletcher's face said he was heading for an ulcer or a heart attack, or both, but she wasn't prepared to leave it there. She poured herself a cup of tea and tilted her head in mock sympathy. 'What have you been up to today, oh Master of the Dog Turd?' It was an old joke, but it never failed to get a rise out of Fletcher. He muttered something and turned away.

'Let me guess,' Young went on, relentlessly prodding him into a response. 'Counting paper clips? Playing receptionist? Photocopying reports? . . . Big responsibility, that – getting the collation right. No?' She thought for a moment. 'Not collation?' She clicked her fingers as if a sudden inspiration had struck her. 'I know what you've been up to. You've been scraping chewing gum off the tarmac in the car park, haven't you?'

Neither man would have guessed it, but Young felt a mixture of anxiety and anger even as she smiled and baited Fletcher. He had almost wrecked her chances of making it as a CID officer. Wrecked her chances and shattered her confidence – she would not allow that to happen again. If Fletcher made the slightest remark to her, she felt the need to slap him down, grab him by the balls and twist. Hard. Because what she feared more than anything was letting him get the upper hand ever again. And if some of the lads thought her a bitch, at least the bitch had teeth.

She took her cup of tea to the Incident Room to type up her report.

'Bloody tart!' Fletcher growled, but only after she was out of earshot.

Thorpe glanced at the closing door. 'Cath?' he said. 'She's all right.' A resentful silence followed, which Thorpe broke. 'So, what *have* you been doing?'

Fletcher's shoulders slumped. He carried too much weight to be comfortable in hot weather and the short-sleeved shirt he wore had large sweat stains under the arms. 'Superbitch was right,' he said.

*Superbitch.* Fletcher hadn't dared call DC Young 'Babe' since last winter, but Superbitch? Thorpe thought she would enjoy that one.

'I've been poncing around doing secretarial work, if you're interested,' Fletcher said.

'Filing?' Thorpe was incredulous: he knew that DI Lawson didn't like Fletcher, but he wasn't vindictive.

'As good as,' Fletcher complained. 'Following up a line of inquiry on the baby's dad. Tobin.'

'Where was he?' Thorpe asked. 'Away from home?'

'*Playing* away, more like.' Fletcher sipped his tea mournfully. 'He's got a little wifey. He just went bareback riding with Amy a couple of times and got caught.'

'You've got a very nice turn of phrase, Fletch – did anyone ever tell you?'

Fletcher shrugged.

'So I take it the baby's dad was at home with the wife when it happened?'

'In Surrey, delivering a lecture. He stayed over with his parents, like the dutiful son. I've just had half an hour of his dear old mum boring the arse off me telling me what a lovely boy he is.'

'So he's got an alibi?'

'He didn't leave Surrey until this morning.'

'Convenient,' Thorpe said.

Fletcher roused himself from bored self-pity to ask, 'Do you think . . .?'

'I dunno, mate, but if you believe the stats, ordering an execution in the twenty-first century is as easy as mail order shopping.'

# IO

Clemence rattled his chair against its stays. 'What's this?' he demanded. 'They screwing down the furniture now? Have you lot gone soft or what?'

'Sit down,' Mr Clemence,' Lawson said.

Clemence didn't comply immediately, but Lawson hadn't expected him to. They made eye contact and held it, and after a few seconds, Clemence lowered himself into the chair opposite Lawson and Sergeant Barton, feet apart, hands on his knees as if he was ready to get up at any moment and leave the room. If all his body language was as easy to read, Lawson thought, they would have an easy time of it. He ran through the introductions. Clemence gave a start at Barton's name – perhaps he hadn't recognised him as the young police officer who had arrested him all those years ago, but then Barton had changed a lot in the intervening time.

Lawson waited a moment, but Clemence did not speak. Lawson repeated the caution and asked if Clemence understood.

'Do I look stupid?'

'Behave yourself, Mr Clemence,' his solicitor warned.

Clemence swivelled in his chair to face the man. 'Or you'll do what, exactly?'

Brent Quartermaine was slightly built, and he would not see the youthful side of fifty again, but he was untroubled by Clemence's aggression. 'The officers are doing their duty,' he said. 'And they are being civil in the execution of it. The least you can do is answer their questions.'

'Well it's good to have you on my side, Mr Quartermaine,' Clemence said.

Lawson knew Quartermaine of old: he had been a teacher before he went into the law and he abhorred bad manners. He maintained rigid standards and felt obliged to correct his clients' social deficiencies.

Clemence turned back to the table. 'What was the question?'

Lawson repeated it for him.

'I understand,' he said with weary patience.

Lawson placed an evidence bag on the table and identified it for the tape. 'Can you explain the presence of this blood-soaked T-shirt in your sports bag?' he asked.

'Cut myself shaving?' Clemence's tone was light and his eyes had the flat, expressionless quality that Lawson had seen scores of times in ex-cons. Hard, cold men who wanted you to believe they were capable of anything except simple human feeling. But Lawson saw the shift in stance.

Clemence leaned back from the table; he crossed his ankles and his hands slipped to his thighs. Not quite ball-cupping terror, but close enough for Lawson to know that Clemence felt threatened.

Barton handed him a second evidence bag. 'This is your sports bag?' Lawson asked, reciting its evidence number.

Clemence gave it a cursory glance. 'Yes.'

'And you don't deny that this is your T-shirt.' The bag crackled under his hand. Clemence shrugged, refusing to look at the rapidly browning stains on the white cotton.

'For the tape, please, Mr Clemence,' Lawson said, with impeccable civility.

He got a glance of approval from Mr Quartermaine.

Clemence sighed. 'How should I know?'

'It was in your bag, which you took from your flat.'

'Yeah . . .'

'Is it yours?'

Clemence leaned forward. 'Would you recognise one of your M&S easy-irons if it was bagged and tagged?' he asked with heavy sarcasm. 'I don't think so.'

'Your bag,' Lawson repeated. 'Your flat. And you were carrying it.' He appraised Clemence with a slow, thoughtful look. 'The T-shirt is very like the one you're wearing.'

'Except for the blood.' Barton had spoken for the first time and it seemed to shake Clemence.

'I'd know if I got blood all over me, wouldn't I?'

Barton clasped his hands on the table in front of him. 'Would you, Mr Clemence?'

They stared at each other, each imagining a scene they had visited many times in the past twelve years, for widely different reasons.

'I'd know,' Clemence said, his voice even and controlled. Funny, Lawson thought, how anger can have a steadying effect on the nerves. And Clemence *was* angry, despite his apparent calm.

Lawson nodded. 'That poses something of a problem,' he said. 'Because you were arrested with a bloody T-shirt in your bag.'

'Was I?' Clemence said. 'Oh, yeah. I remember now.'

Lawson barely acknowledged the interruption. 'So we have to assume one of two things: that the T-shirt is yours and you were trying to dispose of it, or that it's somebody else's and you were trying to dispose of it for them.'

No response, only a dry click as Clemence swallowed.

'Where were you between ten p.m. yesterday and six a.m. this morning?' Lawson asked.

'In bed. Asleep.' Lawson raised his eyebrows. 'Force of habit,' Clemence said. 'And before you ask, I was alone.'

'Does *force of habit* keep you indoors during the day as well?'

'Matter of fact, I was out all day. Alone. I didn't talk to anyone and I don't think anyone saw me.'

'You didn't stop at a café? Call into a shop – buy a newspaper?'

Clemence spread his hands. 'I'm not a big reader. I'm more a visual man.'

'Which explains the camera.'

It was difficult to say if Clemence reacted. Perhaps a

twitch, a brief spasm of the muscles along his jawline, but no readable emotion. Lawson studied the man's face for signs of fear, anger, nerves.

Clemence, in turn, watched his interrogators. He was used to the invasion of privacy, the demands to know the details of his personal life. His rights had been withdrawn for the duration of his prison term. He hadn't yet adjusted to the concept of freedom: freedom of movement, freedom to get up and go to bed when he liked, to go out when he chose. Sometimes, absurd though it seemed, he stood at the front door of the house where he lived, expecting alarms to sound as he crossed the threshold. If these freedoms had been denied him, then he had also been well schooled in the power of silence: it was a right that could not be denied him, and he exercised that right now.

'There was a roll of film in the camera,' Lawson said. 'What's on it?' No reply. 'Officers are searching your flat as we speak,' Lawson went on. 'I've instructed them to take it apart.' He saw a momentary glimmer of something – anxiety? Or anger? 'Best you tell us,' the inspector's tone became pleasant, persuasive, 'rather than waiting for us to find out.'

Clemence folded his arms and stared at the table. 'You could tell them to look out for breakfast dishes,' he said. 'I didn't get around to washing up this morning.' The glimmer Lawson had seen became a gleam of malevolent humour. 'I know,' he said, registering Lawson's annoyance. 'I'm ashamed of myself.'

'We're treating your flat as a potential crime scene,' Lawson said, determined to wipe the smirk off his face.

'If there is blood anywhere – say, for the sake of argument you *did* cut yourself shaving – the Scene of Crime Officers will find it. *Whatever* you've hidden, we'll find it.'

Clemence's face betrayed nothing. After a few moments' silence he unfolded his arms and looked around the cramped interview room, feigning boredom.

'You knew Miss Dennis,' Lawson said.

There was a slight check in Clemence's aimless contemplation of the bare grey walls, then he said, 'Who?'

'The woman who was murdered.' Lawson was careful to keep his tone neutral. He could feel Barton's anger building and it was important that one of them remained coolly objective. He glanced at Barton, and the sergeant produced the 'Arts for Everyone' folder they had taken from Miss Dennis's office.

Clemence paled beneath his tan.

Barton took a sheaf of papers from the folder. The top sheet was closely written, in black ink, in a jerky upright style. 'Maybe you remember writing to her,' Barton said, glancing down at the letter, ' "It sounds like you get to do some exciting assignments with your journalism, but you should watch out – there's a lot of bad people out there". Well, you weren't wrong there, were you, Ian?'

Clemence slouched a little lower in his chair, eyeing Barton with a coldness that Lawson had learned to regard as dangerous.

'I counted twenty letters,' Barton said. 'Not bad for a fifteen-week course.'

'All right.' Clemence took a breath. 'I knew her. *Two years* ago I knew her.'

'And life's such a social whirl,' Barton added. 'It's hard to keep track.'

Mr Quartermaine cleared his throat. 'Sarcasm is neither helpful nor necessary, Sergeant,' he said severely.

Barton shuffled through the pile of handwritten letters and chose one from near the bottom. 'Miss Dennis took you at your word and didn't reply straight away to a couple of your queries,' he said. ' – There were *so many* of them, after all. In this letter where you tell her how much you depend on her. How you hope she'll get back to you more quickly this time. Let me read it to you.' He skipped to the end of the page. '"Get back to me soon. It makes me sort of desperate when you don't answer quick. And you wouldn't want to make me desperate, would you?"'

'I haven't got your way with words, Sergeant – but it wasn't a threat.'

Barton looked into his face. 'You mention in the same letter how you're hoping to get out very soon. I suppose that wasn't a threat, either.'

Clemence didn't respond.

'You didn't look her up when you got out?'

Clemence eyed him coldly. 'No.'

'Not even to try your luck at getting those tutorials?' Barton asked. 'You ask her to give you a few tutorials in' – he sifted through the pile – 'this letter. Along with "extra input", "a few inside tips" – you really were a demanding student, weren't you, Clemence?'

Clemence stared at him, chin slightly lowered. He looked dangerous. He also looked like maybe some part of what Barton said had hit the mark. 'I don't even know where she lives,' he said.

Lawson couldn't say yet that the blood on the shirt was Amy Dennis's, so he phrased his next question carefully. 'She was beaten to death,' he said. 'There was a lot of blood. Is the blood on the T-shirt hers?'

'I wouldn't know.'

'Don't worry,' Barton said. '*We* soon will. Did you know her baby was upstairs?'

Clemence maintained eye contact, speaking slowly as if addressing a stupid child. 'I . . . wasn't . . . there.'

'It was in the papers – oh, but I forgot, you don't read.'

Clemence tensed, and Mr Quartermaine intervened. 'Inspector Lawson, Sergeant Barton is being deliberately insulting.'

'I apologise,' Barton said, avoiding putting Lawson in the embarrassing position of having to admonish him. 'I meant to say that you don't read the papers.' He waited until Clemence had begun to relax before adding. 'You're stronger on the visuals, aren't you? Well picture this, Mr Clemence. A woman with her head caved in. Blood and bone and brain tissue on the curtains and walls and carpets.' He knew that Clemence was back in the dirty flat where he had beaten his girlfriend to death and then slept peacefully next to the corpse. 'Tiring work, beating someone to death.' He leaned forward inviting Clemence to share a confidence with him. 'Think he took a nap before he left?'

Suddenly, Clemence was out of the chair, reaching across the table, grabbing Barton by the throat. Lawson hit the panic button. It took five men to subdue Clemence and carry him back to the cells.

# 11

The solicitor representing the Tobins was willing to push for an early hearing, and they stood a good chance of getting a cancellation, since August was a quiet month for Family cases. Clara had promised to read the file and stay in close touch with them in the build-up to the hearing.

Clara sat at the dining-room table, the Tobin bundle on her left and an A4 notepad on her right. She wrote using the pen her father had given her when she passed her bar exams. Mostly, she didn't think about it, but now, working through the shreds of a family divided, she felt a jolt of recognition. She had worn out dozens of nibs, used gallons of ink since then. The sheen was gone from its barrel and the gold plate had worn off the clip and she kept it safely in its box for much of the time, but it was the pen she chose for reassurance.

Her mother was in India with UNICEF when she was called to the bar. Clara had been out when she telephoned to congratulate her, so she had left a message on the machine. 'Get Daddy to buy you something nice from me,' she had said. It seemed that she had been absent at every milestone in Clara's young life: the summer she sat her GCSEs, her A' level year, the year she passed her finals and was called to the bar. She came for the wedding, when Clara and Hugo got married, but she was off again in days. She seemed quietly appalled when Clara told her she was pregnant, and she could not break her travel schedule to attend Pippa's christening.

It was her father who brought Clara home and spoiled her on the exeat weekends from her boarding school; her father who nursed her when Clara, weak and debilitated with glandular fever, was sent home for fear that she would infect the other girls.

She began calling her mother Sophia on her thirteenth birthday; Sophia was a more comfortable name for this near-stranger. She was always on some mission or other. Sophia had always been better with other people's children – no, that wasn't quite right – she had always been better with children in the *abstract* than with the practicalities of a daughter whose problems seemed trivial in the global scale of things.

Sophia was away when Clara's father had his fatal heart attack. She came home for the funeral and Clara was hopeful that perhaps now she wouldn't feel driven out of the family home by the awkward silences that had characterised their marriage. But she was off again within a fortnight, leaving Clara to speculate just who Sophia had been avoiding all those years.

Clara sighed, turning another page. Did Pippa feel abandoned, too?

The top sheet in the file was an application for right

to access; clipped to it, a copy of baby Helen's birth certificate. Clara's eye skipped to the mother's name. For a moment she couldn't breathe. *This can't be!*

She checked the application. There had to be some mistake. She went through to the kitchen. Pippa was reading *Girl* magazine while Trish prepared dinner. Trish turned and smiled. 'Fancy a cuppa?' Her smile faltered when she saw the expression on Clara's face. 'What's the matter?'

'Where's the evening paper?' Clara demanded.

Trish frowned. 'Haven't seen it – have you, Pippa?'

Pippa didn't even look up from her magazine. 'Threw it away,' she said, with sulky indifference.

Clara stared at her, astonished. 'Why on earth did you do that?'

Pippa shrugged.

Trish wiped her hands on a towel. 'Pippa darling—'

Pippa hunched her shoulders and stared hard at the blocks of brightly coloured text, pretending to read.

'Pippa!'

She pushed her chair back from the table and rolled her magazine. 'Daddy told me to, okay?' Her eyes flashed anger and resentment.

They stared at each other a moment longer, then Pippa edged past her mother, avoiding physical contact and walked out of the room. Trish called after her, but Clara shook her head: not worth the argument.

She took the lid off the bin and began rooting through the potato peelings and eggshells. She found the paper and shook it free of waste.

It was front page news. The *Evening Echo* didn't get much opportunity to report a murder, so a sensational killing pushed community news to the inside pages. She was pretty, the victim, a dark-haired girl with shiny hair and a shy smile. The headline, one word:

## SLAIN

Clara skimmed the first paragraph and found the name. Amy Dennis. The name on Helen's birth certificate. But the front page was dominated by a half-page photograph of Sergeant Phil Barton, carrying Amy's baby out of the house. His Casco baton was still in his hand and he looked bewildered, anguished.

She sat on the nearest kitchen stool.

'Clara?' Trish touched her shoulder.

Clara frowned. 'They lied to me, Trish,' she said. 'They told me it was a straightforward residency order.'

She read the article again, taking in the detail this time. Amy was a freelance photographer. Apparently she had worked for the *Echo* from time to time, and the editor had decided to mount a campaign to bring her killer to justice. There was even a confidential hotline.

Suddenly, Clara was furious. 'I have to go out,' she said.

'What about dinner?'

She looked at the salad and rice queasily. 'I couldn't eat.'

Trish rarely pushed Clara for an answer, but now she took a step forward and asked, 'Where shall I tell Hugo you've gone?'

'Quite probably to talk myself out of a job.'

# 12

As she drove, Clara reflected that this would be her second house call of the day. *Maybe you should advertise*, her inner voice suggested. *Home visits a speciality*. It had its funny side; she even smiled to herself at the thought.

Chris and Diane Tobin lived in a Victorian semi in Hoole. They had a small, tidy garden at the front. The privet hedge had been savaged and all that remained was a few sooty branches. The fence dividing the neighbouring gardens had been recently repaired and two slats of wood gleamed white against the faded brown of the older planking. The light had almost gone but the night was warm and laughter and conversation drifted from the houses on the silky evening air. Clara felt nostalgic for that kind of happiness, for the security of being able to throw open your doors and windows and not fret who might be hiding in the shadows.

Mr Tobin answered the door. He looked frail and tearful but she was in no mood to sympathise.

'Ms Pascal . . .' He looked uncertainly over his shoulder, as if expecting his wife to rescue him.

'May I come in?' Clara asked.

'I . . .' Again, that nervous glance over the shoulder.

Mrs Tobin appeared in the hall, craning to see their visitor. 'For heaven's sake, Chris,' she exclaimed. 'Let her in!'

He stood back and Mrs Tobin led Clara to a sitting room at the back of the house. The scent of honeysuckle and *nicotiana* drifted in through the open French windows. Mrs Tobin invited Clara to sit on a long, creamy-white sofa. Her husband perched on the arm at one end, but Mrs Tobin remained standing. A framed photograph dominated the wall opposite Clara; trees in a mist so dense it looked like poured milk. Beyond the trees, a red October sun hung a millimetre above the horizon. One of Mrs Tobin's Clara thought. How long had she waited for that exact moment – or perhaps she was the sort of photographer who would point the camera, shutter clicking, motor whirring madly, and hope for that one perfect shot.

'Has something happened?' Mrs Tobin asked. 'Why are you here?'

'You know why I'm here,' Clara said.

Mrs Tobin bowed her head. 'Oh.'

'Surely you must have known I'd find out.'

'I . . . I wasn't thinking straight,' Mr Tobin said. 'It's been a terrible shock—'

Clara rounded on Mrs Tobin. 'I offered you every opportunity to tell me the full story, and you gave me half-truths and obfuscation.'

'Don't blame Diane – it's my fault,' Mr Tobin said. 'I was questioned by the police when I arrived home. Apparently, the first person they consider in these situations is the—' He broke off, shooting his wife a guilty look. Was he about to say 'the spouse'? 'The lover'?

'I thought if you knew I was under suspicion, it would look bad. I was afraid I wouldn't be able to see Helen any more.'

'It's in your solicitor's notes, for God's sake! By tomorrow, it will be all over the papers. How long did you think you could keep it from me?'

'I thought—'

'No,' Clara said. 'You didn't think. You weren't thinking then and you're not thinking now. You're casting around for more lies and excuses – and that simply insults my intelligence. Now I want the truth, or I'm walking through that door.'

She expected another flare of temper, but he sat in an armchair and put his head in his hands. When he looked up at her, he seemed near exhaustion. 'I was trying to buy time,' he said. 'I was hoping to convince you to represent us.'

She blinked. 'Diva Legal Services, or me in particular?' she asked. On a number of occasions, ghouls had actually sought her out.

'It's not the notoriety, Ms Pascal,' Mrs Tobin said, understanding at once, and anxious to reassure her. 'We recognised you when you walked through the door, of course, but we're not cynical people. We'd asked around, while we were waiting for the court's decision. You have a reputation for being thorough. It seemed providential that your colleague was away – that the very person we *would* have chosen—'

'Happened through the door at the right time.' Damn Mitch! Had she engineered the whole thing? She wouldn't put it past her even to have persuaded Bethany to take time off so that Clara could be eased into representing Mr and Mrs Tobin.

'People say that once you commit to a case, you don't let go until you get a result,' Mr Tobin said.

'And you thought that you could trick me into committing to this one?' Clara gazed at him with begrudging admiration. 'I'm not sure who I should be more angry with, Mr Tobin – you, or Mitch O'Connor.'

Mrs Tobin blushed and looked away, alarmed. That told Clara all she needed to know: Mitch was implicated up to her smiling Irish eyes. Well they wouldn't be smiling by the time Clara had finished telling her what she thought of her little set-up. She felt a little sorry for Mrs Tobin: it seemed she had been coerced into this situation and she didn't have the constitution for deceit – even when she kept her mouth shut she was capable of spilling the beans.

'All right,' Clara said. 'This is how I see it. The relationship between a barrister and her client is based on trust. Right now, I don't trust you at all – either of you. So when you answer my next question, be very careful what you say.' She paused and Mr Tobin shot her a resentful look. His wife seemed anxious and embarrassed on his behalf.

Mrs Tobin stood near a bookcase cluttered with pottery and knick-knacks, and a stunning bronze sculpture. She retrieved a tissue she had tucked in the sleeve of her blouse and began dusting it. The action, and Mr Tobin's reaction to it, had the mark of a compulsion.

'The Wisdom of Solomon,' Mrs Tobin said, mistaking Clara's interest in her for curiosity about the sculpture.

Mr Tobin seemed irritated that his wife had distracted Clara's attention from him. 'I was delivering a lecture last night,' he said. 'Seven till nine at the University of Surrey's sociology department. Morality in the press,' he added. 'My parents live in Surrey. I stayed overnight with them. Set off at just before seven this morning and . . .' He trailed off.

'He got back shortly after eleven-thirty,' Mrs Tobin said. 'We've been through all of this with the police.'

'The normal course of events is to speak to your legal representation first,' Clara said drily. 'They will have checked with your parents by now. Police relationships, unlike barristers', are *not* based on trust, Mr Tobin,' she added, noting the worried look on his face. Something made her ask, 'Is there anything else you're hiding from me?'

Mrs Tobin glanced at her husband. Clara thought she saw a warning flash in his eyes. 'I can't make a strong argument for you with only half the facts,' Clara said. Mrs Tobin stole another look at her husband; Clara wanted to shout, 'Never mind him – do your own thinking!' Instead, she went on in a quiet, reasonable manner, 'And I will not represent someone who is less than totally honest with me.'

Mrs Tobin seemed to brace herself, it was almost a

visible squaring of the shoulders. 'I think she should know,' she said to her husband.

'Diane . . .'

'The police will find out soon enough, Chris,' she replied. 'Better that Ms Pascal hears it from us.'

He waved a hand in front of his face, abdicating himself of responsibility for what followed. Clara looked at Mrs Tobin. She flicked her hair over her shoulder, a curiously girlish gesture in a woman of her age, then she frowned, nodded, took a breath and said, 'Amy was a colleague.'

'You worked together?'

'At the tech. We sometimes did assignments together and we—' She didn't seem to know how to say it.

'You were friends?' Clara suggested.

Another nod. 'Until . . .'

*He's* unfaithful and *she* feels guilty. Clara glanced at Mr Tobin, sitting slumped in his chair, sulkily chewing his thumb. *Well, why not? After all, she's infertile and he wants a family. What's a man to do?*

'Amy would have wanted Helen to come to me,' Mr Tobin said. 'She knew that the best place for her was here, with me.'

'She was opposing increased access,' Clara said.

'You don't understand,' he said. 'She'd just got herself into a bit of a tizz.'

Clara narrowed her eyes at him. 'Word of advice, Mr Tobin: don't suggest to the judge that Helen's mother didn't want her daughter to see more of you because she was "in a tizz".'

Mr Tobin looked at Clara in resentful silence. She turned to his wife. 'It was stretching credibility to ask the court to believe that you are keen to look after the child of your husband's lover. When they find out that Amy had in fact been your friend—'

Mr Tobin clenched his hands in his lap. 'I don't see what difference that makes.'

Mrs Tobin crouched next to him. 'Listen to what she has to say, Chris,' she said, placing one hand on his knee.

*She's so damned nice!* 'A lawyer in these cases sees what any reasonably astute adult would see,' Clara said. 'The difference is, while most of us would have the tact to keep our observations to ourselves, she – it's likely to be a she, by the way – is obliged to ask those awkward questions, no matter how painful they might be to you.'

Mrs Tobin patted her husband's knee and stood, readying herself for what Clara was about to say.

'It seems you have been extremely tolerant, Mrs Tobin,' Clara said. 'My colleague will speculate on two possibilities: either you are a saint, or a doormat.'

Mr Tobin exclaimed in protest, but his wife nodded. 'I suppose that makes sense,' she said.

'Because my colleague is there to discredit both of you as potential custodians, she will push for the latter,' Clara went on. 'She'll wonder – for the court's edification – if such a woman could be a good role-model for a little girl. She might ask the court to consider whether Mrs Tobin will grow to resent this child and the demands it makes on her time – indeed, will she see it as a symbol of everything that was wrong with her marriage?'

'We don't have to listen to this!' Mr Tobin made a move to stand.

'Be quiet, Chris!' There was a weary impatience in Mrs Tobin's voice. 'Ms Pascal is addressing me.'

He subsided and for a few seconds there was silence, except for the buzz and thump of a moth that had flown in from the garden, attracted to one of the lamps.

'Firstly,' Mrs Tobin said at last, 'Helen is a girl. She's a *she* not an *it*.'

'Quite so,' Clara said, with a theatrical little bow. 'You won't hesitate to correct my colleague in that, will you?'

Mrs Tobin seemed puzzled for a moment, then she responded to the twinkle in Clara's eye with, if not a smile, then a brightening of her expression.

'I was desperate for a baby,' she said. 'If Chris hadn't—' She frowned; this wasn't what she had intended to say. 'If Helen hadn't come along, we would have adopted.'

'You still could.'

Mrs Tobin seemed flummoxed by this suggestions. 'There's no need to, now.'

'And what about the pain your husband has caused you? He had an affair with your *best friend*, for heaven's sake! Are you really expecting the court to believe you *forgave* her?'

Mrs Tobin went to the bookcase and adjusted one of the ornaments, then turned to face Clara. 'When it first

happened, I hated her. I wanted her to pay. But Helen
. . .' She searched for the right words.

'Helen changed your feelings?' Clara suggested.

Mrs Tobin looked into Clara's face, her eyes shining. 'She's so special. She completed us as a family – as
human beings.'

'So,' Clara said, taking the role of devil's advocate,
'you were *grateful* to Amy . . .'

'Of course not,' she answered. 'It's more complicated than that. Helen is a separate entity. She can't be
blamed for what her parents did.'

'That sounds trite, Mrs Tobin. I'm afraid you'll have
to do better than that.'

Clara thought she saw fleeting annoyance on Mrs
Tobin's face. *Good*, she thought. In her experience,
judges didn't believe in saints.

'I never forgave her,' Mrs Tobin said. 'She was
never welcome in this house after – after the affair.
But Helen—' Her smile was pure unembarrassed joy; it
softened her features and gave her a youthful glow.

'You never forgave her,' Clara repeated. 'Do you
still hate Amy?'

Instead of the angry response Clara had expected,
Mrs Tobin grew thoughtful. 'She paid the highest price
and in doing so gave us the most precious gift, Ms
Pascal. How could I possibly go on hating her?'

Clara was relentless. 'And your husband – how do
you feel about him?'

Mr Tobin stared resolutely at his thumb, picking at
the chewed flesh around the nail.

Mrs Tobin seemed to give a mental shrug. 'I wanted

to hurt him as much as he hurt me.' He looked up, startled by this admission. 'I think I did,' she added softly, keeping eye contact.

Something passed between them. Clara couldn't identify what; did she regret hurting him, after all he had done to her? But there was no mistaking the triumphant edge in Mrs Tobin's next statement.

'But he's still here, with me.'

*I'm not sure how much of a bargain you got there, Diane*. Clara smiled and said, 'Helen stays at weekends, mostly?'

Tobin nodded.

'Talk me through a typical weekend.'

Mr Tobin seemed to grasp at last what she was driving at. He became animated and the truculent shoulder-shrugging reluctance to communicate vanished. 'Friday, we don't have time to do much more than bath Helen and put her to bed. Bath-time and bed-time are very special.' He held out a hand and his wife hurried to his side.

*Nice touch, the hand-holding*. She would have to make sure that they were seated together at the hearing. 'Saturday and Sunday are for Helen. We play games, go for walks, we . . .'

'We do normal things,' Mrs Tobin said. 'Like a real family.'

'Drop the "real".'

'I'm sorry?' Clara had put her through a lot this evening, but for the first time, she thought Mrs Tobin had taken serious offence.

'You *are* a real family,' Clara said. 'Maybe not

conventional – but what's conventional these days, anyway? You do normal things like *any* family.'

'Oh,' said Mrs Tobin, dimpling prettily. 'I see.'

Clara felt happier, too. 'Our first priority is to ensure that contact is maintained,' she said. 'Any break in continuity could be misconstrued.'

'Why on earth would we stop seeing her now?' Mr Tobin demanded.

'As I explained this afternoon, your visiting and staying rights remain the same. But the upheaval caused by Miss Dennis's death – the ill-feeling from Helen's grandparents – these things might make you diffident about demanding your rights.'

Mr Tobin gritted his teeth. 'Not a chance.'

'Can they stop us seeing her?' Mrs Tobin asked.

'Not unless there are child protection issues.' Clara took them both in with a long, searching look. 'If there are any proceedings or investigations in train—'

'No!' They spoke simultaneously.

After a pause, Mr Tobin said. 'There is nothing. No proceedings, no hints or allegations to muddy the judicial waters, Ms Pascal.'

'I'm sorry,' Clara said. 'I know this is painful.' Mr Tobin dipped his head in acknowledgement. 'Since there are no . . . impediments, visiting and staying contact will continue as before.'

Mrs Tobin closed her eyes for a moment. 'Thank God,' she whispered. 'You know, I sometimes pretend . . .' She blushed and Clara caught another glimpse of the young girl beneath the slightly sallow skin of the thirty-something woman. 'I pretend that Helen is our baby. Mine and Chris's.' She looked at Clara, her eyes focusing slowly, a camera fixing on its subject. She looked sweet and vulnerable and so full of hope that Clara's heart ached for her.

'She is, in a way – ours, I mean.' She seemed to read something in Clara's expression and went on a little defensively, 'She deserves stability. A proper home.'

'I can understand your saying that,' Clara said, anxious not to hurt her feelings, 'But be careful; Amy is the birth mother, not you. Amy's parents – Helen's grandparents – will be in court. You have to beware of making it seem like you're trying to erase Amy's memory.'

Unexpectedly, Mrs Tobin smiled, exchanging a shy glance with her husband. 'You will represent us, then?'

Clara thought about it. *I'm advising them. Talking to them as clients. Coaching them, for God's sake!* Somehow, without appearing to try, they had retained her services when, in fact, she had come determined to ditch them.

'We've made some headway,' Clara said, falling back on evasive language, creating an escape route, in case of emergency. 'But you have to come clean with the police. Tell them that you and she were friends, Mrs Tobin.'

She seemed uncertain.

'You have nothing to hide – and as you said,' Clara added with a touch of dry humour, 'they're bound to find out.'

Mrs Tobin conferred wordlessly with her husband; after a moment or two, she nodded. 'I'll speak to them first thing in the morning . . . There's one other thing I should tell you,' she said. 'You know the police have arrested a man?'

Clara nodded; she had heard it on the car radio.

'I know him.' She swallowed. 'He was a student, over a year ago – a correspondence course. And . . .' she hesitated. 'And Amy tutored him as well.'

'The media didn't give a name,' Clara said. 'What makes you think it's him?'

She shuddered. 'He got out of prison a couple of months ago. Since then, he – he's been harassing me. Wanting me to organise an exhibition of his work – I can't do that, Ms Pascal! I can barely get my own work shown.'

'It's all right, Diane,' Tobin said roughly. 'You're under no obligation to that thug.'

'But he won't leave me *alone*!' She broke contact with her husband and took a step towards Clara.

'What did you say to this man?'

'His name is Clemence. Ian Clemence. What could I say? He's an ex-convict with no reputation other than the notoriety of his past crimes.' She snorted. 'Of course, these days, *that* sort of background can be an asset.'

'So you told him you couldn't help?'

'I told him I'd look into it. I wanted him out of my house!' she exclaimed, as if expecting Clara to disapprove. 'What else could I do? He knows where I live – he came to my *house*!' She stared fearfully into the darkness outside. 'And . . . I think he's been watching me.'

'You've told the police this?' Clara asked.

'What's the point?'

Clara looked at Mr Tobin. He seemed too absorbed in his own misery to concern himself with his wife's. Clara went to her and brought her back to the sofa.

'Under the terms of the Harassment Act, if you made a complaint against Clemence, the police have to take action. They'll warn him to keep away from you—'

'But they will let him go won't they? He's accused of murder and they'll just let him walk out of the police station a free man.'

'They have a limited number of hours they can question him,' Clara explained. 'But your complaint will give them more to work with. They'll give him a verbal warning, and if he comes near you again, they *will* arrest him.'

'Can't you do something – get an injunction against him?'

'It might not be necessary. Give it a day or two – a warning often does the trick.'

'That's all very well for you to say! How will I know if he's stopped stalking me? I'm afraid to answer the phone in case it's him. I even cut back the hedge so that I could get a clear view across the street. Chris says it won't grow back. How can I be sure he's not creeping around at the back of the house, following me to work, dogging my every move?'

Clara felt a shiver of sympathy. 'I'll find out what I can about him,' she said. *Mistake, Clara. It's not your concern. Leave it to their solicitor.* But she had made the promise; she would not go back on it now. 'If we have to take this to court, at least we'll be prepared,' she said.

'And in the meantime, the police do nothing.'

'They *are* investigating,' Clara said, 'You can depend on it – they're probably waiting for test results. They'll bring him in again when they have more evidence.'

'He's a convicted killer. What more do they need?'

'Past crimes aren't an absolute predictor of future conduct, Mrs Tobin,' Clara said, adding, 'We in the judicial system like to think there is *some* hope of rehabilitation.'

'I don't know why they can't lock him up while they gather their evidence.'

'Because the law won't allow it. We presume innocence until guilt is proved.'

'He killed Amy and now he's terrorising me!'

'Diane!' It wasn't concern for his wife's mental state that prompted Mr Tobin to speak up. 'She's just been talking about child protection issues,' he said, his face red with fury.

Mrs Tobin stared at Clara in horror.

'If there is any threat to Helen's safety, the courts will have to review her contact with you,' Clara agreed.

'He never actually made a threat,' Mrs Tobin said, desperately trying to undo what she had said. 'He never said he would harm me. Maybe I was just overreacting . . .' She stopped, raising her hands and letting them fall in a gesture of defeat.

'It's a material fact,' Clara said, hating herself for adding to the woman's distress. 'I'm afraid we'll have to disclose it.'

Mr Tobin's anger turned to desperation. 'Don't let them take Helen away from me, Ms Pascal,' he begged.

'Nobody is going to take her away. But the court won't place her in a situation were she's likely to be at risk.' Neither looked at her, nor at each other. Each seemed completely alone in their misery. 'Look,' she said, 'It'll be several weeks before we can get a court hearing. Anything could happen between now and then.'

'Yes,' Mrs Tobin made an effort to calm herself. 'Yes, it might. We mustn't let him panic us, darling.' Her husband's only answer was a despairing look. 'Clemence will probably be locked up by then,' Mrs Tobin insisted. 'For good, I mean. We'll be safe.'

'Talk to the police,' Clara said. 'Make a formal complaint. In the meantime, I'll talk to your solicitor, see if we can get an injunction against him. And you should take extra precautions. The French windows, for instance – you should lock them when you leave the room.'

'I'll make sure he remembers,' Mrs Tobin said.

'And deadlock the doors, front and back, even when you're in the house.'

She stopped. They were looking at her in that knowing way people sometimes did – part compassion, part curiosity – wondering, *Is this what* she *does? Is this how she tries to feel safe?*

# 13

DC Cath Young stood in the centre of Ian Clemence's bedsitter and stared at a poster-sized portrait of a woman. Blonde and fair-skinned, no more than twenty, she lay back on the grass, laughing, but startled: her eyes wide, her arms above her head, crossed at the wrists – a clichéd hint at bondage.

Fletcher noticed her rapt examination of the picture. 'Wouldn't mind giving her one,' he said, peering over Young's shoulder, his proximity deliberately offensive.

She looked at him, her expression brimming with contempt, and he chuckled, moving to the bed to strip it of its sheets and blankets. Young glanced again at the picture. There *was* something about it. How did he get that angle? It occurred to her that he must have been standing astride the woman. It would account for her startled expression. She imagined the situation: him at a safe distance, encouraging her to smile, coaxing her to raise her arms – then suddenly he moves in, standing over her, keeping up the patter so that she doesn't get too alarmed, joking with her so that she keeps the pose and he gets the shot he was aiming to steal from the start.

With a shudder, she turned away and went to the tallboy. Starting from the bottom, she pulled the drawer out, clumsy because of the pain in her bandaged hand, but unwilling to ask for help. She emptied the contents onto a small drop-leaf table pushed up against the wall, then turned the drawer over to check for packages taped to the underside before moving on to the next. Clemence had little in the way of clothing: two pairs of jeans, one pair of combats, a pair of chinos. Two black, two white T-shirts. A couple of long-sleeved shirts. His jacket – black leather – hung on a peg behind the door.

DC Chris Thorpe finished clearing the kitchen/dark-room of photographs and began emptying the cupboards, stacking the last of the trays outside the door, then he rolled back the rug in the main room and started checking for loose floorboards. Fletcher turned the mattress and slid the bed away from the wall; when he found nothing, he shoved the bed back in place and bundled the bedding onto it.

Someone had opened the window and street noise filtered in: the shouts of children, the hum of traffic on Hoole Road. Through the wall, the plangent notes of the *EastEnders* theme tune was followed by a brief silence and then a burst of argument.

'Bloody hell!' Fletcher took out a handkerchief and wiped his face. 'What a waste of time.' Neither Thorpe nor Young responded, so he wandered over to the kitchen. 'Someone should have a look behind that plywood,' he said, frowning at the black panels battened against the slope of the stairs.

'You don't look too busy, Fletch,' Young said without looking up.

Fletcher dabbed at his neck with his handkerchief. 'I don't see why we have to work from breakfast to bedtime in this bloody heat. And I've heard no mention of overtime.'

Thorpe continued his painstaking probing of the floorboards; using a screwdriver to try to ease the boards up, he worked a metre at a time, edging slowly forward.

'Have you heard anything about ovies, Chris?' Fletcher persisted.

'No,' Thorpe said without looking up. 'No ovies on this one, Fletch.'

Fletcher thrust his hands into his pockets and sauntered over to the window, but he soon tired of staring at the tiny patch of cracked concrete and the brick wall opposite. He crossed to the centre of the room and gazed at the portrait. 'Nice-looking bint,' he said, lifting it down and planting a kiss on the laughing mouth of the woman.

'You're a hopeless sleaze, Fletcher,' Young said, continuing her search.

Thorpe found a wobbly board near the skirting and worked at it, trying to lever it out. 'Give us a hand with this, will you, Fletch?' he asked.

Fletcher was silent. 'Fletch—'

He looked up and saw Fletcher standing in the middle of the floor with a large brown envelope in his hands.

'Where'd you find that?' Thorpe asked, brushing his hands free of dirt and splinters.

Young turned from the chest of drawers.

'Where'd you think?' He had the framed picture from the wall set on its edge, leaning against his leg. 'Taped to the back of this.'

'You should've let the SOCOs deal with it,' Young said.

'And wait another two hours for one of them to drag his arse out of his comfy armchair?' He turned the envelope over in his gloved hands. 'If you'd been in this business as long as I have, Cath, you'd know that time is of the essence.'

Fletcher no longer had the power to make Young feel cowed by his blustering attempts to pull rank and experience. 'I've got to admit, you're very resourceful, Fletch,' she said, demurely, waiting just long enough for him to start swaggering before adding, 'You find more ways of being wrong than anyone I've ever met.'

'Why don't you go out and get yourself laid?' Fletch asked. 'It might loosen that tight little—'

'Come on now,' Thorpe said. 'Let's keep our minds on the job, eh?'

'You have to *have* a mind to keep it on the job,' Young said. '*Time* isn't of the essence, Fletch. Preserving the evidence is.'

Fletcher reacted without thinking. Turning the envelope upside down, he said, 'Oops,' and let the contents slide out onto the bare boards.

'You bloody idiot!'

Thorpe gave Young a warning glance. It cost her a lot, but she kept quiet: Thorpe was Fletcher's friend, and she could see that anything she said would only make things worse. They all looked at the pictures that had slipped out of the envelope. Six-by-four shots; standard, lab-processed snaps, each of the same small, dark-haired woman. In one, she looked over her shoulder as she slotted the key in the lock of her front door.

'What's the bet she's dead?' Fletcher asked.

Young didn't trust herself to make a reply. She went back to her careful search, looking inside the carcass of the chest of drawers and feeling under the runners to be certain she had missed nothing. Fletcher didn't frighten her any more, but he could still rattle her. She bit down hard on her back molars, thinking how satisfying it would be to clench her hand into a fist and hit the fat oaf hard in his repulsive mouth.

She lifted the empty shell away from the wall. There was nothing behind it, and under it she found only a few dust devils and an old till receipt. She listened with half an ear to the exchange between Chris Thorpe and Fletcher, but couldn't make out the words. As she piled shorts and socks back into the drawers she saw Fletcher leaving.

'Where's he going?' It wasn't to log the pictures – Thorpe was sealing those in a plastic bag.

Thorpe shrugged. 'He'll be back.' He took out his mobile phone and flicked open the panel. He reported the discovery of the pictures and asked for a SOCO to come over, listening to the answers with only an occasional grunt to show that he was paying attention. He finished the call with a terse, 'Okay, fine.'

Young replaced the last of the clothing and rattled the top drawer back in place. 'Are they coming?' she asked.

'No.'

'What did he say?'

Thorpe lifted one shoulder. 'Bag it and tag it. "No point wasting a SOCO's time if you've had your sweaty paws all over it."'

Young shook her head. 'Fletch is a sloppy, idle sod,' she said. 'I don't know why you take the flak for him.'

'He's a mate,' Thorpe replied. 'And he's going through a rough patch.'

'Yeah,' she said. 'So where is he now? Trying to smooth things out with a dead cert?'

Thorpe checked his watch. 'It's a bit late for that, isn't it?'

She held his gaze. 'Yes,' she said. 'It is.'

# 14

———◆———

'These pictures were found in a drying-rack in your dark-room,' Barton said, taking two seven-by-five prints from a buff folder and placing them on the interview room table.

Clemence recognised them immediately: the shots he had taken outside her house. In one, she turned to look down the street, tucking a shank of fair hair behind her ear with a free hand as she rummaged in her handbag for her keys. Funny how women never had their keys ready. Made them easier to ambush. 'So?' he said.

'Who is she?' Barton asked.

'How should I know?' The light had a sharp quality; giving definition to the architectural lines in the picture, and it etched the contours of her face, ageing her. *God it was hot that day!* The stink of privet and the insistent rattle of the sycamore came back to him in a brief, vivid flash.

Barton sighed. 'You took the pictures, Mr Clemence. You must know who she is.'

Clemence looked from Barton to DC Young, who was sitting in on the interview. *They really are asking. They don't know who she is.* 'I didn't ask her name – I didn't even ask her permission,' he said. 'It was an impulse thing.'

'Were you following this woman?'

Clemence looked up sharply. 'No,' he said, slowly and clearly, so there wouldn't be any mistake on the tape. '*I wasn't following her.*' *Give him something more – make Mr Quartermaine think you're trying to co-operate.* He took a breath. 'Look,' he said. 'It was a new lens. I was testing the focus.'

'And you thought you'd test it on a suburban street, on a woman who doesn't know she's being observed.'

'Plenty of reference points,' Clemence said. 'See—' He took the picture and indicated the various features. 'The door frame – that gives straight lines and reflections. Then there's her face – lots of tonal qualities in a face. The fence between the houses—'

'Mr Clemence, I don't need a lesson in photography.'

Clemence replaced the photograph and stared coldly at Barton. 'I'm just giving you a reason,' he said. 'In a park, what have you got? Trees and grass.'

'Where was this taken?'

'Where?' He was stalling for thinking time; he hoped Barton wouldn't notice.

Barton didn't move and he didn't repeat the question.

Clemence tried a smile. So much for stalling. 'I've been away a long time. I'm still finding my way around.'

'So,' Barton said. 'You don't know her, and you don't remember where you took the pictures?'

'Thank you for that clarification, Sergeant Barton,' Mr Quartermaine said. Barton had almost forgotten the solicitor was there, he had been so quiet and restrained during the first part of the interview. 'My client has already answered those points.'

This time, Clemence's smile was real. Barton had asked the question so that in future, if they found out he was lying, they could use it against him. Quartermaine was making it clear in his dry, understated manner, that he knew exactly what the sergeant was up to and he would not tolerate him badgering his client.

Barton nodded and tried another tack. 'You have a lot of pictures of women in your flat.'

'I'm a photographer. I take pictures of women.'

Barton fanned a few of the glossy photos on the interview room table. 'Now,' he said, 'pictures like these, I can understand. They're artistic, tasteful.'

Clemence looked at him from under half-closed eyelids; he wasn't about to spill his guts because of some obvious flannel from a dibble who wouldn't know an *f*-stop from a bus-stop.

Barton took the photographs they had found hidden in Clemence's flat from the folder. Five six-by-fours, each sealed in its own labelled plastic bag, each with an evidence number written on the label. 'These aren't as stylish,' Barton said.

'They wouldn't be,' Clemence said.

'Oh?'

Clemence tapped his temple, widening his eyes to emphasise just how dense the sergeant was being. 'They're not mine.'

Barton exhaled. 'We're wasting time, Mr Clemence. These photographs were found in your flat, taped to the back of the framed photograph on the wall over the fireplace. A portrait you took. In a frame you made. Only *your* fingerprints are present.'

'They're not mine,' Clemence repeated. 'I didn't take them. And I've never seen her in my life.'

Barton looked down at the photographs: a pretty woman of about thirty, her dark hair cut into a short bob. 'Woman going into a restaurant,' he said, sorting through the photographs. 'The same woman getting into a car; and here she seems to be on a patio at the back of a house—'

'I can see,' Clemence said.

'They look like surveillance pictures.'

'You reckon?'

Barton nodded. 'So do these other two.' He touched the two pictures of the fair-haired woman.

'I wouldn't know.'

Young smirked at him, shaking her head.

'I've taken quite a lot of this sort of picture in my time,' Barton said. 'Trust me, I'd know.'

Clemence laughed, turning in his chair to his solicitor. 'He's asking me to trust him . . .'

'You're sure you don't know either of these women?'

In the fraction of a second it took him to swing back to face the sergeant Clemence had himself under control. 'I'm positive,' he said. Nevertheless, his jaw twitched involuntarily as Barton dipped into the buff folder on the desk a third time, bringing out the letters that Clemence had written to Amy Dennis.

'You don't recognise your tutor, Amy Dennis?' he said.

Clemence didn't answer at first; he was thinking furiously. Barton kept paying out the rope and you just helped yourself, didn't you, Clemence? He thought about the roll of film. Was it well enough hidden? And what about Diane Tobin? Once they made that connection, he was done for. But there was always a chance they wouldn't. He knew the importance of luck in an investigation: good luck and bad. Law of averages said that once in a while it had to work in his favour.

If there was one fact Clemence had assimilated during his twelve years in prison – accepting it and making it as much a part of his belief system as his absolute certainty in the existence of God – it was that a grass is the lowest form of life. And the habit of twelve years was too hard to break: you don't grass – especially on yourself.

'Mr Clemence?'

He clenched his teeth and said nothing. He had to be sure that when he opened his mouth it was safe to speak. 'I never met her,' he said at last. 'It was a postal course. I never met her; I didn't know what she looked like.'

'But there are photographs of her in your flat,' Young said.

'*Hidden* in your flat,' Barton corrected.

Clemence looked at Barton. He had a choice: shut down, or explode. He'd got away with grabbing Barton by the throat once, but any more bad behaviour would lose him his legal representation: Mr Quartermaine had made it clear that he wouldn't tolerate 'outbursts', as he quaintly put it. Anger management had taught him a few strategies; visualisation was one. In the past, this skill had been restricted to creating a picture in his mind of smashing his fist into some con's face the second before he did it. In group therapy he had been taught instead to visualise a place where he felt calm and happy. Difficult, inside, to see a sunny hilltop, a deserted beach, but Clemence had been out for two months and he had a strong eye for detail and a good visual memory. He found his own favourite place of escape. And shut down.

Barton halted the interview ten minutes later.

He snagged a mug of coffee from the kitchen then went to Lawson's office to report back. Cath Young caught him up outside the door.

'Sarge—' She still had their copy of the interview tapes in her hand.

'Get those to the exhibits officer before the debrief, will you?' he said, checking his watch. Fifteen minutes to go.

'I'm on my way. But that woman – the fair-haired one—'

Barton recalled the photographs they had taken from Clemence's dark room.

'You know her?'

Young frowned. 'She's familiar. I think I've seen her recently, but I can't remember where.'

'There's a couple of copies on my desk,' Barton said. 'Show them round. See if anyone else can come up with a name.'

Lawson was on the phone, and Barton edged around him to retrieve the photographs for Young.

He finished his call moments later. 'The Super can't make our debrief,' Lawson said. 'There's been an armed robbery in Helsby – he's going over there to lend moral support to the SIO.'

'Anyone hurt?' Barton asked.

'Civilian shot. He's in a coma.'

They paused for a second or two, then Lawson checked his watch. 'All right,' he said. 'What did you get out of Clemence?'

'He clammed up. When I faced him down with the pictures of Amy Dennis, he switched off. He might as well have not even been there. No, that's not quite right – *before* he shut up, he said he'd never met her, didn't know what she looked like.'

'Maybe he didn't.'

'Well, it'd be hard to see a likeness between the photos and the mess he left behind him on his last visit.'

'Woah – wait a minute!' Lawson walked around his desk and closed the office door. 'We don't have a positive link between Clemence and the murder scene and until we do, I don't want to narrow the focus of this investigation with suppositions.'

'He knew her,' Barton said. 'But he denied knowing

her. When he's found out in that lie, he claims he didn't know where she lived. He's got photographs of her in his flat. Blood all over his T-shirt—'

'We don't know if it's her blood. Not yet.'

'He was stalking her, Boss!'

'Possibly. But that doesn't make him a killer.'

'He *is* a killer – that's why he's been banged up for the past twelve years.'

Lawson nodded slowly. 'That was drugs-related, wasn't it?'

Barton's mouth twisted in a grimace of disgust. 'We found him lying on the sofa, staring up at the ceiling, with his girlfriend's body on the floor next to him. Her blood had dried to a crust on him and he was so stoned he just lay there, counting the cracks in the plaster.'

'Is there any indication he's still using?'

'Nothing in his flat . . .'

'And the police surgeon saw no signs of anything more serious than a heavy nicotine habit.'

Barton rolled his eyes. 'Look, sir—'

'If he killed her – *if*, mind you – I want everything we can get before we charge him.' Barton tried to interrupt, but Lawson held up a hand to stop him. 'I've asked the lab for premium service, so the blood test results from the T-shirt should be through by tomorrow. In the meantime, the clock's ticking. When was he booked in?'

'Seventeen-twenty-two.'

'Which means he's been here just short of three hours. We'll have to give him an eight-hour rest break if he's here much longer – that's eleven hours wasted –

add on any consultation time with his solicitor, and our statutory twenty-four hours will soon be eaten up. Is he back in the cells?'

Barton gave him a sheepish look. 'Consulting with Mr Quartermaine.'

'Well, as soon as they're finished, I want him released.'

You can't do that!' Barton exclaimed. 'The man's dangerous.'

'We don't know that.'

'It took four officers to bring him in. You didn't see him in the interview room, Boss.' He could have added *You didn't see the damage he did to Vicky Rees with a claw-hammer*.

It seemed he didn't need to say it for Lawson to know what he was thinking. 'It was a horrific crime, Phil,' he said. 'I've read the reports and I've seen the PM photos. It must have been hard for a young officer to take, but we're looking at a different set of circumstances here.'

'The MO matches the man,' Barton said, stubbornly.

Lawson stared at him without speaking for a moment. 'We've got a contact number for Amy's course leader on the correspondence course, haven't we?'

Barton nodded. 'From her files.'

'Find out if he *did* ever meet her. And if he was given Amy's address. When we have that information, we'll question him again. But we can't do it tonight, and I don't want his sleeping time added to the PACE clock—'

'Sir—'

Lawson spoke over Barton's protests: 'So, when he's finished talking to his solicitor, I want him sent home for the night.'

# 15

Brendan Harris made his first million in 1985, at the age of twenty-six, converting old terraced properties into student accommodation. He worked hard, first to consolidate and later to diversify, and in the process, he had made a lot more money. Now he had reached the stage where money was less important to him than power and control. He worked a sixteen-hour day, slept for only five, and during his leisure hours he preferred high-risk, high-speed activities: go-karting, sky-diving, snowboarding, white-water rafting.

It was after eight-thirty in the evening. He sat behind his desk, talking on the telephone, while his eyes flitted between the close-of-market figures from the Stock Exchange on his computer monitor, and the two TV screens to his right. One was tuned to rally car racing and the other to News 24.

At eight thirty-five, his secretary came in with a tray of coffee and biscuits. She poured in silence, but Harris knew that she didn't mind the late hour: past five-thirty she was paid overtime, and the rates were generous.

As he spoke into the telephone, he occasionally ran his fingers through his hair, relishing the sensation. He was vain about his hair, which was still the thick curly dark auburn of his youth.

Five minutes later, he had drunk his coffee and was near to closing the deal. His secretary returned and stood front left of his desk, avoiding obstructing his view of the televisions. He continued his bantering negotiations, raising one eyebrow to her in question. The look she gave him said that this was important.

He beckoned her forward and she placed a slip of paper on his desk, sliding it across the polished oak until it was in reach. He took it, barely missing a beat as he read it, nodded to her, and she left.

After another few minutes Harris replaced the receiver with a satisfied grin. He gave himself a moment to enjoy his triumph, waiting a little longer for his jubilation to subside – it wouldn't do to be in a good mood when he spoke to his next appointment – then he leaned forward and punched the number for his secretary's extension on the phone keypad.

'Send him in,' he said.

Tom Rivers came into the room looking both belligerent and apologetic. He had the skinny build of a man with a nervous stomach. He was sweating, despite the air-conditioned chill of Harris's office, and he took out a handkerchief to wipe his hands before sitting in one of the leather armchairs.

Harris poured himself another coffee, taking his time, while Rivers fidgeted and sweated.

'What are you doing here?' he asked at last.

'I've been calling all afternoon,' Rivers replied, at once accusing and defensive.

Harris looked at him over the rim of his cup, then placed the cup carefully in the saucer. 'Why are you here?' he repeated softly.

'I wouldn't have to be if you returned my calls.'

'We agreed,' Harris said. 'No calls. No meetings. Communication by courier only.'

'First the girl – and now Enderby's been shot!' Rivers blurted out.

'It's a violent society we live in,' Harris said quietly. 'Burglars carry hammers. Muggers carry guns.' He looked into Rivers' face and was pleased to see that the implicit threat had not gone unheeded.

'They arrested Clemence,' Rivers said, less argumentative now.

Harris took another sip of coffee then pushed his cup and saucer away before saying, 'So?'

'Well, what if he—?' Rivers' eyes darted sideways and he licked his lips.

'Look,' Harris said. 'Clemence is an ex-con. He knows the score. Anyway, he's about to be released.'

'Released?' Rivers looked like the news held little comfort for him. 'It wasn't on the radio.'

'I've got eyes everywhere,' Harris said. 'Clemence is smart. He kept his mouth shut and they had to let him go.'

Rivers took out his handkerchief again and wiped the sweat out of his eyes. 'I'm just a businessman,' he murmured.

'Nah.' Harris waited and eventually Rivers left off wiping his hands and looked up at him. 'You're not just a businessman, Tom. You're a *bent* businessman. Prisons are full of your sort.'

Rivers' sallow colouring became a waxy yellow.

'Go home,' Harris said. 'Stay the fuck away from me. From now on, you wait for me to get in touch. And remember what I said,' he added allowing himself a twinkle of malice. 'I've got eyes everywhere.'

Rivers stared mutely at him.

'What are you waiting for?'

Rivers got shakily to his feet and backed away like an obsequious courtier. Harris turned up the volume on the rally car race and swung his feet up on his desk. He had dismissed Rivers from his thoughts before the door clicked to.

# 16

Phil Barton ate his supper in silence. Fran watched the Channel 5 film with the volume turned low and one eye on her husband. He was edgy and although he ate everything she put in front of him, he seemed to taste nothing.

She waited for him to finish. 'Phil—'

He raised one hand, listening intently.

'I'm just . . . I'm going to check on Timmy,' he said. 'It'll take me two minutes.'

'You checked him when you came in. And again before you sat down to eat.'

'Two minutes,' he said.

'You wake him, you pace the floor with him,' she warned.

She washed up and sat down again in front of the TV, but couldn't settle. When he came down fifteen minutes later, she flicked the off-switch and turned to face him. 'Are you going to tell me what this is about?' she asked.

'What?'

'Checking on Timmy every five minutes, the brooding silence, the bruises on your neck.'

His hand went involuntarily to the tender skin either

side of his windpipe. 'It's hot in the cells,' he said. 'People get fractious.'

'Just an average August day on the mean streets of Chester, then?' She handed him the evening paper. 'You're front-page news. I was kind of hoping you'd tell me yourself.'

He hadn't realised until seeing himself with Amy Dennis's baby in his arms, just how frightened he had been. 'I didn't see the camera,' he said.

'That isn't the point, Phil.'

He rubbed one hand tiredly over the stubbly growth on his scalp. 'You know I can't discuss an ongoing case.'

'You arrested that man, didn't you?'

'No.'

She sighed impatiently. 'Questioned him, then. Why did he go for you?'

'I told you.'

'I don't believe you.'

'He's a vicious thug; they do that sort of thing.'

Fran gave him one of her 'cut-the-bullshit' looks.

He shrugged. 'It was a long time ago.'

'He obviously has no trouble remembering. You know I'll find out, one way or another, Phil.'

He narrowed his eyes at her. 'Have you been watching *The Bill* again?'

'It isn't funny.'

'I know that. I just don't want to talk about it.'

'Great. I spend sixteen hours out of twenty-four with an infant, talking baby-burble and my husband – when he finally does get home – says he doesn't want to talk.'

'I didn't say that – just that I don't want to talk about—'

'About what? About finding the body of a murdered woman, or her baby, alone in the house, or the man who attacked you?'

'Fran—' he began.

'Because let me tell you, Phil, I'm sick of being shut out, kept in the dark.'

Barton closed his eyes. He had kept her in the dark in the past, and he felt guilty about it even now. Fran always knew which buttons to push. He didn't want to talk about this but she was waiting, watching him, her arms folded, implacable and imperturbable, and he knew she wouldn't let it rest until she had an explanation. 'I arrested Clemence,' he said.

'Is that his name? But I thought you said you *didn't*.'

'Not this time.'

She gave a gasp of exasperation and he began to explain: 'I'm talking about thirteen years ago. I arrested him for the murder of his girlfriend.'

Fran gazed at him steadily.

'Clemence was a loser with a habit he couldn't control. So far as we could make out, they had a row. Probably over the drugs Clemence dosed himself with after the attack.' He stared at the blank TV screen, remembering. 'It was a routine call. Domestic – a neighbour dialled triple nine when they heard screams.

'The front door was open. There was no light – most of the windows were boarded up – the place reeked of piss and vomit. I saw him first and I thought it'd all blown over. He was blissed out on that rancid sofa.

The toxicologist couldn't believe he could have so much shit in his veins and survive it.'

Barton hadn't spoken about this in twelve years, not since the trial, but he hadn't been able to get it out of his mind since finding Amy Dennis that morning. 'Then I saw something – just a shape, really. She—' His voice cracked and he coughed. 'She was lying face up.' He blinked, trying to shake the image. 'She'd tried to get away, but he went after her. Finished the job. He beat Vicky Rees to death with a hammer because he thought she'd nicked his stash. She was . . .' He shook his head. 'He cracked her skull like an eggshell.'

Her left eye-socket was smashed and her lips were gone, so that she seemed to be wearing a permanent grin, but nothing in the world would induce him to tell Fran that.

'Amy Dennis was attacked with a hammer, wasn't she?'

He nodded, unable to speak for the moment.

'And you think Clemence . . .'

'He's been out for two months. He wrote threatening letters to Amy. He had a blood-soaked T-shirt in his bag when he was arrested – *and* he resisted arrest. If it was up to me, he'd still be in prison, serving time for what he did to Vicky Rees. He's a danger to women.'

'But he is in custody . . .'

'We had to let him go.'

'Great.'

'It's not up to me, Fran.'

'So,' Fran said slowly. 'He was harassing Amy

Dennis. And he attacked you.' They sat for a few minutes in silence. Then Fran placed both hands flat on the arms of her chair and levered herself up. 'Think I'll go and check on Timmy,' she said.

# 17

---◆◆◆---

Clemence checked every car on the street. No surveillance. But you weren't supposed to see them. They could be in one of the houses opposite – or at the back of the house – which would make more sense, since his bedsit faced onto the alleyway.

He let himself in and shut the door, standing for a few minutes in the hall, listening. The guy in the flat next to his was watching TV, as usual. With the volume turned up too high, as usual.

He thought about knocking, but the mood he was in, he would lose it and end up back down the nick. He decided he would wait a while, sort out and shower, then see if he felt enough in control to make a polite request.

The landlord was supposed to clean the bathroom once a week, which generally amounted to picking the hairs out of the shower cubicle plug-hole and chucking half a bottle of bleach down the bog. But the girl in the flat upstairs always cleaned the bathroom before she used the shower, so it never got too manky. He liked following on from her, the bathroom still steamy and scented with her shampoo and shower gel. There was always a dusting of talcum powder on the floor and, once, she had left a perfect footprint in negative on the floor tiles. Homely-looking girl, but nice tits – and he approved of her housekeeping skills: no slime in the soap dish, no pubic hairs stuck to the glass of the cubicle. Good as a hotel.

The couple on the second landing were at it again. He could hear her laughing, teasing, him panting and wheedling, half-wild with desire. A sudden loud slap, followed by an outraged 'Hey!' Then a rumble and a thud, like they had fallen to the floor, and they were both laughing. Lucky bastards.

He opened his flat door. 'If it bothers you, don't listen,' he told himself. But he knew that he wouldn't be able to stop himself; that next time, like this time, he would stand transfixed, straining to hear like some sad Peeping Tom.

He crossed his room and pulled the curtains closed before switching on the light. The bed was a tumbled mess and the photo of the blonde was gone from the wall, but he had few possessions, aside from his photographic equipment, and there wasn't much out of place.

'You haven't seen the kitchen, yet,' he told himself.

He wasn't quite ready for that so, instead, he went again to the window and looked outside. There was no sign of movement at the back of the house, but the building opposite, a three-storey Victorian gothic mansion, had ten or fifteen dark, shadowy windows, where a cop with a pair of bins and a camera with fast film on the spool could keep an eye on his flat.

He drew the curtains again and slipped the bolt on the flat door before going into his kitchen/dark-room.

They hadn't put the hardboard panels back properly under the stairs and they had obviously removed the blackout boards over the window, because the seals were damaged. He would have to re-tape them. There was grit and dust on the work surfaces; he'd have to clean that lot before trying to develop any more film. They had emptied the drying-racks of photos and taken the negs he'd had hung on a line next to the sink; bastards had even taken the towels off the rail. His light safe stood open, the drawers ransacked and the precious photographic paper he had scrounged and begged from the lab ruined.

'Oh, man . . .' Two months it had taken him to build his stock. Now he would have to start from scratch. His carefully catalogued photographs – the portfolio he had been working on since his release, as well as his earlier efforts when he was inside – all gone.

He lifted the ruined printing paper from the top drawer of his light safe and twisted it, tearing and shredding it. 'Bastards!' He got through most of it before a new dread asserted itself. *The roll of film*.

He opened the wall cupboards. They had been searched and the food shoved back any old way. Had they seen it? The slight difference in depth of this cupboard, compared with the rest? He stacked the tins and packets on the work-surface. They would have said, wouldn't they, if they'd found the hidden roll of film? He examined the backboard: it was flush with the frame. He had made the backboard carefully, sanding away the rough edges, measuring the fit to a hair's-breadth.

He took out his penknife and eased it between the wall and the back of the cupboard, sliding it along until he felt the blade snag against metal. The catch was stiff, but he unhooked it on the third attempt and then repeated the process with the top catch. Light pressure at the base, and the backboard slid inwards, tilting progressively until he was able to lever and lift the board out.

The cylinder was there, but his heart pounded as he reached for it. Was it empty? He gave it a shake. It rattled

*Okay, Clemence, now what? You've got the film. What are you going to do with it? Burn it?* He couldn't do that: too much smoke – poisonous at that – and there was no way he could open a window to let the fumes out. He could dump it, but that would mean leaving the house. And what if the cops were lying in wait?

For five minutes he dithered. After twelve years of other people making decisions on his behalf, it was hard to get back in the habit. He panicked, and panic paralysed him. But after a time, the debilitating wave of fear passed and he knew that the best place for the roll of film was right where he had left it.

He replaced the cylinder in its niche and slid the backboard in place. His hands were shaking, and it took a while to locate the catches. By the time he was finished, he was drenched in sweat. He pulled off his T-shirt and wiped his face, then rubbed the cloth over his body and the back of his neck, swiping under each arm before giving the shirt a tentative sniff. He jerked away, repelled by his own stench, threw the T-shirt in a corner for washing, grabbed a towel and his toiletries bag and went out into the hall.

The girl from upstairs stepped out of the bathroom as he reached the first landing. Pink and clean in a fluffy towelling robe, she was. Her hair still dripping. She gasped and he saw her focus on his naked chest. He flexed his pecs, flashing her a grin, and she fled, her mule slippers flip-flopping as she hurried down the landing to her room.

Still grinning, Clemence draped the towel around his neck and opened the bathroom door. She had opened the window an inch to let some of the steam out, but the room was damp and hot. He flung the sash wide and stripped off, folding his chinos neatly and hanging them over the towel rail before stepping into the shower.

The girl had left her soap in the freshly cleaned dish. He set the temperature to cool, turned on the shower, and stood under the spray for a full five minutes before rubbing shampoo into his hair. Then he reached for her soap and began a slow, sensuous massage.

Thirty minutes later, as he towelled himself dry in his flat, he glanced over at the clock. Eleven p.m. – well after lights-out. Except there was no lights-out here. No lights-out, and no curfew. He dressed slowly: black jeans, black T-shirt.

'You're not inside now, mate.' He didn't have to lie on his bunk, listening to the shouts of the angry and the despairing and the frankly mad, trying to stay awake unable to face the dreams that came, not every night, but stealthily, at irregular intervals, to ambush him.

Clemence tightened his belt and strapped on his watch. *You can come and go as you please.* He closed his flat door using the key, to reduce the noise, checked and double-checked before slipping out of the house, keeping to the shadows, creeping through three front gardens before emerging onto the street from the fourth. Going out on the prowl. Because he could.

———◆———

## 18

The computer fan whirred softly, like a continuous sigh. In her first-floor study, Clara sat, slightly hunched, staring intently at the screen. A desk fan rotated slowly backwards and forwards on its one-hundred-and-eighty degree arc, adding a second note. Clara's fear, faint but insistent, created a third, high-pitched and unsettling.

The windows were locked, despite the heat, and the curtains were drawn; she had woken in the early hours, roused by her own breathless whimpers. She couldn't remember the dream, but she was afraid to go back to sleep and instead gazed fixedly at the hall light, visible though their bedroom door which, as always, stood ajar.

She feared waking in the dark more than anything; afraid that she would be plunged back into the suffocating darkness of her imprisonment and the cold filthy confines of a dank cellar.

Hugo stirred, draping one arm over her and muttering something incoherent. An hour later, every muscle tense, and further from sleep than ever, she had slipped out of bed and in to a cotton dressing-gown. She stopped at Pippa's room to watch her a while, having to resist the almost overpowering compulsion to tiptoe to the window and secure it. They'd had locks fitted that prevented the sashes being opened more than a few inches, but Clara never felt safe with them. She had argued with Hugo about it, but he was insistent.

'Living in terror like this is barely living at all,' he had said.

Sitting in front of the computer, her eyes burning and her throat closing with thirst, and yet unable to relieve her discomfort by opening a window, she had to agree with him.

For an hour-and-a-half she had trawled the newspaper databases, looking for information about Ian Clemence. Most of the agencies she tried, and the websites of the major newspapers, went back only three or four years. She thought she had struck gold with the *Telegraph*: its database went back to nineteen-ninety-four, but Clemence wasn't mentioned. Was this because the nationals hadn't run the story or because the story went back further?

Frustrated, she called up another search engine and typed in 'newspaper database' and began clicking on any site that looked like it might be helpful. She was about to give up when a name caught her eye. Hugo had used this database a couple of years earlier to do some digging on a company that wanted him to design an office refurb on a falling-down Georgian terrace in Liverpool.

She opted for pay-per-download, typed 'Ian Clemence', adding 'murder' as an additional search term, and left the date open. The screen blanked and seconds later she had a list of twenty-nine articles, listed in reverse date order.

|< <Doc1 – 25 of 29> >| Edit search Purchase tagged documents

Purchase tagged documents

☐ 1. Chester Evening Echo, April 15, 1991, pg 1, 228 words. EVIL; Clemence jailed for life.

☐ 2. The Sun, April 15, 1991, pg 2, 427 words. CAGED FOR LIFE; Hammer attack fiend 'must remain behind bars for a very long time.'

☐ 3. Mirror, April 15, 1991, pg 6, 439 words. ROT IN HELL; Mother tells of anguish over diminished responsibility plea.

☐ 4. Liverpool Echo, April 12, 1991, pg 1, 767 words. CLEMENCE GUILTY; Sentencing 'will reflect the horror of the crime' judge says.

☐ 5. Chester Chronicle, April 12, 1991, pg 1, 2364 words. GUILTY; Chester man convicted of hammer murder.

☐ 6. Chester Evening Echo, April 12, 1991, pg 1, 1064 words. GUILTY; 'I didn't know what I was doing,' Clemence weeps as verdict announced.

☐ 7. Chester Evening Echo, April 10, 1991, pg 1, 904 words. BEATEN TO DEATH FOR FIVE POUNDS FIX; 'Hammer was for protection' Clemence claims.

☐ 8. Liverpool Echo, April 9, 1991, pg 4, 253 words. DRUGS CRAZED ATTACK; Alcohol and drugs cocktail 'made accused violent and paranoid', expert says.

☐ 9. Mirror, April 8, 1991, pg 1, 824 words. CALLOUS; Hammer victim lay dying for hours while boyfriend slept.

☐ 10. Chester Evening Echo, April 8, 1991, pg 1, 636 words. HAMMER MURDER TRIAL BEGINS.

Clara scrolled through, clicking on every box to purchase the downloads. If Clemence was threatening her client, she wanted to know everything about him. She read the first article as she waited for the printer to run them off. Clemence was seventeen when he murdered his girlfriend, Vicky Rees. Now he would be almost thirty, with twelve years in prison to toughen him up. She didn't doubt that he was intimidating – Mrs Tobin's fear was real – but she wanted a picture in her mind and web archives provided text only. To-morrow she would pay a visit to Chester Library and request the papers on microfilm – with exact dates, she should be able to get a print-out of the full articles in minutes.

At five-thirty a.m., she gave up reading and decided to take a shower. She would make breakfast for Hugo and Pippa, drop in at Jericho Chambers, as she had promised, and see if she could drum up some work. Hugo was right: she wasn't exactly inundated of late. Nevertheless, she felt unusually positive, despite her lack of sleep. She would never have admitted it to herself, but researching the background on a criminal case had set her mind buzzing.

She towelled her hair dry and padded downstairs in her dressing-gown, feeling more alive than she had done for months: she could help the Tobins and she wasn't going to let Ian Clemence stop her.

Nevertheless, she tuned from the local station to Radio Three before setting about slicing bread and whisking eggs. She finished preparing the mushrooms, wiped her hands and mixed the batter for drop scones then, viewing the carefully prepared ingredients with some satisfac-tion, brewed some tea and took it up to Hugo.

He rolled over and moaned as she came into the room. Half-awake, he picked up his alarm clock and squinted at it. 'How long have you been up?'

'A while.' She had learned to be evasive about her sleep habits since he became impatient with her inability to sleep through the night.

'Come to bed,' he groaned.

'It's nearly seven o'clock. Drink your tea. You'll feel better.' She chose a sleeveless top and cream linen suit from her wardrobe. She wasn't due in court today, but she didn't want the boys at Jericho Chambers to think she had let herself go.

Hugo watched her dress. 'You're not going into work at this hour?' he said. 'You didn't get home till after ten last night.'

'You'll be glad to know that the extra hour or two secured me a couple of clients I was on the point of dropping.' *Why are you doing this, Clara? Why are you picking a fight?*

'Are you avoiding us?' Hugo asked. 'Is that it?' He was wide awake now; stubbly and tousled and grumpy with the heat.

She bit back a tart rejoinder and simply said, 'No.'

'Your daughter barely sees you any more.'

'*My daughter*,' she said, all restraint gone, 'barely speaks to me when she does see me.' She continued dressing, angry and hurt, unable to pull back from the inevitable argument. 'And even then, she's sulky and impudent.'

'Whose fault is that?' Hugo demanded. He stood up and started opening and closing drawers, dragging out a shirt and socks and underwear and throwing them onto the bed.

'Whose fault? All mine, I expect,' Clara said. 'I'm a terrible mother. I can't communicate with my daughter—' She stopped, her throat constricted; she couldn't talk past the pain.

'Clara, I didn't mean—'

'I'll see you later,' she said.

Hugo sat heavily on the bed and pushed his fingers through his hair. The front door slammed.

'Where's Mummy gone?' Pippa stood in her bare feet, teddy bear under one arm and her fringe stuck in sweaty skeins to her forehead.

*She's had another of her bad dreams.* 'Mummy had to go to work,' he said. He could almost wish that Clara could see her like this, vulnerable, achingly in need of her.

Hugo held out one arm and beckoned her to him. She snuggled up next to him, her head against his chest. Pippa muttered something he didn't quite catch.

He kissed the top of her head. 'What, darling?'

'I don't mean to be naughty,' she repeated in a small voice.

'You aren't,' he said. 'Come on, let's surprise Trish and have breakfast ready when she arrives.'

Pippa stared at the neatly stacked bread and the bowls of scrambled eggs and scone mix by the cooker. *Oh, hell* . . . Hugo put his hand on Pippa's shoulder. She wrenched away, shouting at him.

'You should have been *nice* to her! If you were nice she wouldn't've gone! We could've . . . We could've—' She burst into tears and ran off upstairs, back to her bedroom.

# 19

The kitchen window was open wide and the radio played softly. At the far end of the lawn, hard against the fence, a magpie drank from Timmy's paddling pool. Barton made a mental note to tip it out and refill it before he left for work.

Fran crouched in front of the washing machine, her back to him, cramming clothes into the drum. Timmy leaned with one hand on his mother's thigh and they took turns talking. Most of it was incomprehensible to Barton, but Fran seemed to understand Timmy's lisping babble, interpreting some phrases and repeating others clearly, taking his suggestions seriously. Barton felt a fierce surge of emotion, somewhere between pride and love and he was surprised to find tears welling in his eyes.

Timmy turned and saw him and Barton gave him a smile, opening and closing the fingers of one hand. Timmy imitated him, grinning and sticking his tongue between his teeth – a mannerism he adopted when he was feeling particularly pleased with himself.

'There you are!' Fran said, swiping a stray hair from her face. 'What time's the briefing?'

'Eight,' Barton said. 'Plenty of time.' He poured them both a mug of tea from the pot and handed one to Fran, then filled a bowl with muesli.

'It's only healthy if you eat a reasonable amount,' she chided.

'What's reasonable?'

'Four to five spoons.'

He gazed at her in horror. 'I'd starve!'

'You're supposed to be watching what you eat.'

'I do,' he said. 'I do watch what I eat – how else would I keep my shirt-front clean?' He glugged a half-pint of milk onto the cereal and Fran sighed.

He patted his stomach. It was solid. Not all muscle, admittedly, but it didn't hang below his belt either. 'We're big-boned in my family.'

Fran slid him a sideways look. 'Oh,' she said. 'That'd explain why Jelly Baby here wobbles so much.'

Timmy picked up on his nick-name and yelled, 'Delly Baby!'

The letter-box rattled and the newspaper thudded onto the mat.

'I'll get it,' Barton said.

'Al geddit!' Timmy mimicked cheerfully, following him at a rapid waddle, rocking from side to side, feet splayed and arms held out for balance.

'Not so fast, Jelly Baby,' Fran said, sweeping him up and holding him above her head. He squealed with delight, and she jiggled him, just to hear him laugh, then set him in his high chair and plonked his breakfast mush on the tray before he had the chance to complain at his sudden imprisonment.

When Barton returned to the kitchen, Fran was trying to feed Timmy and Timmy was turning his head, refusing to be fed. 'Okay,' she said, closing his fist over the spoon. 'You do it.'

Timmy scooped a spoonful but turned the spoon over at the crucial moment and splodged it on his tray.

'It's gonna be another scorcher,' Barton remarked.

Fran popped two rounds of bread into the toaster. 'I thought I might take him to the P.A.R.K. before it gets too hot.'

Barton felt a tightening in his stomach. 'Oh.'

'What?' she said, puzzled by his silence.

'Nothing. I'd just . . . While things are – the way they are, I'd prefer if you stayed close to home.'

'Didn't do Amy Dennis much good, did it?'

He flinched and she relented a little. 'I'm sorry, Phil. But I won't become a prisoner because this man is free.'

Barton scooped the sodden muesli mash onto his spoon, but his appetite had completely gone and he shoved the dish away from himself. The toast popped up and Fran buttered it, then wiped her hands.

'Watch Timmy, will you, while I go and make the beds.'

Barton grunted a 'yes' and opened his paper.

## AMY MAN TOOK MY PICTURE
### By David Armitage

Police hunting the killer of Amy Dennis have refused to comment on new evidence that the man they quizzed in connection with the murder has been pestering women to pose for photographs.

Pretty Jasmine Unwin, 21, was approached by the man in Grosvenor Park. 'I've seen him a few times,' said Jasmine. 'He only lives up the road from me. He told me he was a photographer.'

Jasmine is now in hiding after she gave the man her address. 'He said he would drop the pictures in to me,' said an anxious Jasmine. 'Now I don't feel safe to go home.'

Single mum, Amy Dennis, was found battered to death in her home on Tuesday. Her baby daughter was found crying in an upstairs room. A local man was questioned but later released on police bail.

Frustrated with trying to keep his food on the spoon long enough to reach his mouth, Timmy banged the spoon into his dish. Startled by the sudden shock of cold, milky gloop on his face; his lips puckered and he frowned while he decided if he felt like crying. When he discovered that he didn't, he tried another experimental bash and chuckled to himself at the effect.

Fran came in as he raised his fist for a third time. She grabbed his hand and guided the spoon from the dish to his mouth. 'Nicely, Timmy,' she said. 'Show Daddy how nicely big boys can eat.' She glanced at her husband. 'You're supposed to be watching him, Phil.'

Barton looked up from his paper. 'I'm watching what I eat,' he said. 'You can't expect me to do two things at once.'

She flashed him a fake smile. 'You don't seem to be doing either very successfully.' Then, when he glanced down at the paper, 'Is that more about the murder?' Timmy seemed to have remembered that he was actually hungry and concentrated on the complicated route from the dish to his mouth, so she slipped over and read the headline splash over Barton's shoulder.

'Puts me right off the park,' she said.

Timmy bashed both fists on his tray and shouted, 'Duck-duck-duck!'

Fran winced. 'Me and my big mouth. Eat your breakfast,' she said and waited until Timmy was tucking in with his fingers, having abandoned the spoon, before scanning the rest of the article.

Timmy said, 'Quack-quack-quack,' as a gentle reminder.

'Jelly Baby is not going to let me off now. It's the park or ructions. Anyway, I'm not letting some creep keep me away.'

Barton folded the paper. If Fran insisted on going to the park, he knew better than to try to stop her. At least if he gave her a general description, he would feel happier. 'All right,' he said. 'He's about five-ten, thirtyish. Dark hair. Muscular. Tattoo on his left arm.'

'And he'll be carrying a camera.'

'We've got his camera.'

She frowned, then her eyes widened. 'Oh, God, Phil! You don't think he took pictures of—'

'We haven't found anything like that,' he reassured her.

He couldn't believe he was feeding her the official line, using the get-out of professional objectivity. Clemence was a killer and he was walking the streets like he had the right to – like he was a normal human being.

Barton realised too late that he should have excused himself from close contact with the man – instead of which, he had asked to be assigned to the interview team. Clemence already had reason to hold a grudge against him as the arresting officer in the murder of Vicky Rees, but Barton had made it personal with his needling in the interview room.

Fran watched him with a mixture of curiosity and concern. 'Should I be packing a suitcase?' she asked.

'I won't let him get within half a mile of you and Timmy,' Barton said. 'We'll find the evidence. And Clemence will go away for a long, long time.'

# 20

The enquiry team had been housed in Castle Square police station, just outside the city walls and near the river. It was a modern, low-rise red brick building, crouched at the base of the hill, overlooked by the castle ruins and tucked behind County Hall – custody suite in the basement, offices on the first floor. The local CID who couldn't be spared to join Lawson's team from on-going investigations had been shifted to temporary accommodation in the duplicating room.

The windowless office Lawson shared with Barton had once been a stationery store. Two desks had been crammed against adjacent walls. Now, he leant against his own desk, discussing the investigation with Detective Chief Inspector McAteer. The DCI frowned at the sheets of paper in his hands, holding them at arm's-length to compensate for the deterioration in his eyesight that he hated to admit to.

'I was wondering about deploying HOLMES2 on this one,' Lawson said.

'We've got a strong suspect in Clemence, haven't we?' McAteer asked.

'Looks like it.'

'And attacks like these are usually personal, aren't they?'

'Amy's face was virtually obliterated,' Lawson said, gritting his teeth against a vivid flash of recall of the post mortem. 'The forensic psychology points towards someone who knew her.'

'We'll run the investigation on paper, for now. No point in paying out for a HOLMES team if we can get by without them.' The Home Office Large and Major Enquiry System was expensive in terms of computer equipment and trained staff to run it.

Lawson nodded. 'All right.' Although he was twenty years younger than McAteer, Lawson's hair was quite grey, while McAteer's gleamed a rich blue-black. Some said he dyed it; Lawson didn't know and didn't care. McAteer might be vain, but you took him for a fool at your own peril; he had led the enquiry into Clara Pascal's abduction, and Lawson respected the man's judgement. 'We could probably use the extra on the forensics on this one,' he added.

McAteer gave a brief nod, wobbling the dewlaps that spoilt the smooth lines of his jaw. 'Whatever it takes, Steve. Whatever it takes.'

They walked to the Incident Room together. This was the first briefing of the full enquiry team. Thirty officers were crammed into a room intended for ten CID personnel. Letterbox windows, high up in the walls, gave poor ventilation and although the door stood open and three desk fans whirred back and forth, the air in the room was sour with overheated bodies. It was too hot and too cramped for comfort: they were eager to get out of the stuffy confines of the room and get started on the day, and Clemence's arrest and the subsequent discovery of the photographs of Amy Dennis in his flat had given them something to aim for, something to compete against.

Lawson stood next to the whiteboard on the wall opposite the door, and looked around the room. Cath Young sat on one of the Formica-topped tables, her long legs crossed and her back straight.

'How's the hand?' he asked.

'Fine, sir,' Young said, blushing slightly.

Chris Thorpe was in a chair to her right. 'Shall I kiss it better?'

She grinned, shoving her bandaged palm in his face, while Thorpe cried a muffled 'Assault!'

McAteer's more stately arrival signalled the need for sobriety and after a preliminary shuffling of chairs, a hush fell, and the only sound was the rush of air from the fans. 'These are photographs recovered from Clemence's flat,' he said, pointing to copies of the surveillance pictures of Amy Dennis blu-tacked to the edge of the whiteboard. He tapped the photograph of the fair-haired woman. 'You all saw this last night. Also found in Clemence's collection. It still doesn't ring any bells?'

Young squinted at the photograph from a few feet away. *Where the hell have I seen her before?*

'Well, think about it. He may have been following this woman as well as Amy Dennis.'

'What about the girls he's been hassling in the park?' Fletcher asked.

'You mean the press revelations?' McAteer arched an eyebrow. 'Taking pictures of pretty girls isn't an offence, Fletcher.'

'Yeah, but—'

'But you're right.'

Fletcher looked so stunned that a few people laughed.

'Clemence said he's a visual man,' Lawson chipped in, allowing himself a quick smile. 'His photographic collection is about as close as we're likely to get to a "Dear Diary" confession. And there's a strong possibility he's been stalking women ever since he got out of prison two months ago – Chris.'

Thorpe stood up and faced the gathering. 'Amy did a bit of postal tutoring,' he said. 'Photography.' A murmur from the rest of the team told him they thought they saw where he was heading. 'I contacted Amy's course leader last night. There's no record of any complaint from Amy. If Clemence was hassling her, she kept quiet about it. He would have known her home address, though. Apparently, they send out address labels to all students – prisoners included.' There were a few exclamations of disbelief.

'Yeah, and Clemence said he didn't know where she lived.' Barton clicked his tongue in mock disapproval. 'He's a tinker, isn't he?'

'They're in the process of changing the procedure for prisons,' Thorpe went on. 'Prison staff will hold the address labels in a secure place, and tutors will be instructed not to include home addresses on letterheads.'

'That's quick,' DC Gordon commented.

'Be nice to think so, wouldn't it?' Thorpe said. 'But the woman I spoke to is based in Stoke – she didn't even know Amy was dead.'

'So why the change?'

'Another tutor in the Chester area put in a complaint. A Diane Tobin. And no prizes for guessing the student who was harassing her.'

DC Young slid from her perch on the table and took a closer look at the photograph of the unidentified woman. 'I knew I recognised her!' she said. 'She came to pick up her husband after he was interviewed – that's Mrs Tobin.'

'Who interviewed Tobin?' McAteer asked.

'Me, Boss.' Fletcher scrutinised the picture before shaking his head. 'I was told to interview *him* – I wasn't paying much attention to her.'

'Talk to her,' Lawson said. 'See if these two knew each other.'

'And we'll need a check on all the other women in his little gallery,' McAteer added.

'We're still doing the garbage sift, Boss.' Fergus Gordon was the team manager liaising with the Information Systems Department and Technical Support. He was a pale-skinned Scot with strawberry-blond hair and colourless eyelashes. 'We've got a couple of thousand prints as well as undeveloped film to process and negs to cross-reference,' he complained.

'We're all working at full stretch,' McAteer said.

'Yes, but . . .' It was evident that McAteer would not

be moved on this one, so Gordon added, 'You could let us have someone to sort the prints – that doesn't need any special expertise.'

This provoked a few cries of 'Ooh!' and 'Get her!'

McAteer located one of the culprits and allocated him to cataloguing the photographs.

Mollified, Gordon said, 'He's written names and addresses on the back of some of the prints.'

'Give them to house-to-house,' McAteer suggested. The officer in charge nodded acquiescence and McAteer moved on.

'Have the lab come up with anything?'

Gordon shook his head. 'No match on the footprint, no fingerprints, some DNA traces, but if you want them prioritised, we'll have to pay Premium Rate.'

McAteer thought about it, then nodded curtly. 'Do it. What about the car?'

'They practically valeted that heap of scrap for him. There's no blood, no fibres, no hairs – nothing to link it with the murder scene.'

There was a general groan of disappointment.

'Only,' Gordon said. 'They reckon he's had it steam-cleaned recently.'

'How recently?'

Gordon shrugged. 'They couldn't say.'

McAteer tugged at one tufty eyebrow. 'Tell them I want that car taken apart. If he's tried to obliterate evidence, I want to know.'

'When do we expect the blood tests back?' Lawson asked.

'Mid-to-late afternoon,' Gordon said.

'Let me know as soon as they come in. What's the status of house-to-house?'

The officer in charge spoke up: 'No suspicious behaviour reported around Amy's house in the last week or two. No unusual activity on the pathway at the back. No strangers in the road.' He dipped his head apologetically. 'In fact, bugger all, so far.' He took a breath, then launched in: 'And if you want us to make a start on door-knocking around the Tobins', we're going to need more bodies.'

McAteer glanced at Lawson as if to say, 'There goes the money we've saved on HOLMES.'

'Who's on the search?' Lawson asked. Half-a-dozen hands went up. 'Okay. Preliminary findings from the PM indicate that the murder weapon was a claw-hammer.' He had another flash of Amy's body on the post-mortem table. He looked from one officer to another, giving himself time. The stench of blood had clung to him all evening, despite changing his clothes and showering. He had even used the trick a pathologist had once taught him, of rubbing lemon juice onto his skin, shampooing it into his hair, but he could not rid himself of the smell. Lawson didn't believe in ghosts, but he did believe the dead haunted the living, demanding justice.

He realised that he had waited too long: his dramatic pause had developed into a silence. 'Amy Dennis was hit at least ten times.' *Professional* he thought. *Keep it professional. Stick with the facts*. 'After that' – he cleared his throat – 'there wasn't enough left of her face for the pathologist to find distinct indentations.'

Nobody moved. It seemed nobody breathed. Even the fans seemed to have stopped turning, though they might have been drowned out by the roar of blood in his ears. 'So,' he said. 'We're looking at someone who knew her. Maybe someone with a grudge. Someone,' he emphasised, 'who wanted to wipe her off the face of the earth.'

McAteer took up the commentary. 'Now I know some of you feel we have our man already. But there is a lot of evidence still to be gathered. Interview her students, colleagues, neighbours. Her relationship with the baby's father may have been over, but if she was seeing someone else, I want him found and interviewed and eliminated from the enquiry. We don't take chances on this one.' He paused. 'Don't get sloppy because this looks simple,' he said. 'Just because Clemence looks guilty doesn't mean we'll get a conviction.'

Barton was talking on the phone when Lawson came into the office. He finished the call and hung up. 'Clemence's solicitor,' he said. 'I thought it'd save time if he was here when we bring Clemence in.'

'Who's gone for him?'

'Thorpe and Young.'

'Good. Fletcher should be on his way to see Mrs Tobin by now. Quartermaine can have his consultation while we wait for her statement.'

'We've already got it,' Barton said.

'That was bloody quick.'

'One of the night team went out after Thorpe spoke

to Amy's supervisor on the postal course, last night.'
He handed Lawson a copy of the report with Mrs
Tobin's statement attached.

'What about Fletcher?'

'I called him back in – sent him to help on house-to-
house instead.'

Lawson grunted distractedly, skimming Mrs Tobin's statement.

'I'd best get off,' Barton said, taking his jacket from
the back his chair. 'I'm interviewing her students today
– all those teenage girls . . .'

'Phil—'

Barton turned.

'Clemence used a claw-hammer, didn't he?'

'Yeah.'

'I never want to go through a PM like that ever
again,' Lawson said.

'Me neither.' They were talking about two different
post-mortems, twelve years apart.

# 21

By the time Clara parked her car at Jericho Chambers, the digital read-out on the BMW's dashboard read twenty-two degrees and rising. The air conditioning kept her cool and for a moment she sat enjoying it. She felt relatively calm now, after her argument with Hugo.

Marcia had said her anger was a defence, and maybe she was right, but it didn't make her words any less hurtful, her anger any less destructive, and she worried that Hugo wouldn't take much more. She sighed, reached for her briefcase in the passenger well beside her, and slid out of the car into solid heat. She eyed the security doors at the rear of the building. It would be easy to slip in unnoticed and establish herself in some quiet corner of her shared office upstairs. *But that's not the point, is it, Clara?*

So she walked to the front of the building, across the pretty cobbled courtyard and up the steps of the Georgian frontage, her head up, performing for the CCTV like it was a screen test.

She swiped her card and the security light flashed through orange and back to red. Frowning, she tried again. Then a third time. *Damnit!* It was tempting to walk away. *Come* on, *Clara. You're here now, don't chicken out.*

She pressed the intercom and was relieved to hear Nesta Lewis's warm Welsh tones. 'My card's not working,' Clara said, trying not to sound like a schoolgirl who didn't get invited to the Valentine's dance.

'Oh, Ms Pascal!' She heard pleasure and alarm in the clerk's voice and her heart sank. Nesta buzzed her in and met her halfway across the dark-brown corded carpet of the foyer.

'Security have changed the codes,' Nesta said, considerately leaving out 'since you were last here'.

'I've got your new card in my desk. Why don't you get yourself a coffee while I root it out for you?'

It was early, but the admin staff were already gathered in the small kitchen to the left of the carousel doors. Their voices drifted out from behind the semi-circular glass partition that divided the foyer off from the offices and consultation rooms on the ground floor. She hadn't been in to Chambers in over two weeks and she knew the staff well enough to be sure that her absence would be a topic of conversation. She was tempted to grab a coffee from the clients' vending machine, but she had to face the pack sooner or later, and now was as good a time as any.

Karl, the office junior, was reading aloud from the morning paper, but he stopped when she came into the room, blushing from his shirt collar to the roots of his hair.

'What's up?' Clara asked, dropping her briefcase near the door.

'Nothing.' He turned the page and took a slurp of tea. The others had fallen silent, but now one of the girls demanded to hear her horoscope and the others concurred, cooing over it and crowding around Karl to look over his shoulder.

Clara topped up the kettle and made coffee for herself and Nesta, puzzling over their apparent embarrassment. After all, it wasn't as if they were talking about her when she walked through the door. A minute later, the room was empty, the newspaper abandoned on the table.

She looked at it for a moment, her head on one side. *Sometimes it's best not to know*, she told herself. But her other self asserted itself. *Bullshit, Clara. It's never best not to know.* She hooked her index finger under the open pages and flipped them over to get a look at the front page.

## AMY MAN TOOK MY PICTURE

*He took pictures* . . . Had he followed Amy, stalked her? What was it Mrs Tobin had said? *I think he's watching me.* The thought made Clara feel ill.

'Oh, God . . .' She leaned with both hands on the table and waited for the nausea to pass.

*They're pictures of girls in the park, Clara. Just a few arty pictures. That doesn't make him a psycho.*

Still, she couldn't seem to catch her breath.

'Ms Pascal?'

She tried to straighten up. but she couldn't: her legs felt weak and she wanted to be sick.

'Come on, love.' Nesta, comforting, loyal, always protective. She guided Clara to a chair.

'I . . .' *Breathe, Clara. Just breathe.* 'This is so stupid. I didn't think it would affect me this way.'

Nesta folded the paper and threw it in the bin. 'Damned idiots.' It was the strongest language Clara had ever heard her clerk use, and she was pathetically touched. Nesta sat and watched for a while, encouraging Clara to take sips of coffee, sips of air.

'You'll be all right,' she said, at last.

Clara smiled, tilting her head back and closing her eyes. 'I wish I could believe that.'

Nesta startled her by grasping both her hands. 'You have to be,' she said, looking earnestly into Clara's face. 'You can't let those – those *men* win.'

Clara had never seen her like this. 'Is this men in general, or do you have someone specific in mind?' she asked.

Nesta held her gaze, but Clara could see that she was already regretting her outburst. 'You're the only lady barrister in this chambers,' she said, pronouncing 'you're' as 'ewer'. 'We rely on you. And . . .' Her courage seemed to be failing her fast, but she took a gulp of air and finished: 'If you let them scare you off—'

'Lord, take this cup away from me!' Clara exclaimed, trying to make a joke of it. She could see that she had hurt Nesta's feelings and she squeezed her hands apologetically. 'Don't make me a role model, Nesta. I'm not some computer-animated babe who can get knocked down and come back badder and stronger.' *And if I mess up*, she wanted to say, *I don't want anyone else's blood on my hands*.

She didn't say it; instead, she asked the question she had wound herself up for since the previous day. She tried to make it sound casual; she didn't succeed. 'Got anything for me?'

'You mean civil cases.' Nesta's disapproval was palpable. 'You missed a dispute over boundaries,' she went on, after an almost imperceptible shrug. 'You should check in at about four o'clock. Things come in during the day.'

A dispute over boundaries. *Things must be desperate if I'm disappointed to have missed* that *one*. 'No family law?' she asked.

Nesta gave an apologetic little moue. 'There was a burglary,' she said, dangling it like a tasty morsel before an invalid. 'Just a two-day slot. Nothing too—'

'Nesta,' Clara interrupted. 'I appreciate what you're trying to do. But no criminal cases, okay?'

For a moment, she thought that Nesta might argue, but then she gave a quick nod: 'Nuff said. Nesta was the soul of discretion, but Clara found the next question even more difficult.

'If you get a minute, could you chase up the Makin account for me?' She took a sip of coffee, to avoid Nesta's sharp look. 'And if you could find out what's holding up the Legal Aid on the Noonan case, I'd be really grateful.'

'Oh, yes,' Nesta said, tutting at her own tardiness. 'That finished months ago. I really should have followed it up by now.'

*Don't!* Clara thought. *Please don't take the blame on yourself.* 'Just clearing the decks before the autumn,' she said.

'Dear me! Are things that tight, Ms Pascal?'

'Mr Warrington . . .' Nesta looked past Clara to the doorway, her face pink with embarrassment for Clara and annoyance at the senior partner's insensitivity.

Clara groaned inwardly. *Warrington! That's all I need.* She carefully composed her features and turned to face the door. 'Every little helps, Mr Warrington,' she said, coolly.

'We could always get Nesta to do a whip-round.'

She smiled and said nothing.

'Actually,' he said. I'm surprised to see you.' He seemed peeved that Clara didn't ask why.

*Find your own straight-guy,* she thought.

'Yes,' he said, spoiling the smoothness of his delivery. 'I thought you'd gone over to working for Michaela O'Connor's little charity.'

'It isn't a charity,' she said, stung at last into a response.

'Well, it could hardly be described as a business, now, could it?'

'And I don't work *for* her, I work *with* her.'

He raised his eyebrows. 'To a greater and greater extent, it would seem. Very worthy, I'm sure. But I can't imagine it's terribly lucrative. And with young – Penny, is it?'

'Pippa.'

'With Pippa almost at that crucial transitional stage. Good public schools do not come cheaply – or were you thinking of sending her to a *state* school?'

*He makes it sound like I'm planning to sell her into prostitution.* 'Mr Warrington,' Clara began. She saw the look of terror on Nesta's face and reconsidered what she was about to say. If she told Mr Warrington exactly what she thought of his kindly advice and paternalistic concern, it wouldn't only be Jericho Chambers that suddenly found that it had a paucity of civil cases suited to her talents. Warrington had considerable influence on the northern circuit.

'Mr Warrington,' she began again, with a reassuring glance at Nesta. 'I am *deeply* touched by your concern.'

Barton settled Clemence into the chair facing the door and went through the formalities as the tape rolled. Clemence listened with half an ear to the wording of the caution, the listing of his rights and studied DC Young. Having your face mashed into the pavement by a girl gave you a warped view of her, but from where he was sitting now, she was easier on the eye than he'd thought. His eyes slid over her body, finishing up at the bandage on her right hand.

She noticed him watching her and covered her right hand with her left. He let his eyes track upwards again. He could make out the lace outline of her bra under her thin cotton blouse.

'You look rough, Mr Clemence,' Barton remarked.

Reluctantly, Clemence switched his attention to the sergeant. 'Your lot dragged me out of bed at crack of dawn.'

'For the record,' Young said, 'we rang the doorbell at

eight forty-five a.m. DC Thorpe waited in your room with you, allowing you time to dress. You accompanied us without need for restraint.'

'Do you agree with those details, Mr Clemence?' Barton asked.

Clemence bit the side of his mouth and said nothing.

'Mr Clemence?'

'Yeah. That's more or less it. But I work late. I keep odd hours.'

'You didn't work last night.'

*Shit, do they know every fucking thing?* 'I didn't get much sleep is all I'm saying.'

'Guilty conscience?' Young asked.

He smiled, letting his eyes wander from her face to that lacy line under her blouse. 'Night on the town,' he said.

'Is this relevant?' Quartermaine asked testily.

'Is it, Mr Clemence?' Barton asked.

Clemence blew air out through his nose and folded his arms.

'You remember in your last interview we showed you these photographs, sir?' Young placed the bagged photos of the blonde on the table.

He took a breath. *They know who she is.*

DC Young stared at him. 'Her name is Mrs Tobin,' she said. 'Another of your "Arts for Everyone" course tutors. You told us that you didn't know her, and you couldn't remember where you took the pictures.'

'Because I knew what you'd think,' he said. *Bad move, Clemence. Let them ask the questions. All you've got to do is answer. Don't make it easy for the bastards.*

Barton rested his elbows on the table. 'What do we think, Mr Clemence?'

'It's obvious, isn't it?'

'Not to me.'

'You said they look like surveillance shots.'

'And what would that make us think?'

'It isn't up to my client to read your mind, Sergeant Barton,' Quartermaine said.

Barton barely acknowledged Quartermaine's intervention. He continued staring at Clemence and said. 'Mrs Tobin says you're stalking her.'

*Stupid bitch!* Clemence looked up at the ceiling; the sound-proofing tiles were faded and yellow. 'Is that what she says?' He kept his voice flat, neutral.

'All documented,' Barton replied. 'She put in a complaint.'

Clemence shook his head.

'You've been pestering her, Mr Clemence.'

'I asked for a few tips. A bit of advice.'

'You phoned her. You sent her letters. You even showed up at her house.'

'Nah . . .'

'We've got the evidence here,' Young said. 'In these photographs.'

'Yeah, well, it gets some women like that.'

Young narrowed her eyes at him. 'Like what?'

'You've been in prison, they think you're a mad axe-man or something.'

'Or a hammer-wielding murderer, maybe,' Barton suggested.

*Visualisation.* Clemence took a breath. He was getting the wrong visuals. *You're supposed to visualise positive things. Relaxing things. That's how you manage your anger.* Trouble was, the most relaxing thing he could think of right now was skinning his fist against Barton's teeth. He was dimly aware of Quartermaine complaining about the line of questioning. He used the time to focus on the shadows behind the wired glass of the interview room door. People passing by, changes in the play of light, and when Barton resumed, he was calm again.

'We've got officers checking every roll of film from your flat,' Barton said.

Clemence felt a quick shimmer of fear convulse the muscles of his face. *Invisible*, he told himself. *Too small to see.* He had seen a TV programme where a psychologist watched a series of interviews on video. Five people, one of them a liar. He said liars betrayed themselves by tiny muscle contractions – micro-gestures, he called them. He caught his villain, but he had to watch the tape virtually frame-by-frame, and even then, he nearly missed it. All Barton had were his own two eyes, and Clemence had been practising keeping his feelings hidden for almost as long as Barton had been a cop.

He was thinking about the roll of film hidden behind his kitchen cupboard. Thinking about the film and beginning to enjoy the fact that it didn't show in his face. 'There's other kinds of control than violence,' the counsellor had told them. 'You have to learn to enjoy the alternatives.' Like watching filth like Barton practically have to sit on his hands to stop himself having a go at an ex-con who wouldn't play his version of good cop, bad cop.

'She said she'd get me a gallery showing,' Clemence said blandly. 'Said she liked my stuff.'

Young smiled in disbelief. 'She'd've promised you a photo-shoot with Madonna for *Vogue* if she thought it'd get you off her back!'

'That's a bit dramatic, isn't it?'

'You said yourself,' Young observed, 'they think you're an axe-murderer.'

'Axe-*man*.' *Pillock! Repeating what you shouldn't've said in the first place.*

'So you played up to her fears,' Barton said.

'I asked her for help.'

'Like a blackmailer asks for a bit of cash – just to tide him over.'

'No.'

'She knew your background and you took advantage of that – you used it to intimidate her.'

Clemence was confused. They were confusing him. 'No,' he said again.

'You don't deny sending her letters on the second and the sixth of August?'

*The bitch has given them everything.*

'Or phoning her twice on the eighth?'

*Every last detail.*

'And do you deny secretly taking these photographs of Mrs Tobin on her own doorstep?'

Clemence felt sweat pop out on his forehead. 'I wasn't stalking her.' *There you go again, pinprick. Why don't you just confess and save them all the bother?*

'The legal definition might just be at odds with your interpretation.'

'What's he saying?' Clemence demanded, turning to Quartermaine. 'What's he mean?'

Quartermaine demanded a break to consult with his client, but Young was determined that this was one answer that would be recorded for evidence. She spoke over the solicitor's protestations: 'My colleague is saying that just because you don't *think* you were stalking Mrs Tobin doesn't mean you *weren't* stalking her.'

# 22

'Clara!'

Mitch's voice ricocheted off the plain emulsioned walls of the corridor and a moment later, she appeared at the door of Consultation Room One.

'How did you know it was me?' Clara asked, leaving off typing another reference onto her laptop for the moment.

'Door was open. Everyone else *closes* the door when they're working.'

'You know,' Clara said. 'Most people would be too polite to point that out.'

'On the premise that your delicate English soul can't take a little honesty?'

Clara fixed her with a stony stare. 'Don't talk to me about honesty, you conniving Jesuit.'

Mitch took a breath. 'The Tobin case.'

'Visiting rights, you said.'

'It is.' She grimaced. 'Technically.'

'It's now a contested residency order linked to a *murder*!'

'It wasn't linked to a murder until yesterday,' Mitch said.

Clara shook her head. 'You're—'

'Resourceful? Persistent? I know, but isn't that part of my charm?'

'I was going to say incorrigible.' Mitch grinned at her and Clara gave up on trying to argue. Mitch was pretty much impervious to her outrage: in their friendship, when Mitch thought she was on the side of right, no amount of disputation could draw her into an argument. She'd just smile and ride the storm and maintain her equanimity.

'How did the unfair dismissal meeting go?' Clara asked.

'Fine.' Mitch never discussed her ongoing cases if they were going well: she had the religious person's devout belief in superstitions. If it was going well, she believed she could turn it around by saying so; when things were going badly – that was the time to talk.

'I'm trying here, Mitch,' Clara said. 'You might at least meet me halfway.'

'Okay. What're you up to?'

Clara looked down at the sheets of paper she had amassed since the previous night: print-outs from internet news archives, photocopies of newspaper articles, her own notes, written in long hand on A4 note paper. 'Research,' she said. *That sounded a touch defensive, Clara.*

'Research,' Mitch said. 'On what?' She picked up a sheet from the desk. Clemence at seventeen; a boy. A child. Hollow cheeks, haunted eyes. His arm around a girl with short, glossy hair and an impish smile. Vicky Rees.

'They had to scrape her brains off the wall, Mitch.' Clara's voice sounded flat and lifeless, even to her own ears. 'They had to scoop it up with a spoon for the post-mortem.'

'Don't you think it's a bit . . . morbid?'

'It's *research*,' Clara insisted.

Mitch stared at her. 'I've got to find something to occupy that fevered brain of yours.'

'Mitch—'

'You're at too much of a loose end – too much time to think.'

'I'm just covering all the bases.'

Mitch sat side-on, with one buttock resting on the desk, crumpling some of the notes Clara had made during the course of the morning. 'You've got to stop blaming yourself,' she said.

'Who says I am?'

'You're talking to an Irish Catholic, here – d'you think I wouldn't recognise a guilty conscience in the act of self-flagellation?'

'You're not funny, Mitch.'

'I wasn't trying to be. You feel guilty and you're over-compensating.'

'What d'you want me to say, Mitch? This isn't a confessional. You can't absolve me. You're not my priest.'

'D'you think if you piss me off enough I'll go away – is that it?' Mitch gave a little shrug. 'Well, why not? It worked with everyone else, didn't it?'

Clara opened her mouth to protest, but Mitch wasn't easy to interrupt – not in the courtroom and certainly not in an argument. 'You've got to get yourself straightened out, Clara.'

Clara looked at the thin screen of her laptop. The screen saver had kicked in and two hairy caterpillars were munching inexorably through layers of ferny leaves. Hadn't Marcia told her to let her friends know – to tell them what she had embarked on so that they could help when she needed it? Now was as good a time as any. 'I am,' she said. 'Getting myself straight, I mean – trying to.'

'You're seeing a therapist? Brilliant – not before time, mind you.'

'And for your information,' Clara said, 'I do feel guilty.'

'Well you shouldn't.'

'People died, Mitch, and it's my fault.'

'That's bollocks and if you had a few hours' sleep, you'd know it.'

'Well, thank you for your candour, Sister Michaela.'

Mitch laughed. 'I must have missed my vocation: first a priest, now a Holy Sister!'

'I said you *weren't* my priest.' Clara allowed herself the ghost of a smile; she was ready to be friends again.

Mitch went to the door and hesitated, looking at Clara with her head tilted. 'Let me know if you decide to take it on – I'll crack open a bottle of champagne.'

'Take *what* on?'

'Clemence's defence.'

This time, she had gone too far. 'I told you, it's research; Clemence threatened my client.'

'You won't get the prosecution,' Mitch ran on. 'Rumour is, the CPS has got someone in mind. They'll appoint in the next day or so. It's a cracker of a case, though, isn't it?' Mitch asked, with a gleam in her eye. 'Why shouldn't you want to know more?'

'He's a convicted killer,' Clara said coldly. 'What more do I need to know?'

Mitch didn't reply.

*She knows you too well,* Clara thought. *She knows you have to have every detail clear before you feel ready to tackle a case.* 'I'm sorry,' she said. 'I've work to do.'

Mitch drummed her fingers on the door frame. 'I'll be in my office, if you want to talk,' she said.

*What's happening to me?* Clara wondered. *Mitch has kept me afloat financially for the last six months. She's bullied and cosseted and joshed me into keeping going. What am I doing, alienating her, like I've alienated Pippa and Hugo. Why do I keep driving people away?*

Mitch turned, bumping into someone. She apologised and side-stepped, leaving the door open.

'Mrs Tobin!' Clara gathered a few of the papers from her desk and stuffed them into a folder, flustered by her client's sudden arrival. Mrs Tobin blinked in horrified silence at the jumble of headlines: **BATTERED – CALLOUS – EVIL – DRUG-CRAZED ATTACK**.

She swayed a little and Clara rushed to help her. 'Here,' she said, turning the remaining sheets over. 'Sit down. Can I get you anything?'

Mrs Tobin shook her head. She pressed her hands together and said, 'I came to tell you – the police were round. They wanted to know about my relationship with Amy. Did you—?'

'Did I what?'

'Did you tell them what we discussed last night – about Amy and me being friends?'

'I'm your legal representative, Mrs Tobin. I'm not in the habit of giving the police confidential information. But if you had followed my advice and pre-empted their visit—'

'I would have!' Mrs Tobin exclaimed. 'I was going to. But they turned up after you left – we were on our way to bed . . . I – I didn't have the chance.'

'All right,' Clara said. 'All right, I believe you. Now what did you tell them?'

She shrugged. 'Everything. About our friendship, the affair. But they were more interested in Clemence. They know he's been harassing me. They think he was stalking Amy, too. They won't let him go this time, will they?' She looked up at Clara, her face pale and strained.

'I don't know,' Clara said. Mrs Tobin's hands fluttered to her throat and Clara continued, speaking clearly and firmly, trying to break through the woman's terror. 'I've been doing some background reading – I thought it might help in the application for an injunction,' she said, needing to explain the detritus on her desk. 'We'll make sure he can't come near you.'

'I want him out of our life,' Mrs Tobin said with unexpected vehemence. 'I want him caged, like the animal he is. While he's free, they'll think it isn't safe – for Helen, I mean.'

'I'm doing all I can—'

'You're wasting time!' she exclaimed. 'On this – this *trash*!'

Clara struggled to make Mrs Tobin understand her. 'The more we know about Ian Clemence, the stronger the case for a restraining order.'

'*Restraining order . . .*' Mrs Tobin looked at her with something akin to dislike. 'I watch television. I know what these men get away with. Stalking and terrorising women; breaking in to their houses. I thought you of all people would understand – I mean would *you* feel safe with him out on the streets if you were me?'

Clara didn't know how to answer: how could she tell Mrs Tobin that she never felt safe, that she imagined men like Clemence waiting around every corner, lurking in every shadow?

Mrs Tobin pulled out a tissue and dabbed at her eyes. 'If they take Helen away,' she said at last, her voice trembling with emotion, 'I've lost him.' A tear spilled over her lower lid and traced a line down her cheek. 'He'll blame me. He'll say it's because of this.' She gestured to the papers on Clara's desk.

Clara again tried to square her own impression of Mr Tobin with his wife's desperate attachment to him. *Not worth it*, she thought. *He's just not worth it.*

'You're good people,' she said, feeling like a hypocrite. 'Mr Tobin is Helen's natural father. You both care about Helen. Nobody's going to take her away.'

Mrs Tobin fixed her with a look of brittle hope and fierce determination. 'if they grant custody to her grandparents,' she said, 'If they take Helen away—' She gathered up her bag and stuffed her tissue into her pocket. 'If they take Helen away, I shall hold you responsible.'

Clara felt a stab of fear. What if she was wrong? What if she messed up? If the courts judged Clemence to be a threat to Helen's security, might they place her with her grandparents?

Given the option, Clara had always preferred to be well prepared, but when circumstances meant that she couldn't be as thorough as she would have liked, she had enjoyed occasionally winging it. Now she was almost paralysed by the need to get everything straight in her mind, to consider all the angles, another reason why Jericho Chambers no longer gave her the 'short' cases – the ones that were allocated at four p.m., prepared overnight, and presented the next morning with minimal notes and calm audacity. She looked in dismay at the jumble on her desk: perhaps if she knew less about Clemence and the harm he might cause, she would be more confident in demanding Helen's placement with her father.

# 23

Lawson placed the photographs side by side: the twenty-storey tower block he recognised immediately. Though its concrete was badly pitted and the windows so grimy that they had ceased to be transparent years before, it represented the most exciting investment opportunity the city had seen for years. The tower block, scheduled for demolition, overlooked both the racecourse and the river: investors were drooling at the prospect of developing the site.

'Where did you find these?'

DC Fergus Gordon nodded. 'Filed under "O" for on-going.' He raised his eyebrows, evidently appalled by the inefficiencies of Amy Dennis's filing system. His team had worked through thousands of photographs in her files and the Information Systems Department had processed dozens more rolls of film.

Lawson studied one of the photographs. The steep camera angle and a backdrop of anvil storm clouds in a darkening sky accentuated the sense of brooding decay. In the foreground a sign read 'Dee View Development. Land for sale. Potential for office and leisure development'. Both the sign and the building were in uncompromising sharp focus. This picture was not intended as an image of sad urban degeneration; it exuded ominous threat.

Lawson flipped the photograph. 'What's this number?' he asked.

'We think it relates to a text file on her computer,' Gordon told him. 'But we've not been able to access the fields yet – they're all password-protected.' In addition to the thousands of photographs in Amy Dennis's garage office, there were thousands more files on her computer disks. Lawson knew that Fergus Gordon was the ideal person to co-ordinate the decoding, sorting, cataloguing and prioritising of the mass of data that would come out of this line of inquiry. He was methodical and thorough, and he wouldn't allow the tedium of the task to distract him from the work.

'This was on the same roll.' Gordon pointed to the second photograph.

'Looks posed,' Lawson said. A group of men and one woman smiled for the camera. All of them wore suits. Two of the men pointed to a plaque bearing the logo of two interlocked, ornately antique letter Ds.

'The development team?' Lawson asked, then corrected himself. 'No, hang on – that's Councillor Rivers, isn't it?' He pointed to a man on the right of the group. 'And this one looks familiar as well.'

'I couldn't say, Boss,' Gordon said. 'They could be one of the bidding syndicates. I could talk to the features editor at the *Evening Echo* – they might even have commissioned it.'

'That's it!' Lawson said. 'That's where I've seen it. In the paper – fairly recently, I think.' When the *hell* was it? He turned the picture over. 'See if this reference number tallies with an invoice number in Amy's files, will you. Or it might be the photo reference to go with the newspaper article.'

'I'll find out,' Gordon said.

'If it is one of theirs, see if you can get a list of names.'

'Boss—' Barton stood at the door of their shared office, looking pleased with himself. 'Blood test results on the T-shirt.' He handed Lawson the print-out. 'An exact match for Amy Dennis.'

'What about his clothing?'

'Well . . .'

'Anything from his flat?'

'The T-shirt is practically sopping with Amy's blood—'

'But there's *nothing* on his clothes, his shoes, no trace of her blood in his flat. I mean, you'd have expected to find blood in the sink, or the shower.'

'So he got changed before he came home. Or maybe he wore overalls. It's not unheard of. And we know the killer wore latex gloves.'

'Yeah,' Lawson said. 'But I'd like some evidence that he was there. His DNA at the murder scene. Even a sighting of him in the vicinity would give us more to go on.'

'Surely you don't think he's innocent?'

Lawson rubbed his temples. The airless enclosure of the room and the mounting heat of the day had given him a headache. 'I think he's hiding something,' he said. 'He was trying to get rid of that bag when he was arrested, there's no doubt about that. But there's no blood on him and there's none in his flat. So maybe he's covering for someone else. Who is he protecting, Phil?'

Barton shrugged. 'Himself.'

Lawson sighed. 'Well he's doing a damned good job. He knows the system – knows how to work it to his advantage.'

'You're letting him go, aren't you?'

'Interview him. Warn him off Mrs Tobin. Present the evidence we've got. Let him make his denials then, yes, let him go.' Barton began to protest, but Lawson interrupted him. 'We've had him – what – ten hours in total, already? And we've got precisely nothing. The PACE clock is ticking, and the only concrete evidence we've got is her blood on a T-shirt that may or may not belong to him.'

'It was in his bag!'

'That doesn't prove ownership of the T-shirt, and the lab says there's too much likelihood of cross-contamination from the bag's interior: any of his DNA they find on the shirt could be from the lining of the bag. We'll need more than that to get a conviction. Juries don't like circumstantial evidence, Phil.'

'So he gets away with murder.'

'No. But we're not going to get a confession out of him. We'll have to rely on forensics and whatever other evidence we can collect to prove he's lying. So, we focus our efforts on finding the murder weapon. We work on his links with Amy. We find someone who saw him or his car in Amy's street at or near the time of the murder.

'He claims he was in work the night she was killed, working the night shift.' he went on, 'But time of death was difficult to establish. Maybe he finished his shift and called in on his way home. Maybe he slipped out unnoticed on a rest break. We'll need to re-interview his workmates and see if we can pick a hole in his alibi.'

'I'll have a word with his boss, after I've given him the taxi fare home, shall I?'

'Look, Phil, I don't like this any more than you do,' Lawson said. 'But I'm not going to screw up this investigation because we've gone in too hard, too early on.'

Barton could see that this was one argument he wouldn't win. Clemence was free and clear, at least for now. He couldn't expect Lawson to understand how dangerous the man was, because he hadn't seen Vicky Rees's faceless body. He hadn't had to listen to fifteen hours of rambling, self-pitying confession and self-justification from Clemence.

# 24

The side gate was open when Clara arrived home and plumes of tantalising aromatic smoke rose from behind the garage. They were having a barbecue. Squeals of laughter from the back garden told her that Pippa had invited a friend over. Clara took her briefcase and jacket from the back seat and locked up.

Trish came into the hall, as she always did – no sneaking off upstairs without saying hello when Trish was around. 'Good day?' she asked.

'Unproductive, I'm afraid,' Clara said.

She had completed her notes on the information she had collected about Clemence, more out of perversity than conscientiousness. Then, unable to procrastinate any longer, she phoned Nesta at Jericho Chambers, hoping that something last-minute had come in: another boundary dispute, maybe, or cover needed for sickness. There was nothing. People went away in August; they didn't launch complicated and lengthy legal proceedings just before jetting off to Spain for two weeks. And the kind of work that proliferated in hot weather – that is violent crimes and burglaries – Clara was unwilling to handle.

'I'll get you a glass of something cool,' Trish said. 'You look like you need it.'

Clara murmured her thanks, still thinking about Clemence's murder trial court records. In all probability, she wouldn't need to know any more about Clemence than she already did. She told herself she didn't *want* to know any more, and yet she had spent the best part of an afternoon getting as much background on him as possible.

*I need to be prepared when we meet.* When? Shouldn't that be *if*? Hadn't she told Mrs Tobin that Clemence would most likely stay away from her – he was in enough trouble with the police without making things worse, hounding his ex-tutor. Why was she acting as if this case would go to trial? *Do you* like *frightening yourself, Clara? Is that it?* She stood still for a minute, trying to analyse the tumult of feelings she was experiencing. The court notes had made grim reading, but she had felt a curious stirring of interest, an excitement she hadn't felt for months, not since – Here, her mind did a little trick she had learned, cutting out the dangerous thought, switching attention to something innocuous. On this occasion, standing in her own hallway, with the smell of the barbecue wafting through the house, she distracted herself with the realisation that she was hungry.

She kicked off her shoes and padded barefoot to the kitchen. The cool of the quarry tiles was instant balm to her aching feet.

'Home-made,' Trish said, handing her a glass of lemonade. 'Hugo's got a bottle of wine on ice outside, if you fancy something stronger.'

Scenting conspiracy, Clara tipped her glass, clinking

the ice against the sides. 'Think I'll just take this upstairs and shower. Maybe have a lie down – it's been a heavy day.'

'Pippa helped to make the barbecue sauce,' Trish said. 'She really wants you to try the spare-ribs.' Her tone was neutral, but Clara thought she could hear a thrill of tension in her voice.

*Why not? Why* not *Clara? You don't have to make everyone else miserable because you are.* 'Hope there's plenty to go round,' she said.

There was more than a hint of relief in Trish's laugh. 'Enough to feed an army.'

Fifteen minutes later, showered and changed, Clara stepped, still unshod, onto the warm stones of the small paved area outside the patio doors. Invisible behind the garage, Hugo worked the barbecue. It hissed and spat and the grey-white smoke puffed like a smoke signal above the pitched roof.

The sun filtered pleasantly through the birch trees on the north-western boundary of their neighbours' property and a hot, dry breeze riffled the leaves, making the dappled shade dance. The girls threw a frisbee over the arc of spray from the lawn sprinkler; they both wore swimsuits and both were soaked, their hair hanging in rats' tails down their backs. They chased forward, then back, like toddlers playing tag with surf on the shingle, laughing and screeching when they mistimed a retreat.

*Annabelle Forrest,* Clara thought. *Year Four's golden girl. Well, well . . .*

Pippa saw her, mid-throw, and stopped. Stopped

playing; stopped laughing – almost seemed to stop breathing. She stood quite still, her right arm hooked behind her back to grip her left at the elbow. She looked awkward. *God help her, she looks shy of me,* Clara thought. It reminded her of a summer holiday in her youth; her mother arrived home early from some trip or conference and Clara's strongest emotion had been alarm: she didn't know what to say to her mother and she was afraid that Sophia would disapprove of her clothes, her friends, the way she spent her time.

Annabelle caught the frisbee, but sensing the change in mood, she dropped her hands to her sides, almost as if she wanted to hide it. 'Hi, Mrs Pascal,' she said.

Clara could see Pippa squaring up to correct her friend, explaining that Mummy doesn't like to be called Mrs; she's a *miz*.

She dodged round the back of Annabelle, swiping the frisbee, and ran. 'Can anyone play?' she shouted over her shoulder.

Annabelle looked at Pippa in astonishment, then hid a giggle behind her hand.

'You're *s'pose* to throw it!' Pippa screamed, outraged. The girls chased after her while she weaved and pranced, evading them briefly. Then Pippa grabbed her around the knees and Annabelle, still not sure of the limits, tugged at her T-shirt while Clara held the frisbee out of reach.

'Daddy, she's *cheating*!' Pippa squealed, simultaneously indignant and delighted.

Hugo rattled the tongs against the barbecue. 'Seconds out!' he called. 'Time to eat.'

The girls ran to the brick-paved area behind the garage, where Trish had laid out a table. Pippa snatched up a plate.

'Not so fast,' Clara said, taking it and replacing it on the pile. 'Run and get changed. And dry your hair.'

'I left a towel on your bed,' Trish said, appearing with a bowl of salad.

'And wash your hands,' Clara added.

Pippa groaned. 'But we've been *playing* in the water!'

'Hmm, let's see. We've got next door's cat – you never know where she's going to leave a little surprise – and that could give you something nasty. And bird poo could give you salmonella. Then there's mozzarella, gorgonzola—'

'That's cheese!' Pippa shouted, laughing.

'Come on,' Clara said, tapping her lightly on the rump. 'Let's all three of us wash our hands.'

They worked steadily through more meat than Clara had seen in a month, and after she had finished, she tore a piece off a bread roll and mopped up the barbecue sauce from the spare-ribs.

'I made them,' Pippa said, her chest swelling with pride.

Clara dug her in the side. 'Didn't know you had spare ribs,' she said. 'Trish, we could save a fortune on food bills with this one!'

'No! I mean I made the *sauce*.'

'Well,' Clara said, popping the last morsel of bread into her mouth. 'It's delicious.'

'*And* I helped with the cheesecake.'

Clara sobbed theatrically. 'My daughter – so talented!' She felt Hugo's eyes on her and when she looked at him, he was smiling. It felt good to make him smile.

'Well – I bashed up the biscuits with a rolling-pin,' Pippa admitted, modesty getting the better of her.

'And I squished them into the tin,' said Annabelle, not wishing to he left out.

'But I didn't do the terracotta cheesy bit because it was too stiff and my arms ached.'

'I should think it would,' Clara said gravely.

Pippa was suspicious; she looked at Trish for an explanation.

'It's *ricotta*,' she corrected gently.

'All right then, ter*ricotta*!'

Hugo snorted into his wine and Clara bit her lip. It was Trish that really set them off. She turned, ostensibly to check on the barbecue, her shoulders heaving silently, but a loud guffaw escaped her and suddenly they were all laughing.

'What?' Pippa demanded. 'What are you laughing at?'

'Don't be cross,' Clara said, the tears rolling down her face. 'Mummy's a bit hysterical, that's all.'

Pippa was not so easily placated. 'Come on, Annabelle,' she said, with the towering disdain of a nine-year-old. 'Let's go and watch the video. *They're* being giddy because they've had too much to drink.'

'Don't be cheeky, young lady,' Hugo said. 'And aren't you going to tell Mummy your good news before you go off for your own giggle-fest?'

Pippa became reticent. She shot Clara a look that said all was not forgotten, nor was it forgiven. A look that said, '*She'll only spoil everything.*'

'You tell her,' she said at last.

'It's your news,' Hugo insisted. 'You tell her.'

'Is somebody going to tell me, or do I have to guess?'

Hugo raised his eyebrows, but Pippa remained stubbornly mute.

'Annabelle has invited Pippa to go to Barbados with her,' he said.

*Oh, God. Barbados. On her own. How will I know she's safe?* Then another, more practical thought: *How the hell can we afford it?*

'Well that's . . . lovely.' She telegraphed Hugo a message: *Tell me you haven't said yes.*

'I think she should go,' he said, firmly.

It was an effort not to let her shoulders slump. *You have to let her escape from you and your neuroses from time to time*, she thought. *Maybe we'll have time to scrape the cash together. If she goes at Christmas . . .*

'She only has two more weeks before the start of the autumn term and we haven't had a proper holiday since— We haven't had a proper holiday in ages,' he corrected himself.

*Surely he can't be considering sending her off during the summer holidays.* 'So we're thinking of . . .'

'Saturday – it was a last-minute thing,' he added quickly, raising his voice a little, anticipating an argument. Pippa glanced anxiously from one to the other. 'Annabelle's parents got a cancellation.'

'Okay . . .' she said, fixing a smile on her face. 'We'll discuss it later.'

Pippa looked defeated.

'Come and give me a hand with this cheesecake,' Trish said, hoisting her out of her chair. She supervised the girls getting changed into their night-clothes and settled them in front of the television in Pippa's room with a slice of cheesecake and a glass of milk, and gave strict instructions that they were to clean their teeth and go straight to sleep after the film.

Pippa tutted and rolled her eyes and promised they would and Trish left them, knowing that they would chatter on till midnight.

Clara and Hugo sat in silence, sipping their wine and listening to the buzz of the barbecue coals cooling, while the night grew dark around them.

At length, Clara sighed and began stacking plates. Trish had already made a start when she took them into the kitchen; the dishwasher was loaded up and the lemonade glasses were washed and sparkling on the drainer. She stood at the bin, scraping the salad bowl clean, humming quietly to herself.

Clara set the plates down on the kitchen table and picked up a tea-towel.

'I'll do it,' Trish said. 'You go and talk to Hugo.'

'I don't think we've much to say to each other.'

Trish took the salad bowl and plunged it into the water, bumping it against the sink walls and splashing soap-suds over the rim. 'Really,' she said, 'I can manage.'

'Don't be silly. You've been on your feet all day, you must be shattered.'

'Will you just *leave* it!' Trish slammed the bowl onto the drainer and a chip flew off it with a gritty *crack!*

Clara was shocked.

'Please,' Trish said. 'For me. Go and talk to Hugo. Make things right between you, Clara,' she said. 'Because it's breaking my heart seeing you like this.'

Trish had supported Hugo throughout the ordeal of Clara's abduction, comforting Pippa and providing a safe haven for both of them in an insane situation. After Clara's return, her work had doubled, because now she had Clara to care for, too. She had done all with her usual good humour, accepting Clara's mood swings and flashes of temper with the calm loving concern that was so typical of her. This outburst was untypical of her: Clara felt ashamed that she hadn't until now considered the strain Trish had been under.

She returned to the patio in subdued and pensive mood. Hugo sat staring into his drink. Seeing her, he reached for the wine and topped his glass up, then raised the bottle to her.

'I'm fine, thanks,' Clara said.

'Try telling that to your counsellor,' he muttered.

*He knows I'm seeing a counsellor?*

He must have caught the expression on her face, because he said, 'D'you think I'm entirely stupid, Clara?'

'No,' she said. 'Of course not.'

He stared at her for some moments, then shook his head, as if regretting his outburst. 'Pippa has had a

bloody horrible time and I think she deserves a holiday.'

'You mean she needs to get away from me.'

'From both of us,' he said. 'From this . . . this
*situation*. She needs to go and have fun and not worry
if Mummy's upset, or if she's cheering Daddy up.'

'I understand,' Clara said. 'I do. But Barbados . . .
Couldn't they have found somewhere more expensive?'

He thought about this. 'Knowing Karine and Roland
Forrest, probably not,' he said, allowing himself a
twinkle of amusement. 'But it's only the air fares
and spends. They've got the rest covered.'

'You don't think the Forrests would fly economy
class, do you? Hugo, I just don't see how we could
afford it.'

'We have to. For Pippa.'

'Where are we going to find the money?'

'I don't know,' Hugo said. 'I don't know. It's been a
struggle since I lost the Melker contract last autumn,'
he said. 'Word gets out you're unreliable—' He
shrugged.

'Your wife had been *abducted*, Hugo. Doesn't that
count for anything?'

'This is business, Clara. What counts is money,
profit margins, investment potential. They expect
you to be available when they need to speak to you.
They expect you to be creative and reliable, to deliver
on time and within budget.'

'So we're goosed, is what you're saying.'

'They'll trust me again. But it'll take time.'

'And in the meantime we've got to fund Pippa's holiday with Beach Barbie.'

Hugo seemed pleased that she was talking as if the holiday was on. He hesitated, then began, 'You um . . .' He seemed to change his mind, even shook his head a little, as if saying, *Bad idea*. Then he took a breath and dived right in: 'I don't suppose you've thought any more about taking on a few criminal cases?'

Her heart stopped. For one chest-clenching moment it actually stopped, then it contracted painfully and she gasped. Alarmed, Hugo set his glass down on the table and half-rose to help her. Clara waved him away.

He looked helplessly at her. 'We need the money,' he said, apologetic, but defiant.

She leaned forward to place her glass on the table, misjudged the distance and it toppled, spilling wine and smashing onto the stone flags. Clara stared at the shattered remains, unable to move. She felt cold – desperately cold – in the humid heat of the evening.

Hugo stood. She followed the fluid movement with blank incomprehension.

'I can't, Hugo. Don't ask me to—'

He placed both hands on her shoulders. 'I'm sorry,' he said. 'I shouldn't have mentioned it. I'll find some other way.'

'I'm working a residency order,' she said, knowing how pathetic it sounded: normally she would have court appearances and consultations booked until December, and new cases coming in every day.

'Just keep doing what you can,' he said. 'It'll come right.'

She didn't believe it, and neither, she thought, did Hugo. But it comforted them for the moment. The lies and the self-delusion had become a necessary part of life since her abduction. They acted as a balm and helped them to get through the nights and days when life seemed almost impossible.

# 25

The locker-room was empty when Clemence arrived. The grey walls and lockers standing on a painted floor reminded him of prison. It had surprised him, when he first started working at the lab, just how little colour there was in the building, when the company prided itself on the vibrancy of its colour prints.

Most people would be down in the canteen by now, having a last-minute cup of tea before the shift started. He was late: the police still wouldn't release his car, and he had no money for the bus fare to get home from the nick, so he'd had to hoof it back to his flat for a quick shower and change. Then he trundled his bike around from where he had locked it against the drainpipe in the back yard and started the half-hour journey to Queensferry.

A puncture almost threw him into the path of a lorry on the A458 and by the time he'd made a temporary repair, he was pretty close to the wire. He got in with only five minutes to spare. No time to eat, but he would grab a packet of crisps and a coke from the vending machine during his rest-break.

He went to his locker for his overall, turned the key and opened the door. Something fell out, hitting him square in the chest. Something solid and round. Green stuff and pink matter spattered his T-shirt.

'Fuck!' He leapt back and it smashed to the floor, shattering, spraying more pink pulp over his trainers and the cuffs of his trousers.

Horror and disbelief and revulsion. He saw Vicky – saw her as if she was in the room with him. Unrecognisable. Inhuman. Monstrous.

He screamed. '*Shit and fuck!*'

He could see what it was now. He forced himself to breathe deeply. Not a head after all – not a head – but a watermelon, its outer shell cracked open, a hammerhead buried deep in its flesh.

He blinked and saw, in that instant, a strobe sequence. A snatch remembered from his dreams. Memories – or an attempt to make sense of something entirely beyond explanation? He had never decided, because the sequence was so terrible that he blanked it out when he woke. But this time he was awake. He saw himself raise the hammer, saw Vicky put up a hand to defend herself . . .

He swore again and grabbed the hammer. Whoever did this was going to pay. Everyone was in the staff room. Fifteen men and women – all of the late shift. Six of them crowded around one of the tables, the rest ranged behind them, facing the door so they could see his face when he came in.

Nobody spoke. A few stared at him, hostile, but most fixed their eyes on the floor. He flung the hammer onto the table. It bounced and skidded across a copy of the morning paper.

'Is this some kind of sick joke?'

Terry Spence sat at the head of the table. He raised his eyes from his coffee cup, fixing his gaze on Clemence. 'I don't see no one laughing,' he said.

*Spence. Pathetic little twat couldn't take me on one-to-one, so he rounded up a posse.* 'Did you dream this up all by yourself, Spence?' he asked. 'I didn't think you had the imagination.'

'The police were in yesterday.' Linda said this – or Lydia – he never could remember her name.

He looked into her doughy face. 'My advice,' he said, 'keep your mouth shut. Ask to see your brief.'

'They were asking about *you*,' she said, offended, slightly flustered.

'The police are asking about a lot of people.'

'Only, *you* didn't turn up for work last night,' Spence said.

'Who d'you think you are, Spence – Hercule fucking Poirot?'

'You like taking pictures of lasses, don't you, Clemence?' Spence lifted up the newspaper, so that he could read the headline:

## AMY MAN TOOK MY PICTURE

The hammer slid off it and landed with a *crack!* on the wood of the table-top, leaving a pink smear across the photograph below the headline.

'Girls like Jasmine, yeah. It's a real pleasure taking a picture of a good-looking girl like that.'

'You're nowt but a bloody pervert,' someone muttered.

'What d'you want?' Clemence addressed the question to Spence. 'A confession?'

'I'll tell you what we want,' Spence said, doing a quick trawl of the room, checking that he had the support of the mob. 'We want you to piss off and let decent folk get on with their lives.'

'Decent folk,' Clemence said. 'You mean folk like you? You mean folk who'd do *this*?' He reached for the hammer, but Spence was nearer and he got there before him.

'What's up, Clemence? Bring back unpleasant memories, did it?'

Clemence was aware of people pressing in, getting too close. Getting too damn close. 'You want to take this outside, Spence?'

Spence stood and at the same time the two men either side of him pushed back their chairs and rose to their feet. Spence held the hammer like a weapon.

One of the women said, 'Hey, come on now, lads . . .' but her heart wasn't in it.

There was a hunger in their eyes – not just the three men opposite – all of them, men and women, young and old. Some he thought he'd got on with; people he had even begun to like. He had seen it a hundred times before on the faces of cons when a fight was brewing. Fair fight, or three onto one, friend or enemy, it didn't matter. They wanted blood.

He clenched his fist, ready to take the first man who came at him, but the canteen door opened and the boss stood in the doorway. Jimmy Torrance was short and balding, with wide hips and a narrow chest.

'The evening shift's waiting to get back to their families,' he said. 'Your shift started' – he checked his watch – 'five minutes ago. Section supervisors have got diaries to check before we get rolling.'

Half a dozen people made their way, shamefaced, to the door. The rest hung back, waiting to see if anything would happen. Spence looked like he might take a swing just to avoid losing face, then Torrance said, 'Just so you know: any overtime I have to pay the evening shift will be docked from your pay packets.'

Spence bared his teeth at Clemence, holding eye contact. 'Later,' he said.

'Whenever.' Clemence watched Spence through the door, the last to leave, just itching for an excuse to lob the hammer.

Clemence made a move to follow, but Torrance gestured for him to wait and closed the door on the retreating backs of the night shift. He sank his hands in his pockets and shook his head, sighing. 'You see how it is, lad.'

'It won't break my heart if I'm not invited to the staff night out, Christmas,' Clemence said. 'I'll keep my head down.'

Torrance took a brown envelope from his pocket and held it out. When Clemence didn't take it, he placed the envelope on the table between them.

'There's an extra week in there,' he said. Clemence stared at it, still refusing to take it.

'Best I could do,' Torrance said, pushing the envelope a little nearer to Clemence.

'You can't do this,' Clemence said. 'This job is all I've fucking got.'

'I'm running a business, lad,' Torrance said, apologetic, embarrassed.

'Right.'

'I'm expecting the police here again in a few minutes.'

'Jesus!'

'I know it's hassle for you, but it's lost money to me. Taking people off the shift makes things run slow, and I can't afford to have this place run slow in August.'

'So put me back on the books. I could run one of those sections blindfold.'

'After what I saw here tonight? And the police aren't going to improve the atmosphere.' Clemence shrugged and Torrance added, 'You weren't exactly Mr Popularity, even before all this palaver.'

'Oh, well, you know I *tried* to make Spence like me, but we just couldn't seem to hit it off.'

'See what I mean?' Torrance said. 'You're your own worst enemy. All lip and bad attitude. I'm doing my best, here. I gave you a chance.'

'And I blew it, didn't I? Got me convicted already, have you, Mr Torrance?'

Torrance sighed again. 'No, of course not. But I've got to think of staff morale. Come on, now. Don't make it any harder for me than it already is.' He picked up the envelope.

This time, Clemence took it. Torrance grinned and offered Clemence his hand. Clemence looked at it and then into Torrance's face, thinking what he could do to the fat little fuck if he just let go of his temper for a second.

'Aye, well, mebbe not,' Torrance said. 'You can cut through my office on your way out, save any . . . unpleasantness.'

'Bit late for that, isn't it?' Clemence said, tucking the envelope into his back pocket. 'I'm gonna clean myself up and walk out through the lab, like I always do.'

# 26

Barton found a parking space just past the loading bay. The boss himself had answered his call – expecting trouble, no doubt, now the press had got hold of Clemence's name. Jimmy Torrance struck him as a man who didn't believe in delegation: he said he would supervise the rotation of staff during the police interviews.

Torrance had told him to use the night entrance, a small door to the left of the huge steel roller shutters that were raised during the day to allow a steady flow of trucks to pick up prints and off-load film for development.

The interview team was due to arrive in ten minutes, but Barton wanted a brief chat with the boss himself. He was off-duty as of twenty minutes ago. He had followed Steve Lawson's instructions, questioning Clemence, telling him to stay well away from Mrs Tobin.

Clemence had smirked at him. 'Haven't you seen the headlines, Sarge?' he asked. 'Diane Tobin isn't my type.'

This visit was to remind Clemence that he was taking a continued and close interest in him.

He clicked the seat-belt release and checked his wing mirror – a driver's reflex. Something moved in the darkness. He did a double-check in his rear-view mirror and finally turned around. He wasn't mistaken; Clemence had come out of the building, wheeling a bike. His T-shirt glistened black and slick in the white arc-lamps of the car park. It looked wet – soaked through – and Barton couldn't help thinking that he had read somewhere that blood looks black in artificial light.

The first pub Clemence tried was full of middle-aged couples sweating over plates of hot food. He thought about staying, seeing how fast he could get paralytically pissed, but the sight of all those fat, middle-class management types filling their faces made him queasy. He moved on to a wine bar near the cathedral, down one of the winding back alleys that seemed to trickle like minor tributaries into the mainstream of St Werburgh Street.

He stepped through the door. *Clemence, lad, you've hit the jackpot!* A row of three juicy peaches perched on stools at the bar, showing their tight little arses to very flattering effect. Strappy dresses, plenty of honeyed skin showing and positively *glowing* in the evening heat. He stood next to them, drinking in their perfume and the faint, pleasant smell of fresh sweat on them. He didn't speak, but when one of them flashed him a look, he smiled.

She smiled back and he left it at that. *Little by little, step by step*. For one thing, after what had happened in work (*Ex-work, Clemence: you're no longer on the staff*), he didn't feel much like making conversation. For another, she looked barely old enough to be out on her own. Funny how it always was girls of her age that really pushed his buttons.

It was like his development arrested at the precise moment *he* was. Like he still saw himself as a seventeen-year-old, hankering for a woman of experience, someone maybe even as old as twenty-one. And it came as a constant shock to look in the mirror and see a man of twenty-nine. Twelve years on and what had he got to show for it?

When he'd first got out, he was filled with impossible optimism, convinced, like a child waking on a summer's morning, that something wonderful was about to happen to him. Sometimes he positively tingled with excitement.

The photo lab was a let-down. He knew that processing was largely automated, these days, but he had hoped that Torrance would see his potential and send him to the digital department to be trained in the use of Adobe Photoshop. He could see himself doing restorations and enhancements, transforming cracked and faded old prints into pristine copies.

When it became plain that wasn't going to happen, he had shrugged his shoulders and concentrated on his own portfolio, working on his printing and development techniques, maybe lifting a bit more paper, a bottle or two more of the chemicals than he would have done otherwise, but ultimately accepting the situation. Prison wasn't good for much, but it taught him patience, and it had made him tough. He had learned to roll with the punches; a man could take a lot of punishment if he learned that trick.

But this, as the Yanks said, was a whole 'nother ball game. The cops, the people at work, that stupid cow Diane Tobin, they all had it in for him. Even that luscious little nymphet Jasmine had turned against him, going to the press and coming on all trembly, like he'd actually done something to her, instead of making her look good.

He swallowed the last of his wine and went back to the bar, feeling a little rubbery around the ankles. *Christ! It never used to affect me like this.* He couldn't get the hang of sipping wine, and his alcohol tolerance was shot to shit by twelve years of virtual abstinence. This time, he ordered a bottle of Bud and took it back to his corner seat to brood.

He had lost his camera and his job in the same week. He had no prospect of an exhibition, judging by what Tobin had told the filth, and no way of building a portfolio to try and get a job he would enjoy doing.

Nobody sat next to him. This both pleased and troubled him. In prison you needed a rep to stop people taking liberties; you learned to create an aura that warned other cons off invading your personal space. But he wasn't inside any more – he still needed to feel safe, true enough – but on the outside, even though it took less to scare people off, it took more to make him feel safe. So he gave off stronger vibes – dangerous vibes – and people steered clear. Which presumably was what Mr Torrance meant when he said: *It's not like you're Mr Popularity around here.*

He needed to make friends, he could see that, but he couldn't seem to get the hang of it. When he tried to make sense of it – and he did now, because he had lost his job and made a few enemies he hadn't suspected – he thought it came down to the fact that the population inside was relatively stable. Cons came and went, sure, but not like they do on the outside. Drifting in and out of your life by the hour, almost by the minute. On the outside, you didn't know anyone but everyone wanted to be your friend.

People smiled at you and you didn't know what they meant by it – if they were being friendly or maybe they were hiding something behind that smile – say you made them nervous or maybe they were planning to do something to you.

Cons were hard to get to know, which made it easier to deal with, because they didn't push themselves at you. You sized them up and they sized you up. You formed friendships slowly and cautiously, because it mattered that you could trust them, as far as you could trust anyone inside.

He watched the three girls all night, taking the occasional chug of beer, thinking about his worries, unaware that he, too, was being watched.

Torrance's bonus money would come in handy. He would need photographic paper, solutions, film, if they ever let him have his camera back. Two weeks' pay wouldn't go far, though. He would have to find something else, but Chester was a small city, and word got around fast.

The girls started getting restless, finishing drinks and

picking up their handbags, ready to leave. Tiny little handbags, barely big enough to hold cash, a stick of lippy and a Johnny. The girl who had caught his eye earlier glanced over. *She fancies me.* His shirt had dried tight on him, accentuating his pecs and the six-pack he'd worked so hard to achieve. She held his eye and tilted her head.

That look said, *Last chance, Stud. Make your move or lose me forever.* As she walked through the door, she thought he saw her give a faint shrug of her shoulders.

*Fuck it,* he thought, glugged the last of his drink and followed them, weaving a little. *Christ, Clemence!* he told himself, *You drink like a girl.*

Where were they going? A club, maybe, or to the pictures. They were dressed for clubbing it, so far as he could tell, being as out of touch as he was. He decided to follow them for a bit, see where it took him.

They turned right out of the bar, then left at the end of the alleyway, parallel with the curving colonnades that sheltered the black-and-white Tudor frontages on St Werburgh Street. The air was heavy and still; a faint whiff of river water drifted up from the south of the city, masked almost entirely by the cascades of strongly scented petunias in dozens of hanging baskets hung under the colonnades. His girl linked arms with the tallest of the three, sharing a secret. He hung back and heard a burst of chatter as the door to the bar opened again.

Without turning, he sized up the situation. Three – no – four lads. Young. Juiced up. Loud, jostling each other. He heard their trainers scuffing the pavement behind him. Shouts, swearing. He walked on, leaving the shadows of the colonnade and moving into the street.

He turned his head slightly, trying to get a glimpse of the youths, to assess the level of threat. Something moved at the edge of his vision and he flinched instinctively. A bottle crashed to the ground a couple of feet ahead of him.

Turn and fight, or keep moving? The cathedral loomed above him on the far side of the road. Spiked railings bordered its edge. The only way out was onwards.

'Hey!' They were shouting at him.

'Hey perve! Clemence!'

*They know me.* But how? For a second, he thought *Spence.* But Spence was still in work – he wouldn't know where he was.

'Leave the girls alone, Clemence.'

The trio were twenty yards ahead, nearing the junction; they turned, nervously looking over their shoulders.

'*Hey, love—*'

Clemence recognised the voice, but couldn't place it. The girls huddled together and hurried on.

The speaker raised his voice: 'He isn't pleased to see you – that's a hammer down his kecks!' This was followed by a burst of dirty laughter.

*Oh, I know that voice. I certainly do.*

When the girls broke into a trot, the same boy called after them, 'Don't run away! We'll take care of you . . .'

They turned left at the top of the road, heading

towards the city centre and Clemence – taking the gamble that the youths would follow the talent, rather than him – turned right, into the sudden open space of the town hall plaza. Behind him, he could hear them shouting, shoving each other, egging each other on. They were following him. He had chained his bike to the railings of the Bluecoat Hospital in Northgate Street, but he didn't stop: they would bring him down like a pack of dogs if he did. *Keep walking – hope they lose interest, or you find somewhere dark to duck into and disappear.*

Barton watched from the colonnade as the four lads moved out into the street. Skinhead cuts, a skinful of ale on-board.

Clemence had been like that once. Loud, cocky, always spoiling for a fight. Barton had been warned to watch out for him; he had even cautioned him and sent him home after he'd got into a scuffle on the street the night he killed Vicky. Barton had often wondered if he'd made an arrest instead, would Vicky be alive today.

One of the lads threw a bottle; if Clemence hadn't ducked it would have hit him squarely in the base of his skull. *Survival instincts of a sewer rat,* Barton thought.

Clemence turned right at the town hall and Barton crossed to the far side of the square, using the loose knots of people as cover. When the pedestrianised area gave way to roadway, he flitted silently from one column to the next alongside the pubs and restaurants of Northgate. It was quiet, almost devoid of traffic, and he could hear clearly the taunts and laughter of the boys as they stalked Clemence. That's all it was for now: a bit of a laugh. Tweaking the tiger's tail. But Barton knew how quickly these situations could turn nasty. He had seen it too many times at football matches and Saturday nights at throwing-out time to ignore the danger.

Clemence passed a couple of side-streets and back alleys that would have given him an escape route. *What's he playing at? Does he think he can take them on? Why the hell doesn't he just run for it?* Then he saw Clemence stagger – not a big movement, more a hesitation, a slight loss of co-ordination.

*Too much ale,* Barton thought. *His judgement's off.* It seemed Clemence couldn't handle his drink any more than he could handle the drugs in the old days.

Suddenly, Clemence dodged right. From his viewpoint across the street, Barton could see he had made a mistake. A few yards on and he could have made the steps carved in the city walls, doubling back along the canal to the north-east of the city, and home. But he had broken too soon, corralled himself in a cobbled alley leading to a dead end. His pursuers assumed he was heading for the walls.

'Get the fucker!' the ring-leader screamed. He sprinted away from the rest.

Clemence realised his error within seconds and turned back, emerging from the shadows as the first of the group reached it. 'You don't wanna fuck with me, kid,' he said. It was dark in the alleyway, but he saw a flicker of doubt in the boy's face, a slight glint of uncertainty in his eyes, and he thought maybe he had a chance. Then the other three arrived, skittering to a halt at the mouth of the alleyway. He was cornered.

Clemence crouched slightly, moving on the balls of his feet. The leader mirrored his posture while the others watched, waiting their chance to move in. A car crawled past, turning right into King Street. For a brief moment, its headlights fixed the group in a tableau. The beam crept up the youth's torso, then onto his neck and face. *The spider's-web tattoo. The boy in the cop shop.* Clemence pounced, knocking the boy to the ground. He threw a punch, connecting. The boy's nose spouted blood.

'Wanna get close to a killer, Spider?' Clemence breathed. 'Is this close enough for you?'

The boy made a wild swing, bruising Clemence's ear. He grabbed the boy's shirt-front, dragging him to his feet. 'You'll have to do better than that.'

A blow to the back of his head sent Clemence crashing to his knees. They were yelling, shouting as the adrenaline screamed through their systems. A kick to his kidneys and one in the ribs and he fell forward. *Get up, you prick. Stay on the ground, they'll kill you.* He got a hold of a foot as it lashed out and twisted. The attacker fell. Infuriated, the others piled in kicking, punching, stamping. The shouting stopped as they concentrated on causing maximum damage.

Barton was thinking about Vicky. The way her mother had gone through her photograph album, showing him Vicky on holiday the summer of nineteen-ninety.

Vicky at her sixteenth birthday party. Vicky the Christmas before she died. As if she was trying to wipe from his mind the image of the bloody mess he had found on the filthy floor of Clemence's bedsit, trying to make him see that Vicky was once a happy girl, her darling daughter.

It only succeeded in making the memory of what he saw more horrific and more real. He had stood in something sticky when he came into that stinking, dimly lit room. Only realising later that there were bits of Vicky's brains stuck to the sole of his shoe. And in the midst of all the horror, Clemence lying on the sofa, blissfully stoned.

Clemence was on the ground, curled into a ball, arms protecting his head, elbows in. *You're not even supposed to be here*, Barton thought. *Who's to know you were?*

The leader staggered back a bit, panting with the exertion, and wiped the sweat from his face. He seemed to cast about for a moment, then stooped and picked something up. His hand went back, getting a good swing and Barton caught a glint of light on glass.

*Shit. He's got a bottle.* He ran, yelling, making as much noise as he could. 'Police officer! Get AWAY from him!'

The youth glanced up, startled. He looked from Clemence to Barton, evidently calculating the risk.

'I've called for back-up,' Barton shouted. 'Now get the *fuck* away from him!'

It wasn't until he was within a few steps of them that

the youth lowered his arm and let the bottle slide from his fingertips. It fell with a hollow *thunk!* and rolled, rattling, into the gutter.

The other three had barely broken their rhythm. They laid into Clemence like they were trying to kick their way out of a burning building. Barton didn't waste any more energy trying to persuade them. He flicked his Casco baton open and hit the nearest hard on the backs of his knees. The boy collapsed, screaming. The remaining two left off kicking Clemence and rounded angrily on Barton.

'I should take that off you and ram it up your arse, mate,' the leader said, wiping the blood from his nose with the heel of his palm.

'Think you're hard enough, son?' Barton said.

'Three lads onto one fat dibble?' The boy looked first at one, then at the other of his mates either side of him. 'I'd lay a fiver on it.' They fanned out, as if on some unseen signal. Barton knew he had to take one more down or he wouldn't stand a chance. They stayed out of reach circling, waiting an opportunity. If he made the first move, he would be open to attack and he had already seen the damage these lads were capable of inflicting.

'Pick up your friend and piss off home,' Barton said, his heart beating hard against his rib-cage. 'There'll be a van-load of officers here any minute.'

The leader cocked an ear, revealing the tattoo in the angle of his jaw. 'I don't hear no sirens,' he said. 'You're all alone, mate.'

They drew closer. The boy he had hit lay still. No

screams, no groans. It seemed he was holding his breath in anticipation of the kicking Barton was about to take. Barton readjusted his grip on his baton. He didn't dare look behind him to try to attract attention from across the street. *Move, Goddamnit! Make your move before it's too late.*

'Hey, Spider.' Clemence's voice. Exhausted and fighting for breath, but defiant, too. 'Don't forget I know you.'

'Shut your fucking mouth, Clemence,' the boy warned.

Clemence laughed. It was a little watery, blurred by blood and pain, but he *did* laugh and the effect was chilling. They all stared at him. He struggled to his knees, still smiling. There was blood on his teeth – more on his T-shirt and trousers. 'Remember what I said, Spider?' He tapped the angle of his own jaw, indicating the position of the boy's web tattoo. 'As good as a bar code,' Clemence reminded him. 'Do like the officer said, and I just might have a lapse of memory.'

The others looked at 'Spider' for guidance. Barton suspected that the name Clemence had just given him would stick with him for life. A crowd was gathering across the street, outside the pub and faintly, in the distance, police sirens whooped.

Spider shrugged. 'I'll see you around.'

He walked as far as the steps to the city walls and then ran for it. The others swarmed after him, up the steps and into the dark, half-carrying the boy Barton had hit.

Clemence fell on all fours. 'Well, who says you can never find a copper when you need one?' he said.

'Don't get carried away,' Barton said. 'I was doing my job.'

Clemence hawked, spat blood. 'What? Protecting the innocent?' He laughed and was racked by a coughing fit.

'Who said anything about innocent? You're going back inside, Clemence, and I'll be there to see you through the gates.'

'You're all heart, Sarge.'

One of the gawpers finally plucked up courage to come over and ask if they needed help. 'He'll be fine,' Barton said, hauling Clemence to his feet. 'Come on, I'll take you to hospital.'

Clemence shook his head, lifting the hem of his T-shirt to wipe the blood from his face. 'That means answering a lot of awkward questions, giving the tabloids another story. Not in my interests, Sergeant,' Clemence said, giving him a long, cool look. 'Not in yours, either.'

# 27

A faint ghostly trace appeared on the paper. Clemence held his breath, as he always did, despite reminding himself not to. Although he knew the chemistry, the process still held a ritual power for him. Within seconds he could make out the curve of her mouth, the line of an eyebrow, her chin slightly lifted, resting on one palm. Amy Dennis as she appeared in the student prospectus.

'Much in demand for her feature photography, Amy's *Photography in Pictures* is a popular beginner's text. She lectures in photojournalism at her local college and tours regularly with exhibitions of her work.'

He had memorised her biographical entry during his many readings of the course book; had studied every line and contour of her face till he had it by heart. Despite the steady hum of the extractor fan, he got a whiff of the ammonium thiosulphate fixer in the third tray; it made him apprehensive: you could have a fabulous picture, wonderfully composed, a perfect balance of light and dark, achingly beautiful tones, but unless you stopped and fixed at the right moment, your efforts were wasted. His hands trembled as he lifted the print out of the developer and slid it into the stop bath.

*What are you scared of, Clem? That she's gonna reach right out of the frame and grab you by the throat?* Although he smiled, his heartbeat counted double the twenty seconds until it was time to move the print to the fixing solution.

He found himself staring at the patterns and play of light on water in the washing tray.

*Missed a step. This is bad. Must've lost your concentration.* Then it came to him: this was a dream. He was gripped by an irrational fear. He struggled, thrashing about like a swimmer in deep water, trying to rise to the surface, but constantly dragged down by the tangle of weeds.

*I've got to wake up.* But he couldn't take his eyes off the ripples of water, stippling and diffracting the image beneath: Amy, smiling. With increasing dread, he saw the image shudder, then shatter. The pieces shifted, realigning, reconstituting into something terrible.

He tried to scream but something heavy pressed on his chest; he couldn't move – could barely breathe. Vicky's image had replaced Amy's. She grinned up at him, her teeth smashed, her lips gone. The water ran red, spilling over the sides of the tray and filling the sink.

A shout burst from him and he sat up, gasping, unable to remember where he was. The room was too big, the sounds wrong. Something flapped to his left and he flinched, sending a bolt of pain through his bruised back.

The curtain flapped again, sending a gust of cool air shivering over his skin.

*Home*, he thought, then repeated it aloud, 'You're *home*, Clemence.'

He lay in the dark, trying to make out the hunched shapes around him. A figure slumped in the single wooden chair next to the table. He made a low sound in his throat, then remembered: he washed his clothes when he got back, letting tepid water run over him in the shower as he tried to tread the blood out of his clothing: since the filth had taken his trousers and T-shirt the previous night, he was already down one set, and he didn't have a huge wardrobe to mix and match.

He realised suddenly that he didn't have to lie quiet in the dark. He could move about his own flat without anyone complaining, switch on his own light with his own light switch – he didn't have to wait on anybody else's routine, anybody else's orders.

He swung his legs over the side of the bed, wincing as he stood, feeling every kick that Spider and his gang had landed on him. He went to the kitchen and flicked the light. The room was empty. All his prints and negs gone, the processing trays stacked neatly on the slatted shelves beneath the wet area of the work surface.

Even so, he had to brace himself to go to the sink, and it was some time before his heart stopped hammering. He rinsed his face, careful not to open the cut over his eye.

The clock on his dresser read three a.m. He paced the room, while the wind blustered against the side of the house and the curtains cracked and flapped, whipping themselves into a frenzy.

'Amy's dead,' he told himself. 'Vicky's dead. They can't touch you.' He didn't believe in ghosts. But he did believe in God and retribution and he had already taken twelve years of punishment. In the distance a glimmer of lightning flashed and, half a minute later, a faint throb of thunder, like a muffled sob.

'Fuck this,' he muttered, slamming the window closed and shooting the catch. It took him longer to dress than it would normally, and he almost changed his mind, but as the wind gained strength, blatting the windows and rattling empty cans along the alley at the back of the house, his determination returned. He felt like doing some damage.

The storm reached its height at four a.m. A dry, crackling display of pink and blue flashes prowled the Welsh hills in the near distance, but although the wind rampaged through the city, tearing tiles from roofs, not a drop of rain fell.

Diane Tobin woke her husband at four-thirty, hissing in his ear. '*Chris! There's somebody outside!*'

He groaned and covered his eyes against the bedside lamp. 'Go back to sleep. It's only the storm.'

She shook him awake. 'There!' she exclaimed, her voice caught somewhere between triumph and terror.

He listened. This time he *did* hear something: a solid *thump!* as if someone had swung a heavy object against the outer wall of the house.

He lifted the covers and eased himself to the floor.

For the first time in ten days, he felt a chill. Cold air was coming in to the house from somewhere. 'Is there a window open downstairs?' he asked, knowing the answer and feeling his pulse pick up in response: he had locked all the doors and windows, checking each one at Diane's insistence before they went to bed.

He reached under the bed and retrieved the cricket bat he had placed there earlier.

Diane caught his arm. 'Don't go,' she whispered, her eyes wide with terror.

He shook her off impatiently.

'You don't know what he's like,' she pleaded.

'This is *my house*,' he said, his voice an angry growl. 'Do you want me to let him get away with this?'

He trod the edges of the risers, avoiding altogether the sixth stair with its creaky board, and paused in the hallway. The back sitting-room door was open. The hairs stood up on the back of his neck. A high twittering sound, not quite like voices, more like animals bickering, came from beyond the door.

A spectacular *crash!* followed by the sound of breaking glass and he jumped, giving a startled yell. He rushed through the open door, shouting incoherently, felt for the light switch and stared wildly about the room.

It was a mess. Books and papers littered the floor, the sculpture lay on its side and the French windows flapped in the wind. One of the hinges had been twisted askew and it was these that gave the chattering, twittering sound as they swung in the gale.

Broken glass from the door and from Diane's

framed photographs made it dangerous to explore further in bare feet and he stood in the doorway, uncertain what to do.

Another *thud!* and he whirled around, the cricket bat raised, ready to defend himself. A pause, then *thud!* The back gate. He began to relax, then felt a second surge of terror. *The sitting-room door!* He had closed it before he went to bed. The intruder could be anywhere. Anywhere at all in the house.

'Diane!' he screamed, running for the stairs. 'Diane – answer me!'

There was no reply, only a breathless silence and the sounds of the storm slamming the gate against the side of the house. He raced up the stairs, almost mad with fear, and blundered into their bedroom.

'Diane!' She was wedged between the wardrobe and the dressing-table, her eyes huge and her face white with terror.

'Why the hell didn't you answer me?' he demanded, his voice raised to a shout. 'I thought something had happened to you. I thought—' She cringed, retreating further into the corner and he realised that in his fury he had been waving the bat at her. He set it down on the bed and bent down, taking her by the elbows and lifting her gently. 'It's all right,' he said.

'I thought he—'

'Shhh . . .' In her present state he couldn't tell her that he thought the intruder might still be in the house, so he spoke to her slowly and quietly, as to a nervous child. 'We'll go downstairs and phone the police.'

She twisted, trying to break his grip, but he held her.

'Come on, now,' he said, ashamed to have made her afraid of him.

'I'm sorry,' she whispered. 'I'm so sorry.'

Her fearful apology hit him harder than if she had used her fists on him. 'God, I'm such a selfish bastard. Forgive me, Diane.'

# 28

---◆---

After the storm, the city had the bedraggled look of a gatecrashed party: shocked and shaken, more than a little sheepish.

Clara drove slowly to work, avoiding roof tiles and hoardings that had tumbled into the road. Shopkeepers swept the debris from the front of their premises, intruder alarms blared in some of the empty properties. Towering bronze anvil clouds retreated into the west, and now the skies over Chester were a high dusty blue. Clara felt optimistic – she might almost have said happy, were it not for a superstitious dread that to acknowledge the feeling would be to banish it.

Mitch's sombre appearance, the tentative, abashed way she came into her office, should have warned her; but Clara was too happy to allow anything to dampen the unfamiliar feeling she had woken with that morning that everything was right with the world.

'Hi.' Clara went to the filing cabinet she had appropriated over the months, and started rooting through it for the Tobin file. Mitch leaned against the door jamb, her arms folded, and stared hard at the floor.

Clara looked over at her, momentarily interrupting her search. 'No doughnuts?' she said, concentrating again on the files. 'No coffee?' Mitch flipped her a look, then returned to her frowning scrutiny of the carpet. 'I'd settle for a hello . . .'

'You won't find it.'

Clara was about to make a facetious remark about finding a greeting in the files, faltered, stopped and looked again at Mitch. The floor seemed to race up to meet her and she held onto the filing cabinet for support. This couldn't be happening. She checked again; the Tobin file was missing.

'I've passed the case back to Bethany.'

'I'm not an employee, for you to "pass" my cases on,' Clara said, 'Mr and Mrs Tobin appointed me—'

'They asked to be reassigned.'

Clara gave a short laugh. 'They were *all over* me! They sought me out.'

Mitch's mouth tightened. 'I'm sorry, Clara,' she said. 'Mr Tobin doesn't like you. His wife doesn't trust you.'

'I don't understand,' Clara said, feeling suddenly weak.

'She thinks you're more interested in Clemence than you are in them.'

'She's wrong.'

'Clara,' Mitch said. 'I was there yesterday when she came to see you. Your desk was practically groaning under the weight of material on Clemence.'

'Preparation,' Clara felt a panicky flutter in her chest. 'Preparation for the restraining order.'

'She doesn't see it that way.'

'I'll talk to her,' Clara said, the panic fluttering like a trapped bird in her chest. 'I'll explain.'

'No, Clara.' Mitch put a hand on her arm. 'She's not inclined to talk, just now.'

'There must be a way.' She couldn't lose this case.

'She won't talk to you,' Mitch repeated.

'Well,' Clara said, gently releasing herself. 'I can always trust you to be straight with me.'

Mitch seemed surprised. 'Wouldn't I be a bloody fool to lie about it?' Another brief hesitation, as if she was afraid that Clara couldn't cope with the next piece of news. 'Someone broke into their house last night.'

'Oh, God . . .'

'Of course they're convinced it was Clemence – and who could blame them?'

Clara felt her way from the filing cabinet to her desk, using the furniture to prevent herself from falling down; finally lowering herself into the chair. 'What am I going to do? I promised Pippa she could go on holiday in two days.'

'She's going?' Mitch exclaimed.

Clara stared at her. 'You know about the trip? Does he phone you for hourly bulletins, Mitch?'

Mitch rolled her eyes. 'God, you're completely paranoid! Hugo called yesterday afternoon to tell you they were having a barbecue. You were at the library or wherever. We got to chatting and . . .' She lifted one shoulder.

Clara searched her friend's face.

'C'mon, Clara. You don't really think we spend our

time having earnest conversations on the phone about you?'

Clara pictured it for a moment, but the image wouldn't stick: Mitch was more likely to face her down and tell her what she thought, than to have whispered conferences with her husband.

She dipped one shoulder. 'Mitch, I thought you cared.'

Mitch frowned, falling momentarily for the look of hurt pride, then she saw the self-mocking lift of Clara's eyebrows and laughed.

Clara sighed. 'Seriously, though. I don't know what I'm going to tell Pippa.'

'Tell her the truth,' Mitch said. 'Tell her that Mummy's not well and she's finding it hard to get work.'

'She's nine years old, Mitch.'

'She's got eyes in her head, hasn't she?'

Clara was startled by the vehemence of Mitch's tone, and her friend relented a little. 'Look,' she said. 'I'll find you something else. Tell Pippa she can go some other time. She'll understand.'

Clara laughed.

'What's so funny about that?' Mitch demanded.

'Imagine you've been invited to spend the weekend at Justice Howell's country manor,' Clara said. 'Imagine there's a hint that you might be offered Silk. You turn it down because you can't really afford a new dress and you can't go without a designer name-tag.'

'It's that serious, huh?' Mitch said.

'It's a once-only, refuse-if-you-dare opportunity to hobnob with the golden girl of Year Four, Mitch.

There isn't going to *be* another time. And she won't ever forgive me if I break this promise.'

'Well,' Mitch said. 'We'll just have to find a way.'

'No. Mitch – you've done too much already,' Clara said, her eyes watering unexpectedly. 'This isn't your problem.'

'All right.' When Mitch had to broach a difficult subject, she mentally rolled up her sleeves and squared her shoulders for the argument. Clara recognised the signs and prepared herself to make a rebuttal. 'Since you've let me off the hook – how about your mother?'

'*Sophia?*' Clara had braced herself, but she wasn't ready for this. 'I couldn't ask Sophia.'

'Why not? She has pots of money, and she's always looking for a good cause.'

'Mitch, she hasn't been near us since – since I was abducted.' *There! You said it.*

Mitch winked. 'Ah, but she did send you a lovely card, didn't she? And if I remember rightly, it said "If you need anything" . . .'

'You've a mind like a steel trap.'

'So people are always telling me.'

'But I couldn't, Mitch. I couldn't just call her out of the blue and ask for money.'

Mitch sighed. 'I hope you aren't hoping she'll make the first call. You could grow old waiting.'

For a long time after Mitch left, Clara sat quite still at her desk. She wasn't ready to talk to Sophia, but there was a call she had to make. Knowing it was unavoidable didn't make it any easier.

\* \* \*

When she arrived at the bistro, it was already busy. Her clerk had found a table near the back, as far from the windows and the bar as she could find. The little Welsh woman stood and took both her hands, but Clara couldn't help noticing her anxious look into the body of the restaurant.

Nesta Lewis sat facing the door and sipped nervously at a glass of white wine, refusing the offer of food. 'They'd wonder what's happened if I don't go down to the staff room with my sandwiches,' she explained, adding, 'I can't stay long, sorry.'

'Nesta,' Clara said. 'If you'd rather not do this—'

'No,' Nesta said firmly. 'You've always been a good friend to me.' She stopped, seemed almost awed by her own frankness. 'Anyway,' she went on, concentrating on a cigarette burn on the table in an effort to avoid Clara's eye, 'it's not like you've asked me to do anything *improper*. I mean, you're a member of Chambers – you're entitled to see what passes through its doors.'

'Quite,' Clara agreed. The fact that Mr Warrington wouldn't have let her within five miles of such an important case, even if she wanted it, was, for the moment, set aside for the sake of Nesta's peace of mind.

'Photocopies,' Nesta said, conscience satisfied. She pushed a manila envelope across the table. 'Everything we've had so far.' She hesitated. 'Does this mean—?'

'Professional curiosity,' Clara said, a little too quickly.

'Oh.' Nesta craned her neck and took a tiny sip of wine. 'Do you mind me asking – how did you know we would be handling the case?'

Clara smiled. 'Mitch told me that the CPS had already appointed prosecution counsel.' She lifted one shoulder. 'Where else would they go?'

Nesta nodded, fondly approving.

'Have they charged him?' Clara asked.

Nesta shook her head. 'But it's only a matter of time, Mr Telford says.'

*Peter Telford.* Clara shot Nesta a sharp look, suspecting her of using Telford as a baited hook. Everyone in Chambers knew of the rivalry between her and Telford.

Nesta met her gaze with calm innocence. 'Mr Telford has been appointed by the CPS. I understand,' she added, taking another demure sip from her glass, 'that Mr Clemence's solicitor is looking for a lady barrister.'

Mitch found her in her office at four-fifteen, reading through the notes Nesta had given her. She camouflaged them with the newspaper clippings and internet print-outs. The door, as always, was slightly ajar and Mitch leaned on it, letting it swing open under the pressure of her fingertips.

'Thought you'd gone out.'

Clara glanced up, sliding the notes under some of the less contentious detritus. 'I did. Now I'm back.'

'Can't you find something more relaxing to do?'

'Like what?'

'I don't know – watch a movie, play some mellow blues on the CD player. Sit in the garden and watch the last rays of sunlight fade to a purple haze. Surrender yourself to the night sounds. Watch moths sip nectar from the honeysuckle and bats slip silently across the moon.'

It was meant as a joke: Mitch sending up her own occasional tendency to hyperbole, but Clara was reminded of the evening of the barbecue. After Trish had left, Clara had returned to the garden and she and Hugo had talked, haltingly at first, then, more at ease, watching the slow slide of day into night, and as the storm gathered around them, they slipped thankfully into a reconciliation. They had made up sweetly, tenderly in the night, their gentle love-making a counter-balance to the raging of the storm.

Suddenly Clara wanted to cry. 'Mitch, you're a poet.'

Mitch tilted her head in regal acceptance of the compliment. 'I'm the product of a great literary heritage,' she said.

She looked at the snowstorm of print-outs and press cuttings on Clara's desk and asked, 'If you're so interested in the case, why don't you take it?'

'Why does everyone want me to take this case?'

'Everyone?'

*She's too sharp for you, Clara. Too sharp and too clever.* 'Never mind,' she said. 'I don't want it.'

Mitch fixed her with a no-nonsense look. 'God knows I value your help here, Clara, but we both know that you always loved criminal cases.'

'Right. Past tense.'

'Rubbish! You're a brilliant criminal lawyer.'

'*Used* to be.'

'It's not something you can switch on or off.'

'No,' Clara said. 'It took a while.' They both knew that she meant the term of her abduction, but it hadn't ended with her release: her confidence had been gradually eroded until she felt that she couldn't trust herself any longer. 'I won't defend him,' she went on. 'I won't allow myself to be used.'

'You're kidding yourself. Every custody case you fight, every child you place with one parent or another, you're being used. One parent using your intelligence and your adversarial skills against the other. That's what it's all about, Clara. You just have to make sure that you're used for the right reasons. You have to be certain that you're on the right side.'

'How can I know that?' She heard the note of desperation in her voice and looked away from Mitch, embarrassed to reveal so much of her inner turmoil, even to her friend. 'I can't know that,' she said, making an effort to keep her voice bland, neutral.

For a long time, Mitch didn't say anything. Clara felt Mitch's eyes on her, but she couldn't bear to look up and see the compassion and frustration in her friend's face.

A faint sigh, then Mitch said, 'So you won't even try.'

'I don't want the responsibility.'

'Don't want it or can't handle it?'

'He stalked her, Mitch.'

'She *says* he stalked her.'

'The papers—'

'Jesus! I can't believe I heard you say that! You're

basing your judgement on what the *papers* say? You're
a lawyer, Clara – you know damn well the papers will
say whatever sells. I'm not denying he made a few
calls.'

'What kind of calls? Nuisance calls? Nice euphe-
mism for scaring the shit out of a woman – "It wasn't
stalking, Your Honour, it was just a *nuisance* call." You
know what, Mitch? A nuisance call is a double glazing
salesman phoning up while you're trying to prepare
dinner, it isn't a convicted murderer ringing to tell you
he knows where you live.'

'You're exaggerating—'

'Exaggerating? Okay. Tell me it's not in the records.
Tell me he wasn't seen outside her house. Tell me – tell
me he didn't phone her, Mitch.'

'Maybe he did. I don't know. I haven't seen the
notes.'

Clara breathed in sharply. *Does she know about my
meeting with Nesta Lewis?*

Mitch went on as if she hadn't noticed Clara's
startled response. 'Look at it one way, and you see a
murderer recently released from prison, badgering and
threatening his ex-tutor.'

'Right—'

'*But,*' Mitch interrupted. 'But Mrs Tobin is the
nervy type. Maybe she took what he said and wrought
it up in her imagination. He's a young man, he's keen –
perhaps even obsessed with his art. Did he make a few
perfectly innocent, if earnest requests for help from his
mentor, or did he demand her intervention with me-
naces?'

'I don't *know*, Mitch! And before you say "There's only one way to find out", I don't think I could ever know. Not for sure. I don't' – How could she express it? – 'I don't *believe* in people any more.'

Mitch was silent for a full minute, and Clara began to gather her papers together, growing restless in the heavy silence. At last, Mitch took a breath and Clara looked up, intrigued, despite herself.

'What if he's innocent?' Mitch asked.

'Based on what evidence?'

'Since when has English Law worked on the presumption of guilt?'

'If he's innocent, what was he in prison for?'

Mitch raised an eyebrow. 'A previous conviction, presumably.'

*Point to Mitch.*

'The man's in trouble, Clara. He needs a good lawyer.'

'Why are you so keen to help him?'

'It's not Clemence I'm trying to help.' She looked into Clara's face, as if trying to read her thoughts. 'The system is fallible, Clara, because *people* are fallible,' she said. 'Mistakes will happen, but when they do, it's the system's failure, not the individual's. You do the best job you can and wait for the verdict.'

# 29

Lawson handed DCI McAteer a sheet of paper. They were on their way to the morning briefing and McAteer kept walking, reading the report as he went.

'Claw-hammer,' he said.

Lawson nodded. 'Carrier bag wrapped around the shaft and another around the head.' They continued down the corridor toward the Incident Room, side-stepping two members of the night team comparing notes. One of them looked up and grinned as if to say, *We've got the bastard!*

'Is it the murder weapon?' McAteer asked.

'There's blood and hair adhering to the head and it was found not far from Amy's house.'

'How the hell did the fingertip search miss it?'

'It was just beyond the outermost grid of the cordon.'

'Who was the informant?'

'A concerned member of the public, out walking their dog.'

McAteer raised his eyebrows in question.

'An *anonymous* concerned member of the public,' Lawson added.

They arrived at the Incident Room and Lawson loosened his tie and popped the top button of his shirt.

'We'll have a result on the fingerprints within the hour, but the blood and tissue-typing will take a lot longer – I've asked for Premium Service, but it will depend on how badly decomposed the material is.'

'Pick up Clemence as soon as the results are in,' McAteer said. There was no doubt in his mind the fingerprints would be a match for Clemence.

Word had got round and they had a full turn-out. The discovery of the murder weapon was just the boost the team needed.

Lawson ran through the facts as they stood. There was a joint exclamation of 'Yes!' when he confirmed the discovery of the hammer. Then McAteer asked for any new leads or lines of inquiry.

DC Gordon stood up. 'We found these in Amy's files last night,' he said, picking up a bundle of computer print-outs and handing them round. 'I talked to the features editor on the *Evening Echo*. Amy took it at a promotional bash for the Dee View Development Project.'

McAteer took out a pair of reading glasses and put them on for a closer look at the photograph.

'The man on the right is Councillor Tom Rivers,' Gordon explained. 'The chap in the centre is—'

'Sebastian Enderby.'

Lawson glanced at McAteer in surprise. 'You know him, sir?'

'He's the shooting victim,' McAteer said, pocketing his reading glasses. 'The investigation I'm mentoring over in Helsby. Enderby was attacked getting into his car on Tuesday evening.'

'D'you think there could be a link?'

McAteer continued staring at the photograph, as if the answer lay in the faces of the gathered group. 'The investigation team think it was a mugging. But we now know that he had at least met Amy, and now she's dead and he's lying in hospital in a coma.' He frowned at the picture of a vigorous-looking man, bulking up to a comfortable middle age. He could not reconcile it with the pale and shattered form he had seen in the intensive care unit on Tuesday night.

He looked up, addressing the whole team. 'I want to know how close Amy was to this man,' he said. 'Talk to her colleagues. Find out if she had a connection, however tenuous, with this poor bugger.'

The night team went home after the morning briefing; the two officers stationed outside Clemence's flat had to wait another half-hour for their replacements to arrive from the station. There was no breath of wind after the storm subsided and at only eight-thirty, the day was sultry and hot. Clemence limped up the steps to his flat at eleven a.m., and the officers that stepped up to meet him were rumpled and irritable.

He came without a fuss, despite some rather rough handling that was more due to the heat and the frustration of a wasted morning than any personal grudge they held against Clemence. The custody sergeant called the police surgeon in to determine the extent of Clemence's injuries, which delayed the start of the interview by an hour. Then Quartermaine requested a consultation and he insisted that lunch be provided for his client before allowing the police interview to go ahead. At two p.m., there was a mild panic because Barton couldn't be found.

McAteer stood at the open door of Lawson and Barton's windowless office and demanded, 'Where the hell is he?' His shirt was buttoned to the collar, and his tie carefully knotted and scrupulously tight; his only concession to the oppressive heat had been to remove his jacket and hang it, buttoned, on a hanger behind his office door.

Lawson looked up from his paperwork. 'He went out to Bodfari to interview one of the women Clemence photographed,' Lawson told him. 'He called in at one o'clock to say he was on his way back. Traffic police say there's a two-mile tail-back on the Queensferry by-pass. We've tried to reach him on his mobile, but he must be in a signal canyon, because we can't get hold of him.'

'Three hours wasted already, Steve.'

'I know, sir.' Lawson thought for a moment. 'Chris Thorpe was in at the original arrest. He's an experienced officer . . .'

McAteer shook his head. 'We need continuity on this.' He sighed and checked his watch. 'Give it fifteen minutes,' he said. 'If he's not back by then, I want you to conduct the interview yourself.'

Barton was, in fact, parked with the car engine idling and the air conditioning at full blast, five minutes away from the station, in Volunteer Street. Despite the icy air around him, Barton was sweating. He did not want to conduct this interview. What if Clemence changed his mind and decided it would be to his advantage to come clean about the events of the previous night?

*Ask Steve Lawson to replace you as interviewing officer.* But Lawson would want a reason – a damned good one. *So? Be honest with him,* he thought. *Tell him you feel your position has been compromised. Brilliant! What does that sound like?* Like a confession, is what it would sound like.

He should have reported the attack on Clemence. But that would mean admitting to unauthorised surveillance of a suspect. Since the *Regulation of Investigatory Powers Act,* covert surveillance required permission of a superintendent. He knew that, and pleading ignorance would only make things worse. He could, of course, say that he saw Clemence acting suspiciously; then he wouldn't have needed to ask for authorisation. *Riding his bike away from his place of work?* That was so ludicrous it might even raise a laugh from Clemence's brief.

Then there was the little detail that Clemence had taken a beating, with an officer looking on for rather longer than was necessary to ascertain that an assault was taking place. And that same officer, who claimed to have 'rescued' Clemence from the thugs, was unmarked. Add to that the fact that the officer in question failed to report his surveillance of a suspect and a serious and unprovoked assault, and you end up with a very suspicious set of circumstances.

Barton groaned. *How the hell did I get myself into this mess?* Clemence knew exactly what he had been up to.

He knew that he could have – *should have* – intervened before the first blow was struck. Clemence had him over a barrel, and Barton had no doubt that he would play his advantage.

*So what are you going to do? Hide from him for the rest of this investigation? Take the coward's way out? There are only so many excuses you can make for not being where you should be.* He thought about this. For five long minutes he thought about it. If he didn't turn up for this interview, he would only have to face Clemence at some later time. This was the crucial first meeting. If he chickened out of this one, he might as well invite Clemence to run every subsequent interview he conducted. He rubbed his hands over his face in a washing motion, smoothing them back over the short fuzz on his scalp, and finishing with his hands clasped behind his head.

'Shit,' he said. But he was reconciled.

Cath Young brought Clemence up from the cells. She took in the cut over Clemence's eyebrow; the police surgeon had put a butterfly plaster on it, because of the danger of it splitting again, and she could tell from the slow, careful way he moved that there was more damage that she could not see. 'What happened to you?' she asked.

Clemence glanced down at her. 'Won't you love me no more if I'm scarred?'

'I doubt if your own *mother* loved you, Clemence.'

'And to think when we first met you had your hands all over me.'

'Yeah,' she said. 'But not in a good way.' She ushered him through the interview room door, feeling pleased with herself. Less than a year ago, she wouldn't have had an answer for Clemence's innuendo. Now . . . well, now things were different.

Barton started by asking Clemence how he got his injuries, reasoning that he might as well get the issue out into the open at the outset.

Clemence flipped a look at Young. 'Sweets here beat the shite out of me in the cells.'

'*For the record*—'

'Spare me, Sarge,' Clemence groaned. 'It was a *joke*, right.'

'So,' Barton said, remaining calm. 'Would you like to tell us how you did come by the injuries listed by the police surgeon in his report.'

'Come by them? Like it was something I popped out for to the local "Eight-Till-Late"?'

Barton heard the resentment in Clemence's voice, and prepared himself for a revelation.

'All right,' Clemence said. 'I'll tell you.' He left a pause, in which he held Barton's gaze. Then he switched his attention back to Young and began speaking, as if he expected her to take out a notebook and start scribbling madly. 'I tripped over a kerbstone.' he said. 'The pavements round my end of town are in a criminal state.' He blinked, once. 'I might sue the council.'

Young glanced at Barton. Surely he wasn't going to leave it at that? The sergeant took a breath to speak, but Young got in before him: 'You're asking us to believe that you split your eye open, and got two cracked ribs, and severe bruising to your buttocks and back from tripping over an uneven flag?'

'You had a sly squint at the Polaroids, did you, DC Young?' Clemence asked.

'I think you were in a fight,' Young said, furious to feel herself blushing.

Clemence's face changed. It wasn't that his expression hardened, it seemed that his face lost all expression. It became cold, flat, unreadable. 'I couldn't give a shit what you think,' he said.

'Where were you last night?' Barton asked.

'What time?'

Barton saw the gleam in Clemence's eye and returned his stare with comparative equanimity. 'Let's start around ten o'clock and go on from there.'

'Start of my shift,' Clemence said, daring him to contradict him. 'I was at work.'

'Your boss paid you off last night. At the start of your shift,' Young said.

'Oh, yeah. That's right. Thanks for reminding me.' He still had that dead look on his face.

'So where did you go?' Barton forced himself to ask, refusing to be intimidated into silence.

'Where would *you* go?' He left enough of a gap to remind Barton that they had gone to exactly the same places last night. 'I mean, if you'd been sacked.' Another, not very subtle reference to Barton's predicament.

'We're different people,' Barton said. 'Very different. Which is why I'm asking the question.'

'Well your *questions* lost me my job,' Clemence said.

'Didn't take much, did it?' Young commented.

'Mouthy bitch, isn't she?'

Young smiled, unperturbed. 'You left work at ten past ten. Where did you go after that?'

For a long moment the tape reel turned and nobody spoke.

'I went into town.'

Barton took a breath.

Clemence stared hard at him. 'Bumped into an old acquaintance, unexpected.'

Barton's eyes moved from Clemence's scraped and bruised knuckles to his face. *Here it comes*, he thought.

'Give us a name, we'll see if he's willing to corroborate your story,' Young said.

A slow smile spread across Clemence's face. 'Would he?' he said, still looking at Barton. 'I doubt it.'

'Give us the name,' Young repeated. 'We'll try him.'

Clemence made a pantomime of trying to recall the name. 'Began with a B, I think. Baker . . . Baxter – something like that.' He screwed up his eyes and focused on a corner of the room. For a brief moment, his expression brightened, then he frowned again. 'Nah . . . it's gone.'

Barton exhaled slowly and deeply through his nose. The danger wasn't over yet. Not by a long way. 'Okay,' he said. 'Your neighbours heard you return home between eleven-thirty and midnight.'

'Great!' Clemence threw up his hands and let them fall with a smack on his thighs. 'They're talking to my neighbours, now!' His solicitor tilted his head: he was sympathetic, but it was only to be expected.

'But you weren't home at five a.m., when the officers called.'

Clemence's anger moderated somewhat and he became wary. 'What are you trying to pin on me now?'

'Where were you between midnight and five a.m.?'

'Out.'

Quartermaine cleared his throat, and Clemence took this as a sign that he would have to say something more. 'I went for a walk. About half three. Took a stroll by the river.'

'Can anyone corroborate this?'

'Not many people about that time of the morning.'

'Strange time to go for a walk.'

'I work nights. My sleeping time is during the day.'

'Nobody saw you?'

'I've just said.'

Clemence looked angry, but Barton thought he saw an edge of anxiety. *He knows what we're building to, and he can't account for his whereabouts.* He made a mental note to congratulate the night team leader for getting someone out to Clemence's so quickly.

*Get him to tell another lie. Something we can use against him.* 'All right. You walked down to the river. Then what?'

'I don't get you.'

'Three-thirty to eleven-fifteen. That's nearly eight hours. Surely you weren't walking all that time?'

Clemence's eyes slid away from his face. 'Not the whole time. I stretched out and had a kip for a bit.'

'And nobody saw you.'

'I wouldn't know. I sleep with my eyes shut.'

'What time was this? When you went to sleep, I mean?'

Clemence held up his left arm, showing a bare wrist.

Barton nodded. 'Was it light? Early? Late? Were there people about?' He saw that Clemence was calculating the best answer to give: if he said there were people along the riverside, he would have to contradict his earlier statement. If he said he found somewhere quiet during the hours of darkness, they would want to know where he found such a place in a force nine gale.

Clemence shrugged. 'I was feeling pretty rough. Maybe I was concussed.' His hand strayed to the cut over his eye.

Barton clenched his teeth. *Slippery bastard.* Clemence gave the ghost of a smile. *He thinks he's won,* Barton thought. *He thinks that all he has to do is plead amnesia.*

'Perhaps,' Mr Quartermaine said, 'you would come to the point now, Sergeant. My client has been very patient, despite being in considerable discomfort. He has answered your questions to the best of his ability—'

'Mrs Tobin's house was broken into this morning.' Barton interrupted.

'And you think I did it?' Clemence puffed air between his lips.

'You just lost your job,' Barton said. 'Maybe you wanted to lash out at somebody.'

Clemence sat back in his chair and folded his arms, stifling a grunt of pain. 'You'll have to do better than that.'

'We can place you at the scene.' Clemence was thinking hard. Wondering who had seen him, what had he left behind.

'Your fingerprints are on damaged photographs, and on a sculpture in the back sitting-room.'

Barton read a moment of blind panic in Clemence's face.

'I was in her house – a few days back. It must've been – it was then.'

'*Must have been?*' Young repeated.

'It *was*. I remember.'

She nodded. 'Mrs Tobin told us about your visit. She told us what you said to her. Every word. She virtually disinfected the place after you left.'

'And I thought we'd hit it off so well.'

Barton had had just about as much of Clemence as he could stomach. 'I'll tell you what I think,' he said. 'I think you had a bad night. Got drunk. Got yourself into a ruck you couldn't handle and needed to take it out on someone. You knew you wouldn't get away with roughing Mrs Tobin up – after all, her husband was at home – so you thought you'd rough up her life instead.'

Clemence didn't answer immediately. Barton thought he saw a flash of anger, but it was quickly quelled, then Clemence said, 'How would you know what sort of night I had?'

*Does he expect me to answer that? Or is he just reminding me that I was part of his 'bad night'?*

Clemence's mouth twitched. 'I mean, you didn't see the other guy . . . did you?' The implication was there, in the pause, in the rising inflection of his tone; it said,

*You were there, Barton, and if you push me too hard, I'm
gonna let everyone know it.*

'Give us something we can believe,' he said, shoving
the threat back at Clemence, *My word against yours,
pal. And who d'you think the courts will believe?*

Clemence moved forward, leaning with clenched
fists on the interview room table. 'I *went* for a walk,'
he repeated, barely in control of his anger now. 'If that
tight-arsed bitch had her way, I'd still be banged up at
night.'

Barton lifted his eyebrows. *She's not the only one.* 'All
right, Mr Clemence,' he said. 'Let's just take it that you
can't account for your whereabouts at the time Mrs
Tobin's house was being broken into.' He didn't wait
for a response. 'You recall that when you were arrested
on Monday, you were in possession of a sports bag
containing a blood-soaked T-shirt?'

'You've already asked me about this.' He turned
around to his solicitor. 'He's already asked me about this.'

'The blood has been matched to Amy Dennis.'

'So you said.'

'Can you account for the T-shirt being in your
possession?'

For a moment, Barton thought he was going to go
through the irritating repetition of 'I don't know,' that
he had resorted to the previous night, but it seemed
that the beating had softened Clemence up a little,
because he chewed the side of his mouth for a while
then began haltingly: 'I . . .'

Barton waited. *Even he knows how stupid this is going
to sound.*

'I found it,' Clemence said.

'You found it?'

Clemence put a hand to his neck and shifted in his seat again. 'In my bag.'

Barton paused, thinking. 'And you don't know how it got there. Are you *prone* to concussion, Clemence?' Quartermaine started to bluster and he apologised.

Clemence stared resentfully at the table-top; he suddenly seemed to be finding it hard to maintain eye contact.

'A hammer was found near Miss Dennis's house yesterday,' Barton went on. 'A claw-hammer.' Clemence's nostrils flared and a muscle jumped in his jaw. *He knows what's coming, all right.* 'Analysis of blood and hair found on the head of the hammer show that it was almost certainly used to kill Miss Dennis.'

Clemence didn't speak; he seemed to be bracing himself for what was to come next.

'Fingerprints found on the shaft match yours, Mr Clemence.'

If the chair hadn't been bolted to the floor, it would have shot back a foot. As it was, the metal frame creaked and gave with the force of Clemence pushing away from the table.

There was a breathless silence. The two police officers tensed, ready to grab Clemence if he kicked off.

'Do you have anything to say?'

Clemence continued staring at the table for a full minute, then slowly, he looked up at Barton. At first his gaze was unfocused, as if he had been day-dreaming, drifted off somewhere remote and dark, but as he fixed on the sergeant, it crystallised into a look of cold hatred.

# 30

'Boss?' Thorpe stood at Steve Lawson's office door.

His desk was elbow-deep in reports and more were coming in all the time: house-to-house, interviews with Amy's colleagues and her students, the new line of enquiry resulting from the burglary of the Tobin's house. He looked up and Thorpe jerked a thumb over his shoulder.

'There's a barrister downstairs, wanting to talk to Clemence.'

'Quartermaine's appointed Counsel already?'

Thorpe shrugged – he was just carrying the message.

Lawson felt mildly encouraged: if Quartermaine had instructed Counsel even before they had charged Clemence, it meant that they were making more of an impact in their interviews than it appeared.

'Is DS Barton still interviewing him?' he asked.

'Quartermaine started on about Clemence working nights and his injuries and all. He's on a rest-break.'

'I suppose he knows his client was prowling the streets through the night?'

'Clemence says it's his normal routine. Says he gets his kip between midday and eight at night.'

'Except when he's doing photo-shoots in Grosvenor

Park,' Lawson muttered, but their hands were tied. If there was any hint that Clemence had not been afforded his rights, there was a risk that Counsel would argue that any admissions were gained under duress. He couldn't refuse Clemence access to Counsel, but an interruption in his rest-break meant the rest period would have to be started over again. An additional eight hours brought him dangerously close to twenty-four hours in custody. And it wasn't unknown for some lawyers to play the game of manipulating the PACE clock, in which case, he might decide to have a three-hour 'consultation' with Clemence as the minutes ticked away. Lawson sighed.

'I'll see McAteer, ask him to get the superintendent to authorise another twelve hours.' He rolled down his shirt-sleeves and straightened his tie. 'Who's the barrister?' he asked.

'Clara Pascal.'

Lawson stopped in the action of fastening his cuff. 'I see,' he said. But in truth, he didn't. Why would Clara Pascal want to represent a man like Clemence? He had heard she wasn't even practising criminal law any more.

Seeing her was a shock. She had lost weight since they had last met. She sat in the interviewee's chair, facing the door of interview room 2, as if terrified that it would slam shut and cut her off from light and air. Too dark in the custody area, he thought. Too many steel doors, too many locks.

'Are you all right?' She was pale and the skin around her nostrils looked pinched.

She shook her head. 'The heat,' she said dismissively.

'I meant . . .' He hesitated, suddenly awkward – he barely knew her, after all. 'Are you coping?'

'Oh.' She seemed to struggle with herself for a moment. *She's used to giving the stock answer. Telling people she's fine, when she really wants to scream.* When she finally looked up at him, there was warmth and – what? Gratitude? Yes, he thought, perhaps gratitude – in her eyes.

'Well, I'm not *over* it,' she said with a self-deprecating smile. 'But coping? Yes, I suppose so.'

He nodded. It was far more complicated than picking up the pieces and carrying on. What happened to Clara had left a gaping hole that had to be filled and patched and tamped down. Is that why she's here? He understood the need – the urge to face down your demons by confronting what you most feared. He had done it himself, since the events of the previous autumn, going into front line positions where firearms were in use, just to test his nerve, just to see if he could still do the job without flinching.

'You wanted to see Ian Clemence?' he asked.

She nodded, a stiff, jerky movement. *She's not sure if she does want to see him,* he thought, *but she thinks she should.*

'You have been briefed?'

'I've read the notes.'

Lawson didn't catch the almost-lie and he put the slight hesitation before she answered as an indication that she knew what Clemence had done to Vicky Rees

– knew it and was appalled by the brutality of it. Nevertheless, he had to ask, 'So you know his previous form . . .'

Another stiff little nod, her jaw clamped shut.

Lawson loosened his tie and sat on the chair that Mr Quartermaine had occupied less than fifteen minutes earlier. 'Look, Clara,' he said. 'If you're thinking of coming back into criminal law, this may be a bad one to start with. The evidence against him is very persuasive and Clemence . . . he's not the easiest of people.'

She relaxed, even smiled. 'I always enjoyed a challenge, Steve.'

Clemence was shown into the interview room and the door was closed. Clara gritted her teeth. *You can't very well have a client consultation with the entire nick listening in,* she told herself. As a distraction, she focused on Clemence. He was not as she had imagined him – not at all the milky prison white she had expected, but he had been out for two months. Nor was he as gaunt as the newspaper pictures she had pored over. *He works out.* The Police Surgeon's report only told half the story. The way he moved, the occasional grunt of pain, told her that Clemence had taken a severe beating. She would not, however, ask him what had happened. That would shift the emphasis: she was here as a representative of authority; she wouldn't take on the role of carer.

'You look wasted,' he said.

*First Lawson, now him. God, I really must look rough.*

'Well, I'm all in one piece, Mr Clemence.'

'This?' His finger traced the cut over his eye. 'It'll be healed in time for committal.'

'We call it PDH, these days.'

He looked at her in question.

'Pleas and Directions Hearing.'

He lifted his chin slightly, filing away this new piece of information.

Clara's eyes were drawn to a tattoo on his left arm: the name *Vicky* and a broken heart; roughly executed. A prison tattoo, the sort done with a sewing needle and biro ink. She leaned across the desk and offered her hand. His was callused; he spent a *lot* of time working out. She thought about the time and effort and determination needed to build a physique like Clemence's and wondered if this was a man prone to obsessions.

'My name is Clara Pascal.' She saw a flicker of recognition. *He knows me, and he's intrigued.* She had seen it a dozen times before: the eager, even hungry look that came over them when they realised they were close to someone with her notoriety.

'Is that a problem?' she asked.

'The custody sergeant just told me my barrister was here to see me. He didn't give a name. I wasn't expecting . . .' He gestured with his upturned palm: her face, her hair, her body. 'Is it a problem? Not for me, it isn't.'

His lazy, insolent manner offended Clara and she felt the need to puncture his ego. 'He told you I was your barrister?' She dipped her head, an insincere mark of regret. 'I haven't decided to take your case, yet, Mr Clemence.'

'So how did you . . .? You mean you bluffed your way in here?' He laughed. 'I like your style.' He watched her closely for a little while. 'So what is this? One exhibit looking at another through the bars of its cage and thinking, "Funny creatures they have at this zoo."?'

'Let's call this an interview,' she said. 'You get the opportunity to sound me out, see if you want me to represent you.'

He was about to speak, but she went on, 'But first, *you* have to convince *me* of your innocence.' Even as she spoke, she knew she was making a mistake. Why was she doing this? To prove she could still do the job?

He narrowed his eyes at her. 'This is a joke, right?'

'I'm not known to be a barrel of laughs, Mr Clemence.'

'I don't have to convince you of anything,' he said. 'You're supposed to defend me. That's it.'

'Right now,' Clara was astonished that she was persisting in this, but she had made a promise to Pippa, so she took a breath and went on: 'Right now, you have no legal representation. The CPS are already building a strong case against you. If you want me to take you on, that's the deal. Convince me.'

'My defence lawyer in my *murder trial* didn't even ask me that,' he said.

She turned. 'Well maybe he should have.'

'What the hell does that mean?' They glared at each other.

'You pleaded not guilty.'

'Yeah . . .'

'But you were – guilty, I mean.'

'That's . . . ' He struggled to express himself. 'You're making it sound too simple.'

'Sometimes it is that simple,' she said. 'Sometimes it really is a question of innocence or guilt.'

'And you're saying if I did it once, it stands to reason I must be guilty now – is that it?'

Clara lifted one shoulder. 'Guilt has a way of tainting a person,' she said

'This is all crap, isn't it?' He shook his head, confused. 'You don't give a shit if I'm innocent – you've just got to convince the jury I am.' He stood, and Clara was almost overcome by the realisation of the potential danger: she was in a small room with a murderer, and she was quite deliberately pissing him off. She set down her pen and laid her hand flat on the table so he couldn't see it trembling.

'It's your job to be clever,' he went on, '– make clever arguments, get people on your side. It's what you do. It's what you enjoy doing.'

'You think you know me, Mr Clemence?' She spoke quietly, injecting a contempt into her voice she did not feel.

'I lost a lucrative case because of you. So by my reckoning, you owe me. And if you don't convince me to defend you, I might just get myself appointed by the CPS to prosecute the case instead.' It was an outrageous lie, since Peter Telford had already been appointed, and Mr Warrington was not likely to change his mind and let her take such a high-profile case based on recent performance, but a man who didn't know a committal from a PDH would not necessarily know that. *If you can bluff an ex-con, you haven't really lost it – is that it, Clara?* And besides, Clemence had frightened her and she wanted to put the fear of God into him. *Vengeance, Clara?* her inner voice demanded. *Vengeance has no place in the criminal justice system.* She silenced its sneering jibes by saying:

'You know my reputation, Mr Clemence. I'm good. I could get you convicted.'

She saw a flash of something sharp, dangerous in his eye, then he looked away, seemed almost chastened. 'I meant lawyers . . .' He paused, then muttered, 'The arguments – the word games – it's what lawyers do. Isn't it?'

Clara was surprised and a little gratified. She had got so used to being afraid of men that she had forgotten what it felt like to be in authority – or more accurately, to be confident in her own authority.

She stared at him for a long time, allowing the silence to answer his question. She had pushed this man harder than she had dared push any client in nearly a year. 'So what's it going to be, Mr Clemence? Should I go away and start building the case against you, or are you going to try to convince me?'

————◆————

## 31

'This is going to get nasty.' Cath Young was reading the *Evening Echo*. Thorpe handed her a mug of coffee and read over her shoulder.

## AMY MURDER: MAN HELD
### Police swoop after 'new lead'

**Police have rearrested a man questioned over the death of freelance photographer Amy Dennis after the discovery of 'new evidence'.**

Detective Chief Inspector McAteer, who is leading the enquiry, would neither confirm nor deny that the 'new lead' is the hammer used to batter the pretty thirty-year-old mum to death.

Milkman Mark Tidswell made the horrific find early on Monday morning on his milk-round. Amy's eleven-month-old daughter is believed to have been in an upstairs room when the attack took place.

The man was taken to Castle Square police station after a police vigil outside his house in Hoole. He is believed to be a paroled murderer, and local people are outraged that he was released without charge after an earlier interview.

'Women aren't safe with animals like that on the loose,' said angry resident, Gavin Jessop.

A strong police presence at Castle Square Station has fuelled fears that local unrest could spark a vigilante-style backlash in this tight-knit community.

'Like the choice of feature story they're running alongside?' She held up the paper for Thorpe to read. Below the main news story was a streamer:

## LICENCE TO KILL?
### Katie Yarrop asks: is sentencing soft on killers?

'Another in-depth report from the Chester *Evening Echo*,' Thorpe muttered.

'They've dragged up half a dozen cases from all over the country,' she said, turning the pages. The centre spread, usually given over to the evening's television, bore photographs of six men. Above their grim faces, the banner headline:

## RELEASED TO KILL AND KILL AGAIN

Below each picture, a catalogue of the crimes they had committed after early release.

'Feel sorry for him, do you?' Fletcher asked, through a mouthful of corned beef sandwich.

'Lay off, Fletch,' Thorpe warned.

'All I'm saying is, some lasses get off on that sort of thing: bad boys, dangerous men.'

Young made the briefest eye contact with Thorpe. That look signalled the clearest message: 'Stay out of this, I can handle it.'

She didn't answer Fletcher at first, merely looked at him. When she was satisfied that he was sufficiently uncomfortable under her scrutiny, she said, 'It's bad enough fighting through the press scrum. Half of Chester will know where to find him now – here, or back at his flat. It'll hamper the investigation.'

Fletcher switched his vitriol to Lawson: he had seen the glint in Young's eye and this was safer territory, since the boss was safely out of earshot in his office. 'If Lawson lets him go after this,' he said, 'he's a bigger fool than I thought he was.'

'The point *is* Fletch,' she said with exaggerated patience, 'Every wide-boy, bad lad, hard man and pot-bellied prat with something to prove will be out to get him – or at least to get their ugly mugs on the telly.'

Fletcher stared at her, chewing slowly; she held his gaze, hoping he knew that the snipe about pot-bellied prats was for him and him alone.

Clemence lay back on the blue plastic cover of the mattress in his cell and laced his fingers together behind his head. He thought he might just be onto a good thing with Clara Pascal. He liked her. He wasn't sure why; maybe it was the fact she had been prepared to lie to get a look at him. Perhaps it was the way she talked straight and looked him in the eye. She had a good rep among the cons – or bad, depending on whether she'd been prosecuting or defending their case. Fact was, she generally won. Even the men she had defended who were given a custodial said she'd managed to get them off a stiffer sentence.

*You've got to play this cool*, he told himself. He was beginning to get the hang of this perspective thing. From *her* perspective, he was a hard case, a wildcard, someone she couldn't trust. He would have to convince her. *But you won't do it by coming over all earnest.* Lawyers like Clara Pascal were immune to ex-cons bleating about their innocence.

Which meant he would have to figure out some other way to make her see what a regular stand-up guy he was. He thought about this for a long time, watching a jumping spider making slow progress across the ceiling, its jerky spurts of movement making it look like a clockwork toy.

*She's clever*, he thought. And clever bints – in his sadly limited experience – didn't like to be told things. They liked to think they had worked it all out for themselves. You had to take the long view. You had to be patient. And if you couldn't learn patience Inside, you ended up seriously twisted.

He could be patient.

The first few months of his prison sentence was in a Young Offenders Institution. One month in withdrawal, with bouts of stomach cramps and diarrhoea like he thought he must have dysentery. Nights spent sweating and shivering in turns, absolutely convinced that he was dying. The next four months he spent stoned on tranx and anti-depressants. He was skinny then. Skinny and soft: an easy target.

Dex Wyatt was cock of the wing. Built like a brick shithouse and twice as ugly. He did what he wanted, took what he wanted and nobody dared stop him. He decided he wanted Clemence's food. So he would sit opposite and jab his fork into whatever took his fancy on Clemence's plate. Of course Clemence complained – he wasn't so far gone that he would let someone take the food out of his mouth without comment – but Dex sorted out that problem by breaking two of his ribs and snapping his little finger. Clemence still couldn't grip weights properly with his right hand.

Dex moved up to adult prison a month before him, but Clemence never forgot him. Dex had a special place in his heart. He waited four years, weaned himself off the tranx, lifted weights, made endless rounds of the gym, shadow-boxing and jogging, eating as well as you ever could on prison food, all because he hadn't forgotten Dex.

He had told the story in an anger management group. To them, Dex was just another con. He didn't give a name: what went on in anger management was confidential, and the counsellor encouraged them to 'take risks', as he called it, but only a fool would give all the facts. He opened up enough to stay in the group, but his instincts were to cover his back. His counsellor asked if he thought he had been preparing for that meeting with Dex. At the time, he told himself that he was lifting weights, putting on muscle, so no one else would try to push him around. But when it happened – when he turned that corner and came face to face with Dex – it was like every pound of iron lifted, every ounce of muscle gained, was all for that moment.

Dex pulled up short. His eyes flicked up to Clemence's face and then away. No apology, but he did step aside, and as Clemence walked past, he felt Dex's eyes again on his face. When Clemence looked back he caught a glimmer of recognition, a tremor of fear. Because Dex wasn't top dog no more. He was the skinny, pimply smack-head and Clemence was the hard man.

That one look kept him going for weeks. Dex kept out of his way but that was all right: Clemence stayed cool, waited his opportunity, knowing that sooner or later, it would come.

Dex got careless. He was already on the downward spiral by then. He'd take anything he could get his hands on: acid, dope – tranx when he couldn't get anything stronger – and coke. Dex loved his nose-candy; made him feel like he used to when he was still cock of the wing, Clemence supposed. But he wasn't above crushing aspirin and snorting the powder if he couldn't get the real thing.

Association time you might have three prison officers guarding three hundred inmates, so order was maintained with prisoner co-operation and screws didn't bother you if you didn't look like you were out for trouble – sometimes not even then. Clemence watched from his own landing, as he had watched for forty-three days, waiting for Dex to make his mistake.

Dex scored and scuttled back to his cell like a fat kid

greedily hiding a bag of sweets. Clemence waited – another thirty seconds wasn't going to hurt after four years of waiting. Thirty seconds: long enough for Dex to get to his cell and begin the ritual that Clemence knew from experience was so absorbing that you forgot everything else – including being careful. He stuck his hands in his pockets and walked slow. Even gave one of the screws a friendly nod as they edged past each other on the narrow walkway.

Dex was on the landing below. His cell door was pulled to. Clemence opened it. Dex was on the top bunk, a square of foil in his hands. He was halfway through opening it; the hungry, gleeful look on his face changed to annoyance at the interruption.

He started to say something then saw it was Clemence and his eyes widened. A muscle at the side of his mouth did a little jig – couldn't make up its mind if it was a twitch or a smile.

He tried again. This time got the words out. 'All right, Ian, lad.' Like they were old mates or something.

Clemence closed the door behind him.

The twitch became a definite tremor. Dex was crapping himself. 'You're not still mad, are you?'

Clemence didn't answer.

'All that was a long time ago,' Dex said. 'We was just kids.'

Clemence visualised the first blow. That was the first time he became aware that he visualised his attacks. He'd always done it before, but he hadn't really *thought* about it. He put it down to the eerie calm he felt at that moment.

'Hey,' Dex said, his voice trembling now. 'I've got some good gear. Why don't we share?'

Good old Dex – still wanting to share after all those years. Clemence smiled and he could see from his face that Dex knew for sure he was in deep shit. His eyes darted around the room, looking for an escape route, a suitable weapon. Even so, he carefully refolded the little square of foil and slipped it into his pocket.

Clemence knew his hand wouldn't come out empty. He grabbed Dex's wrist and pulled him forward, off the bed. The knife clattered to the floor, skittering under the radiator. His right fist cannoned up to meet Dex's face, smashing the right cheekbone. After that, he didn't resist.

Clemence used his fists, knees, elbows, working quietly and efficiently. He'd read somewhere that forensics could match footprints to bruising, which was the only reason he didn't use his feet, but he worked Dex over good. He didn't speak. Didn't utter a single word. Didn't explain why – Dex knew why; words were unnecessary.

The screws found the shiv under the radiator pipes. They found the little silver wrap and they drew their own conclusions.

Clemence was never in the frame: he had never told anyone about Dex, he wasn't into the drugs scene and Dex wasn't talking to anyone. The joke on the wing was he'd got himself beat up for the chance to mainline some quality morph in intensive care.

These days, Dex was a complete fuck-up. Prison worked that way sometimes: straightened some men out and screwed others up good style. Clemence was sure if he hadn't been sent down, he would be dead by now, drugs overdose or stabbed for a five-pound fix by some other sorry loser.

The spider had made its way in spurts from the middle of the ceiling to the top right corner. Slow and steady. *All right,* he thought. *I'm banged up now, but with Ms Pascal's help, maybe not for long.* The trick was not to try and gain her trust all in one go. Give her time to eyeball you, let her do the hard work.

He puffed air between his lips. It was almost funny: the reason he liked her, he discovered, was because she was cautious. She wasn't the usual pushy barrister type, sweeping in with a lot of bluster and telling you what's what; she circled and watched and tested the air like an old con.

# 32

—◆—

DC Young felt Fletcher's eyes on her throughout the telephone call. She finished and hung up, swivelling her chair to face him full-on.

'Did I just grow an extra head or something?'

Fletcher seemed momentarily disconcerted. 'You're interviewing Sebastian Enderby's wife?'

Young thought she heard a slight stress on 'you're'. 'Think you could do a better job?' she asked.

He flushed slightly, emphasising the doughy pallor of his skin. She'd give him two years, tops, before he had his first coronary.

'I just don't get it. What's Enderby got to do with Amy?'

'We don't know yet, Fletch,' she said, deliberately adopting a weary, patronising tone. 'That's why I'm going to talk to her.' Chris Thorpe had told her about Fletcher's new nickname for her, and she felt a mischievous compulsion to live up to it. 'But Amy did take his picture, and he was fronting one of the most favoured bids for the Dee View Development project – before he got shot in the head, that is.'

'He was mugged.'

'He was shot. Motive unknown.'

'They're different cases,' he said. 'Totally separate.'

'Are they?' she asked sharply. 'Know that for a fact do you, Fletch?'

He shrugged, picking up his phone receiver and skimming down the list in front of him. 'If you want to waste your time, help yourself.'

She let him have the last word for now, but as she flashed him an insincere smile and walked to the door, she knew that they would return to this topic of conversation at a later date.

After ten minutes with Mrs Enderby, she was beginning to wonder if Fletch had been right for once in his life. Her husband made the money and she spent it was pretty much how things worked within her rarefied social stratum. It occurred to Young that you don't have to understand the laws of thermodynamics to be able to drive a car, but she was frankly appalled by the level of ignorance that Mrs Enderby was happy to not only admit to, but work at, almost as an ideal to be achieved.

'You've no idea where he got the money for his share in the bid?' She had asked the question minutes before, she just couldn't believe a wife would have no idea and even less interest in how her husband managed to raise a million pounds for a business deal.

'I told you, we didn't discuss money.'

They were sitting in the visitors' room of the ICU. The TV hulked in one corner, grey and hooded, making occasional cracking sounds as if in complaint at being turned off.

Mrs Enderby plucked a tissue from the box on the low pine table and dabbed at her eyes, careful not to smudge her mascara. Young looked at her, wondering at her glossy good looks. Despite days of almost constant bedside vigil, her make-up was perfect and her hair carefully tinted, teased and waxed; she looked like she had been polished and buffed to achieve her healthy glow.

Mrs Enderby sat up suddenly, remembering something, and the bangles on her wrist clacked. 'He said he was thinking of mortgaging the house.'

'And did he?'

Mrs Enderby looked into Young's face, her eyes watering picturesquely. 'I don't know.'

'How much is the house worth?'

She shrugged. 'Four-two-five? Four-fifty?'

*Four-hundred-and-fifty thousand pounds.* 'Weren't you concerned that your husband was risking your home on this deal?'

'Sebastian is a businessman,' Mrs Enderby answered simply. 'He has to take risks.'

'Okay . . . But even if he remortgaged the house for half a million, it'd still leave him shy of another half million.'

Mrs Enderby's brow furrowed. 'I told you: we didn't—'

'Discuss money. I know, you said.'

Mrs Enderby was offended. She stood, smoothing her skirt demurely. 'I think I'd like to go back to my husband now, Constable,' she said. 'If you want to know about money, you should speak to Sebastian's bank manager.'

'I will,' Young said. That didn't produce a reaction, so she went on, 'Did he seem worried about anything? The deal – other business?'

'He had just been awarded Businessman of the Year – what could he possibly be worried about?'

There was no arguing with blind logic like that, so Young didn't try. 'Amy Dennis – the journalist who was murdered? She spoke to your husband before the dinner . . .'

Mrs Enderby frowned in irritation. 'The woman who was taking photographs? She spoke to all the nominees. So what?'

'Mr Enderby didn't seem . . . uneasy afterwards?'

'I *told* you—'

Young thought she saw a tantrum coming on, so she broke in, 'All right. Tell me what happened when you left the dinner.'

'I've already been through this with the other officers.'

'I have to hear it for myself.'

She seemed to consider refusing for a few moments, then changed her mind and sat back down and clasped her hands in her lap, turning her wedding ring round and round on her finger.

'We went home. I made Sebastian a nightcap. We went to bed. It was all very ordinary.'

'And he didn't seem anxious, distant – any different from normal?'

Mrs Enderby stared at her ring, as if willing it to give her strength. 'We'd had a lovely evening, and Sebastian had been honoured and I wasn't really paying attention. I wish I had, but I really can't *remember* . . .'

This time the composure almost fell away and Young got a glimpse of the pain she was feeling. She realised that the perfect hair-style and carefully applied make-up were Mrs Enderby's way of keeping herself together, of being strong for her husband's sake.

*Shit*, Young thought, I really am a superbitch. Maybe Fletch was right about that, too. 'Look,' she said gently, 'I know this is difficult for you, but we want to find the man who shot your husband. So if you think of anything, get in touch with me.' She handed Mrs Enderby her card. 'Anything at all,' she said.

# 33

The phone rang immediately Lawson replaced the receiver in its cradle. Clara Pascal had arrived.

He took her to the canteen and they sipped coffee as they talked.

'Why is he still in custody, Steve?'

'There's a lot of evidence—'

'*What* evidence?' Clara exclaimed. 'It's all circumstantial.'

'It's compelling,' he said. 'And now we have the burglary at Mr and Mrs Tobin's house.'

Clara raised her eyebrows. 'And Mr Tobin says he locked the back gate from the inside before he went to bed. My client has two cracked ribs and severe bruising all over his body. How d'you suppose he scaled a six-foot fence in his condition?'

'We don't know *when* he sustained his injuries,' Lawson said.

Clara bit her lip; she knew that it was impossible to pinpoint the time when the injuries occurred, and since her client was not co-operating in this matter, the police were free to draw whatever conclusions they liked.

'Has his solicitor been informed?' she asked.

'Yes, of course . . .'

She heard the surprise in his tone, the implied criticism: *Don't you stay in touch?*

In fact, Quartermaine knew she was coming to see Clemence; she had told him the previous night. She and Brent Quartermaine had worked together a lot, in the past: he had a reputation for taking on hopeless cases, and Clara for winning them; they were a natural pairing.

She had telephoned immediately after her interview with Clemence, sitting in her car parked in the road outside her own house, listening to Pippa's laughter rising like birdsong from the back garden. Her intention was simply to ask if he had anyone in mind for the defence.

'Why?' he asked with characteristic forthrightness, 'Are you interested?' No intimation that this was a tough one, no suggestion that she might not be up to it – just a straight question. For this, Clara was grateful.

Perhaps it was gratitude that made her say, 'I might be.' Perhaps it was the promise she had made to Pippa. Either way, it was insane: she would be pitting herself against her old rival, and it had been her determination to prove herself equal to Peter Telford that had got her into the mess she was in at present. Reason deserted her, on this occasion; the timidity that had paralysed her during the winter and spring and early summer fled, and 'I might', became, 'I am', and from there it was a short step to accepting the case.

'I'll send the bundle over to you by courier,' he said. 'You'll have it first thing.'

Clara mumbled a guilty 'Thanks'. She'd already had the prosecution's version of the notes from her clerk. 'I'll go in and see him in the morning,' she added.

'No need,' Quartermaine said. 'I'll keep you up to date with developments.'

'No, it's fine,' she said. 'I'd like to see him.'

'There's really no need,' Quartermaine insisted.

'I would like to see him tomorrow,' Clara said equally firmly.

There was a short, offended silence at the other end of the line. 'Well don't expect Legal Aid to pay out astronomical sums because you don't trust me to do my job,' he said.

'Brent,' she said. 'I'm sorry. Of course I trust you. If you want the truth, I don't trust *myself* any more.'

Clara looked up as Clemence was shown into the interview room. The bruising to his face was ripening to an angry purple and his eye looked more swollen and puffy. He moved stiffly and sat with great care, but as soon as the custody sergeant left, he stood and began pacing with restless aggression.

'You know the police are considering charging you with the burglary at the Tobins' house,' Clara said.

'That's bullshit.'

'That they're thinking of charging you, or the charge itself?' He turned and looked at her. 'Just so we're clear.'

He thought about it for a moment, then she thought she saw a mental shrug and he said, 'I might've touched some stuff when I visited her place.'

' "Might have" is not *terribly* persuasive,' Clara said. 'And one has to wonder who else could have broken in to the house. Who else would *want* to?'

He shrugged. 'I wouldn't know.' He stopped next to the table and leaned with his back to the wall. Clara should have asked him to sit down, but she was finding it hard enough just keeping her breathing steady in the claustrophobic space, without having to confront Clemence as well.

'You knew Amy Dennis, and she's been murdered.' Clara spoke as if she was thinking aloud. 'You took photographs of both Amy and Mrs Tobin.'

'The pictures of Amy aren't mine.'

'So you say. You pestered Mrs Tobin with phone calls—'

'I made a couple of calls – since when has that been a crime?'

'When it's coupled with watching the person concerned, sitting outside her house in your car. Taking pictures of her. Showing up uninvited.'

'I just wanted to ask her advice.'

Clara leaned her elbows on the table. 'You frightened her half to death.'

Clemence blew air through his nose. 'She's neurotic.'

Clara stared at him. Did he hold all women in contempt, or was it just Mrs Tobin? Reluctantly, she acknowledged that he was right, in this much at least – Diane Tobin was neurotic. Perhaps she was also prone to hysterical outbursts – perhaps she overreacted when she saw Clemence on her doorstep. 'Did you threaten her?' she asked.

His expression changed to sudden, cold anger. 'Is that what she said?'

Clara leaned back in her chair; an involuntary, defensive gesture. 'She was terrified.'

'Yeah, well, that's her problem.'

'No, Mr Clemence. It's your problem. You're aggressive and you're physically intimidating.'

'It's an advantage in the nick.'

'But not in the dock.'

His eyes widened. 'Aren't you jumping the gun a bit? I haven't even been charged yet!'

Clara paused. 'How long, d'you think, before you are?'

He closed his eyes and Clara sensed that he was counting slowly.

'Got a cigarette?'

'I don't smoke.'

He seemed amused. 'I don't want a smoking buddy, Ms Pascal.' There was a brief silence, then he said, 'God, I could kill for a fag.' He opened his eyes and Clara saw amusement in them. 'Figure of speech.'

'You have a warped sense of humour, Mr Clemence,' she said. 'Now we need to talk about specifics. The bloody T-shirt, the murder weapon with your fingerprints all over it, the photographs of Mrs Tobin and Amy Dennis.'

'Have you got the pictures in that shiny bag of yours?' He jerked his head, indicating her briefcase.

Clara nodded. 'Copies. Why?'

'I want to show you something.' She handed him the two sets and he sat down, placing selected shots side by side. 'The evidence is here in the pictures – you've just gotta know where to look. See the grainy quality on these?' He indicated the photographs of Amy Dennis. 'Shit camera. One of those multipurpose pocket jobs with integral zoom. See the blur?'

Clara leaned closer. Some of the shots of Amy lacked focus.

'Wrong shutter speed,' he explained. 'He's in the shade, she's in the sun. You can't alter the shutter speed manually on cheapo cameras, can't change the aperture. So when she moves, you get blurring.'

'So?'

He looked up at the ceiling and exhaled impatiently. 'Have you seen my camera?'

Clara visualised it – evidence number and all. 'I've seen it.'

'My camera isn't *capable* of taking shite like this.'

She shrugged. 'So you used a different camera.'

'What, you mean I took a few snapshots on a crappy-snappy kiddie camera and hid them in my flat? What for? So I could double-bluff my defence if I got caught? Think too much about that one, your head'll explode.'

Clara had the sense that she was being bamboozled. 'What about the T-shirt?' she demanded. 'How did that turn up in your flat?'

'Same way the pictures did,' he said.

She thought about this for a moment. 'Oh, *really*, Mr Clemence! Are you asking me to believe this is a set-up?'

He pulled his arm back in an imitation of a gambler

at a fruit machine. '*Kerr-ching!* Counsel for the defence hits the jackpot.'

'Steve Lawson?' Clara smiled, despite herself. 'A set-up?'

'Sorry,' he said, 'Didn't know you were pals.'

Clara shrugged. 'We're not friends, but I *do* know Inspector Lawson,' she said. 'He wouldn't—'

'Right,' Clemence interrupted. 'He's with the good guys.'

'He wouldn't tamper with evidence,' she insisted.

Clemence snorted. 'Come off it, Counsel. Everyone does something bent sometime in their life.'

Clara raised her eyebrows. 'Really?'

He gave a short laugh. 'Can you swear you never fixed things to strengthen a case?'

Clara met him eye-to-eye. 'I never needed to. Juries decide on the arguments. Who presents the best case.'

He smiled. 'All you're saying is there's different ways of fixing a case – legal ways and illegal ways. It still amounts to the same thing though, doesn't it?'

That hurt. He was only telling her what she had been saying herself for the past nine months, but she didn't want to hear it from a convicted killer. He had cornered her, manipulated her into defending the legal process, and she hadn't done it well – in fact, she had talked herself into a dead end – and she lashed out, more to get back at Clemence than to get at the truth.

'Your fingerprints are all over the murder weapon,' she said. 'You wrote creepy letters to Amy Dennis before she died. You've more or less admitted to stalking Mrs Tobin.'

'Have I *bollocks* . . .'

'In all but name,' Clara returned evenly. 'Your fingerprints are all over her house.'

'So why's there nothing in Amy's house?'

'The killer wore gloves. Latex gloves. The kind the police found in your dark-room.'

'Yeah? Well it's not just villains who wear latex gloves. Police wear them. Forensics teams wear them.'

'Lawson wouldn't fix evidence,' Clara replied doggedly.

He held her gaze for a few seconds longer. 'So how did they get the photographs? The T-shirt – and what about the hammer?'

'The hammer,' Clara repeated. 'Indeed, yes, what about the hammer?'

He watched her quietly until she spoke again. 'We will have to make a case that somebody took a hammer that you used perfectly innocently. That they used it to kill Amy Dennis and then they left it close to the murder scene, knowing that the police would find it.'

He gave a half-smile. 'You've got me convinced.'

*How can he make a joke of it?* 'The jury won't be quite so trusting,' she said. 'They'll wonder where this mysterious *someone* could have got a claw-hammer with your fingerprints on it.'

He folded his arms, then winced slightly and rested his hands on the table, catching his breath. Clara had interviewed too many hard men to make the mistake of showing sympathy: if he was unwilling to tell her how he got his injuries, then she was unwilling to acknowledge that he was in pain.

There was an ashtray on the table, a red metal disk with crimped edges like a pork pie. He fiddled with this for a few seconds, then began batting it back and forth between his hands as he thought. Suddenly, his head snapped up.

'Wait a minute –' He picked up the ashtray and held it between his index and median finger. 'I did a few alterations around my flat when I first moved in. Fitted a new skirting-board. Completely gutted the kitchen when I fixed it up as my dark-room. I borrowed Walker's toolkit for that – he's the landlord. He had two kinds of hammer, but one of them was definitely a claw-hammer.'

'And why would he want to frame you for a murder?' Clara asked.

'Who says he did? There's plenty of people wouldn't be sorry to see me go back inside. All I'm saying is he's got keys to my flat, and he's been in a few times, snouting through my stuff – I know when the little rat's been in – he leaves a stink behind him. Wouldn't put it past him to let your friendly copper in for a few tenners, turn a blind eye while he plants a few bits of incriminating evidence. But I was forgetting: Mr Lawson's incorruptible, isn't he?'

*He's too slick by half*, Clara thought. *He hasn't just remembered borrowing the hammer – he was ready with it, waiting his chance to tell me.*

He glanced away under her continued and intense scrutiny. 'DS Barton hates my guts,' he said with a shrug. 'You know he was the arresting officer when . . .' He left the rest unsaid.

'He wouldn't risk bribing the landlord.'

'I wouldn't count on it.' He put the ashtray down and stared at it as if trying to divine his future from it. 'All right,' he said. 'How about this? My flat's on the ground floor. Sash window with a simple catch. You can open them with a penknife. And the lock's shot on my flat door. Lean on it and it pops like bubble-wrap.'

'You refitted the kitchen, you put expensive developing equipment in there but you didn't think to replace a faulty lock on your door?'

'I didn't say that. I thought about it all right, but the landlord wouldn't let me change it.'

Clara wasn't convinced. Mr Clemence didn't strike her as the sort of man who would be easily dissuaded once he had made up his mind on a particular course of action. 'I'll get Inspector Lawson to check it out,' she said. 'See if the landlord is missing a hammer. But it still doesn't account for all the other evidence.'

Clemence rubbed a hand over his face, grunting when he caught a tender spot and pressing the area gently, exploring the extent of the damage.

'Sod it,' he said. 'Don't bother. It'd look worse for me if old ratface *was* a claw-hammer short of a toolkit.' He shrugged at her disapproving look. 'You don't think it's funny? You should see it from my side – it's fucking hilarious.'

Clara searched his face: she couldn't decide whether his hubris was an attempt to mask his frustration – even anxiety – or if it reflected a basic lack of human feeling.

'I don't know who I'm kidding,' he went on. 'I killed

her. Stands to reason. I've killed before, haven't I? It must've been me.'

*Well, since he brought it up* . . . 'Why did you kill her?' She made the question deliberately ambiguous.

'It's none of your damn business.'

He seemed annoyed that his play for sympathy hadn't had the desired effect.

'People find all sorts of ways to excuse what they've done,' Clara said. 'Some even claim they don't remember what happened.' She maintained deliberate, insulting eye contact. He returned a look of bland incomprehension but he straightened up a little, as if bracing himself against her searching gaze.

'You know what I think?'

Clemence looked at her through half-closed eyes. 'You know what? I can't bring myself to give a toss.' Clara got the odd but very real feeling that he was visualising what he could do to her even before she moved a finger to hit the panic button.

She exhaled slowly and deeply, forcing herself to hold his gaze. 'I think killers claim amnesia because they're so ashamed of what they've done. It's so much easier to pretend it didn't happen if you claim you can't remember what you did. Killing is a tremendously powerful act. For some, it's the first time in their lives they've felt in control. Of course, they can't *admit* to that, so they say it was beyond their control.'

'Yeah?' he said. 'Well, you'd know all about that, Ms Pascal.'

Clara tensed. *The prison grapevine: more reliable than the World Service.*

He brought the back of his hand to his face and smoothed a line along his jaw. His fingers rasped against a night's growth of stubble. 'Only difference is,' he went on, 'In my case there was one victim, one crime. A bloody corpse and a murder weapon. Easy to point the finger. Easy to punish.'

Clara looked away. He had a point. 'You're right,' she agreed. 'People died because of my arrogance and ambition. I was driven. It made me careless. But what about you? What made you beat your girlfriend to death?'

She spoke harshly, establishing eye contact again, trying to rouse Clemence to an honest reaction. Right now, she did not know if he was innocent or guilty – once, it wouldn't have mattered to her, but now it did. If she believed he killed Amy, she would drop the case. If she dropped the case it would probably signal the end of her career in the practice of criminal law, because everyone in the profession would think she had lost her nerve.

He stood the ashtray on its end and gave it a twist. It spun unevenly on its scalloped edge for a few moments. Clemence watched its collapse, waiting for it to rattle to stillness before answering.

'Like I said – none of your business.' He allowed the silence to lengthen, mocking and challenging her. She stared at him, trying to make him out. Failing.

'I don't understand you, Mr Clemence,' she said. 'I don't understand you at all.'

He gazed back at her, his expression unreadable. 'No . . . you don't,' he said.

\* \* \*

After she'd gone, he thought about her for hours. You could do that inside: think for hours; in fact, he'd found it hard to cope with all the distractions once he was out – another reason why he liked the solitude of the darkroom.

Clara interested him. It wasn't like she was the sort to tell you all about herself at the drop of a hat, so the fact she had been so honest meant something. It hurt her saying those things, telling him she felt responsible for those people dying. But it wasn't like she was asking him to feel sorry for her, or trying to get him to like her; it was an exchange – of ideas, maybe of secrets, too.

He analysed their conversation. She was right: he was too aggressive, but it was hard going, cooped up in a cell, trying to stay cool and be nice to your Counsel, when she didn't believe a word you said.

He'd been an idiot, thinking Diane Tobin would be any use to him, and if he hadn't approached her, would the filth ever have made the connection with Amy Dennis? Diane Tobin's bleating had glued the bastards to his tail.

*Who are you trying to kid, Clemence? If you hadn't panicked, they would never've got hold of the T-shirt. If you'd left it till after dark, been a bit more careful, you could've slipped out of the house, dumped the T-shirt in the Dee along with the bag and nobody would have been any the wiser. They would've still knocked on the door, but without a warrant, the bag would've been safe –* you *would've been safe.*

He put his head in his hands, but thought better of it when the stitches over his eye gave a stab of pain.

Exploring again with his fingertips, he could tell that the flesh around his eye socket was puffy and swollen, but the cut had scabbed.

*That'll look good, going into a committal hearing with a black eye and stitches. How're you going to convince the judge you're no threat to society – safe to be released into the community – when you look like you've just gone five rounds with Lennox Lewis?*

He could just see Clara saying, 'My client was involved in a simple street brawl, Your Honour. Boys will be boys. No harm done.' Except he wasn't a boy no more, and harm *had* been done. Harm he would want repayment for, at some stage. No hurry.

Truth was, he couldn't see Clara taking a stand for him. He couldn't see her standing up in court at all, on his behalf.

*So get yourself another lawyer.*

But it wasn't that simple. Everyone in the country knew Clara Pascal. Everyone knew what she had been through. If Clara Pascal represented him, the jury's sympathies would be with her, and through her, with him. The problem was, that thing – body language, 'physical threat' hadn't she called it? – it was something he didn't even know he was doing half the time. It made people wary, and it made her more than that – it made her dislike him. So he'd succeeded in putting a barrier between him and the one person who could get him out.

*Nice one, mate. Now what are you going to do about it?*

What could he do, but wait? Wait and watch and stay calm.

\*     \*     \*

A fan juddered back and forth, riffling loose sheets of paper and flirting with the wisps of hair that curled at Clara's temples. Clara sat at her desk in Diva Legal Services, reading through her notes, scanning rapidly, pausing when her eye caught some significant detail, scratching in her own impenetrable shorthand.

Hugo recognised the pen her father had given her when she passed her bar exams and he recognised what it signified. It was fragile, battered with age, and Clara only used it when she had a particularly difficult case – when she too was feeling fragile. She called it her 'comforter'.

Her stillness – one might even say her serenity as she worked – was in such contrast to her recent nervous agitation that Hugo felt compelled to leave her undisturbed. The door stood wide, not, he suspected, to improve ventilation, but to beat back the terror of confinement that Clara had not yet mastered and he was pierced with pity for her.

He filled the doorway, blocking the light, and she glanced up absently, a frown dimpling the space between her eyebrows.

'Hugo?' She murmured his name, as she did from time to time in her sleep, and his instinctive response was to reassure her. This time, however, he did not.

He had tanned a little and the blue of his eyes was sharper, more clear against the golden warmth of his skin. She smiled at him, remembering the heat of him on the night of the storm, his gentle strength as he held her, and the taste of salt on his skin, but he did not return her smile.

'I had a call from your clerk,' he said.

'Fliss?'

'Nesta Lewis, at Jericho Chambers. She found some notes she'd forgotten to pass on. Thought you might need them for your case.'

'Oh.' Her shoulders sagged. 'The case . . .'

'When were you going to tell me?'

'Hugo, I—'

'Were you waiting for me to read about your opening statement in the papers?'

Clara closed her eyes and pinched the flesh at the bridge of her nose. 'I haven't taken the case, Hugo. Not yet.'

'*Not yet?*'

'We're . . .' She struggled for the right term, realising how exhausted she was, how little sleep she'd had in the past few days. 'We're in negotiations.' She tried a little smile; tired, self-mocking. 'Anyway, I thought you wanted me to take on criminal law again.'

'There are different levels of crime, Clara. Burglars, car thieves, shoplifters. Why do you have to start with a murder?'

*Because I finished with one?* She didn't say it, but Hugo pushed her for an answer. 'Is it the glamour? The media attention? Why would you expose yourself like this?'

Clara felt a spurt of anger. This was unfair. 'One murder pays better than half a dozen shoplifters,' she said, her voice hard with resentment.

He didn't reply, but she knew the jibe had found its mark. Since her abduction, she sometimes marvelled at

Hugo's gentleness. Despite his size and strength, she had never felt physically intimidated by him, so the hurt in his expression was more painful to her.

'I'm trying to find a way through this, Hugo,' she added more gently.

'All right,' he said, straightening up, ready to leave. 'But be careful you don't lose us on the way.'

He seemed almost preternaturally calm, and this frightened Clara more than if he had lost his temper with her. She felt that he was detaching himself, as one might gently disentangle oneself from an unwanted embrace.

# 34

Marcia Liddle showed Clara through to her consulting room. The evening was sultry and hot, and on the golf course only a couple of die-hards remained, sweltering in the evening sunshine.

'It's good of you to see me at such short notice,' Clara said. She had explained her dilemma briefly over the phone.

Marcia inclined her head. 'It sounded urgent.'

'I just don't know what to do.'

'Clara, I'm a therapist, not a life coach. You should discuss this with your family.'

'I'm afraid I've messed that one up already.'

Marcia waited for an explanation.

'Hugo found out before I'd had the chance to discuss it with him.'

'Did you intend to? Discuss it, I mean?'

Clara put a hand to her neck, it was cold and she realised that she was trembling. Marcia waved her to the chair nearest the window and sat opposite, her facial expression and body language conveying absolute attentiveness.

'To be honest,' Clara said, 'I kept putting it off.'

'Don't you think Hugo can help you with this?'

'I'm not sure he wants to.'

'Perhaps if you asked him, you'd have a clearer idea.'

Clara felt a surge of anger 'I just told you it's too late for that. *Good God*, Marcia! If all you're going to do is state the bloody obvious I might just as well have not come!'

Marcia was silent for a few moments and Clara blushed, ashamed of her outburst. 'I'm sorry,' she said. 'It's hot and I'm tired and I think I'm losing him.'

'Do you see why?' Marcia asked, apparently unruffled. 'You're with your family, now. With friends. You don't have to be angry and you don't have to fight. It only alienates them and isolates you.'

'It gets me out of bed in the morning – it gives me the courage to go out in the street.'

Marcia smiled. 'Then we'll just have to find a more appropriate motivator.'

Clara closed her eyes and felt a buffeting draft of warm air against her cheek. It would be so easy just to lie down and never get up again. It took so much energy to do even the simplest things, and everything seemed futile.

'I can't give them what they want, Marcia. I can't be who they want me to be.'

'What do you think they want?'

'What they've always wanted: Hugo wants me to be his wife again; Pippa wants me to be her mother.'

'Is that so bad?'

Clara gripped the arms of the chair. 'I'm not *capable* of that any more. I'm too tired. I'm too ashamed.'

Marcia leaned forward in her chair. '*Ashamed*? Of what?'

Clara hadn't meant to say that, and she didn't know where to begin. She struggled, making several false starts, but Marcia encouraged her and she tried once more, 'I treated the practice of law like a game – a competition. I set myself challenges and took risks I should never have taken.

'I liked to think of myself as *charismatic*.' She shook her head, in disbelief at her own arrogance. 'Half the time, I didn't see the people I represented – beyond their potential to make me look good.'

'Harsh criticisms,' Marcia said, raising her eyebrows. 'Seems to me you're most angry with yourself.'

Clara thought about this. 'Yes,' she agreed. 'I suppose I am.'

'Then why take on this case – if you still feel that you should have managed things differently, why go back to criminal law?'

Clara shrugged. 'I need the money.' It was true, but it wasn't honest, and Clara could see from Marcia's face, that she wasn't taken in by the lie.

'It's not an easy case.'

'No.' Clara looked at her hands to avoid having to meet her therapist's gaze.

'I suppose if you pull this one off, you could do just about anything.' Clara didn't answer. She found it hard to see further than the next five minutes, so the prospect of a future in which she could 'do anything' was well beyond her imagination. Marcia was silent for a short while, then she took a breath.

'But you're also more likely to fail than if you took a less demanding brief.'

Clara looked up. 'You think I'm setting myself up to fail?'

'Are you?'

'Why would I?'

'It'd get Hugo off your back once and for all.'

Clara sat in silent thought, listening to the birdsong outside the window and watching the two golfers on the hill, wilting in the heat. 'I don't *think* that's the reason,' she said, hearing the uncertainty in her voice.

Marcia waited.

'Doing the reading, researching his background – going to see Ian Clemence today . . .' She paused, trying to disentangle the confusion of emotions she felt. 'I'm more fired up than I've been in months. It feels – it feels like I'm doing something worthwhile – I know that sounds awful – family cases are just as important, but . . .'

'It just doesn't give the same buzz.' Marcia nodded. 'There's nothing wrong with that, Clara. We each have our own strengths, our own spheres of interest. Why not enjoy what you're doing?'

'Because it's selfish?'

'So what, if you're doing some good?' She seemed to consider a moment, as if weighing her words. 'Let me give you an example. I trained as a child psychologist,' she said. 'Worked for education authorities and health authorities for the first five years after I qualified. But I felt constantly frustrated. It wasn't until I started working with adults that I realised what I'd been missing. And I think I've done my best work since specialising in this field.'

'You're saying I don't have to be worthy to be useful,' Clara said. 'I used to believe that. But –' She hesitated to say it, because Marcia might take it as a personal criticism.

'Go on, Clara,' she urged. 'I'm thick-skinned.'

Clara raised her shoulders apologetically. 'It seems . . . hypocritical.'

'Isn't it more hypocritical doing family law because you think you ought to?'

'Ouch.'

'It's what you pay me for, Clara,' Marcia said. 'To ask the difficult questions you haven't the courage to ask yourself.'

Clara sighed. 'I'm still stuck with making this decision, though, aren't I?' She stood, and offered her hand to Marcia. Marcia took it, placing her left hand warmly on Clara's shoulder.

'It isn't too late, Clara. But the clock is ticking. Don't lock your family out.'

Clara nodded.

'And no matter what you decide, you've made great steps with your therapy,' Marcia added, her eyes twinkling with amusement.

Clara frowned.

'You're way ahead of my schedule on the homework tasks,' Marcia said, her voice full of mischief. 'Going into a police station, braving the cells. Tackling a convicted murderer on your own. I'd never have suggested any of those things so early in your therapy.'

'Great,' Clara said, suppressing a smile. 'Now I'm using a major criminal investigation as therapy.'

Marcia laughed. 'I've always felt that all our positive experiences in life are therapy.' She winced slightly. 'That sounds like the sermonising at the end of a chat show, doesn't it? What I'm trying to say is that people find strength and encouragement and reasons to go on in the strangest places.'

# 35

The later editions of the evening papers all carried the same photograph of Amy Dennis, dressed in a suit, her right hand raised, keys at the ready, about to open the front door of a house. She looked over her shoulder, as if anxious that she was being watched. The picture was cropped closely: just the door frame and the lock; no clues to the location. Maybe it was her own house, maybe not.

The evening debrief began in a strained silence. They all knew what was coming. Most had seen the papers and even those that hadn't could feel the electricity in the room like an impending thunderclap.

McAteer positioned himself front and centre and he did a slow, thorough scan of the room. This one, hard look was enough to disabuse anyone of the misapprehension that the DCI was a soft touch.

He held up a copy of the *Evening Echo*. There was a restless shuffle and then the team subsided. 'Look at the headline, ladies and gentlemen.'

## AMY SNAPS FOUND IN SUSPECT'S FLAT

Next to the photograph was more speculation about Clemence's previous conviction.

'I believe that this photograph came from the batch we found at Clemence's flat,' McAteer said. 'I believe that an officer on this team sold it to the local press. I have no doubt it will appear in the national tabloids tomorrow.'

He placed the newspaper on the desk in front of him and smoothed the image flat. Nobody spoke. Nobody even breathed.

'Now I will make you a promise,' he said. 'I will find out who stole the photograph. And I will prosecute them to the full extent of the law.'

Silence. A few officers gazed at McAteer's face, but the majority avoided eye contact – with him and with each other. Someone was going to pay a very heavy penalty for this, and judging by the look on McAteer's face, he was determined it wasn't going to be him. Someone coughed and there was a stutter of noise like a shudder or a sigh.

'DC Young.'

Cath Young spilt her coffee setting the cup down. 'Sorry, sir. What?'

'I understand you spoke to Mrs Enderby today. Would you like to share your thoughts with us?' Nobody laughed. They were just glad that McAteer's sarcasm was directed at somebody else, rather than them.

Young outlined her interview with Enderby's wife. 'She's convinced it was a mugging, sir,' she concluded. 'The business end of town was pretty much deserted when he was attacked. A couple caught a glimpse of the shooter: tall masked man. Dark clothes. He was too far away for anything more accurate.'

McAteer nodded, impatient to move on; he knew all of this from the SIO who was leading the investigation. 'What about his association with Amy? Did they speak at the Awards?'

'No more than she did to any of the other business people. She said he didn't seem worried . . .'

'Is she reliable?'

Young grimaced. 'I think he could've been mainlining valium and she wouldn't have noticed. I've asked for copies of his bank statements, but it could take a day or two for the permissions to come through.'

Chris Thorpe was called on next to report back.

'Amy was working on a reportage – a kind of start-to-finish photo-journal of the development.'

DC Gordon chipped in: 'Her photo files back that up. There's a lot of stuff on the development: pictures of the site, designs submitted by the bidders, that kind of thing.'

Thorpe nodded. 'Amy talked to her editor on Monday,' he said. 'She told him she might have something more juicy than a photo-journal to offer.'

'Details?' McAteer asked.

'Sorry, Boss. She said she had to talk to someone first. Told him she'd go in to the *Echo* office first thing on Tuesday – give him the full story. I could talk to some of the journos who were at the Chamber of Commerce Awards – she might've let something slip.'

'Good idea,' McAteer said. 'Get onto it tomorrow morning.'

Thorpe scratched his eyebrow. 'I could make a start tonight, Boss,' he said, with an earnestness so uncharacteristic that a few people turned around to see what he was up to. 'A lot of them call in at "The Paparazzi" for a swift half on the way home.'

Nobody laughed, but it went some way to defusing the tension in the room.

Lawson saw that McAteer wasn't willing to give any ground and he stepped in: in any investigation the morale of the team was a crucial factor, and it had just taken a hefty knock. 'Just don't let me see it on your expenses claim,' he said.

There were a few chuckles – not because it was a good joke, but because, by lightening the tone, Lawson was sending the message that he knew that only one of them had let the investigation down, the rest were doing all they could to find Amy's killer.

The remaining reports were given with greater formality than usual, everyone was scrupulously polite. The Incident Room emptied fast after McAteer closed the briefing: this wasn't the night for swapping anecdotes or grumbling about long hours. Someone had betrayed their trust and because of this, McAteer distrusted all of them. They resented his suspicion, but they resented the thief more – it wasn't a comfortable feeling, wondering if the officer you exchanged pleasantries with was selling evidence, thwarting the investigation, making fools of the entire team.

McAteer waited until the room was empty then he spoke in a low voice: 'I want an audit done, Steve. Everyone who touched the photographs from Clemence's flat. Anyone who was ever in the same *room* as them. And I want this one back.' He slapped his hand, palm down, on the picture of Amy.

'He'll still be here in the morning.' Fran Barton kissed the back of her husband's neck.

Barton watched his son's restless sleep. His arms twitched and his breathing was rapid and shallow, still congested after a summer cold.

'He's dreaming,' Barton whispered.

'Probably back kicking a ball about in Tumbletots today. You should have seen him.' She chuckled softly at the memory, slipping her arm around her husband's waist.

Barton leaned into the cot and stroked Timmy's cheek with one finger. The boy's eyes opened and he mumbled something. Barton shushed him and he drifted off again, more peacefully this time.

'Come *away*,' Fran urged. 'You'll wake him.'

'He's hot.'

'The temperature outside is still in the twenties – what do you expect? Now stop fretting and come *on*!' She pulled him from the room, leaving the door open a crack.

'Are you sure he hasn't got a fever?' Barton asked, turning again to his son's bedroom.

'Phil, he's *fine*. We're both fine.'

He looked into his wife's face. She always could read him. 'I'm sorry,' he said. 'It's this case . . .'

'I know.' She took his hand and led him downstairs.

They ate supper in the sitting-room with the TV volume turned down. Fran made several attempts at small talk, but Barton couldn't concentrate. At work, he could be dispassionate, think coolly about the situation, but here at home, with his wife beside him and his son sleeping in his cot upstairs, he kept returning to the morning he had found Amy Dennis's little girl, remembering how he had crept up the stairs with sunlight streaming into the hallway and the smell of blood heavy in the air, dreading what he might see in the infant's bedroom.

'Do Social Services think she witnessed it?' Fran asked.

Barton looked up, startled.

'Well, you *were* thinking about the little girl, weren't you?'

He smiled despite himself. 'My wife, the mind-reader.'

Fran arched an eyebrow at him, still waiting for an answer.

He sighed. 'As far as they can tell, she's okay. She's with her grandparents – Amy's parents.'

'What do *you* think?'

He frowned. She wasn't going to let this go until he gave her a straight answer. 'All right,' he sighed. 'She wasn't distressed when I found her. She didn't seem fearful.'

'Well, there you are.'

'What's that supposed to mean?'

'It means you can stop worrying about her. She'll be okay.'

He shook his head. 'It isn't that simple. Some day she'll have to be told. Some day she'll know. What's she going to feel, Fran? A thing like that – what does it do to your view of the world?'

Fran set down her plate and slid up the sofa to him. 'She'll cope. She has people around her who love her.'

He lifted his chin; an equivocal gesture.

'And what's *that* supposed to mean?' she demanded. 'Yes? No? Maybe? I see your lips moving but I don't hear the words?'

Barton rubbed a hand over the close-shaved stubble of his scalp and sighed. 'It means you're probably right – as always.' Something on the TV screen caught his eye and he glanced away from her, simultaneously snatching up the remote control wand and increasing the volume.

A reporter stood outside Castle Square Police Station. '. . . As yet, the man has not been charged,' he said. 'But a source inside the station predicts that this could change at any moment.'

'*News at Ten*,' Barton murmured.

'So?'

'If it's on the *News at Ten*, it's harder to ignore.'

'Oh,' said Fran. 'You're thinking about the national tabloids flocking in like vultures to a kill. Will you move him?'

'I couldn't give a damn about Clemence.' His response was unintentionally sharp and Fran blinked.

'And what about the yobs who hot-foot it down there with their Berghauses bulging with ammunition, hoping to be immortalised on the front page of the *Sun*?'

'In amongst the mob, there'll be ordinary people, wanting to protect their own. People have a right to protection,' he said, his voice harsh with emotion. 'Vicky Rees won't be getting time off for good behaviour. Her family won't get parole from their grief.' It hurt him to think that as the focus shifted towards Amy stumbling on some kind of criminal conspiracy, the probability of Clemence being released became more real.

Fran stared at her husband. 'This isn't like you, Phil.'

'Maybe not.' Once more, his hand went to the fuzz of growth on his head. 'I'm tired. I need a bath. I haven't had a good night's sleep since this started, and maybe all of that has distorted my perspective. I can't look at this coldly, Fran – not after what he did to Vicky Rees. Not after seeing Amy Dennis's brains spattered over the walls of her front room. He's dangerous, and he belongs inside.'

'I believe you, love,' Fran said, placing one cool hand on his. 'I'm just saying he has a right to protection.'

'Society has a right to protection,' Barton said. 'Women like Diane Tobin have a right to protection.'

# 36

❖

Barton was the last to arrive on Saturday morning, looking pale and exhausted. Lawson wondered, not for the first time, if he was just too emotionally involved in this investigation. He did his job, but his dislike of Clemence might be a liability. He liked Phil Barton, they were friends, and taking him off the team would feel like a betrayal, so what could he do?

'Close the door, will you?' McAteer asked.

McAteer had commandeered a large room with a north-facing window, on the cool side of the building. Even so, at eight in the morning, it was uncomfortably hot. The sash had been thrown open and a fan stirred the syrupy air. Distant sounds of city traffic and the more insistent scream of house martins nesting in the eaves of the building opposite drifted in, along with the smell of hot tar and ozone.

'What've you got?' McAteer asked. He was dressed impeccably, as always, in a white shirt and green silk tie. His jacket hung on the back of his chair.

Barton took the offered seat next to Lawson.

'Fletcher, Thorpe and Young searched the flat,' he said. 'Thorpe logged the photos in at the property store.'

'Not Fletch?'

'Not Fletch.'

There was a pause. None of them, it seemed, had expected this.

'How many photographs were logged?' McAteer asked.

'Five,' Barton said.

'And how many has the exhibits officer got now?'

'Five.' Barton held up the evidence bag containing the original photographs.

'If there are none missing, how did the newspapers get this picture?' McAteer glanced at the morning paper. As he had predicted, all of the tabloids had used it on their front pages. Whoever had sold the picture must be making a tidy sum.

Barton cleared his throat. 'I scanned them into the computer after Fingerprints had checked them out, so we could produce copies as needed,' he explained. 'He could've sent the image over the Internet.'

McAteer sighed. 'If that's the case, anyone could have sent it.'

Lawson reached for the evidence bag. 'Let's have a look at them.'

They cleared a space in the clutter of reports and memos on the DCI's desk and spread the pictures out, comparing them with the one in the paper.

Lawson shook his head. 'None of them tally with the newspaper shot. Bastard must've kept one for the album.'

McAteer ran a hand through his hair. 'Nobody logged them out?'

'No, Guv,' Barton said. 'After Fingerprints had finished with them, there was no legitimate reason for anyone to take them out of store.'

McAteer sighed. 'Interview the officers who searched Clemence's flat,' he said. 'Under caution.' He glanced at the flimsy sheet Lawson had placed on the desk while he scrutinised the pictures. 'What's this?' he asked.

'A report from forensics on the hammer,' Lawson said.

'I've seen it. A match with Clemence's fingerprints and Amy's blood.'

Lawson dipped his head apologetically. 'This is new in,' he said. 'And it's not good.'

McAteer scanned the print-out. 'Damnit!' He slammed his palm down on the desk. 'Clemence's defence is going to love this.'

Barton tugged his ear. 'Since you mention her, sir, Ms Pascal is here, and she's asking to see a senior officer.'

McAteer sat down, suddenly looking tired and far less freshly laundered than when they had entered the room. 'Take care of it, will you, Steve?'

'How much do you want me to tell her?'

'About the leak to the press? Nothing, until I've spoken to Complaints and Discipline, and we've conducted the interviews. But you'd better give her the lab results. That should keep her happy for a bit.' He handed Lawson the fax, though from the expression on his face, it seemed he would rather rip it to shreds and eat the evidence.

'Do we move Clemence?' Lawson asked. 'There were a few locals outside the station this morning. It won't be long before they start baying for blood.'

McAteer thought for a moment. 'I'll see if I can arrange a cell at a secure station. But I want this sorted before we move him anywhere else – unless we plug the leak, chances are we'd be in the same position again by tonight.'

'I'll conduct the interviews myself,' Lawson said.

'And I want the missing photograph returned, gentlemen.'

'I spoke to the editor of the *Evening Echo*, earlier,' Barton said. 'He's arguing public right to know.'

'To which you of course replied that this is material evidence in a murder enquiry?' McAteer asked.

'They're pissed off because they helped out with the other line of enquiry,' he said.

McAteer frowned in question.

'The Dee View Development photo,' Barton explained '– they put a reporter onto identifying everyone in it. The way they see it, it's all take on our part and no give. We're not going to get the picture back using strong-arm tactics.'

'Suggestions?' McAteer said.

Lawson was prepared for this; he'd been thinking about it since Barton brought it up as they slurped a quick coffee before their meeting.

'Talk to the news editor,' Lawson suggested. 'See if we can get him on-side. Play the responsibility card. Offer the *Echo* an exclusive interview. They get a story out of it, and it makes them look like heroes. If they're uncooperative, let them know that we'll make sure the rest of the media finds out they're hampering our investigation. They love having a dig at each other on the morality issue.'

McAteer gave a curt nod. 'I'll call the Press Liaison Office after the briefing,' he said. 'And I'll have another chat with the SIO on the Enderby shooting – see if they've come up with anything concrete on Amy and Enderby.'

Young, Thorpe and Fletcher were separated prior to interview. Afterwards, DC Young was sent to DS Barton for the day's allocation. She went to pick up her jacket, avoiding the questioning looks of the few officers who remained to man the phones. DI Lawson was a tough interviewer, and he was evidently heftily brassed off with the three of them. She hadn't lied, but she hadn't exactly told him the whole truth, either. Not because she felt any allegiance to Fletcher, but she didn't want Chris Thorpe caught out in a lie – and she didn't want to break the rules of the game: if you don't know what the questions are for, you keep your mouth shut.

The light had changed from buttery yellow to a dusty gold as Young stepped out onto the car park. Ten in the morning, and already the day had a worn-out, dishevelled feel to it. The heat was intense and the air dense with humidity. She shrugged out of her jacket and steeled herself for climbing into the stifling heat of her car.

Chris Thorpe was ahead of her. His light-hearted

suggestion of the previous evening was forgotten; if he had found anything out about Amy from his reporter friends, he hadn't said so at the morning briefing. She could see that his fists were bunched and his shoulders slightly hunched and she guessed immediately who he was looking for. Fletch was already standing by his car, his keys in his hand.

Thorpe put a hand on Fletcher's shoulder and Fletcher whirled, startled and maybe a little frightened. They were too far away for her to hear, and Thorpe's voice was audible only as a low rumble, but Young could tell he was angry. Fletcher held up both his hands, the gesture unmistakable: *Leave me out of this*. He turned away and Thorpe grabbed his arm; Fletcher shook him off impatiently and got into his car.

Both interview rooms were occupied, so Barton had put Clara in the Parade Room, on the same floor as the office accommodation. Fifteen chairs were arranged in rows angled towards the far corner of the room where a TV and video unit were mounted on the wall. Clara paced the small triangle between the chairs and the walls.

'Ms Pascal?'

Clara stopped and turned to face Lawson, a look of mild surprise on her face. '*Ms Pascal*?' she repeated. 'You must be bringing bad news, Inspector.'

'No,' he said. 'You might consider it very good news, in fact. But first – you asked to speak to me . . .'

'I asked to speak to a senior officer,' Clara corrected, implying in her gently reproving tone that she would not presume upon their previous acquaintance.

Lawson inclined his head, accepting the distinction.

'I wanted to ask when you will be moving my client. There's already a small crowd outside, and from what I saw, it won't take much to get them stirred up.'

'Detective Chief Inspector McAteer has that in hand.'

'I assumed he would,' Clara said, again with that slight note of surprise in her voice. 'But I asked *when*.'

'We hope by this evening,' he said. 'But shouldn't Mr Quartermaine be dealing with this?'

'I think that's a matter for Mr Quartemaine and myself, don't you?'

Lawson was beginning to see how Clara had gained her reputation on the circuit. Taking his lead, she had fallen in with the formality of this exchange, but Lawson saw amusement, even playfulness behind her polite attention to the correct forms of address. For the Clara he had known last winter, he was glad; for himself, he was a little apprehensive.

She was watching him closely. 'Is something bothering you, Inspector?'

Time to come clean. 'We've had a supplementary report on the murder weapon.'

If he had detected any residual nervousness in Clara, any discomfort at being shut in an unfamiliar room, it vanished in that instant. Her gaze settled on him, still and intense. Excitement flashed briefly and was quelled.

He almost had to brace himself to say it. 'There's no blood on the handle.'

Only good manners prevented her from snatching

the copy of the lab report Lawson held in his hand. 'There was blood, bone, skin and brain tissue on the hammerhead,' she said, 'But *nothing* on the shaft?'

Lawson handed her the sheet of paper and she skimmed it, 'Nothing,' she said, 'But my client's finger-prints. Now, how d'you suppose such a messy attack could leave *no trace* on the handle of the weapon?'

'Scientific Support think the handle was wrapped in plastic,' he said. 'There are traces of tape and adhesive near the top of the shaft.'

'So all you *really* have is a hammer that at some time was handled by my client and which was subsequently used in the attack on Miss Dennis.'

'It just doesn't make *sense* to frame Clemence,' he said.

'You read my mind. But "sense" in exactly what context?'

'Why would anyone *want* to frame your client?' he asked, side-stepping the question.

'Why indeed?' She stared at him, her head slightly tilted, amusement shimmering like light in her eyes. Then she seemed to decide to play along.

'This is only a lay-person's speculation,' she said, with just the right note of insincere self-deprecation. 'But I can think of a couple of reasons: revenge is foremost – my client is the sort of man against whom people harbour grudges.'

Lawson's mind flashed to DS Barton.

'I'm less keen on the possibility of a double-cross – but I think you've already considered and disregarded that theory . . .'

Professional assassins don't frame others for their murders, Lawson thought. They move in, do the job quickly and cleanly and get out fast. They don't leave evidence lying around.

McAteer had gone to Helsby to talk to the SIO in charge of the case. They were agreed that Thorpe's information from Amy's editor made conspiracy a definite possibility. The Dee View project would make hundreds of millions for the successful bidders; a few thousand pounds to get rid of a troublesome journalist was pocket-money by comparison.

If she had expected him to fall apart under her interrogation, she would be disappointed: in his time, Lawson had created too many silences that others felt compelled to fill for him to be trapped into saying more than he intended.

Clara, it appeared, realised this. She nodded, and with a sigh, said, 'Well, you'll have to charge him or let him go soon.'

'Oh, we'll charge him all right,' Lawson said.

She seemed surprised. 'Your evidence is looking increasingly tenuous, Inspector. Do you think it likely that the CPS will support you?'

'In the charge of stalking? Yes.'

'Ah,' Clara nodded thoughtfully. 'Diane Tobin. Wouldn't that charge be just as flimsy?'

Had she forgotten the letters, the documented phone calls, the photographs Clemence had taken of Mrs Tobin? Lawson thought not, but he had come up against enough barristers to know that when the facts were against them, they relied on a combination of bluff and bluster. Make a statement with enough conviction and no matter how outrageous it was, they were in with a chance. It might not persuade everyone, might not even convince many, but when it came right down to it, they didn't *have* to convince many – only the twelve jurors, and they were pledged to give un-divided attention for the duration of the hearing.

She was still talking, and Lawson made himself listen.

'If Mr Clemence *was* stalking Mrs Tobin, wouldn't he focus solely on her? I'm not a psychologist, but isn't that how it works?'

'You're right,' Lawson said. 'You're not a psychol-ogist. And neither am I. I'm going on the evidence.'

'The evidence?' She shook her head in disbelief. 'Let's evaluate the "evidence". You say that Clemence was stalking Mrs Tobin – you can back it up with evidence. I would interpret the evidence rather differ-ently, but you would expect that. Ask yourself this: why would he stalk Amy at the same time? And if he *was* stalking Amy, why didn't she put in a complaint?'

'Mrs Tobin didn't complain either – at least not to us. It was pure chance that we found out Clemence had been harassing her. She kept it to herself – she was afraid of what he might do.'

'But if he was, indeed, fixated on Mrs Tobin, how could he divide that obsession between her and another woman? How was it that the T-shirt you found in Clemence's sports bag was drenched in blood and yet not a drop was found in his flat?'

'I'll let you know when we've completed this investigation,' Lawson said. 'Speaking of which . . .' He checked his watch.

'I know,' Clara said. The professional side of the discussion over, she became more relaxed, prepared to talk to Lawson as a man, as well as a police officer. 'You're busy and I'm being a monumental pain in the neck. I just don't want to see the wrong man go to prison.'

'None of us wants that,' he said. But the forensic report on the hammer played on his mind: why would Clemence go to the trouble of taping plastic over the shaft and yet fail to wipe his fingerprints off the murder weapon? Had he simply forgotten? He had known criminals to make more stupid mistakes than this. Or had he, as Clara suggested, been set up? It was possible – for a man just out of prison after twelve years inside, Clemence had succeeded in making an awful lot of enemies. Sacked from his job, harassing his ex-tutors – and just how *had* he come by his injuries on Wednesday night?

'How can I possibly convince you?' she asked, after the silence had gone on an uncomfortably long time.

'You're here to see him now?' She nodded. 'You might try to persuade your client to be a bit more co-operative.'

## 37

Clemence sat on a plastic-covered mattress on the tiled ledge that served as a bed, his eyes dark and unreadable. Clara hesitated at the threshold of his cell.

He had shaved; his hair was wet and glistening and the slightly sour air of his cell was overlaid by the scent of soap.

'Can't they find an interview room?' he demanded. 'I could do with a change of scene.'

She knew what he meant: cream glazed tiles, grey concrete floor. No windows. Her heart began a slow painful throbbing and she had to force herself to speak. 'Both interview rooms are occupied,' she said. 'There was a bit of a scuffle outside earlier.'

' "Bit of a scuffle"?' He grinned. 'You trying to spare my feelings, Ms Pascal?'

Clara didn't answer, but she didn't look away either, and this gave her the nerve to step inside the cell.

'Who's outside?' he asked.

How much should she tell him? *Well God forbid you should spare his feelings, Clara.* 'Press,' she said. 'TV, radio. And a crowd of local people.'

'A mob.'

'Not yet. At least not when I came in.'

'But they've already made a couple of arrests.'

'They're clamping down hard on any unruly behaviour.'

'Well, that's nice to know.'

Clara was beginning to see a pattern. She had been
trying to reassure him, but if Clemence felt he had
revealed too much about himself, he would retreat.
And he wasn't gentle, either; when Clemence wanted
you to back off, it felt something like a hard shove. A
hard shove and harder words: *Stay the hell away from
me. Get out of my face.*

Clara realised she had been staring at him and she
covered by asking, 'How are they treating you?'

'It's the Ritz, this place.' He spread his hands,
inviting her to admire his surroundings. 'Facilities
ensuite' – he nodded towards the three-foot-high modesty panel behind which was a toilet and a wash-basin.
'Breakfast in bed this morning. The works.'

Clara was determined not to let him rattle her. 'You
look – what was the word you used? Wasted.'

He released his grip on the mattress and his hand
fluttered briefly toward his face, then he let it drop and
looked at her, at once amused and aggressive. 'Police
surgeon tells me it's nothing paracetamol and a few
days' rest won't cure.'

The bruising had penetrated deep into the eye socket
and a blood vessel on his eyelid looked swollen and
engorged. More discoloration extended into his hairline at the temple and even the flesh of his cheekbone
looked tender.

'What aren't you telling me, Mr Clemence?'

'You're my counsel. I can tell you anything, right?'

A muscle twitched at the corner of her mouth.

'Oh, yeah,' he said. 'I was forgetting. You want the truth.'

Clara wasn't about to engage in verbal ping-pong, so she kept quiet and after a few seconds he shrugged. 'What makes you think I'm holding back?'

'Someone set you up—'

'I told you that,' he interrupted. 'I said that right from the start.'

'I agree – you were telling the truth about that much – so you must have given somebody a reason.'

'Maybe I did. Doesn't mean I know what it is.'

'Forgive me, Mr Clemence, but you're a liar.'

He lowered his head a little, maintaining eye contact with her. The effect was menacing.

'You're not giving me anything to work with, Mr Clemence. Give me some proof.'

His fingers kneaded the mattress, gripping and twisting, gripping and twisting. Clara waited.

'Tell me what you've got,' he said. She frowned and he went on, 'You reckon someone set me up. So something's happened, some new evidence, am I right?'

She thought about it for a moment. If she told him about the new lab report, it put him back in control. He had conceded nothing, so far. On the other hand, for the moment at least he was her client, and he did have a right to know.

She told him about the hammer.

He sat in silence for a full minute. Clara couldn't

read him. Was his pallor a sign of anger or fear? Or was he appalled to have made such a stupid mistake – covering the handle and preserving his own finger-prints on it?

At length, he stirred, let go of the mattress as if he suddenly realised what he was doing, and rested his hands on his thighs.

'I'd like to do your portrait,' he said.

'I *beg* your pardon?'

'I've taken hundreds of pictures,' he said. 'Men who learned the power of the fist and the foot at their mothers' teat. But I got something else out of them. They bury it deep, but sometimes, when they're off guard, when the light and the angle and time of day is just right, you see a faint shadow of it, like a fish just below the surface of a pond. You've got to be quick, but if you are, you can catch the melancholy, expose the guilt.' He paused. 'I never saw it in a woman before.'

'I find your tone offensive,' Clara said.

'I find your face intriguing.'

'That's it, Mr Clemence. I'm leaving.' She turned to the cell door as a commotion erupted in the corridor outside. An alarm sounded at the desk, a persistent, urgent buzz; someone had hit the panic button in one of the interview rooms. They heard the custody sergeant hurrying to help, then a loud splintering sound as a door was forced and angry voices exploded into the small space. Someone came out of the interview room – not police – and joined the mob.

'They've broken in,' Clemence said. 'They're inside.'

Clara felt a spiteful tingle of satisfaction seeing him afraid.

The custody sergeant was putting up a fight, but he was alone and his shouts were quickly silenced.

'Where the hell *is* everyone?'

'My guess?' Clemence replied. 'Out finding more shit to bury me.'

'Self-pity, Mr Clemence? This is a new tactic.' She reached for the door but Clemence leapt forward and slammed it shut.

'What the hell are you doing?' she demanded, her voice hoarse with fear.

He stood with his back to the door and Clara took a step away from him. 'Let me past.'

Clemence stood to one side and Clara realised that the door was locked.

Clemence smiled. 'No fire exits in this place. "In case of emergency break glass and use key". Doesn't work that way in here.'

'All right,' she said, trying to control the tremor in her voice. 'Let me get to the buzzer.'

'And bring those bastards down on me? No way.'

The roar of blood in Clara's ears almost drowned out the shouting beyond the cell door. Her lips were numb and she felt faint.

A man's voice rose above the rest. 'This way! Let's get the bastard!'

'*Shit!*'

'What?' The terror on Clemence's face brought Clara back to herself.

'Terry Spence – a tosser I used to work with. Jesus, they'll fucking crucify me.'

'What are we going to do?' Her control was slipping.

Clemence stared at her. He was breathing hard and sweat had broken out on his forehead. The men pounded on the door of the first cell in the row and suddenly he seemed to have purpose; he was frightened, still, but he was no longer paralysed by it. 'Take off your jacket,' he said.

'*What?*'

'You look like a lawyer with that thing on. Take off your jacket and try to look scared.'

If she hadn't been so terrified, she would have laughed. In the corridor, they heard the hatch of the cell next to them open. Shouts were exchanged.

'Look,' he said, his voice low and urgent. 'If they think you're on my side, what do you think they'll do? Terry hates my guts. He doesn't give a toss about right to representation. He sees you with me, you're fair game.'

Clara stripped off her jacket and messed up her hair. She kicked off her shoes and flung the jacket over the partition, giving Clemence something more to hide behind.

Clemence jammed himself between the plasterboard and the toilet bowl, grunting in pain when he caught his ribs a hefty blow. As he settled himself in the corner, the hatch opened.

'What's happening?' Clara demanded, her voice high-pitched, breathless.

The man at the hatch ignored her. He bent peering

in at the cell, trying to take in every angle. 'Fuck!' He stood, and all Clara could see through the hatch was his sweatshirt. Somebody shoved him aside and a second face appeared. At first he looked angry, then he grinned, an unpleasant, threatening leer.

'What you in for, love?'

'Either let me out or piss off.' She wasn't much of a mimic, but he seemed convinced by her attempt at a Cestrian accent.

His grin vanished and he stared at her coldly for a moment or two. 'Think I'll just piss off, then.'

They heard sirens as reinforcements arrived and seconds later the mob was gone, leaving behind a raw, angry silence.

'They're gone,' Clara said. Her voice sounded small and hollow in the unforgiving acoustics of the cell.

Clemence came out carefully. He was obviously in pain and he stood with his back to her for a few moments, slightly bent, leaning on the modesty panel for support.

She couldn't bear the silence. 'What now?' she asked.

'We wait for the cavalry.' He straightened up, turned to face her. 'Hope Terry and his mates don't torch the place.'

Clara whirled to the door. They had left the hatch open but she couldn't see any movement. She shouted for help. Nobody came. When she paused for breath she heard a groan: the custody sergeant.

'Why doesn't anybody *come*?'

'Take it easy,' he said.

But she couldn't. She couldn't bear to sit with a door shut in her own home; being locked in like this was intolerable. 'I've got to get out.' She tried the door, pulling at the hatch, shouting until she was hoarse.

'Hey,' he said. 'Hey, they'll come. Don't worry.'

She pressed her back to the door. 'You don't understand. I *can't* be here, I can't—' Her mouth flooded with something bitter and she flashed back to the cellar. It was damp, and when she looked, she saw – not the cream tiles and concrete floor of Clemence's cell – but dirty sandstone, oozing a slimy damp. Despite the heat of the day she felt cold.

'Hey,' he said again. He moved closer, his hands slightly spread, palms down, trying to calm her.

She cowered from him and he backed off, actually returning to the blue mattress and sitting down. 'You've got to think about other stuff,' he said. 'Talk to me. Tell me what's happening at home. You've got a little girl, yeah?'

His voice sounded far away.

'Tell me about your little girl.'

'I don't talk about my family.'

He laughed, and she looked at him, seeing him properly this time. 'Okay,' he said. 'Your choice of topic.'

'I've run out of things to talk about,' she said, unable to suppress a shiver. 'It's your turn.'

For a long time he was silent. At least, it seemed a long time, although when she thought about it later, Clara reckoned it could only have been only a minute. But a minute is sixty seconds, and sixty seconds is a long time locked in a cell with a murderer, with no help at hand and only a booming silence beyond the steel door. It is double sixty heartbeats, when you're afraid. She looked into his face and saw something she hadn't expected. Not pity, exactly, but something akin to it and far more powerful. He understood what she was going through, because he had been through it himself.

'All right,' he said. 'I'll tell you. If it stops you beating yourself bloody on that door, I'll tell you.'

Clara looked down at her hands; she had bruised them on the hatch, trying to lever the door open. When she looked up again, he glanced away, as if he wished to spare her feelings. She forced her hands to her sides, and stood to the left of the hatch, so that she could feel the faint warm stir of air movement in the corridor outside. She could hear, too the moans of the custody sergeant and she prayed they would come for him soon.

'I took some pictures,' Clemence said.

*Pornography*, Clara thought. *Sado-masochism. Blackmail.*

'Pictures of what?' she asked.

'What?' he echoed, then he realised the misunderstanding and laughed again. 'It's not what you're thinking, Ms Pascal. No exchange of bodily fluids involved. Though someone's getting screwed, that's for sure.'

'Don't talk in riddles, Mr Clemence. Who is in the photographs?'

He shrugged, looking past her through the square hatch into the corridor beyond. 'I don't know.'

'More lies?' she asked.

'Believe it or don't believe it. I don't give a shit. But I don't know the target. I was commissioned for this job.'

'By whom?'

'A guy I met in the nick a few years back.' He grunted. 'Said it was an insurance job. He was being ironic.'

'Why didn't you tell me this before?'

'I'm out on life licence, Ms Pascal. I get in any trouble, they can put me back inside to serve the full term.'

She laughed. 'You're facing a murder charge, Mr Clemence. Don't you think that's a bit more serious than taking a few photographs for an underworld pal?'

'No. But it's more complicated than that. I thought the pictures would be my insurance. He wanted the negs, of course but . . .'

'But you kept copies.'

He smiled faintly. 'I took an extra roll.'

She nodded. 'Did you think he would double-cross you?'

Clemence shrugged. 'It's like a reflex. You assume the worst in people, you're not gonna get disappointed. But there was something else.'

Clara had not forgotten that she was locked inside a deserted police station, but her need to know what Clemence was hiding overrode her fear. She didn't even hear the paramedics arrive with police back-up. 'Go on,' she urged.

Clemence shook his head. This time, when he stood and moved towards her she did not flinch. She was curious; she looked into his face as he reached outside and lifted the flap, holding it closed. 'The guy I took the pictures of. I think he's a cop.'

Clara exhaled. 'Hell . . .'

'My, um – boss is working on a big land deal right now. He needs to keep a low profile. He thought this guy was moonlighting – working for the opposition. Drawing attention to him.'

'A big land deal,' Clara repeated. The *only* land deal in Chester right now was the Dee View Development. 'And you don't know the police officer's name?'

He shook his head. 'The face is familiar, but I swear I don't know him.'

'What about your employer?'

Clemence looked away. 'No. Look, I give you his name – I grass him up – I'm dead meat.'

'Looks to me like he's already hung the carcass to ripen,' she said. Clemence looked puzzled and Clara sighed. 'Who d'you think set this up? Maybe this police officer planted evidence, but it's unlikely the decision was his. Isn't it more likely that your employer bribed or threatened him?'

Clemence swallowed.

'Work it out, Mr Clemence: if the man you took the pictures for has the power to blackmail or bribe a police officer, what do you think he could do to you?'

She knew she had got through to him, and a few seconds later, he spoke. 'Brendan Harris,' he said. 'It was Brendan Harris.'

'Harris . . .' Clara breathed. Hugo had told her something about him. He had made his fortune buying derelict properties and renovating them to minimum housing standards for student accommodation. Bad payers were evicted without recourse to the law.

'You evidently know the sort of man you're working for, Mr Clemence.'

'He pays on time and he pays well,' he replied doggedly.

'Two years ago, a building worker was encouraging the men to join a union. He fell from scaffolding on one of Harris's development sites. He died.'

Clemence avoided her eye.

'But you're right. Harris paid generous compensation to the widow. No quibbles, no fuss. The subject of union membership has never been broached since, though.'

Suddenly the hatch was dragged out of Clemence's fingertips; Clara heard a couple of fingernails splinter and Clemence swore.

A policeman peered in through the hatch. 'Everyone all right in there?' Neither Clara nor Clemence answered and he shrugged. 'We'll have you out in a jiffy,' he said.

Clemence held Clara's gaze. He waited until the hatch was clear then whispered, 'I needed the cash. I needed chemicals, developing kit – it all costs. And what I earned at the photo lab barely covered rent and food.'

Clara gritted her teeth. 'The roll of film. Where is it?'

He looked away.

Clara sighed impatiently. 'Mr Clemence, if you want me to get you out of this, you have to trust me. I'll try to find out who the police officer is. Find out exactly how deep in the mire you really are. Now where is the film?'

They heard footsteps returning and the scrape of a key in the lock. 'In my dark-room,' he said.

# 38

―――◆◆◆―――

Clemence's landlord, Mr Walker, was a middle-aged man with a slight stoop. He didn't give his first name, and Clara didn't ask: she would not like to give him the slightest hint that he might dispense with formality. So she introduced herself as Ms Pascal, and referred assiduously to him as Mr Walker.

He showed her to Clemence's flat, directly ahead of the front door, and groped for the key. He wore his key fob clipped to his belt, like a jailer; Clara wondered how that went down with Clemence.

Walker unhooked the clasp and turned to the light, sorting through the colour-coded Yale keys one by one. Clemence's was red. He gave a little gasp of satisfaction on finding it and stood back to allow her through after opening the door.

'You won't find anything,' he said, following her inside. 'Police cleared the place out.'

Clara turned and looked at him. He was standing too close and she could see sharp stubble glistening like sand on abrasive paper in the deep folds of his skin. She wondered fleetingly if it caused him discomfort, but pushed this thought away and actually took a step towards him, forcing him to fall back. 'You can keep the note,' she said. 'Should you need proof that you had permission to let me in.' Clemence had scribbled a letter, allowing her access to his flat.

'I should stay,' Walker said, his eyes roving greedily over the meagre furnishings, 'Make sure nothing's moved. Although there's nowt much left, since the Law were in.'

Clara narrowed her eyes at him and he immediately back-pedalled. 'What I'm saying is, the number of boxes they carried out, there can't be, can there?' He fell silent under her stare. He had been in the place, she was certain; peering into cupboards, rummaging through Clemence's belongings, maybe lifting the odd souvenir.

'My client has a right to privacy,' she said. 'And furnished accommodation or not, he has a right to notice before you gain access to his flat, as well as the right to be present when you cross that threshold.'

'I know the law, love. I respect my tenants' rights.'

Clara smiled. She had to take Mr Warrington's patronising because, as senior partner of Jericho Chambers, he held her career in his hands. Mr Walker had no such power over her. She stood head and shoulders taller than him, and the oily smell from the crown of his head made her feel ill.

'I suspect that your knowledge of the law is as superficial as your professed concern for your tenants' rights,' she said.

Walker bridled. 'There's no need to take that tone with me.'

'Time will tell.' Clara looked over his head, past him,

to the corners of the room. 'If, for example, some item belonging to my client – a photograph, let's say – should find its way into the hands of a journalist . . .'

Walker's shock at the outrageousness of such a notion was as unconvincing as his feigned concern for the rights of his tenants. 'If it does, it won't be from me.'

'Just as well,' Clara said. 'Because I would make it my personal business to prosecute the thief as well as suing for damages in the civil courts.'

Walker swallowed. He made several attempts to look Clara in the face but his eyes kept sliding off her, as if her skin was oiled. He backed away from her and Clara walked to the door, holding it courteously, as if he were a guest about to leave.

'I'll be about an hour,' she said. 'I don't want to be disturbed.' She bolted the door after him and leaned against it, drained by the confrontation. Parents who came to the civil courts, battling over custody or access or maintenance payments were often upset – even angry – but they were angry because they had been hurt, upset because they loved their children and wanted to see them. They might be bitter and hardened by the disappointments of their failed relationships, but they were, for the most part, decent people trying to make the best of a terrible situation. Defending criminals, she was rediscovering, was another matter entirely.

When she had recovered her equilibrium, she turned again to face the room. Bare boards, newly varnished, sparse furnishings – but after prison, a rug on the floor and curtains on the windows would no doubt seem like opulence.

She drew the curtains, as Clemence had advised, before going to the kitchen.

The door opened inwards and for a moment, the velvet dark of its interior seemed to pull her, and she had to steady herself against the sensation of falling.

In the previous two days she had coped with the clammy claustrophobia of police stations and interview rooms – she had even survived with her sanity intact after being locked in a cell. *With a killer*, her malicious inner voice reminded her. Killer or not, it was the confinement she had feared, not the man. She looked again through the kitchen door . . . The darkness was too complete, too uncompromising. No, she wasn't ready for this.

She took two steps away from the kitchen door, unable to drag her gaze from the dark vortex of the interior; fearful, almost, as she had been as a child, fleeing the thing at the top of the stairs, that some malevolent being was waiting for her to turn away, to drop her guard. She shook her head, partly to clear it, and partly in impatience at her own weakness, but still she could not walk through the door.

'This is ridiculous,' she muttered, striding to the chair by the side of the drop-leaf table under the window. She carried it to the kitchen door, wedging it open, then pulled the cord for the light. The walls, floor, cupboard doors and windows were all painted black. He had even found a dark work-surface in imitation granite. The black seemed to suck the light in, draining it of colour and power, and Clara felt an incipient ache behind her eyes. With only the slightest hesitation, she stepped over the threshold.

She didn't give herself time to think, but went immediately to the cutlery drawer and took out a knife. Counting from the end, she opened the third cupboard door and lifted down the neatly stacked cans and packets, pushing them far to the right on the granite work surface, so that she would have access to the back of the cupboard from below, as well as from the front. Clemence was a skilful carpenter, she would give him that: the joins between the carcass and backboard would make a pyramid builder proud.

When the cupboard was empty, she ducked under it and tried to slip the knife between the wall and the back of the cupboard, but it was no good; the blade was too thick.

'Hell!' She slammed the knife down, wishing that she had kept one of the many vows she had made during her captivity: that she would always carry a Swiss army knife.

She pulled open the sink drawer again and rattled through the few items of cutlery Clemence possessed. He kept two of everything – two knives, two forks, two dessert spoons – optimism on Clemence's part, or did the cutlery, like the furniture, come with the room? Frustrated, she dragged the drawer out to its fullest extent and saw something trapped beneath the plastic cutlery tray. Clara reached in and prised it free.

It was a boning knife, its long, tapering blade riveted to a wooden handle bleached by many washings. The blade, too, was worn and had been sharpened so many times that it bowed in the centre and point was paper-thin. Did it belong to Clemence? Why did he hide it? She supposed that in prison, hiding valuables must be almost a reflex. *Oh, and why does he 'value' a boning knife, Clara?* Her inner voice was beginning to sound like her mother: bored, cynical, always tormenting.

'Never mind,' Clara muttered. 'Never mind. Let's just see what's on the film before we hang the man.'

The knife might have been made for the job: she found the catches that held the backboard in place and unhitched them with a flick of the blade, then eased herself from under the cupboard and looked in at the shelves. If he hadn't told her the secret compartment was there, she would never have found it. She reached in and pushed the top of the backboard with her fingertips. It gave slightly; a little more pressure and she was able to find purchase on the lower edge to lever it out. There, behind the board, was the canister of film.

She lifted it down and then set about sliding the board back in place. That was the easy bit; getting the catches back in place was not so simple. It took her an agonising half-hour to finally get both of them hooked on the stays; a half-hour during which she heard Mr Walker creep softly to the flat door and softly steal away a few minutes later.

She replaced everything in the cupboard as she had found it, arranging the cans and packets as before on the shelves. When, at last, she had finished, she stood back appraising her work; it would pass inspection.

She took one last look around the room, her hand already on the cord-pull. Her eye caught the glint of metal: she had left the boning knife on the work surface. Scooping it up, she went to the kitchen drawer and was about to toss it in with the rest of the cutlery, when something made her stop. With a little mental shrug, she lifted the cutlery tray and slid the knife under it, hiding it once more from view.

She stayed in the photographic shop the full fifty minutes it took to process the film.

*Paranoia, darling*, her inner voice chided. *Next you'll be working up some complex conspiracy theory*.

Paranoid she might be, but she wouldn't let the film out of her sight. *Your own private version of police continuity of evidence?*

'Oh do shut up!'

Clara blushed. Had she spoken aloud? The assistant sat at the counter, thumbing through a magazine and chewing with bovine compulsion on her gum, apparently unperturbed and, relieved, Clara returned to her thoughts.

If Clemence was right, and the man in the photographs was a police officer, then a conspiracy theory might not be such an outlandish idea. *Did he convince you with his show of concern, Clara?* He saved my neck in there, Clara retorted. If the mob had broken into his cell – *Ha! He saved his own neck. He shoved you in front of the door and hid behind the lavatory! It was Clemence the mob wanted, not you. He knew that – he used you as a decoy.*

Clara frowned. What about when I panicked? There was no threat to him then – the mob had gone. He could have let me howl the place down, make a fool of myself, work myself into a complete breakdown. But he didn't. He made me focus on something other than the fact that we were locked in that God-awful place.

Even thinking about it made her stomach contract, and her skin felt cold and clammy. The assistant seemed to sense her discomfort and looked up from her magazine. Clara offered a tentative smile and the girl looked away again, a little embarrassed by the contact and Clara resumed her inner argument.

He talked me down. He trusted me with the film. *He trusts you, so you trust him – is that it? Think about it, Clara – what's the balance in this relationship? Tell me, Clara, of the two, who would you trust, given the circumstances?*

Clara stood impatiently and the assistant looked up again, startled.

'Still another ten minutes, yet,' she said.

'What? Oh . . .' Clara tried to think of some excuse for her agitation. 'The fumes,' she blurted out. 'Would you mind if I opened the door?'

Clara felt the assistant's gaze on her from time to time, speculative, wary, as she stood, holding the door open like a hotel commissionaire, standing side-on to allow customers in and out of the shop. But nobody came, and they passed the final few minutes of the developing process in an uneasy silence.

\*     \*     \*

Mitch O'Connor shuffled through the pile of photographs Clara had handed her. They were seated in Mitch's office, the blind half-closed against the sun; Mitch's hair glowed copper and gold in the stray shafts of sunlight that broke through odd misaligned slats. She wore a short-sleeved blouse in burnt orange and a knee-length cream linen skirt.

'This fellow looks familiar.' She stared at the picture of a fat man as if willing it to speak to her. 'I can't think where I've seen him. Looks like a sleazy sod, though. The others . . .' She sifted through the rest. 'They could be anyone. Businessmen, villains – hard to tell them apart these days.'

Clara sighed. 'Don't I know it.'

There were several more of the fat man; one set looked like time lapse, or the jerky images you sometimes see on CCTV: fat man takes an envelope, fat man takes a peek, fat man shoves envelope into his pocket.

Mitch slid Clara a sideways look. 'Where did you get them?'

Clara pressed her lips together and avoided her friend's eye.

'You wouldn't be keeping evidence back from the police, now, would you, Clara?'

Clara stuffed the photographs back into their wallet.

'Clara, if you got these from Clemence—'

'Mitch,' Clara said, 'I'm sorry. I shouldn't have . . .' She closed her eyes for the briefest moment. 'I shouldn't have troubled you with this,' she said. 'It was a long shot. I—' She was on the point of inventing a lie about taking the pictures herself, but found she couldn't. She simply couldn't insult her friend in that way.

Mitch sighed. 'It's none of my business. You'll do what you think is right.'

'I have to go and see Pippa off,' Clara said after taking a few breaths to clear her head, then added as a guilty offering, 'I'll give it some thought.'

'She's unpacked and repacked twice,' Trish said with a wink over Pippa's head. 'And she's put her passport in so many different safe places, I wonder that she'll find it at all.'

Pippa's eyebrows arched in annoyance, belying her studied indifference to Trish's teasing. She retrieved her passport from its most recent hiding-place and slipped it into the front pocket of her Barbie rucksack. 'It's getting late,' she said. 'Where's Daddy?'

'He said he'll meet us at the airport,' Trish said. 'He had a meeting in Frodsham this morning – thought he might as well scoot up the M56 and meet us there, rather than slog all the way home and then back again.'

Pippa looked unsure whether she should be put out by this news, but in the bustle of getting her bags loaded, she seemed to forget about her father's inconsiderateness and worried instead about where she had put her passport and whether she had packed her trainers.

Trish drove, to allow Clara to devote her full attention to her daughter. The following forty minutes was spent reassuring Pippa that she had packed all the essentials, that they would get there on time and that Daddy wouldn't miss waving her off.

*You're not the only one who's had her illusions shattered,* Clara thought.

Pippa fussed over something in her rucksack, rummaging through the carefully packed toiletries and toys and knick-knacks she felt she simply could not do without.

Clara felt a tug that took her back to her daughter's infancy. Hadn't Pippa been at her most vulnerable then? She recalled how she would kiss the delicate, pulsing skin of the fontanelle, feeling the soft peach-fuzz of infant hair growth warm beneath her lips. When Pippa was tiny and fragile, Clara had felt strong, able to tackle anything – anyone – to protect her baby; why couldn't she feel that now? Why couldn't she rebuild the illusion, piece by splintered piece – no matter how false and delicate that shell of invulnerability might be?

Pippa seemed to sense something and looked up. 'What?' She sounded querulous and distracted. Her eyes widened. 'You're not going to *cry* are you?' she asked, dismayed. 'We're nearly there, now!'

Clara understood: Annabelle Forrest would be there and her manicured parents with their pristine luggage and their perfectly managed lives, and it would be just too *embarrassing* if her mother broke down sobbing in front of them and made a scene.

'I'll make you a deal,' Clara said, blinking hard to clear the tears blurring her eyes. 'I won't if you don't.'

'No,' Pippa argued, '*I* won't if *you* don't.'

Trish smiled at Clara in the rear-view mirror.

They kept their promise – almost.

Hugo met them, as arranged, and Pippa relaxed a little, even dragging him to Boots to try and wangle a new pair of sunglasses out of him, but the effort was half-hearted and she was back a few minutes later, looking pale and anxious. At the international departures gates, Pippa pulled a small box from her pocket.

'It's for you,' she said.

Clara looked in wonder at Hugo and Trish. Hugo, it seemed, was as mystified as Clara, but Trish simply raised her eyebrows, smiling. Clara opened the maroon box.

Inside was a penknife. She held her breath.

'Well, you're always saying you need one,' Pippa said.

'For the garden,' Clara added, her heart swelling with love and regret. Pippa was leaving this as protection, because she wouldn't be there to look after her mummy.

'And *stuff*.' Pippa said.

How did she know? How did she know just how fearful Clara was for most of the time?

*It's hardly a state secret, now is it, Clara?* She silenced the savage voice in her head and hugged her daughter. 'It's a lovely present,' she said. 'I'll use it this evening for pruning the roses.'

'You could just have it in your pocket – just in case,' Pippa suggested. A slight note of desperation had crept into her voice.

A talisman, Clara thought. She wants it to be a

talisman. 'Always,' she said, slipping it safely into her trouser pocket.

And that was when the tears began to flow. Pippa left on her big adventure in a state of excitement and grief she hardly knew how to contain. Hugo agreed to take Trish home so that Clara could have the car.

'What's so urgent?' Hugo asked.

'Mountains are built by ignoring the molehills, as my mother used to say.'

This surprised a laugh from Hugo. 'Your mother would *never* employ anything so vulgar as an aphorism.'

Clara had almost forgotten how good it was to hear him laugh. 'Well, she should.' She smiled back at him. The photographs were in her briefcase, in the boot of the car, and they felt like a physical presence, constantly nudging her in the back, demanding to be dealt with.

# 39

As Steve Lawson reached for his telephone, it rang.

'Thought you'd want the good news, Boss.' He recognised DC Gordon's fastidious Edinburgh intonation. 'They've cracked Amy's password.' Lawson had sent Gordon to Information Systems an hour earlier to see if he could hurry things along.

'Fantastic!'

'But—'

'There's bad news as well?'

'Someone from the Financial Investigations Unit came in at the crucial moment. Wanted to know what we'd got from Amy's hard drive.'

*The FIU?* 'Did they say why they're interested?' It was looking more and more like something dodgy was going down at the Dee View Development project.

'He wasn't that chatty. But he said he wanted everything we pull off the drive.'

'Oh yeah?' Lawson felt a muscle tighten in his jaw. 'Who's the SIO?'

'DI Hill. Came in himself, to impress on us mere mortals just how important this request is.'

DI Hill. Lawson knew him of old. They had worked together as DSs in Runcorn. He didn't like the man then, and he couldn't see age improving his manners and temperament. Lawson felt a little acid-burn at the lower loop of his oesophagus. Hill had got there ahead of him, swooping in and snatching the prize like a scavenging gannet. And since the FIU didn't get out of bed in the morning for anything less than a million-pound fraud, Hill would think himself justified in crashing in on witnesses. Witnesses who, given the right encouragement, might have been helpful to their murder investigation. Lawson knew Mark Hill's bullying and blustering techniques well enough to be able to predict the level of hostility he would create in his wake.

'Well,' he sighed. 'It isn't a competition, Fergus. We've a duty to co-operate with other inquiries.' He knew how unconvincing he sounded but he couldn't summon the energy to act like he meant it.

'Aye, and I've assured him of our co-operation, Boss.'

Something in DC Gordon's tone gave Lawson a glimmer of hope. 'I'm glad to hear it,' he said, warily.

'As soon as I've emailed the files to you, I'll get a copy over to his office.'

Lawson grinned. 'You didn't give him the files . . .'

'He didn't ask nicely.' There was a pause, then he added. 'You know how it is – we were right in the middle of things when he arrived and I didn't like to give him half the story.'

'Commendable,' Lawson said, swallowing a laugh.

'And DI Hill is mentioned in Amy's notes.'

'Oh?' Suddenly, it didn't seem so funny.

'I think you should judge for yourself, Boss.' The

implication being that Hill had, indeed, been holding out on them.

'But you will get the stuff to him just as soon as is feasible.'

'Och, yes. When I've found his card in all this forest of paper, I'll get it to him *tootsweet*.'

Good. They understood each other. 'You don't happen to recall, do you, where he's working from?' He knew McAteer would ask, and he would have to provide an answer.

'They had to rent an office in the city. Shortage of space at HQ. I *cannot* for the life of me remember where.'

'Thanks, Fergus. I owe you one.' Grinning, Lawson hung up. Never piss off a meticulous man, he thought – if he decides to be sloppy, he'll do it with scrupulous attention to detail. Lawson could rely on DC Gordon to give them an hour or two head start; in the mean time, he would get DS Barton to make a few desultory phone calls to try to locate the Financial Investigations Unit led by DI Hill. He was whistling as he went to pick up Amy's faxed files from the Incident Room.

DS Barton sat in front of an integral TV and video unit, watching the tape of the assault on the station, while Cath Young sat two desks away, ticking off names as she slowly worked her way down a list of phone numbers.

Barton shifted in his seat, leaning closer to the TV screen to get a better look, rewound, pressed play, then froze the frame. At the head of the mob, he thought he had seen somebody. He wasn't sure of the face – one skinhead looks much like the next – but as the youth punched one policeman, he turned, giving an over-arm gesture for the others to follow. At that moment, his neck was exposed, the tattoo clearly visible: a tattoo of a spider's web.

'Anything useful, Phil?' Lawson asked.

Barton pressed fast-forward. 'I'm working on it,' he said. 'I'll let you know.'

DC Young called Lawson away to take a phone call from Clemence's landlord; he considered it his 'civic duty' to tell them of Clara Pascal's visit to her client's flat. Lawson thanked him and hung up, intrigued. He stopped on his way out, but by this time the mob had breached the outer doors of the station building and the cameras and booms of the media were caught, as if jousting for the prize of a televisual scoop, trying to follow the rioters inside the police station. He told Barton the good news about Amy's files and asked him to start tracking down DI Hill.

'No rush,' he said. 'When you've finished trawling the tapes.'

Barton wound the film on, relieved that Lawson hadn't seen the image of Spider on the videotape. He felt a presence to his left, a little out of his line of vision, and turned, scowling.

'You hovering, Cath?'

DC Young licked her lips and laced her fingers together, nervously kneading the knuckles.

'Can I have a word, Sarge?' she asked. 'In private?'

\* \* \*

Amy Dennis's files were exhaustive, and although her journalism files were password-protected, her student records were not. Officers had been working through them since they lifted the PC from her office on the day her body was found, but this was the first glimpse they'd had of her journalistic notes. She had password-protected her diary, too: dates and names of contacts were mixed in with appointments for baby clinic and vaccination dates for her daughter. Someone else would sift through that, but before he passed the papers on, Lawson was curious to see if there was anything in her last few days – any reference to Clemence, for instance, or to the Dee View Development – that might explain her death. Lawson flicked through the bundle of sheets to the end.

Background: Dee View Development        A. Dennis
08.02


Foremost Investments
Syndicate members
Officially: Sebastian Enderby, (Ex) Councillor
Thomas Rivers, Russell Jacques, in conjunction
with English Heritage. Lottery money a strong
possibility.
Unofficially: Brendan Harris, John Ridley. Maybe
others?


Harris is bad news: Calls himself a property
developer. Implicated in university accommodation
scam in the 1980s. Accused of unlawful eviction of

tenants from redevelopment sites. Case collapsed
when witnesses refused to testify. Either he's Teflon-
coated or he scared the shit out of them.

Ridley: hard man. London refugee. Got out after a 4
year stretch for robbery and found young bucks
had taken over his territory. Gone soft, or easier
pickings here in Cheshire?

## Sebastian Enderby

Enderby squeaky-clean: business awards,
environmental sponsorship with BTCV, links with local
schools. But where's the money coming from? He's
wealthy, but not rich. Ridley? Harris? Front-man?
Naive or knowing? Think he's softening up. Seems
nervous of Ridley. Will talk to him again at the awards.

## Thomas Rivers

Long-standing member of the council until bids were
invited for the development. Stepped down end of last
year. Business man: Cash and Carry, a small road
haulage business. He bought up and redeveloped
Lache business park, attracting computer/
technology businesses a couple of years back. Well
respected, but the haulage business isn't doing well
and he's been looking for new areas to invest.

## Russell Jacques

Still working on Jacques. On board of numerous
charities since retirement from bank management.
Joined English Heritage in March 2001.

Syndicate gains:
Inward investment? Certainly. Legit business to
launder drugs money? Possibly. Dee View a
potential gold mine.
Site alone easily worth £8 million prior to
development. Proposals include hotel, leisure
complex, casinos, conference facilities linked with
racecourse – irresistible.

English Heritage have guaranteed up to £750,000
for excavation of Roman remains and maintenance
of site in first 4 years.

Lottery funding likely to be way in excess of this.
Tender put in for educational facilities. Worth?

Police investigation?
Had a visit from a DI Mark Hill, Tues (13.08).
Wanted to know what I was working on. Wasn't
prepared to explain why. No frank exchange for DI
Hill. And no warrant. All cold-eyed suspicion and
veiled threats. Charming man. Didn't respond well
to being told to get stuffed.

Think maybe I'm being followed. Saw the red car again.
And someone was in the garden last night. Don't <u>think</u>
I'm being paranoid. Should I go to the police? Can't see
them being sympathetic after I blew off DI Hill. Would
have to tell them what I know. Risk losing the story.

D: \work\inv\DVD

Lawson's mind flashed back to his conversation with Clara Pascal. Here was proof that Amy was being stalked – together with an explanation as to why she didn't report it. He hoped that DC Gordon would have considerable trouble finding Hill's business card. He arranged for officers to interview the key figures mentioned in Amy's notes. DI Hill, he would deal with himself.

Word came through that Clara Pascal was waiting to see him. He completed his calls, then went downstairs to the reception desk himself to collect her. She seemed anxious, looking into the faces of every officer they passed, as if searching for someone. He showed her into his office and shut the door. He saw a flicker of alarm and she looked like she might object, but she seemed to think better of it, and took the offered chair, angling herself so that she could see the door. He had to admire her guts: in her quick inventory of the tiny room, she had noted the lack of windows, but she had managed to remain composed.

'You said you were looking into having my client moved,' she said.

Lawson nodded. 'We've sorted out a secure station outside the city. I'll give you the details before you leave.'

With the door shut, the room heated up rapidly and Clara slipped off her jacket. 'What about the leak to the press?' she asked.

'We've got a lead on that.'

'I want him suspended with immediate effect.'

'I didn't say it was a police officer.'

Clara gave a quick, tense smile. 'I'll bet you give the CPS value for money in the witness box.'

Lawson wasn't feeling susceptible to flattery. 'Was there something specific you wanted to talk about?' he asked.

Clara didn't answer. He was suddenly sure that there *was* something – that Clara Pascal had come to him with information about the case.

'Clemence is very lucky to have such personal attention from his barrister,' he said.

'I haven't too many demands on my time, right now.'

'Did you come to an agreement?' Lawson asked. It couldn't be coincidence that she had just been to her client's flat.

Clara frowned. 'Concerning what?'

'Concerning how much you would tell me.'

Although she remained stubbornly mute, Lawson sensed that Clara was ready to talk, given a shove in the right direction.

'I could arrest you,' he said in a speculative tone, as if testing the idea.

'What?'

'I could charge you with withholding evidence.'

'What "evidence"?' Her pallor belied her disbelief.

'The evidence you collected from Clemence's flat.'

Clara closed her eyes. When she opened them again, she looked directly into his. 'Walker?' she asked.

Lawson nodded.

Clara's shoulders slumped. 'Can't you cut me some

slack, Steve? You must see the difficulty I'm in – I could be implicating my client—'

'I *will* arrest you, Clara.'

'I'd be betraying a trust.'

He felt for her but he deliberately hardened his voice. 'I'll arrest you and I'll put you in a cell. You won't like it.'

He saw fear flash in her eyes again, swiftly displaced by frank contempt, and she retreated into the safety of stiff formality. 'I need to be sure that my client will be protected from prosecution in this matter, Inspector.'

Lawson smiled, matching her, civility for icy civility, title for title. 'You know I can't make any such undertaking, Counsel.'

'If I assure you that my client is innocent of any illegal activity?'

Had she really forgotten so much about the cut and thrust of criminal law? Not for the first time, it hit Lawson just how much Clara had come through since last year – and how much courage it must have taken to be shut in his tiny cell of an office after what had happened to her only that morning.

'I'm sorry,' he said, and his regret was sincere. 'Defence Counsel's recommendation of her client's good character wouldn't be enough to convince my bosses. But if Clemence is exonerated from criminal involvement, I think we could put in a good word.'

'Not enough.'

He raised his eyebrows. She really was full of surprises – start to feel sorry for her and she was liable to kick you right where you were vulnerable.

'I want a guarantee that he won't be hounded, that you'll find him alternative accommodation—'

'Now wait just a minute,' Lawson interrupted. 'You haven't forgotten that he's still facing charges of stalking and possibly even murder?'

Clara seemed to withdraw into herself. She was silent for some time, then she sighed. 'Tell me this,' she said. 'Was Amy Dennis investigating some kind of fraud on the Dee View project?'

Lawson gazed at her; she might have lost her nerve, but she was still sharp. 'What makes you think that?'

'Are *you* investigating?'

He smiled. 'You know I can't discuss confidential police matters with you.'

She closed her eyes, briefly. 'At least tell me you're keeping an open mind.'

He hesitated and she looked at him. Lawson gave a reluctant nod. 'We're exploring every available line of enquiry,' he said.

'All right.' She lifted her briefcase onto his desk and glanced anxiously towards the door before opening the lid and taking out a photo-processing wallet containing Clemence's surveillance pictures.

Lawson studied each picture carefully, making no comment. He made an effort to keep his expression neutral, but perhaps she saw the tension in his jaw, or sensed his anger from his stance.

'You know him.' It was a blunt statement of fact.

Lawson looked at the sharp, clearly defined image. There was no mistaking the paunchy figure. He only wished their own surveillance pictures were always as unequivocal. 'Yes,' he said. 'I know him.'

# 40

---◆---

'Boss?'

McAteer and Lawson had their backs to DS Barton.

McAteer looked around, first alarmed, then irritated by the interruption.

'Don't you knock before entering a senior officer's room?' he demanded.

'Sorry, Boss – but this is urgent.'

McAteer stared balefully at him and Barton started to back out of the room, apologising again.

'Since you're here,' the DCI said, waving him in impatiently.

Barton stepped smartly into the room and shut the door. It was hot, as it was everywhere in the building, but the north-facing aspect meant there was no direct sunlight and a fan hummed quietly in one corner of the room, so the heat was bearable. Somehow, Barton thought, McAteer always seemed to manage things so that he was comfortable.

McAteer turned back to his desk and shuffled a few papers before giving Barton his full attention. If he guessed rightly, the two senior officers had been discussing sensitive new evidence. Word was, the password-protected files they'd pulled off Amy's computer

were very interesting. Barton forestalled another iras-
cible remark from McAteer by handing over the photograph he had personally accepted from the news editor
of the *Evening Echo*.

'The original of Amy,' he said. 'The one that's been
in all the tabloids.'

'I don't suppose he told you where he'd got this?'
McAteer said.

Barton shook his head. 'Protecting his sources,' he
apologised.

'They'll run this as an exclusive tomorrow,' McA-
teer said. 'How they've provided the police with vital
evidence.'

'The boss asked for a photo-opportunity. You with
the news editor.' Barton waited for the outrage to
register in McAteer's face before adding, 'I offered
them one of you slapping the cuffs on him.'

Lawson laughed; he didn't quite raise a smile from
McAteer, but the DCI looked less worried and dys-
peptic for an instant, which Barton took for approval.
'They said they'd run the story without an official
police comment.'

McAteer passed the picture on to Lawson. The
newspapers had cropped the image tightly, narrowing
the focus to Amy's anxious expression and tense body
language. Uncropped, there was a lot of additional
information that would help them find the location.

'It's not Amy's place, that's for sure,' Lawson said.
'Her house is a bog-standard 1960s semi. This looks
like a two- maybe three-storey Edwardian.'

The bottom of the first-floor windowsills were just

visible and it was certainly possible that there was another floor above these three, evenly spaced windows, but it was impossible to tell from the photograph. The red tiles of the front step alternated with black along the outer edges; some were cracked, and together with the unruly hedge and the damaged fence between this and the adjacent property, it seemed unkempt.

'So where is it?' McAteer asked.

Lawson shook his head. 'Someone on house-to-house might recognise it.'

'I'll get it scanned into the computer,' Barton replied. 'Zap off enough for the whole team.'

'And make sure Ms Pascal and Clemence's brief get a copy,' McAteer added.

'What – *now*, Guv?'

'Yes, Sergeant, now. Ms Pascal is being extremely helpful,' McAteer said.

The words bubbled up before Barton had the chance to suppress them: 'What about the CPS – do they get to see it, or aren't they being "helpful" enough?'

'That will do, Sergeant.'

McAteer didn't need to raise his voice for Barton to know he'd been reprimanded. He took a breath and waited until the anger subsided before allowing himself to speak. 'There's something else you should know. The other snaps of Amy? DC Young reckons Fletch found them.'

McAteer and Lawson exchanged a look. Barton saw it and his eyes flicked to the desk behind the two senior officers. McAteer stood square in front of it, so all he could see was one edge and a wodge of pink flimsies: duplicates of forms.

'She thinks he passed the photos to Thorpe,' he continued, mildly distracted, less angry than curious, now.

'Why would Fletch do that? It'd look better for him if he'd logged them.' Lawson said. 'Unless he pocketed one,' he added, answering his own question.

'She says Fletch left shortly after talking to Thorpe. She thinks he had a pressing appointment with his bookie. Thorpe was doing him a favour.'

'You're sure she's not seeing how deep she can drop Fletch in it?' Lawson asked. 'Those two do have a history.'

Barton shrugged. 'Sure, Fletch made it hard for Young on the Clara Pascal investigation. But Cath made her mark on the team. I'd say she's pretty much even with Fletch by now. Her theory is Thorpe is covering for Fletch – he knows he shouldn't have logged the evidence in the first place, but he's just too macho to admit when he's made a mistake – her words, not mine.'

McAteer thought about this for a few moments. 'A bookie's appointment, she says?' he asked.

'Yes, Guv, but she didn't actually hear what was said.'

'And she didn't see how many pictures Fletch handed over?'

'No.'

'So Thorpe could, in fact, have slipped one from the pack himself. Or they could be in on it together.'

Barton didn't answer immediately. 'Fletch is a gambler,' he said. 'Not a good one. And he's drinking heavily.' McAteer's surprise was evident: the sergeant wasn't the sort to bad-mouth his fellow officers. Barton shrugged. 'I'm just saying that Fletch is a better suspect than Thorpe.'

Lawson spoke up. 'Sir?'

McAteer hesitated, nodded, then stepped to one side. Lawson lifted a few papers and retrieved a set of photographs. Barton took the pack and began sorting through them. The silence lasted a full minute.

'*Not* a trip to his bookie, then.' It wasn't funny, wasn't funny at all, but what else was he supposed to say? That he'd never have thought it of Fletch? Truth be told, it was more of a shock that he'd not succumbed earlier.

'We don't know when they were taken,' Lawson said. 'Ms Pascal might be co-operating, but her client is less well disposed towards our investigation.'

'*Clemence* took these?'

Lawson gave a brief nod and Barton returned to his stunned shuffling of the photographs.

He looked at the picture of Fletcher stuffing a fat envelope into his pocket. 'Fletch backs a dead cert . . . What are the odds of that?' he muttered, tilting the picture to the light. 'Isn't that John Ridley handing over the money?'

'What d'you know about him?' Lawson asked.

'Worked out of Lewisham. Lost his niche in his own smelly little pond when the Rude Boys took an interest in his business concerns while he was inside.'

'Yes,' McAteer said, as if expecting him to continue.

'Clemence took these . . .' He shook his head. 'I don't get it – was Clemence blackmailing Fletch?'

'Clemence says he was working for Brendan Harris.'

Barton blew air through his nose. 'Now why doesn't that surprise me?'

'Clemence claims he was paid to take a few pictures,' Lawson said.

'What kind of pictures?'

'Amy's notes list both Ridley and Harris as secret backers of the Foremost Investments bid for the Dee View project,' Lawson said. 'Harris said he needed the pictures as "insurance" – maybe he thought Fletch was playing both sides against the middle.'

'And what's Fletch been doing for these upstanding citizens?' Barton asked, placing the stack of glossy prints carefully on the desk.

'What do villains generally want from cops?' Lawson asked. 'Lost files, misplaced evidence, advance information.' He spread his hands. 'Forewarned is forearmed. But the truth is, Phil, we don't know.'

'And it isn't our job to investigate,' McAteer reminded them. 'Complaints and Discipline will take it from here – they'll be working alongside the Financial Investigations Unit.'

'So, is Brendan Harris implicated in Amy's murder? Is Fletch? I mean, the money . . .'

McAteer sighed. 'There are certainly common denominators. But a correlation isn't necessarily a causative factor.'

Barton stared blankly at the DCI and Lawson spoke

up. 'Ever sneezed just when the whole house was plunged into darkness?'

'This isn't coincidence,' Barton said.

'You could be right,' Lawson agreed. 'But it isn't straightforward, either.'

He couldn't argue with that. 'What do I tell DC Young?'

'Tell her we're looking into it.'

'And Thorpe?'

'He's not in the clear, yet.'

'No, but Fletcher thinks *he* is.'

'Which is about the best we could hope for, until Complaints and Discipline have had the opportunity to gather evidence, don't you agree?' McAteer said. 'Can Young be trusted to lay off him in the meantime?'

'I'll have a quiet word,' Lawson said. 'But Clara Pascal will want to see some action on this, or she might make waves of her own.'

'What have you told her?'

'That we'll investigate, of course, but she's already demanding Clemence's release.'

'On what grounds?'

'On the grounds that he was measured, suited and sewn up for this by Fletcher.'

Barton could believe that Fletch sold out to Harris, but Clemence as a lamb to the slaughter? That was too hard to take. 'So Fletch slipped the photos of Amy into an envelope and hid them in his flat, I suppose.'

'That's the general idea, yes.'

'But *why*? It doesn't make any sense, Boss!'

'We haven't got all the facts, yet. Maybe the consortium needed someone to take the fall for Amy's death – draw attention away from their activities, weaken the ties between her and Mr Enderby.'

'You can't believe Fletch is a killer?'

'No, Lawson said. 'I don't think he would go that far. But he *is* an opportunist, and on the evidence of Clemence's photographs he's almost certainly bent.'

Barton couldn't believe it: they were going to lose their prime suspect. 'There's a hell of a lot more against Clemence than a few poxy photographs!'

'I agree with Sergeant Barton,' McAteer said. 'Clemence is still a strong suspect.'

'And on his own admission he was working for Brendan Harris – just about the sleaziest landlord since Rackman,' Barton added.

'I'm not suggesting we let him go,' Lawson said, 'Just that we consider all the options.'

'Fair enough.' It seemed McAteer had heard sufficient from both sides to make up his mind. 'We need to get this paperwork from Amy's computer sifted and shifted, first. Get DC Gordon to do a search of the computer files, make sure there's no reference to Fletcher. This is for him and him alone to know. Any' – he waved a hand as if swatting a fly away – 'sensitive material comes to me. The rest can be dished out to whoever, as long as it's not to Fletcher.' He paused briefly. 'Or Thorpe.'

'It's about time I had a chat with DI Hill, find out what their investigation has turned up,' Lawson said. 'Mrs Enderby called earlier; she found Amy's business card in her husband's wallet – with DI Hill's phone number written on the back.'

McAteer nodded. 'And it would help if we knew the location of the house in this picture. DS Barton – make that your priority. We can't do anything about Fletcher, except keep him away from anything that might prove "saleable", so there's no point arguing about him.'

He checked his watch. 'Now, Clemence is due to be moved to the secure station at six – we'll send out a van as a decoy, then an unmarked carrier with him in the back. He'll be protected by armed officers – this morning was a PR disaster. Tonight, gentlemen, we take no chances.'

# 41

DC Thorpe was tasked with interviewing former councillor Tom Rivers. Rivers had been ranked low priority, so it had taken two days since the discovery of the photograph to get to it. He had been reassessed after his mention in Amy's notes, but as Actions went, this one was one rank above photocopying.

Thorpe was in no doubt why he had been allocated the job: he had logged the photographs of Amy Dennis which meant that he was high on the list of suspects for having stolen the one that got into the newspapers.

Since their conversation in the car park, it was clear that Fletch had no intention of pulling his orbs out of the fire, and Thorpe was not in the best of moods when he pulled up outside Rivers's road haulage offices.

They were housed in a shabby one-storey concrete building, converted from a roadside greasy spoon café. Plenty of parking space for the rigs and conveniently placed on an arterial road, yet it was evident that business was slow: Thorpe counted four lorries and trailers idle in the yard as he locked his car.

He flashed his warrant card and asked to speak to the boss. Rivers's secretary was bright and pretty. She invited him to take a seat and buzzed through to

Rivers. There was a long silence, then Rivers said, 'What does he want?'

The girl turned to Thorpe and began to ask, but Rivers interrupted, the intercom's squawk sounding like an exclamation of alarm.

'Never mind,' he said. 'Send him through.'

She gave a little shrug and nodded to the connecting door.

Rivers looked unwell. He had the kind of scrawny build that never truly looks healthy, but Thorpe guessed that he was looking worse than usual. Councillor Rivers had something on his mind. This simple fact was enough to displace Thorpe's resentful mood and replace it with an aggressive curiosity.

It was warm in the low-ceilinged room, but not uncomfortably so. An electric fan whirred on the desk and all the windows stood open, allowing a cooling breeze to blow through. Despite this, Rivers was sweating and his hand trembled as he waved Thorpe to a seat.

DC Thorpe remained standing.

'I'm very busy,' Rivers said, his voice not quite steady enough to strike the patronising tone he was trying to convey. 'Is this important?'

'It's about a murder,' Thorpe said. 'Is that important enough for you?'

Rivers licked his lips. 'I didn't know her.'

'Know who?'

Rivers blinked and his eyes widened momentarily.

*Like he just realised he opened his big mouth too soon,* Thorpe thought.

'This is about Amy Dennis, isn't it?' Rivers asked.

'Matter of fact, it is,' Thorpe said. 'And you did know her.'

'Look, Constable, I think I'd remember if—'

'She took your photograph last week,' Thorpe interrupted. 'It was in the *Chester Evening Echo*.'

Rivers said, 'Oh,' and shuffled a few papers on his desk before rallying. 'A lot of people take my photograph. That doesn't mean I know them.'

'Bit of a celebrity, are you, sir?' Thorpe asked, with a deliberate sneer.

'I was a councillor for ten years; I have business interests in Chester and—'

'Oh, yeah,' Thorpe said. 'You've put in a bid for that new development over by the racecourse, haven't you?'

'I'm one of the syndicate,' Rivers corrected him.

Like it mattered that he wasn't the only one. Like he wasn't willing to take all the blame. 'Sebastian Enderby was also on the syndicate, wasn't he?' Thorpe said.

'He still is,' Rivers said. 'But I don't see what that has to do with Amy Dennis.'

'She was putting a story together about the whole set-up.'

Rivers bristled. '*Set-up?*'

'Before she was murdered, yeah.' Thorpe laid emphasis on the word 'murdered' and Rivers deflated like a burst balloon.

'Terrible thing,' he said. 'Terrible thing.'

'Did she interview all of you when she took the photograph?'

'In a general way – whether we thought the bid would be successful. What our bid offered over and above the rest.' Rivers made an attempt at a smile: it seemed he had given up on bluster and was trying to down-play the situation.

*Too late, pal,* Thorpe thought. *Way too late for that.* He stared at a bead of sweat trickling from Rivers's hairline down his forehead. Rivers flinched as the salty drop ran into his eye, then he took out a handkerchief to mop his face.

'She was at the Chamber of Commerce Awards on Monday,' Thorpe said. 'Did she speak to you then – in a general way?'

Rivers wiped his hands. 'I really can't recall,' he said.

Thorpe's mood was beginning to improve. 'Not to worry. We're working though her notes and computer files.' It was cruel, but Thorpe's improved mood hadn't made him feel any more kindly disposed to Mr Rivers, so he added: 'In the meantime, I'd like you to come in.'

Rivers's hand went to his throat. '*Now?*'

Thorpe left it longer than was strictly necessary before he replied. 'Tomorrow will do.' He flicked his card onto Rivers's desk. 'If you remember something of a more . . . *particular* nature, my number's on there.'

Rivers slumped back in his chair and stared at the office door. *They can't touch you if you keep your mouth shut,* Harris had said. He was wrong – Rivers had the feeling that this policeman would come back again and again.

He reached for the phone, but his hand jerked violently and he knocked the receiver off the hook. He stared at it for a full five minutes, giving a little yelp when the three-tone warning sounded; listening stupidly to the operator's exhortation to *Please hang up and try again.*

If only it was that simple.

# 42

The Financial Investigations Unit had set up shop in a modern glass-and-concrete office block on City Road. One of Hill's DCs buzzed Lawson in and he took the lift to the third floor. The DC's instructions were to turn left out of the lift and buzz again at the second doorway along the corridor. The door, solid oak, set into grey, fluted concrete, had no sign, only a number.

The office faced onto the main road, but no sound penetrated the sheet-glass windows. The blinds were drawn, angled to let in natural light while cutting down the glare of afternoon sunshine. The three desks in the room would have looked a little lost in the vast expanse of oatmeal carpet, were it not for the ranks of filing cabinets and the bookcases stuffed with box files and legal texts. An officer sat at one of the desks, munching a sandwich while he ploughed through a Home Office report on the allocation of Lottery grants.

The DC who had answered the door directed Lawson to the end of the room, which was divided off from the rest by a floor-to-ceiling panel of glass, etched with abstract shapes, vaguely suggestive of the human form, the pearly opacity of the figures giving privacy to the superior officer.

Outside, the air temperature was twenty-six degrees and rising, and the oppressive humidity made the city feel like an unventilated greenhouse; in the FIU's temporary accommodation, though, the thermostat struggled to get past seventeen.

Hill was talking on the telephone. He glanced at Lawson, then swivelled the chair slightly away from him and carried on talking. As Lawson had predicted, age hadn't improved Hill's manners. The uncharitable thought crossed his mind that Hill was talking to a dial tone. He pulled up a chair and sat down. Several folders lay scattered on the desk; one was marked A. Dennis. Lawson tried to catch Hill's eye, but Hill was assiduously ignoring him, frowning at a reporter's notebook on his lap and muttering into the mouthpiece of the phone.

Lawson gave up trying to be polite and, picking up the file, began to riffle through. It contained nothing more than the documents lifted from Amy's hard drive. With a flash of annoyance, he guessed that Hill had left the file on view as a tease, to get him salivating over material his investigation already had. Glancing around and seeing him with the folder, Hill hastily finished his conversation and hung up.

'What the hell d'you think you're doing?' he demanded.

Lawson looked up from the file. 'Hello, Mark. It's been a while.'

'Give that to me,' Hill said, ignoring the greeting. He was a big man with close-cropped brown hair, a wide, flat nose and a look of permanent irritation etched between his brows.

Lawson squinted at the label on the front of the file. 'Says A. Dennis, here.' He tilted the file so that Hill could read it. 'You know the rules, Mark. We share.'

'Like DC Gordon "shared" Amy's computer files with this office?'

'They're all here, as far as I can make out,' Lawson said, fanning the contents of the buff folder.

'Thanks to Gordon, my people are a couple of hours behind yours on every interview, every new lead.'

'We had a few officers spare,' Lawson said, as if modesty forbade him to brag. 'We were just a little quicker off the mark than your team.'

'I'm going to put in a complaint about DC Gordon's conduct,' Hill said.

'Do that,' Lawson replied, 'and I'll put in a counter-complaint that you hampered a murder investigation.'

The two men locked gazes. Hill seemed to be trying to gauge the seriousness of Lawson's threat. There was no shrug, nor sigh, nor even a nod his head, but Lawson knew Hill had conceded defeat before he spoke.

'I don't want your lot interviewing any more councillors,' he said at last.

'Don't worry,' Lawson said. 'I've briefed them carefully. My team have strict instructions *not* to ask if anyone has bung-money stuffed under the mattress at home.'

'This isn't a joke, Lawson.'

'No,' Lawson agreed, feeling a surge of anger. 'It's a small matter of a murder – the attempted murder of Mr Enderby is not in my brief, though Helsby CID might have a few questions on that score.'

Hill rolled his eyes. 'You haven't gone and told *them* about this?'

'Police on connected investigations sharing information – it's a radical idea,' Lawson said, ladling on the sarcasm. 'But you know, I think my governor might just have mentioned it.' He tossed the folder back onto the desk and took a card from his top pocket and placed it on the desk. 'Amy's business card,' he said. 'Mrs Enderby found it in her husband's wallet.'

'So?'

'We're sharing, Mark.' Lawson turned the card over. 'Your number,' he said. 'In Amy's handwriting.' He paused, but Hill remained silent. 'The way this works is you tell me why Enderby had your number.'

'I really have no idea,' Hill said.

Lawson exhaled. 'Given that I accept that – which I don't – why would *Amy* have your number?'

Hill glanced left. 'I spoke to Ms Dennis,' he said.

'And?'

'She wasn't very co-operative.'

'She told you to get stuffed – I know that – it's in her notes. And I can't say I blame her. What I'm interested in is, what put you onto her?'

'She was poking about, asking questions, upsetting our targets.'

'I want a list.'

Hill gestured towards the boxes of paperwork around him. 'This is money. Big money. Money on a grand scale.'

Lawson expected him to start drooling any minute. 'Money is a pretty good motive for murder,' he said.

'I'm working on a conspiracy,' Hill said.

Hill's mind ran on a narrow track, Lawson realised. *Okay, let's give him something that might interest him*. He took a breath. '*Amy's* death is looking more and more like conspiracy,' he said. 'Could be the people you're investigating also conspired to get Amy out of the way. If we co-operate, we might just get a result. What do you say, Hill? Think we could work together?'

Hill picked up Amy's folder and dumped it into a tray already stacked high. 'As if I had a choice.'

Lawson waited and Hill opened another folder – red this time – took out a sheet of paper and pushed it across his desk to Lawson.

'You know the background of the Dee View Project – multi-million pound development – leisure complex, luxury hotel, conference centre, possibly a casino, too. The racecourse on the doorstep, quaint, walled city for the tourists. And to keep the Cheshire Set from screaming vulgar commercialism, a Heritage site bang in the middle of it.'

Lawson grunted acquiescence as he skimmed the list of names on the sheet. 'These are the backers of the Foremost Investments bid?' he said.

Hill nodded. 'Officially, it's just Mr Enderby and Councillor Rivers – who, incidentally, has stepped down in order to avoid a conflict of interests – but those two haven't got the financial muscle to pull off something like this on their own. The Magnificent Seven at the top of that sheet are completely off the record. If the council had any inkling that their premier land development project had been hijacked by the likes of Harris and Ridley, they'd have a collective heart attack.'

Lawson scanned the rest of the list. 'There *are* a couple of councillors here, though . . .'

Hill shook his head. 'Strictly Sunday League. They may have taken a back-hander for shuffling the Foremost Investments bid to the top of the pile, or fed Rivers a tasty morsel about the selection board's particular preferences, but that's as far as it goes. They'll be useful witnesses when it comes to court, that's all.'

'Was Enderby in on this?' If he was, then Amy had signed her own death warrant when she spoke to him.

'We think Enderby's clean. He put up a million of his own cash for the project, but a development of this size, a million isn't much more than a goodwill gesture. Rivers was supposed to come up with the real cash. Which ostensibly is why he stepped down from the council. Rivers's road haulage business has suffered because of problems with freight in the Channel Tunnel, and blockades in France. Despite this, his bank balance has swollen by fifteen million in eight months.'

'Have you traced the source?'

'It's Brendan Harris. He's a—'

'I know who he is,' Lawson said.

'Then you'll know he's not easy to pin down. But we'll get him.' He took a photocopied bank statement out of one of the folders on his desk and passed it to Lawson. 'Rivers extended Enderby a loan a few days before he was shot. Three and a half million. No contract, no repayments. Just a loan between friends.'

'And you think Enderby is *clean*?'

'I didn't say he wasn't stupid. I think the penny dropped when Amy started asking questions. Anyway, that's when he got nervous.'

Lawson recalled Amy's notes, carefully hidden and password-protected on her computer files. She had been unsure of Enderby. 'Naive or knowing?' she had written. It was beginning to look like Enderby was naïve enough to have tackled Harris, and got himself shot for his impertinence.

'They had several meetings,' Hill went on. 'We got one of their conversations on tape.'

'And?'

Hill snorted. 'He was scared shitless – not that I blame him.'

'He was scared . . .' Lawson repeated. Hill had suppressed material that might have prevented Amy's death. Even after her murder, and the attack on Enderby, he hadn't come forward.

'We've got your man entering and leaving Harris's business premises on –' Hill reached for a folder and flipped it open 'Four occasions.'

Did he mean Fletcher? Lawson knew better than to give Hill a name. 'My man?' he repeated.

Hill paused a few moments, apparently waiting to see if Lawson would crack. Then he shrugged. 'Clemence.' He passed Lawson the folder he had just picked up from the pile. 'These are minor players. What you might call facilitators.'

'There are police officers on this list,' Lawson said, struggling to keep the anger out of his voice. Fletcher was there, as he had expected; he had been working on a murder case in which he might be implicated and Hill hadn't been bothered to pick up the phone and let somebody know.

Hill met him eye to eye. 'Paid for insider info, or to look the other way.'

'It goes without saying that you've passed these names on to Complaints and Discipline . . .'

'As of this morning.' As of the moment Hill knew that he would be held to account.

Lawson shook his head. 'You had all of this and you kept it to yourself.'

Hill shrugged. 'We're running a covert operation, Lawson. The fewer people in the know, the better.'

Lawson folded the sheet of paper and put it in his pocket. 'I want everything you've got on Amy Dennis.' He spoke softly and slowly. 'Everything on the Foremost Investments bid, Sebastian Enderby and the syndicate – official and unofficial. Files, faxes, photographs, taped conversations –' He stood and leaned over Hill. 'Everything.'

He paused at the door of the office. Hill wasn't a man who would feel shamed by his actions, and Lawson had seen him wriggle off the hook enough times to know that Complaints and Discipline wouldn't catch him out, but he understood politics, and he was vain enough to crave media attention.

'You won't have noticed in your chilly little ice-box,' he said. 'But it's hot outside. People have been frightened by Amy's death. The city's a potential powder keg. We had one incident this morning, and the media are circling like piranhas, waiting for something big to happen. So think about this as you contemplate your conspiracy theories: if I find you've kept so much as a discarded *sweet-wrapper* from my investigation, I'll feed you to them like so much live bait.'

# 43

'That's it,' Clara said. 'I'm phoning the hotel.'

Hugo followed her into the hall where she opened her briefcase and searched for the slip of paper on which she had jotted the number.

'Clara, you're overreacting.'

She stared at him. 'She hasn't rung, her mobile's switched off – they should have touched down half an hour ago – why hasn't she rung?'

'She probably forgot to switch it on again after they landed,' Hugo said. 'Baggage collection, Customs, the drive to the hotel – it could take them an hour or more. Give it some time.'

Clara found the slip and held it tight. 'She promised she'd ring,' she repeated doggedly.

'And she will. Give her breathing space.'

'So I'm suffocating her, now, am I?'

Hugo raised his hands. 'I didn't say that. But if you phone her sounding anxious, *she'll* be anxious.'

*Rein back, Clara. Rein back.* She took a few deep breaths. *It's not anger that's making you bite Hugo's head off, it's worry.*

'Of course you're right.' Clara remembered Pippa's obsessive checking and rechecking of her bags before they left home; the constant reassurance she had needed that she hadn't forgotten something, that Daddy would be there to say goodbye, that she wouldn't miss the plane.

Hugo stroked her upper arm with the back of his hand. 'I just want her to be able to relax.'

'So do I, Hugo.' Relieved, this time, that she sounded softer, less argumentative.

'I know,' he said. 'I know you do.' In the silence that followed, a reconciliation was forged. 'Why don't we sit in the garden, swat a few midges, sip a glass of wine?'

Clara smiled. 'You make is sound so appealing, but . . .' Her eyes strayed to her briefcase. 'I couldn't sit still. Not until I've heard from her.'

'And you think work might be the best distraction?'

She tilted her head apologetically. 'Maybe.'

'The glass of wine is still on offer. It's chilled . . .'

Clara felt a sudden release of tension: they were talking to each other without the threat of argument and the pall of guilt that had hung over their lives like a dark shadow since the previous autumn. 'A glass of wine would be lovely,' she said.

The evening was hot and she opened the dining-room windows before setting to work. A week ago, such an idea would have been unthinkable: to be alone in a room without locking the windows would have induced a panic attack. She felt stronger, happier now, than she had for many months.

She set the photographs out on the table, grouping them as if dealing cards for a game of Patience. Somewhere close by a lawnmower hummed, faltered, spat and was silent. The evening seemed to hold its breath, then a blackbird tried out a tentative three-bar melody in the lower branches of the oak at the end of the garden.

Clara examined the photographs. They were divided into three sets: a selection from Clemence's portfolio, the pictures of Amy which the police had found hidden in Clemence's flat, and photographs of the police officer taking payment for services rendered. She had yet to tell Clemence that she had shown these photographs to Lawson. She had put off going to see him, telling herself that the move from Castle Square to Forest Lane Police Station made the trip more difficult but the real reason was that she was fearful of Clemence's reaction.

For several minutes, Clara lost herself in the portraits of Clemence's portfolio. Most were angry men, furious that they hadn't been given the breaks they needed, that they had been caught. Many were hard men, who settled an argument or closed a deal by laying their opponent out. Some were bad men, hell-bent on self-destruction. In one or two, she saw the unmistakable mark of madness. But Clemence had coaxed something more from them: a human quality. Was it vulnerability, or sadness, or regret? Clara wasn't sure: it seemed to shift as she studied the pictures, as capricious as reflections on water.

The door opened. Hugo stood behind her and gently squeezed her shoulder. Clara turned, pressing her face against his hand.

'Feeling better?' he asked, the surprise and delight at this spontaneous show of affection evident in his voice.

'Feeling wonderful,' she said, surprised in turn that she actually meant it. Hugo handed her a glass of wine and she took it, savouring the first cold sip. He left his hand on her shoulder and Clara moved closer, feeling his body heat and relishing the light tangy scent of his cologne. For a brief moment she closed her eyes, thinking, *Yes, I remember this feeling: this is how it used to be.*

'He's good, isn't he?' Hugo stared at the photographs of the cons. 'He's captured something in them.'

Another wave of relief washed over Clara: he had forgiven her for taking on the case; even for having kept him in the dark.

'It's as though he's found the boy of seven in the face of the ruined man.'

'That's it,' she agreed, slipping her arm around his waist as naturally as if they had never spent months lying side-by-side in bed at night, an invisible barrier as cold and hard as steel between them, preventing them from touching, even by accident.

'I couldn't quite work it out, but that's precisely it: he's found the hidden core of neglect and wrongs that turned the injured little boy into the brutish adult.'

They contemplated the photographs for a few minutes longer and then Hugo broke the silence. 'Are these police photographs?' He tapped one of the pictures of the police officer taking an envelope from a cold-eyed man in a suit. 'They look like surveillance shots.'

Clara nodded. 'I got them off a roll of film hidden in his flat.'

Hugo twisted to face her and she laughed. 'The police have copies, Hugo. It's all above board.'

'I knew that,' he said, grinning sheepishly. But she had felt his grip on her shoulder tighten, even if it was only momentarily.

'Look at this,' she said, laying one of the pictures of Amy next to it. 'Clemence says the photos of Amy aren't his. He says they were planted in his flat.'

'They don't have the same look,' Hugo conceded. He pointed to one of the grainy shots of the murdered woman. 'Isn't that the one that's been in the papers?'

A nervous Amy, looking over her shoulder. Clara felt a stab of sympathetic anxiety. Who was behind the lens of the camera? Her killer?

'He was right, Hugo.'

'About what?'

'I thought all that paranoia about him being set up was fake – a story to get me on his side. But it's looking more and more likely that he's telling the truth.'

'What convinced you?'

Clara hadn't told him about the incident in the police station – and she wouldn't – but in truth, it was Clemence's compassion when she panicked that had tipped the balance. She picked up the photograph of the fat man and the cold-eyed gangster. 'This man is a police officer,' she said. 'And he's taking a bribe.'

Hugo looked at her, his expression sombre. When he opened his mouth to speak, she pressed one finger to his lips. 'It's perfectly safe,' she said. 'Steve Lawson is investigating.'

Hugo continued to search her face. She shouldn't have told him, but the strain of the day, the wine and the intoxicating warmth of him next to her, had made her drop her guard. She hadn't gone so far as to mention Harris's name, but that was sheer luck. 'It's something to do with the Dee View Development project,' she said. 'Nothing scary.'

Hugo's eyes widened. 'Dee View?' He held her at arm's length. 'Have you any idea how much money is riding on that project? It's huge, Clara. People will do anything for that kind of money. *Anything.*'

'Truly, Hugo. I wouldn't take any risks.'

His eyes brimmed with all the worry and pain of the previous months and Clara reached on tiptoe to kiss him. He didn't respond immediately but then he seemed to realise that she meant it and he bent to her, sliding his hands from her shoulders to her waist and pulling her to him.

Clara broke contact first, pulling away gently. They looked into each other's eyes breathless, perhaps a little shocked. Then they laughed – a burst of pure, joyful excitement: there *was* hope.

'I was planning to leave this till after dinner, but –' Clara felt suddenly awkward, unsure how to broach the subject. She riffled through the pockets of her briefcase and handed him an envelope. He opened it and took out a cheque. The bemused expression on his face made her want to kiss him again.

'Guilt-money,' she said. 'I called my mother. She

was *devastated* that she hadn't had time to come and see me, since my "unpleasant episode", but she's been *desperately* busy . . . Of course, if there was *anything* she could do . . .' She knew she sounded bitter and she forced herself to stop.

'I know how hard this must be for you,' Hugo began.

Clara shook her head. 'No. I've been selfish. I knew I only had to ask. Thing is, it wasn't money I wanted . . .'

Hugo kissed her forehead, but she eased away from him, determined to say what she had meant to say. 'It's all she *can* give, Hugo. It's all she knows how to give.

'I shouldn't have put you and Pippa through this. It wasn't your argument. It was futile and destructive.'

'It's natural to want to be loved, Clara.'

'I know. And it's foolish to waste your love where it's not returned. I have people here who love me.' She looked into his eyes; they were shining with love and longing. 'Second chance?' she said, aching with the pain she had caused him.

'As many as you need.'

He opened his arms and she slipped easily into his embrace. For a few seconds, she pressed her face to the cotton of his shirt, feeling his skin warm through the fabric, finding comfort in the regular thump of his heart.

'This is ten times what we need to pay for Pippa's holiday,' he said, reading the cheque once more over her shoulder.

'Poor Sophia's riddled with guilt. And I may have laid it on a bit thick.' She felt a laugh rumble in his chest. 'It'll keep us going until you get your next contract – and I build up a solid caseload.'

'What changed your mind?'

She shrugged, feeling rather foolish. 'Mitch sowed the seed. But ultimately, it was Pippa. Seeing her at the airport. Four-foot-nothing of gossamer and sunlight and desperate to protect me. I thought I was punishing Mother, letting the silence grow, being too proud to ask for help. But I was only punishing myself. All of us.

'D'you know what she said? "It's only money." Which, of course, is true, until you try to live without it.'

He touched her cheek gently and smiled. 'I'll make a start on dinner.'

For a few minutes, she listened to him clattering around the kitchen, the noise carrying window to window on the densely perfumed evening air. She took another sip of wine and turned her attention to the six, slightly blurred six-by-four shots of Amy. It occurred to her that, judging by the roll of film he had ferreted away behind the kitchen cupboards, Clemence knew a thing or two about hiding things. Why on earth would he leave such sensitive pictures where they were so easily found?

She kept coming back to the shot of Amy calling at someone else's house – it wasn't her own – there had been pictures of Amy Dennis's house in the papers the day after her body was found; hers was a small, modern semi with a square patch of front lawn and a concrete driveway. The house in the picture was much older, a little seedy, the hedge overgrown and the fence in need of repair.

'The evidence is in the pictures,' Clemence had said.

'You've just got to know where to look.' So she looked – long and hard. Most were of Amy arriving or leaving somewhere: a restaurant, a house, a public building. There was one of her sitting in the back garden of what Clara imagined must be her own house. Another of her getting into a car. She picked up the photograph. *She's smiling.* At what?

She went to the junk drawer of the dresser in the alcove by the window. In the kitchen, the radio was tuned to a classical music station; an aria from Cosi Fan Tutte, full of yearning and the poignant certainty of disillusionment.

The cold water tap came on: a short, harsh hiss of sound. Clara pictured Hugo standing at the sink, a tea towel over one shoulder and she felt a surge of love for him. He had tried so hard – to be there when she needed him, to back off when she needed to find her feet, to care for Pippa when she, Clara, was incapable. He tried to hold the family together even when he found it hard enough just keeping himself from falling apart.

Her emotions threatened to overwhelm her and she returned to her search in an effort to banish the feelings that were too raw to face. She dragged open a drawer and turned its contents upside down in her search. Rolls of sellotape, odd batteries, a box of matches, rubber bands, out-of-date raffle ticket stubs. She pulled them out and then shoved them back, frustrated. She found it under a notepad at the bottom of the accumulated rubbish. A magnifying glass. Tilting the photograph to the light, she passed the glass over it; the dark blob she had noticed on the driver's side of the car resolved into a silhouette.

'She's not smiling at some*thing*,' she muttered. 'She's smiling at some*one*.' There was somebody waiting for her in the car.

Harris was involved in the project in some way. Had he got pictures of Amy talking to someone who could harm him? Was Clemence a convenient scapegoat?

If Harris intended to set Clemence up for Amy Dennis's murder, he could hardly have sent Clemence himself out to take the photographs they would use to frame him. Did Harris know about Clemence's connection with Amy? – The prison grapevine was faster than email for disseminating information, and Harris certainly had some close contacts inside. Or maybe he had sent somebody to check out Amy's records and stumbled across the information serendipitously. She shook her head: the newspaper reports had said there was no sign of a break-in. Which brought her back to how *un*likely a suspect Clemence was, when you really scrutinised the situation: what woman in her right mind would willingly let an ex-student who also happens to be an ex-prisoner – and a convicted murderer – into her house in the dead of night?

So somebody else took the pictures. One of Harris's men? It would have to be somebody with surveillance skills. She felt a sudden chill at the notion that the happy-snapper might be the fat policeman in Harris's pay: after all, a woman wouldn't hesitate to let a police officer in to her house in the dead of night, would she?

Clara pressed a hand to her midriff to stay the flutter

of nervousness in her stomach. Other people have surveillance skills, she thought, it didn't have to be the policeman. She went to the hall and took the *Yellow Pages* from the window ledge.

There weren't many detective agencies listed in Wirral and Chester *Yellow Pages* and she tried them all, working through them alphabetically. Despite the late hour, most of them were open for business and those that weren't gave an emergency mobile number. Clara made arrangements to see the people she spoke with directly and left a suitably ambiguous message, together with her mobile number, on a couple of answer machines.

Now the difficult part: tackling Hugo.

'Will dinner be long?' she asked, lingering in the kitchen doorway to facilitate an easy escape.

'I'm making risotto.' He was chopping onions next to the open window, his back to her. 'Why, are you starving?'

'I thought I might slip out for a while.'

He turned to face her.

'Just to talk to a few private investigators,' she said. 'I've had an idea about the photographs.'

Hugo tilted his head, waiting for an explanation.

'It's a long shot,' Clara said. 'I'm probably way off the mark.'

'What makes you think they'll talk to you?'

She shrugged. 'It's a reaction I'm looking for, not a confession. Something to take to Steve Lawson. Something to make him listen.'

Hugo wiped his hands. 'I'll come with you.'

Clara laughed. 'No you don't! What will they think when they see me with six-foot-four of muscle in tow? I wouldn't even get past the introductions.'

'I could follow at a distance,' Hugo suggested.

'I'm seeing licensed PIs, Hugo – not shady security guards with a pedigree in the penal system. I'll ask a few questions and then leave. It'll take me an hour at most.'

'All right,' he said. 'But you leave your mobile switched on, and you ring me if you're at all nervous.'

Most of the offices were located near the city centre, so Clara parked at the top end of Foregate Street and walked from one appointment to the next. By seven p.m., she had visited four agencies; the brief hiatus between shopping crowds and evening clientele was over and the streets were filling with groups of people strolling towards the restaurants and bars in the centre, laughing, arms linked, gearing up for Saturday night.

Clara walked up to The Cross, turning left into Watergate Street. The agency she was heading for was accessed via a flight of worn stone steps onto the raised wooden walkway of the Rows. A little further down, towards the main road, and just past an estate agency, she found a glistening black door. The brass plaque on the brickwork to the left read 'Morrow's Detective Agency'.

She rang but the intercom remained stubbornly mute. She pressed the bell push again; still no answer. *Damnit!* As she turned away from the door, her mobile rang. She fished it out of her handbag and answered.

'Ainscough Security.' A man's voice. 'Peter Ain-scough. You left a message.'

'Thank you for getting back to me,' Clara said. 'Can we meet?'

There was a pause. 'It's late . . .'

'I know, and if there's a consultancy fee, I'll pay it.'

'What's this about?' He sounded doubtful.

'Photographs,' Clara replied. 'I'm trying to find out who took them.'

'Look,' he said, 'Don't shoot the messenger, okay? If you've got problems in your relationship, talk to your bloke. All we do is collect the evidence.'

*My 'bloke'?* Clara pulled a face at the handset. 'It isn't like that,' she said. 'I'm a defence lawyer. You might be able to help me – and as I said, I'll pay a fee, of course.'

'Contact me during office hours.' She had said the wrong thing. Apparently, he didn't like lawyers.

'My name is Clara Pascal,' she said, raising her voice. She paused, listening; he was still on the line. 'You may have heard of me.'

His silence told her that he had.

'Meet me,' she repeated. 'At your office – a wine bar – anywhere.'

'I don't know about you,' he said, 'but I could do with a drink.'

His tone was quite altered. Some men seemed to get a vicarious thrill from talking to her, knowing what she had been through. *There you go again, Clara: using your notoriety to get what you want.* What would Marcia make of it? Was it a good or a bad sign?

She shrugged and set off, back the way she had come, toward Bridge Street. There were tables set out on the pavement outside Café Renouf, but she would have to go in to order. The main body of the restaurant was in a basement of one of the Rows buildings: scrubbed brickwork and groyned ceilings, a remnant of the thirteenth-century buildings that had once stood in the walled city centre. The low ceilings and faintly musty smell reminiscent of a crypt. Or a cellar.

Clara stood outside for an agonising few minutes, breathing deeply, visualising going down the wrought-iron staircase into the gloom, telling herself, as her counsellor had advised her, that it was safe, that she could walk out whenever she chose. It didn't help much, but it got her down the stairs to order a bottle of wine and back out again without a panic attack.

She hurried outside, into the light and air to sit at an empty table and wait. She sipped her glass of cold wine slowly, grateful that the sun had already sunk over the westerly edge of the rooftops and the street was in shade. Nevertheless the evening was warm and she slipped off her jacket and draped it over the back of her chair.

Twenty minutes passed and there was still no sign of Ainscough. What was keeping him? Clara felt a sudden prickling unease and she glanced to her left, peering into the darkness of the Rows opposite. People walked along the raised walkways from time to time; she had caught their fleeting shadows from the corner of her eye. As she watched, something detached itself from the gloom of a shop doorway on the raised level, coalescing and gaining form. It was a man. He trotted down the wooden steps opposite her, his hands in his pockets.

Clara's heart-rate picked up, but she forced herself to remain still.

He was tall, and he looked like he kept himself fit. 'Mr Ainscough?'

'The same.'

She smiled, inviting him to sit, and poured him a glass of wine. Feeling his close scrutiny, she made eye contact, challenging him.

He had the wary eyes of an ex-cop who had seen everything and believed nothing. They raked her face, trying to make her out, while revealing nothing of himself. 'You're not what I expected.'

'Really, Mr Ainscough?' she said. 'What *did* you expect?'

He laughed. 'A barrister, Clara,' he said. 'And call me Pete. Me – when I think "lady barrister", I think hard-faced cow. Or maybe my ex's lawyer has soured me.'

'I don't do divorce cases,' Clara said. 'And I'm harder than I look.'

'Yeah,' he said, pensively stroking the stem of his glass, slipping her a sympathetic look. 'You'd have to be.'

Clara clenched her teeth. Bloody hell! *Well what did you expect when you go flaunting your tragic history at him?*

'I'd like to show you some photographs,' she said, keeping her voice pleasant. 'Perhaps you can tell me if your agency took them.'

Ainscough looked away from her. 'Can't promise anything,' he said, apparently offended by her rebuff. 'But get 'em out by all means, let's see what you've got.' The *double-entendre* was deliberate and it was intended to provoke.

Clara kept the pleasant, rather bland expression on her face while she found the wallet of photographs in her handbag. She watched Ainscough closely as he sorted through them. There was a flash of something in the first instant, extinguished too rapidly for her to analyse.

'You recognise them?' she asked.

'It's Amy Dennis. She was in the papers.'

She picked out the photograph of Amy on somebody else's doorstep. 'This one was used by the press.'

'Was it?' he frowned. 'I don't get much chance to read the papers . . .'

Was he afraid of admitting he had taken them? Certainly the police would want to know why he hadn't come forward.

'Mr Ainscough – Pete –' Clara said. 'I'm not looking to blame anyone here. I just want to help my client.'

'Commendable,' he replied. 'But I don't see how I—'

'I know you took these.' Again, Clara saw a flicker of something.

Ainscough gave her a half-smile. 'Yeah?' he said. 'What makes you so sure?'

Clara couldn't answer that convincingly, so she didn't try. 'My client is accused of murder, Pete. Please – you don't know how important this is.'

Again, he looked away for a fraction of a second. 'You're a lawyer, Clara,' he said. 'As a lawyer, you should understand I can't break client confidentiality.'

'If I say a name—'

'*No*,' he interrupted, a little too loudly. A few heads turned and he took a gulp of wine, hunching himself against the unwanted attention. After a moment or two, he looked into her face. Clara did not speak.

'Look . . .' He gave her an embarrassed smile. 'I've already said more than I should have.'

Clara held his gaze. 'Was your client Brendan Harris?'

This time he didn't flinch. Didn't so much as blink. But as he stared back at her, refusing to comment, Clara thought she saw relief in his eyes. And she knew she had been right.

# 44

DC Thorpe spilt scalding coffee over his fingers lifting the plastic cup from the dispenser. He swore softly and comprehensively. It was seven-thirty p.m. and he was already late for the debrief.

'Here, mate.' Fletch offered him a paper tissue.

They were alone in what was generously termed 'the kitchen': a room which had been chosen for the purpose because it had a sink and a window that opened. It was furnished with a table and chairs, and equipped with a kettle, a microwave and a vending machine that dispensed hot drinks of an indeterminate nature.

Thorpe eyeballed him, transferring the cup to his left hand before flicking the now cooling coffee from his right. 'What do you want, Fletch?'

'Don't be like that, Chris.' Fletcher lowered his arm, absently crumpling the tissue into a ball in his fist.

'*Don't be—?*' Thorpe shook his head in disbelief and made to walk past, but Fletcher caught him just above the elbow. Thorpe didn't resist; he looked at Fletch's fat fingers gouging the flesh of his upper arm, then slowly tracked up to Fletch's face. Fletcher let go.

'I just wondered if you'd heard anything.'

'I hear a lot of things, Fletch. You'd be surprised: every day, something new.'

'I mean about the pictures.'

'What about them?'

'It's just – people have been looking at me funny.'

'You want to try sprucing up your wardrobe,' Thorpe said. 'Summer sales are on.'

'I'm *serious*, Chris.'

'So am I.'

Fletcher paused for a moment, and then continued with an effort. 'I'm sorry, all right? I've gotta cover my back—'

'So long as you're all right, eh?'

'But I'm not.' Fletch smiled, a small, frightened twitch of the mouth. 'Barton's keeping me out of the loop – counting bloody paperclips while the real work gets passed to a frigging fourteen-year-old on work experience.'

'Well, I'd better not be seen with you, had I?' Thorpe said. The disparaging reference to Cath Young did nothing to endear him.

Fletcher shifted from one foot to the other. 'Look,' he said. 'I panicked a bit. But I wouldn't have let it go too far.' He spread his hands. 'I wouldn't let them put you in the frame.'

'But I am, Fletch. I am in the frame. And *you* put me there. I'm under suspicion because I did a favour for a mate. And guess what – he shafted me.' He placed his coffee, untasted, on the table and looked at Fletcher.

'It's my name in the log. Mine. As far as Lawson is concerned, I nicked police evidence and sold it to the tabloids.'

'I'll tell them –' Fletcher began impulsively, but he didn't go on, so Thorpe pushed him.

'Yeah? What're you gonna tell them, Fletch?'

Fletcher's gaze shifted a little to his left, then back again. 'I'll tell him there were only five photos – Clemence probably sold one before we found them.'

Thorpe laughed. 'For a minute there, I thought you were going to come clean, Fletch. You sold the picture. I know it, you know it, and soon Lawson'll know it.'

Fletcher licked his lips. 'Look, I didn't—'

'Don't lie to me, Fletch – I may be a mug, but I'm not a complete idiot.'

Fletcher coloured a little. Thorpe left it until Fletch's neck was as red as the rest of his face.

'Don't worry,' Thorpe said at last. 'I won't grass you up. But not because I feel sorry for you. If I tell Lawson, it makes me look criminally stupid instead of just plain criminal. It would embarrass me to have to admit I was a prize pillock. But I won't have to tell him – he'll work it out for himself. And when he does' – he prodded Fletch in the chest – '*you* are on your own, mate.'

'I'm sorry, all right?' Fletch moved close enough for Thorpe to smell the whisky from his lunch-time top-up, soured by fear. 'We all make mistakes.'

Thorpe remembered how Fletch had shaken him off in the car park earlier in the day, refusing even to discuss the photographs when he had thought that Thorpe would take the blame for the theft of the picture.

'Yeah,' he said. 'My mistake was trusting you.'

'If you'd let me explain . . .'

'I don't want to hear it. You fucked up, and you want me to bail you out. Like I always bail you out.'

Thorpe turned to leave, but Fletcher grabbed his arm again. 'You don't understand.' His fingers felt clammy and slippery. 'It's not the poxy picture.'

For a couple of seconds neither man spoke. Fletch was frightened of something far more terrifying than simply losing his job. His eyes were red-rimmed – hangover or emotion, Thorpe couldn't tell. 'What the hell have you done?' he asked, almost awed by the man's terror.

Fletch passed one hand over his face. When it came away, his eyelashes were wet. 'Been a bit careless,' he said.

Thorpe almost gave in then. This was new on him: Fletch actually admitting to his own stupidity, acknowledging his fault in whatever scam he had allowed himself to be sucked into. If he had left it at the admission – if he had waited for Thorpe to make up his own mind – he might well have found an ally, but he couldn't stay silent. He couldn't simply ask: Fletch had to demand help.

'You've gotta listen to me, Chris,' he said.

'That's where you're wrong,' Thorpe answered. 'I don't have to listen. I don't have to help you out, or give you a break, or do you a favour. I don't owe you a thing.'

# 45

The City Keys was a proper pub, in Terry Spence's reckoning. No poncy themes, no posy soap star celebs, hoping to be recognised – just good ale, plenty of games machines, a pool table and live footie by satellite. No food, but you could always get a meat pie from Sayers up the road. A traditional pub, where you could have a quiet pint with your mates.

The doors were open and the jukebox music throbbed into the street, hard and slow as his pulse. He was hot and thirsty despite the lager he'd been drinking steadily since the abortive raid on the police station that morning. Him and half a dozen others who had the sense to run instead of trying to take on the dibble reinforcements when they arrived.

He'd found a new friend in Spider – he might be only a kid, but the lad had a head on his shoulders. For the first hour they congratulated each other on their respective roles in the assault.

'This guy,' Spider said, 'was awesome. Straight in there with his baseball bat. Dibble one *boom*! Dibble two *twat*! and we're in.'

'Did you see the look on that copper's face when we came through the door?' Terry asked.

'He crapped himself, I swear.'

The lads round the table laughed. Somebody brought a couple more drinks over for Terry and Spider.

'What about that hooker, eh?' Spider said.

'The hooker?'

'The girl in the cell.'

'You should've sprung her, man. She was up for it.'

'You reckon?'

'Gagging for it.' Spider looked around the group. 'She says "Let me out or piss off". *He* says, "Think I'll just piss off then".' More laughter.

Terry thought about it. He'd had quite a lot to drink by this time, his head felt loose on his neck, and thinking was getting to be a complicated process. 'Don't think she was a hooker, though.'

Spider laughed into his pint, spraying foam over his companions. 'The voice of experience,' he said, wiping his mouth with the back of his hand.

Terry smiled crookedly. 'Stick with me, kid – you might learn something.'

'I'm not ready to sign up for me Stakeholder Pension just yet, mate.'

They joked and swapped insults for the next hour, arguing over who had led the charge. The make-up of the group was fluid: some came, some left, off to do their afternoon shift, or out for a bite to eat. It wasn't Terry's regular pub, so mostly it was Spider's mates. People came in just to get a look at the lads who'd stormed Castle Square Station. A few returned later in the day, bringing bags of chips and news off the radio. Terry felt like a minor celeb himself.

They watched the TV for a while. Man U lost and for a while they kept depression at bay by slagging off Victoria Beckham and speculating what they might do to her, given half a chance.

'I wish he would've been there, though,' Terry said.

'Clemence?' Spider asked.

'No – David bloody Beckham, who d'you think?' He felt suddenly irritated by Spider's stupidity. He was hot and uncomfortable, he needed a shower and bloody Spider was asking daft bloody questions.

'Me and this lot kicked the shit out of him once already.' Spider looked to his mates for confirmation.

Terry screwed up his eyes to get Spider in focus. He didn't look like he was joking. 'When was this then?'

'Wednesday night,' Spider said.

One of the lads squared his shoulders. 'He was stalking some girls, like.'

Terry jerked a thumb in the direction of the speaker. 'Regular knight in shining armour, your mate, isn't he?'

Spider drew his eyebrows together. 'He was, though. We saw him follow them girls out the bar didn't we?' His friends agreed readily. 'If that fat dibble hadn't stuck his oar in, we'd've finished the job.' He suddenly remembered something and said to the boy opposite, 'Show him your leg. Bastard dibble near broke his leg, didn't he?' He wasn't satisfied till the boy had yanked down his trackie bottoms and showed everyone the bruising on the back of his knee where Barton had hit him.

By the time the whistles and catcalls died down,

Terry's growing sense of frustration and general discomfort had solidified in a slow-burning anger. This kid was telling him he had battered Clemence. For two months Terry had listened to Clemence's smart-arsed comments, he had put up with his constant needling; he had watched Clemence swagger around the workplace and he hadn't so much as landed a punch. He was pissed and he was pissed off, and hearing Spider boasting about his exploits wasn't improving his mood any.

'Nearly hammered him meself,' he said. 'Same night.'

'Nearly?' Spider was sneering at him. Terry's temper turned up a notch. This snot-nosed seventeen-year-old skinhead was *sneering* at him.

'No,' he said, compounding his mistake. 'I nearly did. With a hammer.'

Spider was curious. 'So what stopped you?'

'The boss came in . . .'

There were guffaws around the table. 'I could understand that, mate,' Spider sympathised. He looked round at his pals, making sure they were all listening. 'Threaten to keep you in at playtime, did he?'

Laughter exploded and Terry got unsteadily to his feet. 'You arrogant little prick,' he said.

Spider stood up and his mates fell quiet, watching, ready for a ruck.

One of Terry's mates, freshly showered and changed ready for his shift came in off the street. He sized up the situation: Terry and Spider head-to-head. One of Spider's gang lightly fingering a beer bottle, ready to switch grip to use it as a club if it came to anything.

After the slightest of hesitations, Terry's mate carried on walking, speaking over the jukebox. 'You heard they moved him?'

'Moved who?' Spider said, not taking his eyes off Terry.

'Clemence.'

'Is he thick, or what?' Spider addressed the question to Terry; it was intended as an insult: *even your mates are dense*. 'They moved Clemence this morning,' he said, keeping his eyes on Terry. 'He wasn't there when we took the station.' Sounded good that: 'Took the station' – had a nice ring to it.

Terry's mate was unfazed. He pulled out a stool and straddled it. 'You're wrong, lad. When we stormed the Bastille, Clemence was still there. The mouthy bint was his barrister.'

Spider turned to face the speaker. 'She was locked in his cell with him?'

There was hush, then Terry said, 'Blimey – I thought she sounded a bit breathless.'

That broke the tension. Everyone laughed – even Spider's mates; the adrenaline rush was still working in them; it wouldn't take much to make their anger boil over into violence, but now it was directed at their proper target: Clemence.

'Where is the bastard?' Terry demanded.

'Secure station,' his friend said. 'We wouldn't get within a hundred yards.'

Terry smiled slowly. 'We can still hit him where it

hurts. Bring the empties,' he said. 'We'll be needing them.'

Spider didn't move. His gang waited for his signal. 'We don't take orders,' he said.

Terry shrugged. 'Up to you. I just thought you wouldn't want to miss out.' His smile broadened. 'You see, I know where Clemence lives.'

# 46

Clara checked her watch again. It was seven forty-five and she was anxious that she might already have missed Pippa's telephone call.

*You could go home* . . . She could, but she knew she wouldn't. The police *had* to act on the information she had gleaned from her conversation with Ainscough. If they got to him quickly, he wouldn't have time to think of ways of covering up. If she spoke to Lawson, she knew she would be able to convince him.

She returned to the reception desk and asked what was keeping the inspector. The constable lifted the receiver wearily and punched an extension number. He listened for a moment, then turned the receiver to her, so that she could hear it ringing unanswered. 'Still in his meeting, ma'am,' he said, contriving to make a perfectly civil explanation sound decidedly *un*civil.

'Can't you try the Incident Room?' she demanded. 'This is urgent.'

He replaced the receiver and gave her a blank stare. *He's been working on that look,* she thought.

'The inspector should be out in twenty minutes, maybe half an hour,' he said, as if there could not be a more convivial way to pass the time than sitting on a bench in the hot and grubby reception area of a police station.

Reluctantly, Clara went and sat down again. She couldn't wait half an hour. She wondered whether she should go to see Clemence at the secure station in Boughton but indecision nibbled at her resolve, telling her to go home, to talk to her daughter. She had the sense of compounding one mistake with another, but she couldn't see a way out.

A couple of police constables came through the door to her right heading for the exit; the door swung to under the weight of the spring and she heard the lock click. A phone rang in the inner office and the officer on desk duty went to answer it. Half a minute later, the two officers who had stood duty at the station entrance for the past two hours came in for their break. Although Clemence had been moved, they had kept a high uniform profile at the station. One of the officers called through and the duty officer popped his head around the door.

'Get it yourself, will you, mate?' he said. 'I've got my hands full.'

The officer leaned over the desk, hooking his hand under the counter to press the door release. It buzzed and his partner pushed it open. They both went through, barely glancing at Clara; she had become almost a fixture in the place over the last couple of days. As the door swung closed, Clara stretched out the tip of her toe to catch it. She watched for the duty officer's return, listening to the two constables' chatting as they walked down the corridor, waiting until they went through a second door before she slid off the bench, ducking low. She crept through, closing the door behind her.

She knew the way to Lawson's office, and took the back stairs, her heart thudding at the thought of meeting somebody. But it was late; the night duty officers had already started their patrols, those involved in the murder enquiry were in their debrief, and the building was quiet. Lawson's office was empty, but she heard his voice coming from a room further down the corridor.

She would pass a message to him via one of his officers, asking Lawson to come and speak to her – if he was handing out work for them to do, they should follow up on Ainscough tonight. She went to the door and stood at the entrance.

Thirty people were crammed into the limited space, some sitting on chairs and tables, a few standing at the back.

Lawson was at the far end of the room. He saw her almost immediately and stopped talking. Twenty or more heads turned, following his line of sight. 'I'm sorry to interrupt,' she said. 'I have—' Her eye strayed to a table to the right.

*My God, it's him.* It was the man in Clemence's photograph – the police officer. She stared from Lawson to the man and back to Lawson. Her heart hammered in her throat and she felt the familiar, unpleasant tingling in her fingertips that preceded a panic attack, and yet, from somewhere in the rational part of her being, her inner voice spoke up.

*Would you stop gawking at the man?* Not her mother's censorious carping this time, but Mitch, talking sense, as she always did. Clara dragged her eyes from the man's face and made an effort to seem calm.

'I . . . have some information – it can't wait,' she said.

Lawson was leading the briefing in DCI McAteer's absence; they had just received news that Sebastian Enderby had died. McAteer was meeting with the SIO on the case, to discuss strategy. Lawson turned to Sergeant Barton.

'Take Ms Pascal to my office,' he said. 'We'll talk after the briefing. Now, let's get back to business.' His brisk, sharp manner drew the attention back to him.

'DC Young, what's the score on Brendan Harris?'

'Harris, five, Young, nil.' She was playing it down, but Lawson could see that she had been shaken by the encounter. 'Oily bastard asked me to convey his heart-felt good wishes to the investigation team. He says he's keen to do whatever he can to assist in the police inquiry.'

Lawson nodded. 'Keep on at them. We keep shaking the tree till something falls out.'

It was no more than twenty paces to Lawson's room, but it was a feat of will for Clara to make it. Her legs seemed unwilling to support her and she felt suddenly and devastatingly cold. Twice before this had happened – both times she had blacked out.

*It's all right, girl. Stay calm and don't forget to breathe.* Mitch again, dispensing good advice.

Barton stood back and Clara walked through the door, feeling the room tilt as she lowered herself into the nearest chair.

'He shouldn't be too long,' Barton said, folding his arms and blocking the doorway with his bulk.

*Say something, Clara.* 'Some of those officers worked my case, didn't they?' Her voice sounded thin and tinny.

Barton nodded. 'It happens.' No change of facial expression.

'I wish I'd had the opportunity to thank them all.'

'Getting you back safe was thanks enough.' The words sounded flat, insincere. She couldn't read him.

Lawson had told her that he was investigating and she had trusted him to do just that. Yet he had allowed the man to remain in post – working on an investigation of a murder in which he might well have been involved. She should have left it at that, but she had a perverse and rather foolish notion that if she knew his name, it would protect her in some obscure way.

'The dark-haired woman near to Inspector Lawson,' she said. 'I recognised her.'

'DC Young.'

She nodded, smiling, her heart rate picking up as she added. 'And the chunky fellow to the right of the door . . .' *God Almighty, you'll need a crash course in cross-examination skills, if you ever get back in a criminal court.*

Barton didn't answer at once. She noticed this. She also noticed his reluctance when finally he supplied the officer's name. 'DC Fletcher,' he said.

Clara nodded. 'Of course.' She had never heard the name, but she shook her head, as if to say, 'How could I forget?'

Barton narrowed his eyes at her.

*He knows I'm dissembling.* Suddenly, the queasy, panicky feeling returned. Barton stood in the doorway, blocking the light, sucking the air out of the room, and she felt she would suffocate.

'I'll come back later,' she said standing rather uncertainly.

'Like I said, the boss won't be long,' Barton reassured her. He didn't budge.

Clara's terror threatened to overwhelm her. She swallowed, making an effort to slow her breathing; she had learned during her captivity that there are degrees of terror, that she could control her fear – although since her release, that notion had become more a theoretical concept than a practical skill.

This time, however, she managed it; she turned it down a notch or two, but she found her rationality no help at all. Ainscough Security photographed Amy Dennis for Brendan Harris; Harris was involved in some crooked manipulation of the Dee View project; DC Fletcher was in Brendan Harris's pay. Who was to say DS Barton didn't work for him as well? There was a lot of investment potential in Dee View. Plenty of money to grease any squeaky wheels. And for anyone who couldn't be bribed, Harris knew plenty of other ways to buy silence.

Clara looked Barton in the eye. 'I'll talk to Inspector Lawson tomorrow,' she said. 'I'm expected at home.' It

was absurd, but making even an oblique reference to
Hugo made her feel safer.

'Up to you,' Barton said, but still he didn't move. 'If
you want to leave a message – or maybe there's something I could help with?' She thought she heard something unpleasant, insinuating in his tone.

'No.' She tried to sound firm, rather than belligerent.
'It can wait.'

His forehead furrowed briefly. 'You sneak past our
security and gatecrash the evening debrief and suddenly it doesn't seem that important?'

Clara walked straight at him, thinking for one crazy
moment of Harry Potter, racing towards a wall at
King's Cross Station. Faith saved Harry from crashing
into solid brick and breaking his head, and faith saved
Clara: at the last moment, Barton gave way, standing
aside to let her through.

Steve Lawson found Barton alone in their office a few
minutes after the briefing. 'Bloody hell, Phil! Couldn't
you have kept her a few minutes longer?' he demanded.

'I tried, Boss, but she was spooked.'

Lawson dumped his notes on his desk and slumped
into a chair. 'Fletcher,' he said. 'Where did she go?'

'Home, I think.' Barton shrugged. 'I'm sorry, Steve,
She's a hard woman to turn once she's made her mind
up.'

'Don't I know it.' Lawson flicked through the pile of
documents on his desk with a sinking heart. 'She's
convinced Clemence was set up.'

'She's been wrong before.'

Lawson gave him a searching look. 'I daresay we all have, Phil.'

Barton flushed. 'You only have to look at the evidence.'

'Give it a rest, will you?'

But Barton would not be deflected. 'For God's sake, Steve! We've got the murder weapon with his fingerprints all over it.'

Lawson shook his head. 'Fletch—' He bit off what he was about to say, closing the door before starting again. Keeping his voice low, this time, he took Barton's arguments point by point. 'Fletcher could have planted the pictures. We got the T-shirt, fine – but there's no sign of blood in Clemence's flat. The murder weapon has got Amy's blood on it all right, and Clemence's fingerprints. But the distribution of both is all wrong. And what about the unidentified footprint? We've tried matching it to everyone who might have gone anywhere near the scene – including you. And Clemence. No match.'

'So he got rid of the shoes,' Barton said. 'Clemence may not be very bright, but he was in the nick long enough to do the basic forensic awareness course.'

'He disposed of the shoes but kept the T-shirt? He'd have to be dense, Phil. And Clemence may be a lot of things, but he's not dense.'

Barton sat and brooded for a while. Lawson gave up on him and started working through the reports and correspondence in his in-tray, skimming and prioritising, restacking the urgent to the left, non-urgent to the right.

'Say he was set up,' Barton said. 'That's not to say he's innocent – just that he was the right man to take the fall.'

Lawson floated the next flimsy onto the urgent pile. 'He's an obvious target,' he agreed.

'But who's to say he didn't do the job for Harris or whoever and then they double-crossed him? Who's to say he didn't kill that poor bastard Enderby, as well? It's not like he's going to hold his hand up to murder. And even Clemence has got the sense to know that he wouldn't survive a month inside if he grassed up Harris.'

Lawson thought about it. 'I don't see him jeopardising his freedom after two months on the outside. It's not like he's a career criminal: he seems to take his photography seriously.'

'Yeah. Seriously enough to scare the shit out of Mrs Tobin. And don't forget, I saw his dark-room. It takes money to buy kit like that. A lot of money.'

'He reckons he scrounged or scavenged most of it.'

Barton snorted. 'I believe him.'

'This is far too personal, Phil,' Lawson said.

Barton avoided his eye. He realised he had spoken more sharply than he had intended. Lawson riffled through the Rolodex on his desk, searching for Clara's number, picking up the phone with his free hand as it rang.

He listened for a few moments, then asked 'When?' Clara forgotten, he rooted for a pen under the flurry of papers on his desk, then jotted down a few words.

'Who's dealing?' he asked.

He slid the notebook to Barton. *Attack on Clemence's flat*, it read. *Possible casualties*.

Barton felt sick. This wasn't supposed to happen.

# 47

Clara turned off Handbridge into Queen's Park Road, wondering what Hugo would say if she asked him how he would like to do that bodyguard job, after all. The fact was, she didn't feel safe going back to the police station alone.

Almost home. The radio was tuned to Gold Coast FM and as the dance tune faded, the news jingle cut in.

'Just in: police and fire crews are called to a disturbance in Hoole.'

Clara slowed down, leaning across to turn up the volume. The headlines continued with a background drum beat and four-note spacers, designed to heighten the dramatic effect. She barely heard the other news items for the clamouring in her head.

'Fire crews are tackling a blaze in Hoole, just outside Chester city centre tonight,' the presenter said. 'Crowds gathered outside the house earlier this evening, after rumours that a man arrested in the Amy Dennis murder hunt had been released.' The urgent back-beat continued. 'Jamie Dillon reports live from the scene.'

'The house is still on fire, John.' The young reporter was finding it hard to keep calm, his voice was pitched too high and breathy. 'The mob won't let the fire service near – they're throwing bricks and stones. You might be able to hear the shouting.' A pause, while he held the microphone to the night. As if aware that this was their cue, the screams grew louder and something shattered nearby.

'Can you tell us, is anyone hurt, Jamie?' the station presenter asked.

'Police evacuated the house an hour ago. There's nobody left inside. But unless they get the rioters under control, the fire service fears the entire house could go up—'

Clara snapped the radio off and turned her car into a driveway, reversing so fast that her front spoiler caught on the slope, crunching metal on brick. She turned back the way she had come. *Bastards!* He didn't have much – but they had to take it, anyway. They had to teach him a lesson, didn't they?

Her anger at the rioters was mitigated by a burning shame: hadn't she condemned him with the rest – treating him as a 'type', a vicious animal beyond change or redemption?

Forest Lane Police Station was at the back end of the city, beyond the walls and out of range of the centre's more picturesque influence. It was a narrow, red-brick building, the reception area was only large enough to seat two people; it had two cells and one interview room.

The interview room was a small, windowless box, and Clara had to brace herself to shut the door. *God, it's as airless as a coffin,* she thought. The notion shocked her. *Where the hell did that spring from?* In all the days of her incarceration, in all the months of recovery and counselling, she had never had this thought before. *Now is not the time, Clara. Save it for the counselling sessions.*

She waited fifteen minutes, fighting the claustrophobia induced by the soundproofing boards, the securely anchored furniture and the stale, dead air of the windowless room. If the light bulb had failed in those fifteen minutes she would have gone mad: started screaming and simply been unable to stop. But she held on, controlling her fear minute by minute, fighting the cowardly impulse to leave and give Brent Quartermaine the dirty work of telling Clemence.

At last, she heard a brief muffled conversation outside the room and then the door opened.

'Seems your client isn't too pleased to see you, Ms Pascal,' the custody sergeant said. He stood close to Clemence, as if concerned that he might kick off at any moment.

Clemence held his hands limp at his sides, his shoulders slightly slumped. The swollen blood vessel on his damaged eye had gone down, but the eye socket was black and the bruising at the edge of his hairline had spread, purple and livid, to his forehead. His eyes were dark and angry.

'You've not brought a clerk with you, then?' the sergeant said, intimating that he thought the omission irresponsible.

'It would seem not.'

'Are you going to behave yourself, Ian?' he asked.

'Model of good manners, me, Sarge,' Clemence replied, keeping his eyes on Clara.

'Please sit down, Mr Clemence,' Clara said, returning his gaze.

He seemed to think about it and then, with a slight shrug, he took the two steps to the table and lowered himself into the chair opposite her. It seemed the bruising to his body was still causing him some discomfort. It didn't show in his face, however; he sat with his feet apart, hands resting on his thighs, eyeing her coldly.

'Thank you, Sergeant,' Clara said, careful that nothing passed between her and the police officer that might be misconstrued as collusion.

'You got the fags I asked for?' Clemence asked.

The sergeant switched his attention to Clemence. 'Thought you were the model of good manners,' he said, fishing in his trouser pocket for the cigarettes and matches.

Clemence shrugged. 'What d'you expect from my sort?'

The desk sergeant stacked the packet and the box of matches on the table and left with a backward look of warning to Clara.

After a silence calculated to give the sergeant time to return to his desk, Clara said. 'I'm sorry I didn't come back sooner.'

'Got the pictures?' She might not have spoken.

She handed them over without further comment and he sifted through them in silence while she waited. 'Have you shown these to Quartermaine?'

'I wanted you to see them first.'

The hard glitter of anger returned to his eye. 'Yeah?'

'You were right about him being a police officer,' she went on.

'How would you know that?' he asked.

'I spoke to Inspector Lawson.'

He didn't comment, but she could see him notching it up as one more betrayal in a long list of betrayals.

'He is investigating.'

'Oh, well, that puts my mind a rest. One dibble investigating another who stitched me up. Very reassuring.'

'You can trust him, Mr Clemence. Talk to him.'

'I've already done that.'

Clara caught her breath. 'He questioned you about Fletcher?'

He absorbed the revelation of Fletcher's name without comment. 'It was a wide-ranging discussion,' he said.

Ignoring the sarcasm, Clara said, 'He shouldn't have questioned you without legal representation.'

'I waived the right.'

She stared at him dumbfounded.

'Well, I wasn't going to talk to Quartermaine, 'cos them pictures were just between you and me, weren't they? We agreed, didn't we? And you weren't around, so what was I supposed to do?'

Self-destructiveness: Clara hadn't expected that in Clemence; she had thought self-preservation his prime instinct. He lit a cigarette and Clara had to fight a wave of nausea. Cigarette smoke and confined spaces – bad combination. She took her time, slowing her breathing, aware, nevertheless, of the trickle of cold sweat tracing a path down her spine. 'What did you tell him?'

He snorted. 'What d'you think I told him? Nothing. *Fuck all* is what I told him. And I wish I'd told you the same, *Counsel.*'

Clara felt a sudden flash of anger. 'What are you afraid of, Mr Clemence? That I might work out what you've really been up to?'

'Oh, yeah,' he said. 'I forgot. It's all-important to you that your client is innocent, isn't it? The guilty don't have a right to representation.'

'I didn't say that.'

'Maybe not, but it's far too mucky for you to dirty your hands with.'

'I just don't want to be responsible for letting a guilty man go free.'

'And what exactly d'you think I'm guilty *of*?'

'Okay,' she said. When she drove to the police station, full of righteous indignation on his behalf, she had been convinced of his innocence. Now, seeing the man, talking to him, she was as unsure of him as she had ever been. She had a sudden insight into her mother's strange ambivalence towards her: at a distance, she was easier to love, because there were no real demands – of emotion or time. At close quarters, things became too messy, too complicated.

'Okay,' she repeated. 'If you really want to know.' She spoke fast, not taking time to organise her thoughts. 'I keep thinking maybe you did the job, and then he planted the T-shirt and photos to incriminate you. Or perhaps he gave you the pictures so that you would know what she looked like. Of course, he knew the police would suspect you – an ex-student. Fresh out of prison. He's got people on the inside. They would know your connection with her.'

Clemence's expression hardened. 'What are you on about? *Who* planted the T-shirt? *Who* gave me the pictures? *Who* set me up?'

'Brendan Harris.'

He seemed genuinely nonplussed. 'Why would he do that?'

'I'm saying Brendan Harris hired you.'

'Of course he hired me – I took the pictures of Fatman taking a bung, didn't I?' He stopped, suddenly realising the full implications of what she had said. 'You think he took out a *contract* on Amy Dennis?'

'Happens all the time.'

'*Why*, for Chrissake?'

'Because she was making waves. Because if she published a story she had been working on, he would lose a contract that might cost him millions.'

For a few seconds, he said nothing, merely stared at her, then he said, 'I had nothing against her.'

Clara's heart rate picked up: he had said something similar when questioned about the murder of his girlfriend all those years before. There was nothing in his face to say he recognised the echo of those words.

'You said yourself, the photolab didn't pay well. You need equipment, chemicals, materials for your work.' she said, 'And you strike me as the kind of man who, when you need something, you just go out and take it.'

His face was taut with anger, and when he spoke, his voice was harsh with bitter emotion. 'Even if that means taking a life?' he asked.

'What's a life?' Clara said, with deliberate cruelty. 'Life is cheap.'

'You think you can take someone's life like you steal a parking space at the supermarket?' he demanded. 'A bit of shouting, a bit of push and shove, maybe, and then just find somewhere else and forget about it?'

The lives Clara had ended through her arrogance meant more than that – much more – but she found it hard enough telling her therapist how she felt, and she certainly wasn't interested in sharing her guilt with Mr Clemence. She wanted to know the value *he* placed on a life – a life not his own.

'Forgive me if I sound cynical,' she said. 'But you took a life for a five-pound fix.'

He stared at her. 'You want an explanation?' he said. 'A neat, logical reason why I killed Vicky?' He flinched, saying the name, as if it caused him physical pain. 'What can I tell you? I was Jonesing for a fix? How could I be, I was already off my face – crack, booze – I'd just been home and robbed my mum's DGs, for Chrissake! Left an old woman in pain because I was hurting, and that's all I gave a shit about.' He stubbed out his cigarette savagely and lit another.

'Fact is, I don't know why I killed Vicky. I don't . . .' He looked up and Clara saw a shadow, a faint after-image behind the eyes of the man, which revealed the haunted, horrified face of the eighteen-year-old boy. He exhaled, almost a sigh. 'I don't remember.'

Clara wanted to make him stop. She had heard enough, seen enough. She couldn't bear his suffering as well as her own. But she couldn't find her voice.

'Life doesn't come cheap, Ms Pascal.' he said. 'It costs. It costs the poor bastard whose life you stole. It costs her friends, her family – even people who barely knew her.'

He didn't seem to realise he had switched to saying *her*. For a long, tense moment, he said nothing. He simply sat, staring at his hands as if they didn't belong to him. As if they still had Vicky's blood on them.

'It costs you,' he said softly, '– in night terrors and sleepless nights, loss of self-respect, lost friends . . . lost time. You're not who you were before. It's like that life was blown away with hers.'

Clara looked at the badly executed prison tattoo on his left arm, the tattoo with Vicky's name and the broken heart. They used to brand criminals, she thought. Was this act of self-mutilation his way of marking himself as an outcast, a criminal? He looked at her and beneath the mask of self-possession she thought she saw a struggle for composure.

'You take a life, you lose a life,' he said.

Clara didn't trust herself to speak, and a long, painful silence followed. At last, Clemence nodded. Leaning against the back of his chair, he returned to his customary expression of cool cynicism. 'You don't believe me.'

'No,' Clara insisted. 'No – I do. I think I did even before you told me all this.'

'So what the *fuck* was that all about?' His anger was sudden and hot.

'I – I wasn't sure,' she said. 'I'm sorry. I was wrong once before, and –' She was about to say *and people died because of it – because of me*. She shook her head. 'This time, I had to be sure.'

'Well, now you're *sure*, Ms Pascal, you can piss off to your nice home and your nice life with a clear conscience.'

He couldn't be more wrong: a clear conscience was for people who had no regrets, who never made mistakes. 'Mr Clemence—'

'Are you still here?' he said.

'I know you're angry – you've every right to be—'

'You're not listening to me, Counsel. I just fired you. Now piss off out of here.'

No. This could not happen. She had gone through too much to be told, now that she finally believed in the man, that she was off the case. 'Why?' she demanded, raising her voice. 'Because I know too much about you?'

He sneered at her. 'You know *fuck all* about me.'

She stopped feeling sorry for herself and started feeling angry at him. 'Oh, I wouldn't be so sure. I bet I got more of an inside knowledge in the last five minutes than you gave in months and years of attending your anger management groups – am I right?' He seemed startled by her knowledge of his life inside.

She blushed, a little ashamed of her outburst. 'I told you, I had to be sure.' He seemed undecided and Clara continued, her voice low and urgent, 'I've seen your portraits, Mr Clemence,' she said,. 'I've seen you lay a man bare to the bone with the camera lens. Don't you think your subjects *resent* being exposed in that way?'

'That's different,' he said. 'I'm trying to . . .' He trailed off. They both knew what he was about to say: that he was trying to find the truth that lay behind the mask of toughness and indifference. They had each been searching for truth in their way; he in his sitters, she in Clemence's account of events.

He was calmer now, and Clara tried again. 'I lost faith in my abilities as a lawyer,' she explained. 'More than that, I thought that maybe I was' – she shrugged – 'I don't know . . . dangerous.' He remained silent. Clara ran a hand through her hair. He wasn't speaking to her, but he hadn't walked out, either.

'You're a skilled carpenter, Mr Clemence – those cupboards in your kitchen. The hidden compartment. But wasn't it . . . difficult, picking up a hammer for the first time after – after what happened?'

For a long time, he said nothing, but she felt sure that he was thinking about what she had said, that she had made some impression. He swallowed and something clicked at the back of his throat.

'First time I picked up a hammer, I went weak. All the strength went out of my arms, and I – I felt sick. The kind of sick where you can't even stand up. Truth is, I didn't feel safe holding that hammer in my hands, you know?'

'Yes,' Clara said with gentle compassion. 'Yes, I do know.' The law might be a blunter instrument but, as she had found to her cost, it was just as powerful, just as deadly. With a shock of realisation, she knew that the reason she felt sick whenever she went near a criminal court was not because of the sort of people she might meet there, but because she was afraid of her own capacity for destruction.

There was a shift of perspective after that moment. They understood each other, and despite the fact that they knew so little of each other, they formed a bond. After a time, Clemence stirred and sighed.

'You'd better tell me why you're here,' he said. Clara's puzzled expression made him smile. 'You leave here at ten in the morning. You come back at eight o'clock at night. All you had to do was get some prints developed at a one-hour processor's. I know you passed them on to Lawson. You weren't going to come and see me. So, why the change of heart?'

He raised his eyebrows, waiting for her answer, and Clara had a breathless moment of indecision. She *did* want him to look at the photographs of Amy again – the photographs she now knew were taken by Ainscough detective agency for Brendan Harris; she hoped that Clemence would find something she had missed. Maybe Harris had said something that might help their case. But shouldn't she first tell him about the mob attack on his flat – after all, wasn't that what had brought her here? If she kept that news from him, wouldn't she be manipulating him again? And wouldn't she risk losing his trust for good?

He gazed at her, curious, unsuspecting. 'It was on the radio,' she said, with an effort of will. 'Your flat . . .'

He closed his eyes briefly. When he opened them, he

seemed surprisingly calm. 'Terry Spence. He said he'd get me one way or another.'

Clara knew she had to tell it all, having started, but the words came reluctantly. 'They – threw a petrol bomb through the window.'

He looked past her, assimilating this piece of news. Then he nodded.

'You don't seem too concerned.'

He shrugged. 'The police have got most of my gear stored as evidence.' He focused on her face. 'And you've got my portfolio.'

'Yes.' Clara exhaled. She was confused; she had thought she had the measure of the man, but she realised now that Clemence's character would be a difficult knot to unravel. 'It's . . . It's quite safe. Nobody was hurt,' she went on.

Another curt nod. 'Can you do me a favour?'

'If I can,' she said.

'Find out if they've got my enlarger in store.'

'Of course.' Was he so hardened that all he cared about was his photographic equipment? Was home no more to him than a place to sleep, somewhere to set up his studio? Wasn't he concerned that others might have been injured? She gave a mental shrug. Why not – nobody had done him any favours since his release. He had been arrested, freed, beaten up and arrested again. Nobody believed him when he said he was innocent, including his legal representation. And where exactly was home for him? He must have lost count of the number of times he had been moved from prison to prison without warning during his twelve years inside –

perhaps that rootlessness was something he had learned to accept.

'So,' he said. 'What did you want me to help with?'

For a second or two, she stared at him stupidly, then realising what he meant, she opened her briefcase and spread the photographs of Amy out on the table.

'I don't get it,' Clemence said. 'I've seen these before.'

'Do you know who took them?'

'I know it wasn't me.' There was a pause, then he realised something important was happening and he leaned forward, resting his forearms on the table. 'What have you found out?'

'They were taken by a PI firm called Ainscough Security,' Clara told him. 'Mr Ainscough did the job himself, I believe. They're surveillance photos. I think he was employed by Brendan Harris because Amy was investigating his business investments.'

Clemence was silent. Watching her.

'What do you know about that?' she pressed him.

'What would I know about Harris's investments?'

'You tell me.'

'If I have to keep convincing you I'm with the good guys every question you ask, we'll be here till morning.'

'You don't have to convince me, but I need the full picture,' Clara said.

He sucked his teeth. 'All right. One last time. He told me he had something big going down. He didn't want anything to jeopardise that.'

'That's all he said?'

'Men like Brendan Harris aren't big on small talk.'

'The pictures were found in your flat.'

'They were *planted* in my flat. By the fat cop – Fletcher – taking the bung.' His fists clenched on the table in front of him. 'We've already had this discussion – I thought you said you trusted me.'

'I know. I *do* – but I've got to find a reason why those pictures were planted on you and—'

'And all you can think is Amy was attacked with a hammer.'

Clara rubbed tiredly at the frown-line between her eyebrows. She felt ashamed of herself. She didn't know who to trust any more. She had simply lost the knack.

She placed the picture of Amy that had been re-turned by the *Evening Echo* on the table, next to the rest. 'This one is bothering me,' she said.

'Is this part of the set?'

She nodded. 'It was . . . misplaced for a while.'

Clemence picked up the uncropped photo of Amy at the door of a house. 'Why's it bothering you?' he asked.

She stared at it. 'There's something niggling at me, but I can't think what. I was hoping you might notice something I'd missed.'

He shook his head. 'There's nothing special about it I can see.'

She sighed. 'OK. I'll go back to see DI Lawson. I should have told him earlier.'

'Told him what?'

'That these don't belong to you – and I can prove it. I'm going to make him talk to the private investigation firm. I'm going to make him find out the truth.'

'Why didn't you tell him this before?'

'I wanted to speak to you, first.'

He frowned, but she saw a glint of bitter amusement in his eyes. 'You showed him my pictures without asking me, but you needed to show me a shot of Amy that's been all over the papers – I'm not stupid, Ms Pascal. You didn't talk to him because you thought I was guilty.'

'That's not true,' Clara said. 'I was confused, yes. But I did go to the police station to tell Lawson about the detective agency's involvement.'

'Only you had a change of heart.'

'Only I got into a blind funk and ran out before I spoke to him.'

His raised his eyebrows in question. Clara looked away from him for a moment. *What the hell? If you're going to be honest, you might as well be completely honest.* 'The fat man you photographed . . .'

'The cop—'

'He's working on the murder investigation.'

Clemence put a trembling hand to his face. 'Jesus,' he said. 'I am so completely fucked . . .'

# 48

Clara signed out and walked slowly to her car. Dusk was falling, a pale lilac glow suffusing the westerly sky. It remained oppressively hot, and anything more energetic than a gentle stroll would have been an act of madness.

She felt peculiar – light-headed, almost – but it wasn't the heat. She was ready to put it down to drinking wine on an empty stomach, when, abruptly, she recognised the feeling: she was elated – buoyant, even. She had faced up to Clemence and she hadn't shattered into a thousand tiny pieces as soon as he raised his voice. More importantly, she had made a judgement about her client and had been right.

She heard the faint whirr of an electric motor and turned. A CCTV camera, part of the station's heightened security, was focusing in on her; she had been standing stock-still.

She half smiled to herself and walked on, savouring the feeling. *Hugo has been saying that I needed to get back to criminal work, Mitch has been hassling me for weeks. God, what'll I say to them? They'll be unbearable if I admit they were right.* She groped in her handbag for her keys and tossed them triumphantly into the air.

They rose, twisting, flipping over, the BMW fob flaring briefly in the light of the car park's arc lamps. The moment seemed to go on, like a sequence in a dream; she watched the keys fall, stretched out her hand and caught them.

She felt she could achieve anything. As she slid behind the wheel, it occurred to her that the best way to make it up to Clemence for not having believed him was to get him released. The evidence connecting him with Amy's murder was looking more and more flimsy, but the police still had him on the stalking charge.

*Don't do it.* Mitch's voice rang like an alarm bell in her head. *Whatever you're thinking, don't do it.* She would talk to Mrs Tobin, explain to her that Clemence could not have broken into her house. Where was the harm in that?

*Are you entirely mad?* Mitch again, on the side of reason. *You could get yourself disbarred for this.* It was true. Mrs Tobin would be the chief prosecution witness if the charges of stalking ever came to court, but Clara felt sure that they would not, and meanwhile Ian Clemence was in a police cell. Diane Tobin had a forgiving nature: hadn't she taken her husband back – supported and sustained him – when she might have been forgiven for taking a pair of shears to his tender parts?

Driving toward the city, heading for the Tobins' house, Clara changed her mind a dozen times, almost talking herself out of her suicide mission, telling herself that Clemence was hardly an innocent in chains; he was a murderer, he had spent twelve years in prison – a few more days would make no difference. But she couldn't shift the image – the last sight she had of him – afraid and in pain. Diane Tobin would understand that – understand and perhaps identify with it.

All her reasoning and rationalisation did not make it any easier to ring the doorbell, however. It was almost dark; a yellow moon hung low in the eastern sky, magnified by the dust in the torpid evening air. The house was quiet and dark, and Clara was on the point of leaving when light spilled into the hallway and she heard footsteps hurrying from the back of the house.

Mrs Tobin opened the door. She glanced at Clara, then half-turned, looking over her shoulder, momentarily striking a pose that was disturbingly similar to the press photograph of Amy. She was dressed in a pale blue floral print dress and she looked sweet and fragile.

'What do you want?' she asked, her voice unexpectedly harsh.

Clara blinked. She hadn't expected a welcome, but neither had she expected outright hostility. 'May I come in?' she asked.

Mrs Tobin hesitated, gripping the door tightly as if Clara might try to force her way past. Then she seemed to reconsider, and stood back, holding the door as Clara stepped into the hall and closing it quietly behind her.

Clara heard voices from a room further down the hall. 'Is Mr Tobin here?' she asked.

'He's visiting his – visiting Helen.' She had caught herself in time, but she had nearly said '*his daughter*'.

Clara hoped their new Counsel would warn against that. It wasn't her business to tell them. *Any more than it's your business to be here*, her inner voice told her.

'It's good he's keeping up his visits,' she said, following Mrs Tobin through to the back sitting-room. She felt awkward and embarrassed; she really should not be intruding like this.

Mrs Tobin stopped suddenly, turning on her heel and confronting Clara face to face. 'Look, if it's Chris you want—'

'No,' Clara said, surprised and a little flustered, 'I came to see you.'

She searched Clara's face. 'That's what I thought.'

Clara tried to read Mrs Tobin's expression: she seemed fearful – there was always a frisson of nervy energy about the woman, but there was a suspicion of something else – contempt, perhaps. Clara didn't blame her: for Mrs Tobin, the simple fact was that her own appointed Counsel, who had sworn commitment to protecting her against a man she perceived as a threat, was now defending that same man, supporting and advising him, finding excuses for him.

Mrs Tobin gathered her composure about her like a cloak. 'Well,' she said. 'What do you want?'

Clara glanced at the radio: the source of the voices she had heard when she came in to the house. The news desk was reporting the latest on the arson attack and riots in Hoole. 'I think we both know why I'm here,' she said.

Mrs Tobin met her gaze, cold, hard-eyed. 'I should call the police,' she said. 'Have you thrown out.'

'But you won't.' Clara sensed that Mrs Tobin felt some responsibility for what had happened to Clemence.

She didn't answer at first. She stared out through the open French windows and then back to Clara. She seemed to be waiting, so Clara began to explain:

'My client is innocent, Mrs Tobin. He shouldn't be in prison.'

'What do you expect me to do?'

'Drop the charges of stalking.'

She seemed to consider this carefully. After a pause, she tucked her hair behind her ears and drew herself up, meeting Clara's eye in what seemed almost a gesture of defiance. 'And if I don't?'

'Then I won't answer for the consequences.'

The storming of the police station, the riot and the burning of Clemence's flat were all because of public fears that a dangerous predator was loose in the city. If Mrs Tobin persisted in her claims, worse would surely follow.

Mrs Tobin bridled. 'You think you can come here and threaten me—'

'*Threaten* you?' Clara was incredulous. 'I would hardly call it that. I'm simply pointing out that there could be . . . repercussions if you—'

'Oh, *please*,' Mrs Tobin interrupted. 'Spare me the lecture. He broke into my house. He smashed my things . . .'

'That isn't true,' Clara said slowly and carefully. 'Ian Clemence was attacked and severely beaten the night your house was burgled. He can barely walk, even now.'

'Do you expect me to feel *sorry* for him?'

After all that had happened, that was exactly what Clara had expected. But it seemed that Mrs Tobin had Ian Clemence pegged as a murderer and, as a murderer, he must be guilty of anything else he was accused of.

'I didn't want to have to say this, but . . .' Clara shrugged. She needn't *name* him. 'I spoke to a private investigator today.'

Mrs Tobin listened, watching her face intently.

'He admitted taking the pictures of Amy that were found in Clemence's flat,' Clara went on. 'He wouldn't say how they got *into* Clemence's flat, but I can hazard a guess.'

Still, Mrs Tobin made no comment.

'Ian Clemence was not stalking Amy and he wasn't stalking you.'

Mrs Tobin plucked a tissue from her dress pocket and began dusting the sculpture of Solomon with compulsive assiduousness. Clara stifled an urge to snatch the tissue from her hand.

'Are you listening to me?' she demanded. 'I know who the private investigator was working for. I know why he took those photographs of Amy.'

'Do you?' Mrs Tobin looked up briefly from her polishing, her eyes filled with bitter resentment.

Clara understood: she was asking Mrs Tobin to realign her position on a man whom it was not easy to like or to trust. If she could make her see that Clemence was as much a victim as Amy had been—

'Ian Clemence was set up,' she said. 'Somebody

planted the photographs in his flat. That same somebody planted the other "evidence" — I shouldn't be surprised if it was they who telephoned the police to let them know where to find the murder weapon.'

Mrs Tobin stopped altogether, screwing the tissue into a tiny ball in her fist. 'Somebody?' she said.

They stared at each other for some moments. Clara would not name Harris: it was one thing to put her own career on the line, but she would not compromise a police investigation.

'Somebody,' she repeated.

# 49

Clemence stopped and turned when he heard the cell hatch open. He ducked to squint through the slot at the custody sergeant.

'What's up, Sarge? Am I bothering you with all this restless pacing?'

'Someone here wants a word with you. You did ask.'

He scooped up the photograph of Amy. 'At long bloody last!' When he saw it was Barton, he skimmed the photograph back onto the bed, disgusted.

Barton said nothing.

'Are you waiting for me to crack?' Clemence asked. ''Cos I've gotta tell you, Barton, it'd take more than the evil glint in your eye.'

'*You* asked to speak to *me*, remember?'

'I asked to speak to a senior officer. But see, now, that's the trouble with your modern police force – ask for a bloodhound, you get Scooby-Doo.'

'Look,' Barton said. 'I don't want to be here, any more than you want to see me.'

'But you're here, all the same.' A slow smile spread across his face. 'I get it,' he said. 'You thought I wanted to spill the beans about our friendly fist fight with Spiderman and his mates.' A frown creased his brow briefly, as if he was disappointed that Barton could think him so fickle. 'A promise is a promise, Sarge – I told Spiderman I'd forget his name. Mind you, that was before he stormed the police station and torched my flat.' He tilted his head. 'Think we're even now?'

Barton said nothing; it was hard enough trying to control the urge to reopen the cut over Clemence's eye without having to hold a conversation with him.

'Oh!' Clemence said, as if making a sudden recollection. 'You're thinking about our unspoken deal: you save me from a kicking and I keep my mouth shut about the fact you watched for a bit before you decided to help out?' He sucked his teeth. 'I don't mind telling you, Sarge, this place is enough to make a man break his word. Crap ventilation, poky as hell – and as for the view—' He glanced up at the thick glass blocks that served as a window.

Clemence, Barton had to admit, was not as dense as he had first thought. When they got word at Castle Square that Clemence was screaming 'material evidence', Barton had volunteered to make the journey to the secure station for precisely the reasons Clemence had outlined.

'Are you going to tell me why you dragged me all the way over here,' Barton said, 'Or is the plan to bore me to death?'

In answer, Clemence picked up the picture from the bed and handed it over.

'It's the one the press have been using,' Barton said, half-expecting an accusation. 'What about it?'

'A woman looking over her shoulder can say one of

two things,' Clemence told him. ' "I'm frightened, help me", or "I'm available, take me". Whoever it was gave the papers that picture, they made a good choice.'

Barton met his gaze with a blank stare. *It'd take more than the evil glint in your eye, an' all,* he thought.

'Look at it, Barton. It's all there in the picture. Ask yourself who she was looking *at* over her shoulder.'

'She was looking to see if she was being followed,' Barton said.

'I thought you blokes were trained to look for evidence.' Clemence leaned over Barton, his animosity forgotten in the excitement of the moment. 'Look at the bottom right of the frame. There's a faint shadow – could be a second person. Someone just out of shot.' He watched Barton studying the picture for a moment or two, then began again, following his original line of thought. 'Ms Pascal thought she knew the place, but couldn't remember where from.'

'And you do?' Barton scrutinised the untidy privet bushes along the low wall, the dilapidated fence between the adjoining properties and the peeling paint of the front door.

'She's painted the front door since,' he said. 'And she'd already cut back the hedge by the time I arrived,' Clemence said.

'She?'

'That's Mrs Tobin's house,' he said.

'Mrs *Tobin*?'

'Ms Pascal would've seen the place after she'd tidied the lot up. I reckon these were taken two or three weeks ago.'

'What makes you think that?'

'Because before she invited me, I did a recce of the place and the first time, it looked pretty much like this.' He stared past Barton, remembering the pictures he had taken of Mrs Tobin: she was locking her car, her pale hair and skin stark against the dark green blur of the privet hedge.

'It *could* be the same place,' Barton said, interrupting his thoughts. 'Of course, it could be the same photographer.'

Clemence shook his head in disgust.

'You went to see her,' Barton said. 'When was this?'

'I don't keep a diary, mate.'

'A rough estimate.' Barton eyed Clemence coldly.

'I dunno. A couple of weeks back. Middle of the week, maybe. She invited me round. Told me to bring my portfolio.'

'And she invited you?'

'Why doesn't anybody listen? I just told you. She said I could call in the afternoon. She talked me through the pictures. Made some suggestions—'

'So,' Barton said. 'You fetch up on her doorstep and . . .'

Clemence was silent for a short time. 'Whatever she told you, she's lying,' he said. 'She. Invited. Me. She wasn't scared of me. *She* asked *me* over. Get it? She was pruning the bloody *hedge* when I arrived. Well,' he corrected himself. 'I say "pruning". She'd practically hacked it to death.' He realised the connotations of what he'd said, and shrugged, embarrassed. 'She was fine,' he repeated doggedly. 'Look – I even helped her with the fence—'

'*You helped her?*' A possibility had occurred to Barton. Something that made him feel sick to the very core of his being. Diane Tobin was pruning the hedge when Clemence arrived. Hacking the privet back and hammering planks to fill the gaps in the fence.

'I helped her,' Clemence repeated. 'So?' He stared at Barton. Barton waited. He wasn't about to hand Clemence an escape route that easily.

The truth hit him like a sledgehammer, winding him, and he had to sit down. 'Oh, Jeez, you pillock . . .' Clemence muttered to himself.

'I fixed the two new planks into the gaps for her. I took the claw-hammer out of her gloved hands and fixed the gaps and packed it away nice and neat in her toolkit, to save her the effort.' Neither spoke for several seconds.

'You've been royally screwed, Clemence,' Barton said at last. He wasn't sure which was the more terrible: believing that Diane Tobin could do something so horrible, or that Clemence might be innocent. Barton had to reconcile himself to the fact that, indirectly, he had helped her to set Clemence up, bringing the press into the equation by providing them with the photograph of Amy, turning the white-hot spotlight of media attention onto Clemence's crime and his presence in the community, and in doing so, casting Diane Tobin into the shadows. The photograph in the papers every morning of a fearful Amy, looking over her shoulder, had backed up Mrs Tobin's story of being stalked.

'You had all the right credentials for all the wrong people,' he said. 'Me included.'

Clemence lifted his head. 'Was that an apology?'

'Like I said, you had the right credentials – but you earned those yourself. My instincts still tell me you're the worst kind of sewer slime.'

Clemence clasped a hand to his heart. 'I'm touched.' He thought about it for a minute. 'She trussed me and stuffed me like a fucking Christmas turkey, though, didn't she?'

Barton lifted one shoulder. 'If it makes you feel any better, you weren't the only one. I just might lose my job over this.'

Clemence raised his eyebrows. 'Should we be taping this conversation, Sarge?'

Barton smiled, pocketing the photograph. Any confession he chose to make would be to DI Lawson and him alone. 'So where's Ms Pascal?'

Clemence shrugged. 'She left half an hour ago. Said she was going to talk to Lawson – tell him about the PI.'

'Woah, woah, woah! Back up a bit,' Barton said. 'What PI?'

'He was working for—'

A confusion of images flashed into Clemence's mind in rapid succession. Their first meeting, Clara Pascal nervous, yet defiant; laughing, surprised and angry at something he had said; that probing, somehow *disappointed* look she sometimes had when she wasn't sure if he was telling her the truth; the blank horror on her face that morning when, locked in his cell, she had faced demons far more terrifying than the mob.

'She *thought* he was working for Brendan Harris,' he said. '– keeping tabs on Amy Dennis, but . . .'

'Chances are, he was working for Diane Tobin,' Barton finished for him. He dipped in his inside pocket for his mobile phone. No signal. He ran to the custody sergeant's desk, not bothering to lock Clemence's cell door. When Clemence limped into the corridor a few seconds later, Barton had already spoken to DI Lawson. They made eye contact and Barton gave a slight shake of his head.

'Shit.' Clemence leaned on the wall for support. 'I've taken a lot of pictures,' he said. 'You see people in a different way. You see what's going on behind the eyes . . .' He shook his head. Barton wouldn't understand, and he certainly didn't know how to explain.

'Find Clara, Sarge,' he said. 'Find her safe.'

# 50

'Where are you going?' Mrs Tobin's voice was high, panicky.

'I'm wasting my time. You won't change your mind,' Clara said. 'It was a mistake. I shouldn't have come here.' She turned to leave.

'No!'

The cry was so anguished, so distressed, that Clara stopped.

'I only wanted to keep my family together,' Mrs Tobin said. 'Me and Chris and Helen. We *are* a family, even though I'm not her biological mother. And I'll take good care of her.'

Clara didn't doubt it, but neither did she understand. If Mrs Tobin dropped the charges against Clemence, the Family Courts would be less likely to quibble with a residency order placing Helen with her father. 'I don't see how your family unit depends on an unsubstantiated and frankly flimsy charge against Ian Clemence,' she said.

Mrs Tobin continued as if she hadn't heard. 'I went through hell for Chris,' she said, tears welling in her eyes. 'Miscarriages, in-vitro fertilisation, years of pain and intrusive procedures and disappointment. In the end, he said it didn't matter.' She found an invisible blemish on the face of one of the women in the sculpture and began working at it, rubbing and polishing with her tissue.

'I believed him.' She seemed astonished at her own gullibility. 'But he dotes on the child – so evidently it *did* matter, just a little.' Her face twisted into a bitter grimace.

'Mrs Tobin—'

'I'm trying to explain!' Her young-old face was wet with tears, the colour of her skin yellow and sickly in the lamplight. She stroked the belly of the infant, lying between the two women. 'I love Helen too – I was happy to give her a home. But he lied to me. He lied and humiliated me. Going to her behind my back. Carrying on the affair. Bringing her to my home.'

*Oh, my God. Oh, my God!* What was she saying? Clara experienced a terrible moment of recognition. She saw a vivid image: the photograph of Amy on the doorstep of a house not her own, glancing over one shoulder, eyes wide with fear. Or excitement?

Mrs Tobin saw the look and misinterpreted it. 'Yes. He brought her here. To this house.' Her hand closed over the form of one of the women as if she was trying to obliterate it.

The sitting-room door was only a few feet from her. Clara backed away a step or two. 'The private detective was working for *you*,' she breathed. Amy getting into a car, smiling at someone in the driver's seat. 'The man in the car . . .' Her voice had no strength.

'Chris,' Mrs Tobin said. 'He met her. Took her out.

*Courted* her, after telling me it was finished. He betrayed me and lied to me – humiliated me.'

'That didn't give you the right to take her life – *dear God!* Her baby was sleeping upstairs.'

'He was planning to leave me.' Mrs Tobin seemed hurt and bewildered. 'You have to be prepared to protect what you cherish. I thought you would understand that.'

'I understand love – the will to protect those you love,' Clara said. 'But this isn't about *love*. It's about possession.'

'I took care of him,' Mrs Tobin exclaimed. 'For years I had to be the strong one. I supported him through university – squandered my own talents to make sure that he had what he needed.'

'You murdered a young woman and framed an innocent man.'

'Innocent? He's a convicted killer.'

'Well that's not the only kind, is it, Mrs Tobin?' Clara spat back.

'You think you can sit in judgement on me?' She wrenched and strained at the sculpture as if she would tear the true mother from the base. 'Do you know what he did, my brave husband, when he found his lover dead? He ran. He ran back to me.' The triumph in her voice was mingled with contempt. 'He ran, leaving his baby alone in that house, not knowing if the killer was still there.'

Clara stared at her in horrified disbelief. ' "The killer",' she said softly, 'was *you*.'

Mrs Tobin used the screwed-up tissue to wipe her

face. It left a smear of greyish metal dust under each eye. 'You have to protect what's yours,' she repeated stolidly. I managed everything, as usual – arranged his alibi with his dithering parents. Got rid of the evidence.'

'Evidence?' Had they both planned it? 'He knows?'

Mrs Tobin gave her a pitying smile. 'Do you think he'd stay with me if he knew?' She flicked her hand in a dismissive gesture. 'He had blood on one of his shoes. I had to get rid of them. You have to understand that, in Chris's version of the universe, he is at the centre, making it turn, and he thinks that everyone around him – his wife, his lover, even his baby girl – exists to make him happy. The idea that I might do something that would be so destructive of his happiness simply would not occur to him.' She paused, considering. 'To be fair, he was pathetically grateful. I disposed of the shoes, kept him calm, sorted out the custody situation. I fielded questions and patted his hand, while he grieved for that bitch—'

'You've been very resourceful.' Clara agreed.

Mrs Tobin heard the barb in her tone. 'Do you think this is easy for me?' she demanded. 'I didn't ask for this – any of it. I just wanted my life back.'

Clara had thought that Mr Tobin was the manipulator in the relationship, the blood-sucker, but now she saw that they were well matched – a true couple.

'Did you really think you could get your life back by killing Amy Dennis? she asked.

Mrs Tobin broke down, sobbing. 'I don't deserve

this,' she sobbed. 'You have no right to judge me. I'm not a bad person. I didn't set out to hurt anyone.'

Clara had heard enough. She turned on her heel and made for the front door. She reached it, but fumbled the catch.

Light exploded in her skull; the pain came a second later. She fell, smashing her cheekbone against the door jamb. She brought both hands to her head, felt warm blood ooze between her fingers. Mrs Tobin stood over her, the Wisdom of Solomon in her hands.

Clara's vision blurred, then snapped back into sharp focus. The base of the sculpture glistened red. Solomon, his face stern and unyielding, raised his sword two-handed over his head.

'You tried to talk her round,' Mrs Tobin said. 'But she wouldn't listen. They never listen. They just keep on and *on* until you can't stand it any more.'

Clara kept her eyes on Mrs Tobin's face.

'Don't do this, Diane,' she pleaded. 'You don't have to do this.' She slipped her hand into her trouser pocket. The knife Pippa had given her at the airport nestled in a fold of fabric. She found the groove in the blade and plucked at it with her thumbnail.

'You do your best. You work *so hard* and what happens?'

Clara's fingers were slick with blood and the blade began to slip and close. She gasped, pressing the point into the fabric of her trousers to save it, nicking her fingertip in the process. It held and she levered it open.

'You always have to clear up after him. At home, at work; his messy emotional life . . .'

Clara moved, trying to sit upright, and a rush of debilitating weakness flushed through her system. *Don't pass out. Don't you dare pass out, Clara!* Had it been her mother's voice, Clara might have given up there and then. But it wasn't her mother, it was Mitch: furious, foul-mouthed and fighting mad. *Are you going to let this loony feckin bitch best you?* Clara closed her eyes and tightened her grip on the knife.

'Why couldn't you leave us alone?'

Clara opened her eyes. Mrs Tobin wasn't talking to some bloody memory of Amy Dennis any longer, she was talking to her. She looked at the sculpture in her hands and seemed surprised to find it there.

The Sword of Justice gleamed dully in the hall light. She raised her arms in an imitation of Solomon's double-handed grip.

Clara struck, lunging forward, sinking the knife deep into Diane Tobin's thigh. She screamed, dropping the sculpture, gazing in horror at the knife jutting from her thigh as Clara braced herself against the front door and eased herself to her feet.

Mrs Tobin wrenched the knife out, screaming again as the police sirens wailed down the street. She looked around her in dismay. 'Look at this mess,' she said, pressing one hand to the wound.

The sirens were shut off and there was a brief pause. The lights flashed, tingeing Diane Tobin's skin a cold, deathly blue, then doors slammed and footsteps clattered up to the house. Mrs Tobin looked Clara in the eye; she was serene and completely lucid. She turned her wrist to expose the flesh of her inner arm and calmly gouged a line from the base of her thumb to the crease of her elbow.

Clara screamed, fighting with the door latch, struggling to open the door as Mrs Tobin fell. Shouts – a gasp of dismay – another magical pause: the hush before the thunderclap. Then more sirens. An ambulance sounded a counterpoint, and Clara knew this wasn't the end; this was where it all began.

# EPILOGUE

DI Lawson supervised Clemence's release himself. He hadn't expected relief or gratitude and he got neither. The system had failed Ian Clemence and he was out of a job and a home because of it. Part of it was down to a callous and manipulative woman who had built a case against him before coldly murdering Amy Dennis, but there were also failures and abuses of police privilege.

Diane Tobin would answer for her acts, although it would be months before she was fit to stand trial. Many of the newspaper headlines featured the word 'remorse' in the telling of her suicide attempt, but Lawson suspected a far less noble motive had prompted her to try to take her own life. The private investigator had admitted helping her to gain access to Clemence's flat, but Diane Tobin had done the rest: planting the photographs, the T-shirt, leaving the murder weapon near the scene – she had even made the anonymous call to tell them where she had dropped it. And she alone had murdered Amy Dennis.

There were disciplinary matters Lawson knew he would have to deal with, too. Fletcher was DI Hill's problem; he was co-operating with Hill's investigation, but as Hill said, he was strictly Sunday League. They wouldn't get Brendan Harris on the murder of Sebastian Enderby, but Tom Rivers had turned quite conversational and Hill was confident the charges of fraud would stick.

Phil Barton was another matter entirely. He had let his emotions get in the way of reason. He said he had stolen the photograph from the pack on impulse, with no plan in mind. Lawson believed him. The one thing in his favour was that he hadn't accepted payment for it. He had given it to the *Evening Echo* on a point of principle: appointed himself judge and jury against Clemence. He was so convinced that Clemence had killed Amy, so haunted by the day he had found Vicky Rees's battered body, that Amy and Vicky became one: victims of Clemence's brutality.

Lawson knew it was easier to believe in the guilt of a convicted villain than to think badly of nice people who lived in nice houses and had respectable jobs, but Barton had gone further than that: he had stolen the photograph, allowing other officers to take the blame – perhaps Fletcher deserved it, but not Thorpe. Barton had set up his own surveillance oppo on Clemence without permission. He had failed to report a serious assault, even when he knew it would exonerate Clemence at least of the burglary of the Tobins' house – worse still, *because* it would do so – and he had hidden the identity of one of the rioters who had attacked the prison the previous day.

Lawson sighed, watching Clemence lope across the car park. He had known officers do worse than Phil Barton, and for less honourable reasons, and he would try to protect the sergeant, but the painful truth was that he would never be able to trust the man again – not completely.

Clemence walked out of the custody area and paused, blinking in the early morning sunshine. He moved a little stiffly, still feeling the effects of the kicking that Spider and his mates had given him a few days before, but he looked fit. The bruising on his face was beginning to fade and when he tilted it towards the warming rays of the sun, Clara could barely distinguish the damaged tissue from the tan.

When she saw him, Clara leaned off the bonnet of the car.

Hugo ducked his head to talk to her through the open window. 'Are you sure about this?'

'I'm certain,' Clara said, without looking back. She wanted to tell him that she owed Clemence her life, and more. She had tried to explain it to him during the long night in casualty, and the sleepless hours later, when they held each other, afraid to let go, but she didn't have the words, and maybe she didn't need them after all; maybe Hugo understood, otherwise, why was he here?

She walked toward Clemence, still feeling a little woozy from the injury to her head. Clemence saw her, faltered and stopped. After a few seconds' indecision, he sauntered over to her, his hands in his pockets.

'Didn't expect to see you.'

Clara smiled a little. 'Didn't expect to be here.'

He bent at the waist, peering into Hugo's car, some fifteen feet away from where they stood.

'My husband,' Clara said, adding as an after-thought, 'Hugo.'

'Big bloke,' he commented. 'He your minder for our little heart-to-heart?'

In answer, Clara gave him her card. 'My home number,' she said. They made eye contact. 'If you ever need a lawyer.' She shrugged, adding awkwardly, 'Or someone to talk to.'

A storm of emotions chased over Clemence's face and were quelled in an instant. He took the card and nodded his thanks.

'Have you arranged accommodation?' Clara asked.

'You offering me a bed for the night?'

She laughed and he seemed pleased – perhaps because she took it as a joke, perhaps because she hadn't felt threatened. 'Council's fixed me up. It'll do for now.'

'I could put you in touch with someone who'd give you a good price on a studio . . .'

'Yeah?' He was careful to hide any eagerness he felt.

Again, Clara felt that unaccountable shyness. 'Hugo knows a lot of people in property – you'd probably have to do some upgrading, but that wouldn't be a problem, would it?'

'No problem at all. And if you want a family portrait doing, I'd give you a preferential rate.'

'I'd like that,' Clara said, feeling a pricking of tears at the back of her eyes.

'Best wait a week or two, though,' he confided. 'Give the bruising a chance to fade.'

She smiled again, feeling the skin tighten around her left eye and cheekbone. 'I wanted to say—'

'No need,' he interrupted, his tone brisk and a little rough. Then he seemed to relent and offered his hand. She took it. 'You're all right, Ms Pascal,' he said.

The calluses on his hands from lifting weights, the tattoo on his arm, the hard-man act that wouldn't allow her even to thank him were all symptomatic, she knew, just as much as her panic attacks and anxiety. She felt compelled to ask, 'How are the nightmares?'

He frowned, as if she had broken some social taboo.

'You can tell me,' she persisted. 'We're cell-mates, aren't we?' He looked at her and she looked back, unafraid.

'Yeah,' he said at last.

'And?'

He laughed, exasperated. 'You don't give up, do you?'

She grinned. 'That's why I'm still here.'

For a moment she thought he wouldn't answer, then he said, 'Improving.' He looked at her a while longer. 'How about you? Are your demons sleeping any quieter?'

Now she understood his reluctance to answer. Weakness was hard to admit to. 'Not yet,' she said at last. 'But who knows, given time?'